WISP OF A THING

BOOKS BY ALEX BLEDSOE

Blood Groove
The Girls with Games of Blood

The Sword-Edged Blonde
Burn Me Deadly
Dark Jenny
Wake of the Bloody Angel
He Drank, and Saw the Spider

The Hum and the Shiver
Wisp of a Thing

WISP OF
A THING

ALEX BLEDSOE

TOR®

A TOM DOHERTY ASSOCIATES BOOK

NEW YORK

This is a work of fiction. All of the characters, organizations, and events portrayed in this novel are either products of the author's imagination or are used fictitiously.

WISP OF A THING

"Wrought Iron Fences" written by Kate Campbell, Ira Campbell, and Johnny Pierce copyright © 1996 by Large River Music Inc. (BMI)/CedarSong Publishing (BMI). Used by permission.

A Tor Book
Published by Tom Doherty Associates, LLC
175 Fifth Avenue
New York, NY 10010

www.tor-forge.com

Tor® is a registered trademark of Tom Doherty Associates, LLC.

The Library of Congress has cataloged the hardcover edition as follows:

Bledsoe, Alex.
    Wisp of a thing / Alex Bledsoe.—First Edition.
        p. cm.
    ISBN 978-0-7653-3413-8 (hardcover)
    ISBN 978-1-4668-0826-3 (e-book)
    1. Musicians—Fiction. 2. Magic—Fiction. 3. Great Smoky Mountains (N.C. and Tenn.)—Fiction. I. Title.
    PS3602.L456W57 2013
    813'.6—dc23

                           2013003720

ISBN 978-0-7653-7693-0 (trade paperback)

Tor books may be purchased for educational, business, or promotional use. For information on bulk purchases, please contact the Macmillan Corporate and Premium Sales Department at 1-800-221-7945, extension 5442, or write to specialmarkets@macmillan.com.

First Edition: June 2013
First Trade Paperback Edition: March 2015

Printed in the United States of America

0 9 8 7 6 5 4 3 2 1

To Lynne and Michael Thomas
for the faith

SPECIAL THANKS

Jennifer Armstrong
Jen Cass
Charles de Lint
Lisa Germano
Jennifer Goree (the first honorary Tufa)
Seanan McGuire
Lucy Mogensen (RIP)
Sile Shigley
James Travis Spartz
Paul Stevens
Marlene Stringer
Miriam Weinberg

and

Kate Campbell, now the second honorary Tufa

and always,

Valette, Jake, and Charlie

WISP OF
A THING

1

Peggy Goins stepped out into the cool dawn behind
the Catamount Corner motel. As always, she was perfectly coiffed and dressed the way a stylish Southern
woman of a certain age should be. Her black hair,
streaked with dignified gray, held its own against the
wind like the Confederates at the Battle of Brentwood.
She drew on her cigarette, leaving lipstick stains on the
filter, and luxuriously released a breath made up equally
of smoke and condensation. It was still late summer
elsewhere, but here in Needsville, high in Appalachia,
fall was coming; for the last three mornings, she'd been
able to see her breath.

The woods, which started twenty feet from her back
door like a solid wall, showed only hints of the impending autumn. A few leaves near the treetops had turned,
but most remained green and full. Visible in the
distance, the Widow's Tree towered above the forest.
Its leaves were the most stubborn, tenaciously hanging
on sometimes until spring, if the winter was mild. It

was a transitional period, when the world changed in its cycle and opened a window during which people might also change, if they had the inclination.

Peggy smiled and hummed a song she'd known all her life. It was her way of thanking the world for its gifts.

Something clattered in the big green Dumpster. She threw down her cigarette, ground it into the gravel, and shouted, "Hey! Y'all get out of there! I mean it!" When nothing happened, she walked over and slapped the metal side. It boomed in the silence.

A teenage girl peeked over the Dumpster's edge. Her eyes, wide and blank beneath a boyish mop of ragged black hair, stared at Peggy. "Don't give me that look," Peggy said impatiently. "Get out of there, young lady. Ain't nothing in there for you."

The girl slithered over the edge and dropped to the ground. She wore a tattered old orange sundress, and nothing else. Dirt smeared her exposed skin, and candy wrappers from the garbage stuck to one thigh. Breath shot from her nostrils in rapid little puffs, but otherwise she showed no sign that the chill affected her. She growled softly, like an animal, then dashed into the trees. Peggy called after her, "One of these days somebody's liable to run you off with a shotgun, you know that? Then where'll you be? Dead in a *ditch*, that's where!"

When she was certain the girl had gone, Peggy went back inside, through the Catamount Corner lobby and out the front door. She walked two buildings down to the new post office. The place didn't open for another hour and a half, but an old man with a bushy white beard already sat in one of the rocking chairs on its porch.

She put her hands on her hips and stared at him. "So when do you plan to do something about that crazy girl in the woods?"

The old man said nothing.

"It can't go on like this, you know. She's losing her fear of people. Before long, she'll be running down the highway, chasing cars like a dog." Peggy paused and shook her head contemptuously. "And that beard makes you look like some demented ol' Santa Claus. You planning to keep it?"

By way of reply, he leaned to the side and spit into the bushes. The tobacco left a faint smear in the white whiskers.

Peggy looked up at the sky, still laced with pink clouds from sunrise. "Something's coming. You know it just like I do, just like everyone with the true in them knows. Careful whatever it is doesn't trample you on its way through."

"I'd best be worrying about myself if I was you, Peggy."

"Don't you threaten me, Rockhouse Hicks. You're up to something, aren't you, old man? All this time, and you still ain't learned your lesson. You're going to try something else, just like you did with Bronwyn Hyatt, and when it all goes to hell, you won't care who you take with you, will you?"

He smiled. "Peggy, darlin', I didn't know you cared."

"I'm just tired of finding that girl in my Dumpster," she snapped. "Get it stopped, or I'll stop it for you."

In a drawl so slow, it seemed to suspend time, the old man said, "When the last leaf falls from the Widow's Tree this year, she'll be done for good. No coming back. No bothering anyone no more. Nobody'll find her bones, and before next spring, nobody'll even remember her. She'll just be a wisp of a thing."

Peggy looked toward the tree, now hidden behind a low patch of morning cloud. She breathed out hard through her nose. "That's a terrible thing to do, Rockhouse. Even for you, even to her."

"Set in motion a long time ago," he said blithely. "Just took this long to finish up."

"Not everybody's afraid of you, you know. Eventually somebody'll stand up to you. Then where will you be?"

"Right here on this porch, Peggy," he assured her, and patted the chair's arm with one of his six-fingered hands.

"Hmph," she said, and stamped away. The old man smiled, with no amusement and more than a little contempt.

Peggy returned to the Catamount Corner. She poured some coffee from the machine in the dining room, then went behind the desk and began sorting the day's paperwork. The honeymooning couple in room 6 would be checking out soon. They had conceived no children—she always knew when it happened under her roof—and she'd have to strip the bedclothes, wash the disgusting little private hairs out of the shower, and make sure no condom wrappers had fallen into places where another guest might accidentally discover them.

She stared at the swirling pattern of cream and sweetener atop her coffee. A change was coming, all right, one that had nothing to do with the seasons. Needsville changed so slowly, most people—even those with true Tufa blood in them—barely noticed. But this would be a big change. She could sense no details of how that change would manifest or what its results would be. It felt like that moment just before a car crash, when you see the other automobile coming in slow motion, you know what's about to happen, and yet you can't do a thing about it.

And then, inevitably, comes the shrieking thunderous impact.

In their double-wide trailer located in the shadow of the mountains just outside Needsville, Doyle Collins awoke to the sound that had become his alarm clock: his wife vomiting.

He rolled over and sat up on the edge of the bed. The thin

trailer walls let him enjoy every gasp, gurgle, and splash. As he rubbed his eyes, he reflected that if this were morning sickness, he'd actually feel a manly pride in her nausea. He had nothing to do with this, though. This was caused by the other men in her life: Jim Beam, Johnnie Walker, and Jack Daniel.

He pulled on his jeans, went to the kitchen, and started the coffee. He looked up as Berklee emerged from the bathroom, gasping, red-eyed, and pale.

"Mornin', Glory," he said.

"Don't yell," she mumbled. "I need coffee."

"It's brewing."

She pushed past him and reached for the aspirin in the cabinet above the stove. She wore one of his undershirts and a pair of baggy cobalt blue panties. He recalled when they fit her snug and tight, a second satin skin on her smooth, firm behind. "Still losing weight, I see," he said.

He was pretty sure his tone was neutral, but she still glared at him with all the fury her weakened state allowed. "I've had the flu, you know. I can't keep anything down."

"Except whiskey," he said, then instantly regretted it.

She threw the aspirin bottle at him. "Don't *mess* with me this early in the morning, Doyle!"

He flinched a little as it bounced off his chest. At least the bottle was still closed. The sadness that had grown in him for years kept any anger at bay. "Sorry," he mumbled. "I'm going to get dressed. I got to pick up Dad and get to work."

"I'm sorry, too," Berklee said quietly, standing over the sink. Her hair obscured her face.

As Doyle pulled on his coveralls, he fought the overpowering sense of helplessness. His wife, whom he dearly loved, had been spiraling downward since he'd known her, but he always thought his steady affection could somehow forestall it. Now, though, as anything does in a whirlpool, she was moving faster as she neared the center. If something didn't change, and change soon, she would be lost to him down that great cosmic drain that swallowed wayward souls like hers.

In the distance, a coyote howled its final cry before sliding into its burrow for the day.

And something howled back.

High in the mountains that overlooked Needsville, Bliss Overbay stood on her deck and looked down the hill at her lake. Mist rose from the surface of the water. In the shadow of her big house, the night's chill remained, and she cinched her robe tight against it. She sipped her tea and considered again the images left over from her dreams.

Music.

Being held in a stranger's arms, his lips about to touch hers.

A hand clawing up from a grave.

And a final confrontation between two people who, should they ever fight, would irrevocably change everything, no matter who won. One wore a white dress splattered with blood.

She finished her tea and glanced at the leaves at the bottom of the cup. They bore out the sense of impending transformation she'd gotten from the dream. She thought about calling some of the other First Daughters of the Tufa, to see if they'd experienced anything similar. Perhaps Mandalay had a different interpretation. But her own ability had never failed her, and she had no reason to doubt it now.

Bliss closed her eyes, weary from the knowledge she alone had been chosen to bear. For an instant, something big and dark broke the surface of the lake, disturbing the insects swarming there. Then, like Bliss's dream, except for the ripples it was gone.

A cool breeze touched her. From the forested slopes, a distant coyote howl broke the dawn silence. It startled the birds into life, and they burst from the treetops and sailed overhead. A moment later, another cry—closer but definitely not a coyote—sounded in answer to the first one.

Then she went back inside, to shower and get ready for work.

2

Rob Quillen tried to check the map on his iPhone and still watch the road as it hugged the landscape's rolling contours. The morning mist that surrounded him left no more than ten yards of visibility. Clingy clouds like these gave the Smoky Mountains their name, but they made it a bastard for strangers to navigate. Modern roads blasted their way straight through annoying hills, but this path was older than Rob could imagine, and protected in ways he'd never believe. Even the state DOT could only pave it, not alter it.

Suddenly he emerged into a clear spot bathed in bright sunlight. To the right loomed a big rectangular sign halfway up the hillside. At the instant he looked away from the road to squint at the words, a gust of wind blew leaves in front of his car, obscuring something that dashed across the pavement. He slammed on the brakes and steered hard to the right.

His car stopped with a thump as one front tire dropped into the shallow ditch. He turned off the engine and jumped out, but saw no sign of the animal. It *must* have been an animal, he told himself, despite the fact that what he glimpsed seemed upright and flesh colored. After all, why would a mostly naked human being, wearing what looked like a ragged orange dress, run across the road in front of him and then vanish?

Once his heart stopped thundering, he again looked up at the sign. In big, friendly calligraphy it read, *Welcome to Cloud County, Tennessee.* Crudely painted mockingbirds flew in the corners. Beneath this was the line that he's squinted at: YE CAN DO NO HARM WHILE YE BE HERE. It must, he reasoned, be some obscure Bible verse used as a civic motto. He took a quick photo with his iPhone.

Wearily he returned to his car, slid into the driver's seat, shut the door, and turned the key.

Nothing happened.

Closing his eyes, he tried again. Nothing, except the faintest series of clicks.

"No, no, no," he whispered, and pressed his forehead against the steering wheel. He should've insisted on the Jeep he'd reserved and not accepted the four-door sedan the rental agent pressed on him, especially one that was bright red. Everyone knew red cars were bad luck.

He opened the glove compartment, found the rental agreement paperwork, then took out his phone again. There was no signal.

All of this should have worried him. After all, no one really knew where he was. Instead, though, he accepted it with weary resignation. Like everything else in his life, none of this seemed real. Nothing had, since Anna died.

We're so sorry, Rob. Everyone pitched in to sign this card. Now, we need you to sign this waiver. . . .

With no warning, that awful image came to him again: the

moment just before her plane hit the ground. He saw the look of terror as Anna realized what was about to happen, and the way the ground rushed up through the window beside her. He heard her helpless final scream. None of that had any basis in fact, of course; no one would ever know what truly happened during the plane's final minutes. "Mechanical failure," the official report said. But Rob was a songwriter, and so was blessed—or in this case, cursed—with a vivid imagination. And he knew Anna very, very well.

And yet, here he was at the border of Cloud County, the one place he might find the solace he sought. The man in the sequined jacket had been certain: Here among the Tufa, he could find the way to heal his broken heart. Here he could find, carved in stone, *the song.*

He opened the trunk and pulled out his guitar. He knew he'd eventually have to deal with the mundane aspects of car repair, but for now, he sat on the fender and began to play, sad minor chords that sounded like thin tendrils of the agony inside him.

After a few moments, his fingers froze in mid-chord. He definitely felt watched.

He saw no sign of people, and mentally ran through the list of large animals in his guidebook. Neither coyote nor deer would attack an adult, even a solitary one, it promised. But a *bear,* now that was a scary thought. Had his car stalled near a hidden den with a cub? Was he about to be slashed open and devoured by five hundred pounds of black-furred maternal fury? Careful to make no sudden moves, he placed his guitar back in its case and slowly closed the trunk.

Then he spotted his watcher.

A boy about ten years old stood where the road curved at the bottom of the hill. He had straight black hair and dark skin, and wore jeans and a faded T-shirt. Even at this distance, Rob could tell the eyes were fixed on him.

Rob laughed with relief and waved. "Hi."

The boy said nothing.

Rob gestured at his car. "She broke down on me. Am I anywhere close to Needsville? I know this is Cloud County, but it's hard to tell distance from my map. Those straight lines don't go up and down like the real roads do around here."

The boy cocked his head like a puzzled animal. He had the right hair and skin tone, Rob observed. "Hey, can I ask you something? Are you . . . a Tufa?"

The boy did not respond. Then abruptly he ran off into the forest.

"Wait!" Rob cried, but the boy had vanished.

He laughed at his own reaction. Like an idiot, he'd expected the first Tufa he encountered to be identical to the ones in that famous century-old photograph he'd found online. He anticipated something far more mysterious than a bored country kid skipping school.

A Ford Ranger pickup emerged from the mist, passed over the very spot the boy had stood, and climbed the hill toward Rob. The vehicle had a camper shell and the name COLLINS AUTO SERVICE stenciled on the side. It slowed as it approached.

Rob swallowed hard. *Locals,* he thought. *Just be cool. They're more scared of you than you are of them.*

". . . and then ol' King of the Hill, he put on that devil costume and started down the street, trick-or-treating," Doyle's father, Finley, said, laughing. "That old crazy Christian woman, she just got all puffed up like a bullfrog 'cause all them kids starting following him instead of her."

Doyle nodded patiently. His father always assumed the title of any movie or TV show referred to the main character. It worked okay with things like *Matlock* and *Shane,* less well when he insisted that Bruce Willis's name in the movies was really Die Hard, and Angela Lansbury played a woman called Murder-She-Wrote. He said, "Glad it was a good show, Dad."

"You and Berklee should watch it. Give you something in common."

"We got plenty in common, Dad."

"Not too much. I ain't tripped over no grandchildren yet."

"Everything in its own time. Berklee's not ready yet. She wants to get promoted at the bank before we start a family."

"Son, you ain't never 'ready' to have kids, you just have 'em and hope for the best. Hell, I was five months laid off from the timber mill when you was born, you know that?"

"Remember it like it was yesterday."

Finley scowled. "You must've got that smart mouth from your momma."

"Hey, look," Doyle said.

Finley leaned forward and squinted through the dust-coated windshield. "Appears that fella's got car trouble. Looks like a Tufa. You know him?"

"Nope," Doyle said. He slowed down as they approached. "Better see if he needs a hand, though."

The pickup truck stopped. Rob stood mock casually beside the car, radiating all the self-assurance he'd learned from his weeks on TV. The glare on the dirty windshield hid the driver, but the old man in the passenger seat grimaced, an expression that, if he'd had all his teeth, might have been a smile. He leaned out the window and said, "Car broke?"

"Yeah, it's been out of work for a while," Rob said.

The old man laughed, a barking sound bracketed with wheezes. "That's a good'un!"

Rob smiled. "Thanks. I had to stop quick, and now she won't start back up." He patted the fender like the car was an old, usually reliable friend.

The old man spoke to the driver, who shut off the engine and stepped out of the truck. He was about thirty, tall and thick bodied. His hair was light brown, which meant he wasn't a Tufa. He carried a toolbox almost as large as Rob's guitar case, and the oval name patch on his blue work shirt read DOYLE. "I can take a look at it if you want. If you need a tow, my garage is just down the road."

Rob stayed between Doyle and the vehicle, like a warrior defending a fallen comrade. "No, that's all right, really. I can call Triple A."

Doyle stepped to one side, and again Rob jumped in front of him. Doyle frowned, then saw the Kansas license plate. "Sorry. Didn't realize you was from out of town."

"He ain't from Needsville?" the old man called from the truck.

"Nope. From Kansas," Doyle said.

"He sure looks like one a'them high-yeller Tufa nigras, don't he?"

"*Dad,*" Doyle said sharply. To Rob, he added, "Sorry."

"I'd probably be pissed off if I knew what that meant, wouldn't I?" Rob said.

"Probably," Doyle agreed. "He don't mean nothing bad by it, that's just how old folks are around here. When he was my age, white folks didn't stop to help coloreds. Everybody stayed with their own."

"I'm 'colored'?" Rob repeated, unable to keep an outraged chuckle from the word.

"That's just the way my dad thinks. It's that Tufa hair of yours. To me, you're just a fella who needs help, I don't see no color."

Rob shook his head. His experiences observing racism first-hand as he drove the length of Tennessee had completely startled him. His skin *was* darker than most "white" people, due to a Filipino grandmother brought to America by his grandfather after World War II; she'd also passed down his jet-black hair. So far in the South, when he wasn't recognized from the TV show, he'd been mistaken for Mexican or part African American, referred to as "boy," "son," and "Paco," and once even actually denied use of a restaurant bathroom when other, more Caucasian-appearing tourists were allowed. ("I said it's out of order, boy. You lookin' for trouble?") And now came the ultimate irony: being mistaken for one of the very people he sought.

"I won't charge you nothing for just looking at your car, if that's what you're worried about," Doyle continued. "And I know you Yankees depend on them cell phones, but you'll have a hard time getting a signal out here to call Triple A. Once you get down into the valley, it's fine, but there ain't enough towers to get down into these hollers. And even if you *did* get ahold of 'em, they'd probably just send me anyway. Not a lot of garages around here; most people fix their own."

"Well . . . all right," Rob said, and stepped aside. He quickly added, "But let's talk some more before you *do* anything, okay?"

Doyle opened the hood. As he studied at the engine, Rob looked back down the road for either the boy or the mysterious creature that had caused him to swerve. It had really and truly seemed, based on just the blur of movement, like a mostly naked girl in a tattered dress.

"Yep, it's the starter," Doyle said. "Lucky for you, I got one at the shop that'll fit." He closed the hood; the unnatural metallic noise echoed among the trees. Somewhere a dog or coyote responded with a sharp, yipping cry. "We'll tow it in, and I can get right to work on it. Won't take too long, and," he added with a grin, "I won't charge you the usual Yankee price."

"The rental company better pay for it," Rob said.

"I imagine so." Doyle looked at him oddly. "You sure *do* look familiar. Did you used to live around here?"

"Nope," Rob said. He hoped they wouldn't press the issue. He was quite ready for his fifteen minutes to be over. "Grew up in Kansas."

"Same place as your rental car," Doyle observed.

"That's where I got it. Left straight from home."

Doyle and his father quickly chained the car to the truck, Rob squeezed into the cab with them, and fifteen minutes later, they pulled into the station. It wasn't much: two gas pumps outside a cinder block building divided into a garage and a tiny convenience store. The faded sign read, COLLINS AUTO SERVICE STATION AND SCRAP METAL, with an added placard at the bottom stating, WE BUY FUR. Doyle opened the garage door, while his father shambled over to unlock the store.

"So you're a long way from Kansas," Doyle said as he returned. He carried a round mechanical device Rob assumed was the replacement starter.

"That's the truth," Rob agreed. "But please, no Dorothy jokes."

Doyle popped the hood again. "What brings you here?" When Rob hesitated, Doyle added, "I've got my hands under your hood, you know. We're practically engaged."

Rob laughed. "Met a fellow who told me about Needsville, and I thought I'd see it for myself."

"Told you *what* about it?"

"Well . . . about the Tufa."

"You didn't believe them stories, did you?"

"Didn't tell me any stories, really," he lied. "Just said it was an interesting place, and the folks were good musicians if you could get them to open up."

"We do like our music," Doyle agreed. "What do you play?"

Inside, Rob sighed with relief. Doyle didn't recognize him. "Guitar, mostly. Mess around on keyboards sometimes. How about you?"

"Me? All I play is the stereo."

Rob recalled something his college music history professor once said during a class: "In primitive societies, everybody sings. In agrarian societies, most people sing. In modern societies, hardly anybody sings." Since Doyle knew about cars, had it cost him his cultural heritage? Or was Rob just generalizing about things he really didn't understand? "So you don't know any Tufa songs?"

"Everybody knows all the old mountain songs, but I don't recall ever hearing a song that was specifically Tufa."

"Huh," Rob said noncommittally. "Well, how about . . . cave carvings?"

"Cave carvings?"

"Yeah, you know, like . . . words carved into the walls of a cave. Or a cliff somewhere, like that giant bird in Ohio."

"Uh, I hate to break it to you, but we don't have any cavemen or giant birds around here. The Tufa ain't no different from anybody else: They live in houses, they got bills and cable and the Internet."

Rob realized how patronizing he sounded, yet he'd come all

this *way*. . . . "Anyone who might know about it? Either one, Tufa music or rock carvings—?"

Doyle crossed his arms, and Rob was suddenly conscious of the other man's considerable physical size. "You know, we get a few strangers now and again coming through Needsville poking into the Tufa. They write books, put up Web sites, make their little reality shows for the History Channel, and promise the people here things that ain't never gonna happen. If you smack even a dumb dog enough times, he learns to see it coming. We've been smacked a fair bit."

Rob put up his hands. "No smacking here, I promise."

"You say that now. But when you have to choose between either keeping your word to a bunch of strangers back in the hills, or signing on the dotted line in Nashville or L.A., you might not remember. I've seen it happen. There's a song on the radio I know for a fact a fella who lives over on the highway toward Bristol wrote, but you don't see his name on it. And ain't no checks in his mailbox."

The mechanic resumed work, and Rob tried to think of some way to convince him he meant no harm. But he wasn't sure that was the truth. If the sequined man's ludicrous story turned out to be right, what Rob sought here needed to be shared with the world. What would he do if he did find it, if it actually worked, and if he could, in fact, take it for his own?

Doyle dropped the ratchet handle in the toolbox. "Slide in there and try the ignition."

Rob did, and the engine snapped to life. Doyle moved his toolbox and shut the hood. He listened to the car idle . "There you go. Sweet as."

"What?"

"Huh?"

" 'Sweet as' what?"

"It's just a saying." Doyle wiped his hands on a rag, then spotted something on the ground by his foot. He picked up a penny, faceup, and wiped the dirt from Lincoln's profile. The omen seemed to indicate Rob could be trusted, if he read it right; certainly his grandmother had drilled him enough on signs and omens that he *should* read it right. Had the penny been facedown, it would've meant the opposite, and he wished that had been the case. It was always easier to send strangers on their way. He said, "I reckon I *could* introduce you to some people."

"I'd appreciate it."

Doyle looked hard at him. "You *sure* I don't know you from somewhere?"

"I'm sure I don't know you," Rob said truthfully.

Doyle held up a small can of spray paint. "There's a scratch on the right fender. I know how rental places are, so I'll touch it up for you, if that's all right. No charge."

"Sure."

It only took a second. Doyle gave the can to Rob. "Use this if you get any more dings."

"Thanks."

Doyle looked him over thoughtfully, and finally said, "So do you know where you're staying in town?"

"I have a reservation at a motel called the Catamount Corner."

"I know Mrs. Goins, the lady who runs it. How about I call you there when I get off work? Maybe we can go grab a beer or something, check out where some of the local boys play and sing."

"That'd be great," Rob said with genuine appreciation. "Really. Thanks."

Doyle held out his hand. "Well, my name's Doyle Collins."

"Rob Quillen."

Rob waited for the look of recognition, but it never came. Doyle said, "Pleased to meet you."

Rob laughed. "Really?"

"Well, truthfully, I don't know yet. But I bet I'll find out pretty soon."

An old pickup truck with a bunch of black-haired kids riding in the bed pulled in as Rob left the station. He knew he couldn't keep his past a secret—somebody would eventually recognize him, he was sure—but he wanted to hold it off as long as he could. People got weird around famous people touched by tragedy, especially people famous *because* they were touched by it.

3

As he drove, Rob noticed something in the yard of an old shack ahead on the right. At first he thought it was one of those elaborate homemade mailboxes, fashioned into the shape of a tractor or a gas pump. Then it stepped into the road and blocked his way.

He had plenty of time to stop. The emu, an ostrich-like bird six feet tall and brownish green in color, stared at Rob's vehicle with mildly stupid curiosity. Rob knew some people raised these birds for their meat, but this one appeared to be roaming loose, and in no hurry to get out of the road. Rob used his phone to snap a quick picture.

A wiry, dark-haired man in jeans and a denim jacket ran out of the shack. He had the distinctive Cloud County look, just like the boy. "Hey, *hey*! *Git outta here!*" An aluminum baseball bat flashed in the sun.

Rob's muscles tensed in anticipation of a fight, but the man's rage was directed at the emu, which took off and disappeared into the woods across the road. The man shook the baseball bat menacingly after the bird, then skulked off the way he'd come. He never even glanced at Rob.

Rob let out his breath in a long, heavy rush. Welcome to the land of the Tufa.

The road rose and fell several times before it topped a final hill and descended into the valley where, at the center, awaited Needsville, Tennessee.

Needsville's "main street" was simply a wider stretch of the highway with buildings along either side. A lone traffic light flashed yellow to control access to a road winding up into the forested hills. Beneath the sign that identified the city limits, a smaller homemade placard advertised the Catamount Corner Motel, half a mile ahead on the left.

He found it easily enough and parked out front. The steps up to the porch sagged a little, but otherwise it seemed in excellent condition, with all the wood recently painted. He'd been afraid of some run-down fleapit used by truckers and fugitives.

The staggering reality of the scenery hit him anew. The horizon in Kansas was impossibly distant and flat; here it loomed over him. The rounded mountaintops were daubed with spots of yellow and orange as the trees began to turn. Beyond them, the far peaks rose ponderously, clothed in somber hues of spruce. Where the forest had been cleared from the slopes, the hills swelled with lush grass. Tiny dwellings perched here and there, some visibly new, most as old and gray as the rocks beneath them. Cell phone towers poked into the sky along the ridges; they reminded him of hairy moles on an old woman's chin.

He immediately tried to find metaphors for the beauty, words that captured the overwhelming sense of massiveness and antiquity. He imagined the first European settlers reaching the top of one of these ridges and seeing the valley in which he now stood. Whether they'd been English, Scotch-Irish, or German, they would have been overwhelmed by the vista before them: all this untouched virgin land just waiting to be cleared, built on, and developed.

And when those first settlers arrived, they found the Tufa already here.

The wind shifted direction, and he shivered. His guidebook said the temperature change could be extreme in late summer and early fall, from the high seventies during the day to the thirties at night. He grabbed his bags and quickly went inside.

The lobby smelled like potpourri and fresh flowers; lace-edged country knickknacks covered every surface, and one corner was set up with displays of the same items for sale. He stepped up to the desk, carefully propped his guitar case against it, and less carefully dropped his duffel bag to the floor. "Hello?" he called.

A woman in her fifties, with dark skin and ebony hair touched with gray, appeared from the office. She wore a T-shirt decorated with appliqué hearts. "Hello, young man. Can I help you?"

"I've got a reservation. Robert Quillen. Hope I'm not too early to check in."

Peggy Goins looked him over with the practiced evaluation of a woman who had never lost touch with her inner horny teenager, the one who'd spent a single glorious summer in the 1960s traveling and fucking all along the eastern seaboard. This Robert Quillen was slender, with a thick head of black hair, an easy smile, and dark, piercing eyes. She'd seen eyes like that before; they spoke of the capacity for furious anger, and other furies far more intimate. He carried a single bag, which meant he traveled alone, and a guitar, which said he was musical.

Although he looked like one of them, she knew immediately there was no Tufa blood in him. It happened occasionally; people ran across the "Tufa mystery" on the Internet or in a book and imagined they, too, were somehow connected. But there was more to it than just physical resemblance. After all, the Tufa weren't the only ones in the world with straight black hair and a swarthy complexion. But this boy sure did look the part, and folks in Needsville with less of the true in *them* might easily assume he was, especially since he was a guest at the Catamount Corner. Peggy's establishment survived on the desire of anyone with even a drop of Tufa blood to return to Needsville. It was similar to the call of Mecca, or a bird's urge to migrate, except that it was more subtle, usually unconscious, and could be resisted without too much effort. Those who answered it, however, often learned things about themselves they'd never imagined.

She flipped through a recipe box and pulled out a three-by-five index card. "Here you are, Mr. Quillen. And how long will you be staying with us?"

"Probably three nights, but maybe more. Is that too vague? I mean, if I need to stay on longer, will that be a problem?"

"Not at all. We only have one other couple coming in this weekend. Now, next month, when the leaves really start to turn, then it'll be a madhouse here. Nothing but Canadians and Texans until Thanksgiving." She handed him the guest registration card. "Fill this out for me, if you would."

She took his Visa card and ran her fingers over the signature on the back. She sensed only vague things from it, but they made her frown nonetheless. She was right about his temper; it would burst out soon, and affect a lot of people in town. She also saw disturbing flashes of blood, and the ghastly image of a pale hand clawing up from a grave. But mixed in were smiles, strains of music, and the sighs of lovers. She remembered her own omens at sunrise and wondered how this newcomer would figure into them.

Rob quickly filled in the other information, but paused at "emergency contact." Normally, it would be Anna. Now, he had no idea whom to put down. He left it blank.

As she waited for the card's authorization, Peggy asked, "Here to trace your family?"

"People keep asking me that. Do I really look that much like a Tufa?"

She waved her hand. "Oh, honey, looks got nothing to do with it. Tufa's like Cherokee, you can be blond and blue-eyed and still have enough in you to count. It's just that we get people in here, prowling the cemeteries, looking for ancestors. They take pictures and videos and rubbings and such."

"Well, not me. I'm a musician."

She nodded, and then her eyes widened. "Oh, my goodness, you're Rob from the TV show!"

His cheeks burned. This never got easy. "Yep, that's me."

"I am so sorry, I didn't recognize your name at first. Oh, you poor thing, bless your heart."

"Thank you. Do you mind if we keep this just between ourselves for now?"

"Of course, whatever you need." She patted his hand. "But if you want to talk, I promise you, I can listen with the best of them, and I keep secrets like a beehive keeps honey from a bear."

"Thank you," he repeated.

She returned his credit card, but when he reached for it, she said, "Would you mind if I had a look at your palm?"

"Are you going to tell my future?"

"Oh, no, nothing so silly. No one can predict the future. Every blink of every eye changes it. I can just sometimes tell what your next few days might be like."

"Well . . . I suppose." He put his card back in his wallet, then let her hold his hand, palm up.

Most of her evaluation was empirical. Rob's hand was small, but by its weight, she knew the muscles were built up the way only prolonged musical practice would develop them. His nails were short and neat. One knuckle felt larger than normal, probably a healed injury from the temper she'd already sensed. But then came observations and impressions that had no material source, but that she trusted as much as any physical sign. After a moment, she released his hand and nodded.

"Did I pass?" he asked, amused despite himself.

"Of course. It looked to me like your time here will do you a world of good. Everything will be different when you leave."

"That's a tall order."

She patted his hand. "You just wait and see. But I've got to warn you: Not everyone you meet will be as honest as me."

"I've worked with TV producers. I'm ready for anything."

He followed Peggy across the lobby. He stopped at a framed newspaper clipping on the wall that showed a dark-haired young woman in an army uniform gazing sternly into the camera. He recognized her at once. "Bronwyn Hyatt is from here?"

"Oh, yes. She grew up here. She lives out at her family's farm."

"Huh. Imagine that." He remembered the media circus surrounding her rescue in Iraq and her return to the States in the spring, and the way that she completely dropped out of the public consciousness since. Maybe he should look her up and ask her how she did that.

Upstairs, Peggy unlocked room 17B with a simple key, not one of those ID cards used in chain motels. Then she stepped aside so he could enter.

The room brought him up short. Lace edged *everything*, from the writing desk to the telephone receiver. Little painted animals in overalls and straw hats ran along the baseboard, and the bed sported an enormous canopy and a huge, thick mattress. When Rob tossed his guitar on the bed, it bounced a foot into the air.

"That looks comfortable," he observed.

"We don't get many single young men coming through," she said. "Usually couples."

"I bet they appreciate that."

She handed him the key. "I hope you enjoy your stay with us and manage to get some rest. There's a café menu on your desk. Local calls are free, although Lord knows who you'd call around here. But you've probably got one of those fancy picture-taking cell phones anyway." As she went out, she added cheerily, "If you need anything, just holler. I'm usually in the office behind the desk during the day, and my husband and I live out back."

"Thanks. I should be fine for tonight." As she turned away, he added, "Did you know you have wild emus around here?"

"Yes," she said with disgust. "They used to belong to old Sim Denham. He bought a whole gaggle of the nasty things. Thought he'd make a fortune with them. Then the bottom dropped out of the market and he just let 'em go. Now the darn things are everywhere."

"I nearly ran over one today. Are they dangerous?"

"No, but they give me the whim-whams the way they just *stare* at you." She shivered. "Well, if you need anything, you just let me know."

Rob closed the door after her, and noticed an odd wooden

device mounted to it. It looked like the neckless body of a tiny mandolin or guitar, with four strings stretched across the hole. Small wooden balls hung so that they'd strike these strings whenever the door closed. It made a soft, comforting sound.

He cleared the complimentary stationery and postcards from the desk and placed his laptop on it. As he waited for it to find the network, he took in more details, like the small fireplace in the corner and the lack of a television. On the wall over the desk hung a framed cross-stitched quote attributed to William Blake:

GREAT THINGS ARE DONE WHEN MEN AND MOUNTAINS MEET.

It was stuffy in the room, so he opened the window. His view looked out at the woods, which grew thick on the slope of a rising hillside, giving him only a limited view of the sky. A small piece of irregular blue glass lay discarded on the sill. He tossed it in the trash can by the desk, then sat down to check his e-mail.

He was startled to see, not his Gmail account, but the Tufa Mysteries Web site. He forgot he'd made it his home page just before he left Kansas. The splash page featured the classic vintage picture of these enigmatic people, the one in every book, article, or blog. It was black-and-white, scratched and faded with age, but sharp with the detail those old huge cameras captured. Three women held their babies and stood grim-faced before a rough-edged mountain cabin. In front of them, three men sat in straight-backed chairs; they clutched a rifle, a guitar, and a windup phonograph, respectively. They looked like European Gypsies: dark skin, straight black hair and eyes haunted by mistrust. Yet the caption read, "Gorvens family, Cloud County, TN, 1898."

This picture—the original was held in the Museum of Appalachia archives—was the touchstone for anyone interested in the

Tufa mystery. Rob had seen the same photo in many other books, often with conflicting information about its origin. About the only thing the different sources agreed on was the family's surname, Gorvens, and that the clan had vanished into the mountains shortly after they'd been convinced to sit for the photo, never to be seen again by the outside world.

The guitar in the photo had first caught his attention as he surfed Web sites on music history late one sleepless night. Most sources insisted guitars weren't generally used by the mountain folk until after 1910, yet here was one, in a blatantly musical context, at least twenty years earlier. The picture tangentially confirmed part of the sequined man's story, enough to convince Rob he should make the pilgrimage.

After reading about the Tufa into the wee hours, the idea that he might just throw things in a car and head south struck him as he stared at the ceiling. Why the hell not? He had money, and time. If the tale of heart-healing magical music turned out to be bullshit, which Rob knew *had* to be the case, he'd at least get a change of scenery, which God knew he needed. And if it were *true* . . .

He glanced at his reflection in a small mirror across the room and compared it to the faces in the photograph. There *was* a general resemblance, but these Gorvens had something in their eyes entirely missing from Rob's. It was too vague and insubstantial for him to name, but its reality was unmistakable, like seeing a shadow but not the thing casting it.

He logged on to Facebook and updated his status. This was his personal page, with fewer than two hundred friends. His "Like" page had more than twenty-five million. He never even looked at it now; twenty-five million messages of sympathy and condolences just left him numb.

Arrived in Needsville today, he typed.

My car broke down, but one of the locals helped me out. Here's a quote from my official Tennessee guidebook that really captures the feel of the place: "Nestled in the northeast corner of the state, deep in the Smoky Mountains, the area's rugged landscape features many high ridges and narrow valleys that remain mostly untouched by the modern world." And I tell you, it's the truth. It's like entering another world, similar to ours but with small, subtle surprises. Like this.

Then he posted the photo of the emu.

He closed the computer and took out his guitar. Seated on the edge of the bed, he softly played one of the tunes he'd written after passing through Erwin, a town noted for a bizarre incident in which a killer circus elephant was hanged with a railroad crane. It was his latest attempt at a true folkish story-song, and although it was awful (he rhymed "elephant" with "the hell it can't"), he understood that it was a step on the road to competence.

But, as with everything he wrote these days, that song morphed into another, one of many he'd written about Anna. He sang softly, feeling the rhythm of the words link inextricably with the melody.

> *All the screaming girls*
> *Said they love me*
> *All the screaming girls*
> *Said they want me*
> *All the screaming girls*
> *Fade into the dark*

And I'm the one screaming
For you.

He yawned, and realized he was thoroughly exhausted even though it was barely lunchtime. He'd left the Cookville motel before dawn, and now could not keep his eyes open. He leaned back on the bed, intending to just shut his eyes for an instant, and didn't even put his guitar away. He was asleep in moments.

Peggy's husband, Marshall, came in from the back carrying a box of disposable coffee filters. "You ain't never gonna guess who's upstairs right now," his wife said.

He put down the box on the front desk and looked at her. "That's likely."

"Well, go ahead, guess."

"You said I ain't never gonna be able to."

"That doesn't mean you shouldn't try."

"I don't know. Kevin Sorbo."

"Kevin Sorbo? Where'd that come from?"

"Can you just tell me? I have a bunch of stuff to unload."

"Rob Quillen."

"You're right, I never would've guessed that. Who's Rob Quillen?"

"That poor boy from *So You Think You Can Sing?* His girlfriend was flying out to surprise him at the final show, and her plane crashed?"

"Oh, yeah. There's some tough luck for you. Why is he here?"

"I don't know. Remember how we all thought he looked like one of us? Well, he ain't got a drop of Tufa in him, I can tell that for sure. But he does have the look."

"That could be trouble. Not everyone can tell the difference."

"Oh, he's harmless. He probably just wants to get away from all the publicity, like Bronwyn. Can you blame him?"

"Reckon not. He picked the right place to do it."

Marshall carried the box into the kitchen. Peggy tapped her finger on the desk. Marshall had reiterated something she'd thought earlier: Not every Tufa, even some of the true bloods, could tell if someone else was one of them. If a person had the look, like Rob, then he could stumble into things he was never meant to know.

She picked up the phone and dialed Bliss Overbay, then hung up before it rang. Bliss was fine for most things, but she was merely the regent, not the leader. For something like this, Peggy needed someone with a direct line to the night winds.

She dialed again. A moment later she said, "Leshell? May I please speak to Mandalay? Oh, that's right, school did start last week. Well, could you tell her to call Peggy Goins when she gets home? Thanks."

4

After lunchtime, Doyle went into the convenience store beside the garage. His father sat on a stool at the register, chin in his hand, elbow on the counter. He was snoring. Behind him, Gretchen Wilson reclined suggestively in a poster thumbtacked to the wall.

Doyle picked up the phone, dialed the bank, and asked Bella Mae for Berklee's extension. "Thanks for calling the Bank of Needsville," his wife said when she picked up, "where interest rates are—"

He interrupted the mandatory spiel. "It's me."

"Hi." There was no feeling of any sort in the word.

"Met an interesting fella today. Guitar player from Kansas, staying down at Peggy Goins's motel. Thought I might take him down to hear Rockhouse and the boys tonight."

"Sure, go ahead."

He had to lick his suddenly dry lips before speaking again. "Thought you might want to come along."

There was a long pause. Doyle heard the noise of the

pneumatic tubes at the bank's drive-through window, and he knew exactly what his wife was thinking: *He might be there.* Finally Berklee said in a small voice, "Okay. That'd be nice."

He felt a tingle in his chest, but wasn't sure if it was relief or apprehension. "'Kay. See you at home, then."

"'Kay. Love you."

"Love you, too."

He hung up. Gretchen's slightly stoned, slightly horny expression hadn't changed. He turned so he wouldn't have to look at her, and watched through the connecting door as a squirrel poked its head into the garage, sniffed the fume-laden air, and scampered away. It was a nice symbol for how he felt whenever he approached Berklee these days. Something inside her was dying, decaying, and she tried to cover the stench with alcohol and bluster. Unlike the squirrel, though, he couldn't wrinkle his nose and just scurry away. He loved her.

Doyle parked his truck beside Rob's car in front of the Catamount Corner. The sun had just crept behind the mountains, and darkness would, as always, fall like a thick shroud thrown over everything. Berklee sat beside him, her eyes scanning the street outside the way they always did in town. She looked fantastic: tight jeans, a blouse unbuttoned just enough to display her cleavage, her long hair loose and combed to shiny perfection. And, as some sort of concession to the evening, she'd consumed only three beers during the time she spent getting dressed. He knew if he mentioned it, she'd mock him and turn it into an argument, so he simply filed it away. These scraps of effort, meager as they were, made him recall the girl he loved, and kept the spark inside him alive.

Peggy Goins glanced up at them as they entered, then smiled. "Well, the happy Collinses. And how are the night winds treatin' the two of you this evening?"

"Fine as always," Doyle said. Berklee said nothing, her eyes continually drawn to the windows that looked out on Main Street. "We're here to pick up one of your guests."

"Must be Mr. Quillen, he's the only one I've got right now," Peggy said. "I'll ring his room for you." She picked up the phone, punched the numbers, and waited for an answer. "You have company, Mr. Quillen. Doyle and Berklee Collins. Okay, I'll tell them." She hung up. "He said he'll be right down."

Berklee took a seat in one of the padded high-backed chairs, elegantly crossed her legs, rested her hands in her lap, and resumed staring out the window.

Peggy took Doyle's arm. "Come along, then, we'll go hurry him up." She pulled him toward the door that led to the stairs.

"But he said—"

"*Come along,*" she repeated, and cut her eyes at Berklee. Doyle wearily nodded and allowed her to lead him into the stairwell.

Once the door closed behind them and they were halfway between the two floors, Peggy stopped. "She's getting worse, Doyle."

"Everybody drinks a little," he said with a weak shrug.

"I don't mean the drinking, and you know it. She hasn't taken her eyes off the street since you got here. I bet she hasn't let the two of you have marital relations in months."

"That's kinda personal, Mrs. Goins," he said, annoyed. He respected Peggy as both an elder and because of her status in the Needsville community. But some lines no one was allowed to cross.

"You need to cut bait, Doyle," Peggy said seriously. "There's nothing you or anyone can do. It's got its hooks in her, and they won't pull out. They just work their way in deeper."

"She don't drink *that* much."

"Stop trying to make this about her drinking," Peggy said. "I'd drink all the time, too, in her shoes. I can't believe she's lasted as long as this. But, son, you *have* to know where this'll end up. No matter how much you love her, it'll never be enough. You should start letting go of her now, before she pulls you down with her."

"You give everyone such good advice?"

"Doyle Collins, don't you take that tone with me. I knew you before you could wipe your own behind. Same with Berklee in there. You think it doesn't break my heart to see her like that? I'm giving you the advantage of my . . . Oh, what do you call it when you look at something different from everyone else?"

"Perspective?"

"Yes. The advantage of my perspective. I wouldn't be able to close my eyes at night if I knew I didn't try."

"Then you should sleep like a baby."

He said it flatly, with no blatant malice, but his irritation was plain. Peggy scowled again, then decided to change the subject. "How did you meet that boy upstairs, anyway?"

"His car broke down. Dad and I helped him out."

"Do you know who he is?"

"Said his name was Rob Quillen."

"Yes, but do you know who he *is*?"

Doyle shook his head.

Peggy opened her mouth, then remembered her promise. Her almost biological need to gossip warred with her sense of honor, until finally the latter won. "I reckon he'll have to tell you. I promised I wouldn't."

"Is he famous or something?"

"Closer to 'something.'"

Doyle shrugged. "Whatever. I can find my way from here."

———

When the phone woke Rob, it was dark. He knees ached from dangling off the side of the bed. He lay half-curled around his guitar, the same way he used to spoon with Anna. After talking to Mrs. Goins, he stood, stretched, and felt his back and shoulders pop. Then he went to the still-open window.

Darkness thicker than any city night had fallen, and he heard nothing but wind, crickets, and the occasional owl. A brief, spooky shudder rippled through him as he realized how cut off he was from real civilization.

As if to emphasize this, a coyote chose that exact moment to howl its shrill, vaguely mocking cry. That made him smile, and his paranoia retreated. It was, after all, the twenty-first century, and even here, he had wireless access. How isolated could he really be?

He adjusted the window to block most of the chilly night breeze. His solitude enveloped him anew, a pressure that seemed to leave him weightless and insubstantial. Would anyone care if he vanished from this room? Would he inspire more than a knowing "tsk" from anyone who knew him? At best, he'd become the answer to a trivia question, a footnote in pop-culture history.

He was so engrossed in these self-pitying thoughts that he jumped at the knock on his door. "Come in," he said when he got his breath.

Doyle opened the door. He'd changed from his gas station clothes and now wore jeans and a University of Tennessee T-shirt. "Hi, you about ready?"

"Yeah. Fell asleep. Sorry."

"There's some local boys got a pickup bluegrass band playin' down at the Pair-A-Dice tonight. My wife and I generally go for a while, so I thought I'd see if you might want to tag along."

"Definitely, thanks." He splashed some water on his face, combed his hair, and touched up his deodorant. Then he carefully wiped his guitar's strings and put the instrument back in its case. He wished he could spend just five minutes alone with his music; playing always grounded him.

Rob followed Doyle downstairs. In the lobby, a young woman rose from one of the overstuffed high-backed chairs as they entered. Tall, willowy, with jet-black hair and dark skin, she reminded Rob of the cliché image of an Indian princess from one of the souvenir plates his mother collected.

"Hi," she said, and snuggled into Doyle's embrace when he put his arm around her shoulders. To Rob she said, "You must be the fella with the bad starter."

My starter's working just fine, Rob wanted to say as he surreptitiously admired her, but instead replied, "Yeah. Quite a handy husband you got there."

"He'll do." She was almost as tall as Doyle, and jabbed him playfully. "So are you going to introduce us, or should I just call him 'Yankee guitar boy,' like you do?"

Doyle had noticed Rob's reaction to Berklee; every man had the same one when they first met her. As always, he let it slide. "Rob Quillen, this is my wife, Berklee."

Rob shook her hand; it was small and strong, with elegant nails. He wondered what she did for a living. "Berklee like the music school?"

"No, Berklee as in my daddy, Berk, really wanted a son and had to make do with me. But it's spelled like the school." Her eyes narrowed. "Excuse my rudeness, but . . . do I know you?"

"I don't see how." He smelled beer on her breath.

"It's probably just that black hair. You look like you could be a Tufa."

" 'Fraid not," he said.

"So are you going to sit in with the boys at the Pair-A-Dice tonight?" she asked.

"Nah, I'm just going to listen." Rob had learned the hard way that showing up with his guitar did not automatically gain him entrance to a local music scene. If anything, his TV fame often just pissed them off. They felt, quite correctly, that it was only dumb luck that he'd been chosen over them, and probably resented the tragedy that had overtaken him and made the spotlight even brighter.

"Well, if we want a decent leanin' spot on the wall, we better get on down there," Doyle said.

Rob nodded, followed them out the door, and after an inadvertent glance at her gracefully swaying rear, made an inner vow to stop thinking of Berklee as a human woman right then and there.

Peggy rested her chin in her hands and watched the night through the window. She felt guilty for almost breaking Rob's confidence, but also a heartrending sympathy for him. It was the biggest Tufa weakness: the ability to empathize all out of proportion to the relationship. She barely knew the boy, but his plight caused her almost physical pain.

Had he been even part Tufa, she would've known what to do.

WISP OF A THING

But he had no blood in him, despite his appearance. So she was at a loss.

Then she had an idea. She reached for the phone and dialed a number she knew by heart.

"Chloe? It's Peggy. Is Bronwyn there?"

49

5

The Pair-A-Dice was a rectangular cinder block building, windowless and with only one visible door, set back from the highway in the center of a dirt parking lot. Only the two enormous cutouts of dice on the roof, visible as Doyle's truck topped the hill, implied that it was anything other than someone's old work shed.

Rob spent the whole ten-minute ride jammed against the passenger door, as it seemed prudent not to press himself too closely against his new friend's wife. Now, as his tennis shoes hit the gravel, he heard banjo, fiddle, and guitar mingle in a swirling bluegrass spiral metered by enthusiastic clapping. This moment just before entering a new music venue always gave him goose bumps, and the fact that he couldn't immediately name the song sent extra adrenaline rushing through him. Maybe this band played songs he'd never heard before. Maybe—he couldn't help but hope—*Tufa* songs. Maybe even *the* song. Could "carved in stone," as the man told him, have meant inside a concrete building?

Cars and trucks formed an irregular circle around the place. The air smelled clean and fresh, helped by the wind's faint autumn bite. When he looked up, Rob saw a pinpoint ocean of stars, with the crescent moon waiting like a cup to catch any that fell its way.

The moon had risen behind a distant, incredibly tall tree. "What kind of tree is that?" Rob asked, pointing.

"That's the Widow's Tree," Berklee said.

"What does that mean?"

"Widows carve their husband's name on it. It helps them get over the loss."

"Really?"

"They say. Don't have any experience with it myself."

"And I'm glad to hear that," Doyle said. He indicated the full parking lot. "Looks like a good crowd."

"Rockhouse brings 'em out of the woodwork," Berklee added, forcing her gaze to the ground. "Both sides come out to hear him."

"Both sides of what?" Rob asked. When no one answered, he added, "So, I take it they play bluegrass?"

"Bluegrass is what they call it in Nashville," Berklee said disdainfully. "Everything needs a label there."

"If we're real lucky, Bliss Overbay'll sit in with 'em," Doyle said. Immediately, he regretted it.

Berklee jabbed him with her elbow in a gesture that appeared playful, but was a bit too emphatic to be a joke. "If she does, you better be as far away from her as that room allows, my friend. I shit you not."

"You'd have to eat me first," Doyle said. He grabbed Berklee's hand and held it tight. Like her drinking, her jealousy had grown much worse lately, and Doyle prayed she wouldn't make another scene if Bliss did show up. The last time, he'd had to carry her out like a child having a tantrum.

The music surged out when Doyle opened the door. Not only was the band loud, but everyone in the packed room seemed to be clapping along and stomping in unison as well. To Rob, it was both a cliché and a wonder. "Wow," he said. It was the only appropriate word he could think of.

A young, giddy couple on their way outside pushed awkwardly past them. " 'Scuse us!" the boy called back over his shoulder. The girl kissed him and, without letting go, practically yanked him around the corner of the building. Both had jet-black hair and Tufa features.

"Is this a rowdy bunch?" Rob asked Doyle over the music.

"It's a golden retriever, on a dog scale."

"On a what?"

"Dog scale. Worst is a Rottweiler, best is a collie. A golden retriever is pretty easygoing until you get out of line. These folks are like that."

"You're big on animal metaphors, aren't you?"

Doyle laughed.

The crowd was so thick near the entrance that they could barely close the door behind them. Other than the eager young lovers, people weren't trying to leave, though; rather, they had backed up to clear the small dance floor. Beyond them, Rob saw the bobbing heads of the actual dancers.

Berklee stood on tiptoe and looked around almost frantically. At last she sighed, settled back to her feet, and sagged with disappointment.

"Hey!" a short, round woman called to Doyle and Berklee. "Y'all lookin' mighty fancy tonight!"

Since the woman appeared to be wearing every cosmetic

known to man, Rob thought this quite a statement. She wedged through the people standing near the door and hugged Doyle around the waist. Then Berklee bent to receive her embrace.

She looked up expectantly at Rob, then realized she didn't know him. Her too-small dress buttoned up the front, but just barely, and she apparently wore nothing under it. "And just who's this handsome blade of grass here?" she asked.

"Rob Quillen," he said, and shook her hand.

She brushed his hair back from his face and scrutinized him. "Hm. I figured he was from another ridge somewhere, but he don't talk like us. One of them people comin' through lookin' for your roots?"

"No, ma'am, I'm pretty sure I know my roots."

The woman's eyes shone from alcohol. "Well, it's nice to meet you, anyway. I'll save a dance for you." Then she bulldozed past them to hug someone else.

Doyle responded to Rob's quizzical look with a shrug. "That's Opal Duncan, She's always here."

"She work here?"

"No. She's just . . . always here."

"She fell out of the ugly tree," Berklee added, "and hit every branch on the way down."

"Be nice," Doyle said. "We can't all be pretty as you."

Rob followed Doyle and Berklee to the bar, where they all ordered beer. Doyle and Berklee both drank healthy swallows, but Rob put his tongue over the bottle's mouth so it only looked like he was drinking. He liked to stay mostly sober in strange bars.

The walls were lined with wood paneling that should have ruined the acoustics but somehow didn't. Torn, stained posters and faded photos lined the walls; some went back more than sixty years, to a time when giants like Hank Williams walked the earth in a haze of whiskey-drenched loneliness. Rob felt a, tangible connection to this history, and imagined the way Bill Monroe's cowboy boots must've sounded as they walked across this floor, or the snap as Earl Scruggs opened his banjo case. Back then, no one knew they were creating a whole new form of music; hell, people barely grasped the true scope of it now.

The room buzzed with energy, and it surprised him how many kids he saw, many of them too young to even be in a bar. He wondered if they came for the social aspects, the lack of alternatives, or if they, too, were drawn by the music.

Rob stood on tiptoes to see the band on the riser in the corner. Two old Peavey amplifiers were stacked on either side of the stage, and a single dim spotlight hung from a bracket on the low ceiling. He saw no mixing board anywhere, or any sign of monitors. He wondered how they heard themselves over the crowd.

Three men and a woman were onstage. All looked to be in their fifties, although he'd read that age could be deceptive among the mountain folk due to their hard lives. Two of the men, the fiddler and the guitarist, were dressed in Western-style finery, with big cowboy hats and pearl-snap shirts.

The lone woman stood facing the fiddler, her back to the room. She wore a long denim skirt and her black hair pulled up into a bun atop her head. She held two knitting needles, and hammered out a rhythm on the fiddle strings while the fiddler played the melody. Rob had never seen anything like that before.

The third man played banjo. He wore overalls and a baseball cap turned backwards, and sported a thick white beard. The banjo's skin face cover was stained dark in the center from years of use.

"I got you now, you old rascal!" the guitarist called out.

"You got it goin' on, I tell ya!" the fiddler yelled back.

Something about the banjo player drew Rob's eye, but he couldn't identify it. Had he seen the man's picture somewhere? No, there was something different about the way he played. Not how he held the instrument, not the way he picked, it was—

He had six fingers on each hand.

Rob stared as the bearded man ran them up and down the banjo's neck and plucked expertly at the strings. He'd never seen anyone with extra digits before, and the fact that they all seemed to work added to his surprise. With a flourish, the band finished their current number, and the banjo picker threw his hands up in mock supplication, as if his skill was a gift from heaven. The sight of the twelve fingers spread wide was even stranger.

The crowd applauded, laughed, whistled, and stomped their approval.

"Thankee, thankee," the guitarist said as the applause faded to an excited murmur. The woman took her knitting needles, picked up the canvas bag at her feet, and left the stage. She sat nearby in an old folding chair and began to work on one end of a sweater sleeve.

The banjo player stage-muttered, "Boy, I tell you what, I'm gonna kick the ass of the fella that thought up mountin' a set of strings on a damn drumhead."

"'Cause he made you love it," the guitarist fired back. To the crowd, he said, "We're about to bring a special guest up here now to join us on this next song. Y'all all know her, so let's have a big round of applause for Miss Bliss Overbay."

This time the response, if possible, was even louder. The banjo picker scooted his stool to one side, but not very far, as if he resented sharing the center spot.

A slender woman stepped onto the stage. She had long jet-black hair in a single braid that fell down her back almost to her waist.

Her dark face had deep smile lines bracketing her wide mouth, which made guessing her age difficult; she could've been anywhere between twenty and forty. Her eyes were dark, but Rob swore they actually *twinkled* like they were illuminated from within. She wore a long, dark skirt and a simple sleeveless blouse that hinted at the same tough, exquisite shape so many rural women possessed in their girlhood: broad shoulders, narrow waist, wide hips, and strong legs. A snake tattoo ran around her upper arm and disappeared under her clothing. Through a momentary gap in the crowd, he glimpsed her bare feet.

"Well, if it ain't Miss La-Dee-Da," Berklee sniffed.

"Stop it," Doyle said patiently, as if he'd said it a million times before.

Bliss faced the packed room. Her decision to sit in with the boys had been sudden and inexplicable, one of those urges sourced somewhere deep inside, beneath her veneer of civilization. She'd taken a change of clothes with her to work, something she almost never did, and headed straight to the Pair-A-Dice instead of home. *One song,* she told herself; *one song to honor the night wind and the eternal truce between her people and the others, and then back home, straight into the shower and then to bed.*

She smiled as the applause, and the energy it generated, rippled over her like a thousand caresses. Not all these people liked her, and some rightly feared her, but they all appreciated her musical skill; the songs were the common ground where all the Tufa met. She let her eyes drift over the crowd, observing the faces that had changed and the ones that hadn't.

"Wow, thank you," Bliss said. "Before we get started, just wanted to mention that there's a yellow Chevy Nova outside with its lights on. Also, the kitchen's closing in about ten minutes, so if you're hungry, you better make up your mind now." She looked down, and her demeanor shifted from casual to something more serious. She exchanged a long, enigmatic look with the six-fingered banjo player, then spoke. "This is one of my own, which y'all have been nice enough to ask us to play before. Hope you like it this time, too."

She began to sway, her skirt waving against her body; then she counted four. The band came in behind her with practiced precision. Their tightness impressed Rob; they clearly played together often. He imagined them as young boys on a mountain cabin porch making music for barefoot girls in long summer dresses, who swayed to the music with their eyes closed just as Bliss Overbay now did.

Then Bliss stepped to the microphone and let out a long, deep wail, a counterpoint melody to the banjo and guitar. The fiddle came in as harmony, soaring over the woman's smoky voice. The sound quieted errant conversations and stilled the dancers as everyone turned their attention toward the stage. Rob got chills that had nothing to do with the weather.

She wrapped one hand lightly around the microphone on its stand and began to sing.

I'm driving down the mountain
As the sun begins to sink
I've got the music blasting off the ridges
So I don't have to think
I hear the wind in the pines moan low under the beat
For the price of my heart, I'd trade these wheels for wings,
But I dance in the dying daylight as I sing
The song that reminds me of you.

The guitar kept the rhythm, while the banjo plucked a metronomic counterpoint. The fiddler wailed softly beneath the woman's full voice.

The crowd was absolutely rapt. Even Berklee and Doyle kept their eyes on Bliss. Rob had never seen anyone so thoroughly command a crowd's attention. Even the packed audiences at the TV show tapings had not been this riveted. The cliché said that at a good concert, each audience member felt as if the performer sang directly to him or her; here, that was no cliché at all.

Bliss closed her eyes and bent her head back, letting her long braid sway with the music. She knew that, when she sang right and truly embodied the music, she *was* beautiful, that all the empty superlatives slathered on her were, at that moment, entirely true. If the song was graceful, so was she; if the words were biting and yet playful, her smile shone the same way. The twinkle in her eye gleamed like the notes flying from the banjo, and she swayed like the fiddler's bow. The clunky, flesh-bound bulk of her life was made bearable by these freed-spirit moments when she became what the Tufa ultimately were: a song. Then she slowly twirled, the skirt flaring around her, and timed it perfectly so that her hand slid back around the microphone as she began to sing again.

> *Tell me what's remembered or forgotten*
> *When my heart hits the ground*
> *There's things I can't get out of my mind*
> *And they're pulling me down.*

She threw her free hand into the air, and the band stopped instantly, except for the plinking beat carried on the banjo.

> *I tried to run for the hills*
> *But they were here and I was already theirs*
> *I wanted to crawl into my grave*
> *Give up my time to the things I can't bear*
> *But your voice called me from the edge*
> *As I looked down into the comforting dark*
> *And now I huddle at your feet*
> *Bruised and bursting the seams of my heart.*

Then the band thundered back, or at least as much as a bluegrass trio could thunder, carrying the melody as Bliss sang wordlessly in a style half yodel, half blues wail.

When they finished a measure later, the place went nuts.

Rob applauded and whistled through his teeth, as impressed by her presence as by her song. He'd just encountered a whole new genre; it was fucking *Goth bluegrass.*

And for a brief moment, the pain and loneliness no longer enveloped him.

The appreciative noise fell over Bliss like an old, comfortable blanket until a sharp whistle stood out from the rest. Her eyes flitted among the familiar faces until, this time, she spotted the new one. He had black hair and Tufa-dark skin, although like Peggy Goins, she instantly knew he had no Tufa blood in him. He watched her with the inadvertently blatant look she knew so well.

She didn't know *him,* though; how had she missed him earlier? His presence recalled the previous night's dream, and that connection sent a rush of panic through her. Suddenly the room felt small, hot, and dangerous. Hiding it as best she could, she made for the exit.

Rob leaned close to Doyle and shouted over the noise, "Who is that again?"

"Bliss Overbay," he said with real admiration. "Something, ain't she?"

"Yeah, she's something, all right," Berklee said, "and it rhymes with 'rich.'" She finished her beer in one long drink, belched, and waved to the bartender for another.

"She just does one song and then *leaves*?" Rob asked.

"It *is* a weeknight, and she lives pretty far out of town," Doyle said.

"Good thing, too," Berklee added as she took a drink of her fresh beer. "Much closer, and I don't think you boys could stand it."

"I have to meet her, man," Rob said. "I have to tell her how good she was."

"Oh, for God's sake," Berklee sighed.

"You better hurry, then," Doyle said. "She's probably already gone."

Bliss saw the stranger break away from Doyle and Berklee Collins and move toward her, hindered by the crowd. It panicked her even more. She moved her fingers in a certain way, taught to her by her mother and stretching back in her family to a time when the rolling mountains grew jagged and tall into the ancient sky. It had the desired effect of hiding her from non-Tufa eyes, and she made her escape.

Rob pushed through the crowd as politely as he could. Outside, he saw no sign of Bliss, or dust from any recently departed vehicle. He rushed around the building, surprising the giddy young couple in the bed of a truck. But he saw no trace of the elusive dark-haired girl.

He walked to the highway and looked for taillights topping any of the hills in the distance. Gradually the excitement dissolved, and he realized how uncharacteristically he'd behaved. It was too soon after Anna, he reminded himself. Sure, he'd noticed how hot Berklee Collins was, but that was normal and he could handle it. He'd never seriously pursue a married woman, and he wasn't the kind of man to inspire thoughts of infidelity in them anyway. But Bliss Overbay was something else entirely, and he couldn't even identify what about her attracted him so strongly: her voice, her smile, her eyes, or her song. It was as if she'd simply sent out some kind of emotional tentacle and wrapped it around him as she sang.

But as his breathing slowed and he felt the cool night air on his sweaty skin, that intense hold faded. He turned and walked back to the Pair-A-Dice, his footsteps loud on the gravel.

6

Inside, Doyle and Berklee huddled together. Their expressions and gestures told Rob they were arguing. Not wanting to intrude, he detoured around the wall, until he tripped over the feet of the six-fingered banjo player.

The old man sat by himself on a wall bench, sipping coffee from a faded, stained mug. Even in the crowded, noisy room, he radiated a kind of earthy calm, and everyone seemed to respect his personal space. He looked up sharply as Rob nearly fell over him, and swung the cup away so it wouldn't splash on his lap. "Careful, son. This is hot."

"Sorry," Rob said. When he realized who this was, he added, "Wow, you guys were great. I really enjoyed your set."

The man had the same sparkly eyes as Bliss Overbay, only the skin around them was drawn tight and deeply lined with crow's-feet, giving him the gaze of a Spaghetti Western cowboy. When he turned his head a certain way he reminded Rob of someone, but it faded before he could place it. "Thank you, son," the old man said. "You a musician, too, I see."

"How could you tell?"

"Only place you got work muscles is from the elbow down. If you just had 'em in one arm, I'd reckon you spent a little too much time in your room, pluckin' your own banjo. But since you got 'em in both, I figure it's from playing the gee-tar or something."

"Good eye."

"I been around a long time."

Rob nodded at the empty space on the bench beside him. "May I join you?"

"Reckon not. I figure you'll want to talk about music and all, and I just ain't interested. Talking about music is for the folks who can't play it."

Rob paused, startled by the blatant rejection. Did the guy secretly recognize him from the TV show? "Well . . . I play, *and* I talk about it. What does that make me?"

"You must not do either one of them too well, I reckon." Then the old man turned to watch the people across the room, and Rob knew he'd been dismissed.

Annoyed, he worked his way back to the bar, where Doyle now stood alone, scowling into his beer.

"Where's Berklee?" he asked.

"Pissed off," Doyle answered with no apparent malice. "Apparently, I didn't blink enough while Bliss was singing, so she thought I was staring."

"Hard not to," Rob acknowledged.

"Yeah," he agreed with weary admiration. "But you'd think after damn near twenty years of knowing that me and Bliss ain't never going to be nothing but friends, Berklee would be *over* this. I mean, we all grew up together, it's a little bitty town, and if I ain't hooked up with Bliss before now, I ain't likely to, you know?"

"Women are funny."

"True enough."

"So what's this Bliss girl's story? She live around here?"

"Other end of the valley, up the mountain." He pointed with his beer. "Her family used to own a lot of land around here, and she managed to hang on to some of it, including that big ole house."

"What does her husband do?"

He smiled. "Bliss ain't the kind to let a man have too much influence, you know?"

"She's gay?"

"Naw, she ain't gay, or at least I don't think she is. She's just . . . comfortable being alone. She's a big deal in the Tufa. What they call a 'First Daughter.'"

Berklee pushed through the crowd and stood before them, arms folded. "I'm sorry," she barked, in the same way another woman might've said, "Go to hell."

"Ah, me, too, honey," Doyle said magnanimously. He stepped aside and gallantly gestured at the empty space against the wall. She slid into it, still glaring. "That's how she apologizes," he explained to Rob as he handed his wife a fresh beer.

"My whole life, every guy in this goddam town has wanted to get in Bliss Overbay's blue jeans, and it's just getting old." Berklee said sulkily. "It ain't solid gold down there, you know? It just ain't."

"I don't want in anybody's blue jeans but yours," Doyle said patiently.

Rob took a long drink of his beer, unable to get the image of Bliss out of his mind. As the band began to play again, he found himself picturing her standing at the front of the stage, swaying to the music, dancing alone like a pagan priestess in her circle.

Doyle and Berklee dropped Rob off at the Catamount Corner just before midnight. He had to use the buzzer to get Mrs. Goins to let him in. He was a little drunk, and as he undressed, he felt the usual pangs of loneliness begin. He thought about shutting the window, but the slight chill made the prospect of the thick blankets even more inviting.

So, as he had done so many times in the past three months, he carefully turned off all the lights, crawled into bed alone, and cried himself to sleep.

Bliss sat on the short, age-warped dock that extended out over the lake behind her house. Her bare feet dangled in the cold water, and she held her guitar across her lap. She idly picked notes as she watched the ripple patterns, losing herself in the rings of reflected moonlight. The sky blazed with stars occasionally blocked as small clouds scudded along with the night wind. Insects and frogs provided a steady accompaniment, and the owl that lived across the water called out to its mate. Mosquitoes swarmed about her, but none landed to feed. They knew better.

Suddenly she realized she was playing the song that had been stuck in her head all week, "Wrought Iron Fences" by the Mississippi singer-songwriter Kate Campbell. Her tentative picking grew stronger, and she sang:

Tangled vines cover the lattice
They creep and crawl around the house
Nobody lives there
Only ghosts hang around

She reviewed the night's events as she played. She'd gone to the Pair-A-Dice on a whim, wanting only to sing and feel the musical blood rushing through her. Nothing ever replaced performing in front of people, especially *her* people, who knew just how crucial music could be. She'd seen Doyle and Berklee, and noted again the woman's deteriorating condition. The hateful glares Berklee directed at her held no threat; Bliss understood their source. She wished Doyle did, and would admit it, and take the only action possible. She'd known Doyle all his life, knew both his goodness and weakness, and hated to see the former suffer due to the latter. But there was nothing she or anyone else could do. Some things were irreversible.

Doyle's heartbreak hadn't brought her to the water this night, though. The boy with them, the stranger, *obsessed* her. He looked vaguely, distantly familiar. Who *was* he? He had Tufa hair and Tufa skin, but he wasn't Tufa; of that, she was sure. Why had he stared at her with such intensity? She was attractive, sure, but no great beauty and certainly not worthy of that sort of attention. She knew after one song that she had to get out before he approached her, but now she couldn't get him out of her head. What would he have said to her?

She finished "Wrought Iron Fences" and closed her eyes as the music changed, grew softer and more sensual. She was a First Daughter, and more than that, she was the regent for her people until Mandalay reached her majority. She was resigned to the solitude those roles demanded, and any feelings that arose and made her reconsider it were, she knew by now, mere fleeting hormones. The feel of the cold water on her toes was all she needed to endure it. She'd never see the boy again, and the urgent thoughts would fade, and Needsville would return to its routine.

But on this night, under the moon, she could almost howl with frustration.

As if reading her mind, a distant cry echoed through her little wooded hollow. She stopped playing immediately and listened for any subsequent sound. She thought she heard one, but it was much farther away and may have just been the wind. Sometimes even she couldn't be certain.

It broke the moment. She went inside, leaving the night to its creatures, and the night wind to its riders.

Rob snapped awake.

Every muscle tight with anticipation, he listened again, unable to clearly recall what awoke him. An echo seemed to hover in the room, but it faded before he could identify it.

In the distance, a screech owl cried. Somewhere a car crunched gravel. But these were normal sounds, and too faint to rouse him out of his exhausted sleep. What had he heard?

Somewhere a coyote faintly yipped. It sounded amused.

It must have been a dream. Maybe the airplane nightmare again. Or just noise in the building, another guest or something. Or someone outside in the street, although at this time of night, Needsville seemed abandoned to its ghosts.

He took several deep, regular breaths and closed his eyes.

Then the sound came again, and he sat straight up in bed.

It was a cry similar to the coyote's, with the same rhythm and timbre. But it was in a somewhat higher range, and had an unmistakable human quality. Somewhere outside, fairly close, some*one* was howling back at the night.

Then the sound turned into a long, despondent wail, a new sound not native to the wild. It was the sound of a human being in true pain, of someone demanding answers from a God who refused to reply.

The cry faded into the night. After a few moments, the crickets and other insects resumed their music, and the real coyote yelped once, as if to acknowledge the human crier's superior torment. Rob lay awake for a long time, but the noise never came again.

7

"Yeah, I'm on my way," Bliss Overbay said into the phone. She watched dust float in the sun blazing through the window over her sink. "Just wanted to warn you I'll be a few minutes late, I have to run through town and pick up some things. Okay. Bye."

She hung up the ancient rotary phone and leaned against the kitchen wall beside it. She remembered that same phone from when she'd been a child in this house, ringing with the good and bad news that marked transitions in her life. She yawned, then padded across the hardwood floor, leaving wet footprints from the shower. She'd lied to her boss: She had nothing to pick up in town. She did, however, have a major sense that something important required her presence there, and she knew better than to ignore it.

In the bathroom, she undid the towel from her hair and let the water-heavy black strands fall down her bare shoulders and back. The unadorned face she seldom showed to the world looked out from her mirror. To her, she looked as old as the hills around her, and far less graceful.

As she brushed her hair, the snake tattoo coiled around her biceps seemed to move independently of her arm. Its one visible eye watched her in the mirror.

She yawned again, this time so hard, her ears popped. She'd slept only in fits, and in between had endured the entirely inappropriate desire she'd felt since making eye contact with that strange boy at the Pair-A-Dice. At last, just before dawn, it faded enough for her to get a bit of deep, dreamless sleep. Then her alarm clock yanked her back to the mundane world.

Now she slowly braided her hair, her movements as lethargic as her thoughts. She needed coffee, and clear air, and a song to get her connected back to this existence. The coffee was brewing, and she opened the window to allow the cool morning breeze to caress her still-damp skin. And as for the song, there was only one that would do.

Her voice, the one she used only for occasions when the song meant life or death, rang through the empty old house. The air trembled the way it always did, and she felt the presence of those the song summoned, praised, and kept in their proper places.

> *Oh, time makes men grow sad*
> *And rivers change their ways*
> *But the night wind and her riders*
> *Will ever stay the same. . . .*

"Oh, God," Berklee said, her arm draped across her eyes. "There ought to be some exercise to thicken your eyelids so the sun can't get through. Do you think every time you blink, you wear them down a little?"

She lay in bed, naked except for her bra and one sock. Doyle stood at the closet holding a clean shirt. He'd slept on the couch once he saw that Berklee was going to toss and mutter all night, and even in the other room, with the door shut and the air conditioner running, his wife's drunken snoring kept him awake until nearly dawn.

"I can put some tinfoil over the windows if you want," he said.

She sat up, blinking. "No, that's just stupid. Besides, I have to go to work. Is there coffee?"

"Same as every morning."

She scooted to the edge of the bed. Her hair was matted where she'd sweated out the effects of the alcohol. She stumbled into the bathroom, and he heard her throw up. It wasn't an epic puke like some mornings, but it was enough to envelop him in sadness. She emerged wrapped in her bathrobe and went into the kitchen.

He followed, pulling on his shirt. "So how'd you like Rob?"

"Who?" she said as she poured herself some coffee. She ignored his empty travel cup waiting beside the machine.

"The guy we took to the Pair-A-Dice."

"Oh. He was all right, I guess." Then her memory grew a bit clearer. "Wait—did he run off with Bliss?"

"No, we took him home. Alone."

"Oh."

He gently nudged her aside and filled his cup. "You know, he was a nice guy. Thought we might have him over for dinner tonight. I could grill out, maybe he'd bring his guitar and play for us."

"You planning to invite Bliss, too?" she said. Her hangover kept her sarcasm from being too venomous.

"No, just him."

She nodded, careful with her tender head. "Okay. I'll pick up some stuff after work. Maybe start a casserole or something when I get home."

He wondered why she was so accepting of this. Was she just grateful for an excuse to go through the motions of normality? Was it one more way she denied there was any problem?

He snapped the lid onto his travel cup. "Well . . . I have to go."

"Have a good day," she said in a small voice, like a little girl playing at being a wife.

"Do my best," he assured her.

Peggy Goins stretched toward the sky and yawned. Her feet twisted with the movement and crunched the gravel beneath them. The exhalation from her first cigarette of the morning trickled out of her open mouth like incense from a brazier.

She finished her sunrise smoke and started to go back inside when she heard the faint sounds of a guitar. She paused, ground her butt into the gravel alongside years of its comrades, then peeked at the porch around the corner of the building.

Rob sat in one of the front porch rockers, his guitar across his lap, picking so faintly, she could barely hear it. He had an easy touch with the instrument; his fingers slid on the neck with little of that annoying screech some players produced when they changed chords.

She mainly watched his face, though. She believed a musician's expression when he played in solitude told you more about him than anything else. Some made exaggerated "stage" faces even when alone, while others looked bored with the tedium of main-

WISP OF A THING

taining their skills. Rob's face, though, mirrored his music. The old perennial tune he played now, trickling softly through the cool air like a brook over its rounded bed-stones, exactly reflected the sad, weary look on his face.

> *Oh, listen to my story, I'll tell you no lies,*
> *How John Lewis did murder poor little Omie Wise. . . .*

No one who knew his story could doubt what inspired this choice of song. Tears unexpectedly welled up and she slipped back out of sight, not wanting to be caught spying.

She wiped the corners of her eyes, then checked her fingertips for mascara. The boy's tragedy had seemed abstract and distant until this moment. She imagined how she'd feel if Marshall died that way, and the guilt that would come with knowing he was coming to surprise her. They had sat together on the couch, holding hands as they watched Rob, on TV, struggle through George Jones's "He Stopped Loving Her Today" while the celebrity judges, even that smug English one, openly wept. The obvious choice of song, the fact that it was on TV, and the overall falseness of the show had kept her from feeling anything at the time. Now, though, it came in a rush and threatened to overwhelm her.

When she emerged behind the motel desk, she was surprised to see another young man on the other side. This one, though, she recognized immediately. "Reverend Chess," she said.

Craig Chess, the young Methodist minister from nearby Smithborough, said, "Hey, Ms. Peggy." Then he saw her red eyes. "Are you all right?"

"Oh, I'm fine, Reverend." There were no churches in Cloud County, and never would be as long as the Tufa lived here, but

Craig had quietly earned the Tufa's trust by not proselytizing or evangelizing. He simply lived his beliefs, something the Tufa understood and accepted even if they didn't share them. "Bronwyn gave you my message, then?"

"She did."

"Well, I sure do appreciate you coming by."

"Always glad to help. What can I do for you?"

"Did you see that young man on the porch?"

"The one playing guitar? Yeah."

"Did you recognize him?"

"Ms. Peggy, I've only lived here a little while—"

"No, not from here, he's not one of us."

"He's not? He's got the look."

She leaned close and said quietly, "That's *Rob Quillen*."

Just as softly, Craig asked, "Who's Rob Quillen?"

"That boy from the TV show, *So You Think You Can Sing?* The one whose girlfriend died flying out to surprise him at the finals. Remember?"

"Oh, yeah. I read about that, I didn't watch the show. That's tragic."

"Yes, exactly. And it's eating that poor boy up, I can see it just as plain as I see you." She leaned closer and said, softly and urgently, "He was just playing 'Omie Wise.'"

Craig's expression told her he didn't get the significance.

Peggy continued, "If he were a Tufa, if he had even a drop of Tufa in him, I'd know what to do to help him, but I don't. I was hoping you could point me toward something."

He smiled sympathetically. Peggy's genuine desire to help this stranger reminded him why, despite their prickly and evasive attitude toward strangers, he'd continued trying to earn the Tufa's trust. "Ms. Peggy, I wish I had a simple answer for you. Grief hits everyone differently. All you can do is let him know that you're here if he needs anything, especially if he wants to talk. That old saying about how grief shared is grief halved is usually true."

She nodded. "Thank you, Reverend."

Craig looked out the front window, where he could see the back of Rob's head over the rocking chair. "Tell me, though. If it's not rude to ask, why is he here if he's not a Tufa?"

She shook her head. "He's looking for something. I don't know what, yet. I don't think *he* truly knows. A little peace away from the fame, maybe. Like when Bronwyn came home from the army. How is she, by the way?"

"You'd never know she'd been hurt. Even the scars are fading."

"That's wonderful."

He narrowed his eyes in playful suspicion. "Go ahead and ask. I know you want to."

"Why, I don't know what you mean, Reverend," Peggy said in exaggerated innocence.

"I'll tell you anyway. We've gone to the movies a couple of times, and her family's had me over to dinner. She still hasn't come to hear me preach, though she keeps promising she will. And that's as far as it's gotten."

Peggy patted his hand on the counter. "You do still like her, though."

"Yes, ma'am. Quite a bit."

"You just keep doing what you're doing, then. And thank you for getting up so early to come talk with me."

"I'm going fishing with Bronwyn's father and brother anyway, so I had to come through town. Always glad to stop and see that pretty smile."

She blushed despite herself. "You are a charmer, Reverend Chess. You sure are."

———

Rob watched the other man climb into the car with the blue CLERGY sticker in the corner of the windshield. He looked nothing like a Tufa, yet he also seemed thoroughly comfortable in town. He waved as he drove off, and Rob nodded in return.

The dawn shadow crept down the mountains as the sun rose. The harsh golden light instantly aged the buildings as it touched them, removing the blemish-hiding dimness that disguised cracked windows and peeling paint. What passed for a quaint village in the dimness became in full daylight an aging, impoverished small town. He played softly out of respect for both other guests and the general morning vibe.

A few men stood talking outside the convenience store across the street. They glanced his way on occasion, and even at this distance, Rob sensed their suspicion and hostility. They were also all of the same physical type: dark hair, olive skin, and wiry bodies from their hard lives. Classic Tufas, he thought, at least based on what he knew about it. And damn if he *didn't* look like one of them.

Their distinctive appearance was the most obvious aspect of their mystery. Most other Appalachian natives descended from pale, fair-skinned Europeans. The Tufas, though, came from somewhere else. Some sources said their ancestors were mutinous Portuguese sailors marooned on the North Carolina coast by Columbus. Others said they were the result of interbreeding among Native Americans, freed African slaves, and various European ethnic groups. Naturally, a few errant voices called them survivors of Atlantis, Lemuria, or the Lost Tribe of Israel.

The census practices of earlier times, when people were classified as simply "white" or "other," blurred their history ever more. Those who could pass as white did so, and denied or buried their

Tufa heritage so that it was almost impossible to do significant genealogy. The only thing most experts agreed on was that the Tufas were undeniably *there*.

No one knew exactly why they were called "Tufa," either; the common assumption was that it was based on a corruption of the word "tooth," and referred to their surprisingly strong dental constitution in an area noted for significant tooth decay. "Grinning like a Tufa" literally meant smiling so wide, it showed all your teeth; more symbolically, it meant hiding your true feelings behind that smile.

He looked up as the front door opened with the slightest creak. Peggy Goins emerged and placed a coffee cup atop the decorative butter churn beside his chair. The cup rested on a matching saucer, complete with a little lace doily. Printed on the side of the cup were the words, TAKEN BY MISTAKE FROM THE CATAMOUNT CORNER, NEEDSVILLE, TN.

"You're up awful early for a musician," she said.

"It's my best thinking time," Rob said as he sipped the coffee. "Mm, thank you. That hits the spot." He noticed that her pink fur-lined jacket matched her pink fur-lined boots. "So what is there to do around here first thing in the morning?"

"Like I said, most of our visitors tend to be here doing genealogical research. Or they spend their time in their rooms, honeymooners and such. Like the two folks opposite you. They checked in while you were out last night, I hope they didn't bother you. Sometimes young couples can get a little overexcited."

Could that have been the source of the cry that had awakened him? No, he was absolutely sure it had come from outside the building, from a distance. "Never even knew they were there."

"Good. They left before dawn to go prowling in graveyards and such."

He took another sip and said, "Wow, this is *great*."

"I'm glad you like it. I grind it myself every morning. I sing a special song over it."

"It's sure worth it. But let me ask you about something. Do you know of any place nearby where there might be . . . stone carvings?"

"I beg your pardon?"

"Places where people might have carved words into rock. A cave, maybe. Or one of those boulders that stick out of the ground."

"Mr. Quillen, I can truly say I've never heard tell about anything like that. Do you mean like caveman paintings?"

"I'm not really sure. Someone told me to look for the stone carvings when I came through here. Maybe on a hill?"

"They must've been pulling your leg. There's nothing like that in Cloud County."

"Is there anyone around here who's older than you who might know of something?" He realized how it sounded, and could only hope she didn't take offense.

"The only one who might know is old Rockhouse Hicks. But good luck getting a civil word out of him."

Rob perked up at the name. "Does he play the banjo? And have six fingers on his hands?"

"That's him."

"I saw him at the Pair-A-Dice last night. He was awesome."

"Well, if you're feeling brave, you can find him down on the post office porch. He likes to watch people coming and going, so he can keep up on all the gossip."

"Is his name really Rockhouse?"

"That's what we've always called him." She leaned close and lowered her voice. "When we were kids, we called him 'Rock-*head*' behind his back." She smiled as if this were privileged information.

Then she looked wistful. "Course, the kids now, what with cable and the Internet and all, call him Rock *A-s-s*, pardon my French. The world's just harsher than it used to be."

"Sounds like you don't care for him."

"He'll say anything to anybody just to get a rise out of 'em. I remember being a little girl, and him making fun of my daddy for being 4-F for the draft. If somebody had cleaned his clock a couple hundred years ago . . . Well, he's just a mean old man now, isn't he?" Without waiting for a reply, she went back inside.

He chuckled to himself. *A couple hundred years ago.* He loved the way Southerners used exaggeration to make their points.

He recalled the way the old man blew him off the night before. This time, Rob would use all his considerable charm, the very thing that got him through the *SYTYCS?* audition process when more blatantly talented performers were ruthlessly weeded out. At the time, he'd felt no remorse about it, since everyone was entitled to use whatever gifts he or she naturally had. Now he wished that the show truly judged people on talent, instead of just paying that idea lip service. He'd never have made the finals, and Anna would still be alive.

Peggy reappeared with a cordless phone. "You have a call, Mr. Quillen," she said. "And please bring the phone back in when you finish, they get left all over the place if I don't keep an eye on them and then the batteries run down and it's just . . ." She finished the sentence with a fluttery hand gesture before going back inside.

A sticker on the phone sported the same TAKEN BY MISTAKE warning as the coffee cup. "Hello?"

"Hey," Doyle Collins said. "Something told me you were an early bird. How's it going?"

"Pretty good. So did Berklee make you sleep in the truck?"

"Nah, we always fight like that. It's part of our rustic charm.

Speaking of which, want to come out to our place for dinner to-night and see some more of it?"

"Do you use paper plates, or should I just wear a helmet for when she starts throwing the china at you?"

"I promise we'll behave. And she's a heck of a cook, really."

"What time?"

"Seven. Kind of late, but I've got to replace a head gasket today and my dad's helping. That doubles the time it takes, but it makes him feel useful."

"Okay. I was going to poke around town today anyway. I'm not in my room right now, so call me on my cell later and give me directions." He gave Doyle the number.

When he returned the phone, he considered asking Mrs. Goins about the howling, but decided against it. He'd seen too many movies in which outsiders encountered strange phenomena and were ridiculed by the locals. He put his guitar in its case, picked it up, and headed to the post office in search of Rockhouse Hicks.

8

A single pickup passed Rob as he negotiated the uneven sidewalk. It was the same one he'd seen the day before, when he left Doyle's service station. In the bed, three dark-haired, dark-skinned teenagers stared blankly at him. Two of them, boys around fifteen or sixteen, were so thin, they reminded him of famine victims. The other one, a girl of about twelve, was bigger than both of them combined.

The brand-new post office was a brick square with bright blue mailboxes out front and a flagpole that gleamed silver in the sunrise. A narrow covered porch ran the length of the building. The plaque next to the door stated that it had been built four years earlier on the site of the original post office. Rob assumed the ancient rocking chairs that lined the porch had been inherited from that prior building.

The customer service window wouldn't open for another hour, but Rockhouse Hicks already sat in one of the rockers. The chair creaked in the morning silence;

his banjo case hung on the back and occasionally tapped the brick wall behind him. At the opposite end of the porch, a shrunken elderly woman sat working on a huge quilt that covered her lap and pooled at her feet.

"Morning, Mr. Hicks," Rob said as he stepped onto the porch. He also nodded at the old woman. "Ma'am."

She did not look up or respond.

Rob continued, "Looks like it's going to be a fine day once it warms up, doesn't it?"

Rockhouse glanced up at him. His beard hid any change in his expression. "If it ain't the talking musician."

"Mind if I join you?" Rob said as he took the empty chair next to the old man.

Hicks's expression, whatever it was, stayed hidden in the creases of his face. "You one of them people coming around to see if their family tree goes back to the Tufa?"

"No, sir, I'm just here . . . Well, I'm looking for a song."

He smiled, or scowled, depending on the way the light hit his face. "You can find a song on the radio, or one of them fancy lap computers."

"Not this kind of song."

"And what kind would that be?"

Rob suddenly felt self-conscious under Hicks's withering, unspoken contempt. *On a hill, long forgotten, carved in stone,* he wanted to say, but chickened out at the last instant. He laughed nervously and said, "Ah, never mind. I see you've got your banjo; why don't we just jam a little bit?"

Hicks laughed scornfully. "Only jam I know is what I put on my toast with my sorghum. Besides, I don't reckon we know too many of the same tunes. Can you play 'Hares on the Mountain'?"

Rob knew that the same folk song could have half a dozen different titles. "No, not as such."

Rockhouse closed his eyes and leaned his head back. His voice was surprisingly high and clear.

> *Young women they'll run*
> *Like hares on the mountains,*
> *Young women they'll run*
> *Like hares on the mountains*
> *If I were but a young man*
> *I'd soon go a-hunting.*

Hicks smiled smugly, and then the old woman, without looking up from her quilt, sang:

> *"Young women they'll sing*
> *Like birds in the bushes,*
> *Young women they'll sing*
> *Like birds in the bushes.*
> *If I were but a young man,*
> *I'd go and rattle those bushes.*

This made Hicks grin even wider. "Do you know that one?" he challenged.

"I do now," Rob said, and bent to open the guitar case.

A heavy foot slammed down on it. "This the boy you said was bothering you, Grandpa Rockhouse?"

Rob looked up. The backlit figure looming over him was broad shouldered, square headed, and the size of a portable toilet. Slowly Rob sat back in the chair until he could make out the face, and realized this was a woman.

"Yeah, he's one of them song-catching Yankees, I think," Hicks said dismissively.

"Huh," the woman said. Derision filled the single syllable.

"Ma'am, would you please take your foot off my guitar?" Rob said. His stomach began to tighten with fear. He hadn't heard the old man say anything about being bothered, let alone summon help. Where had this woman come from?

"I'll take my foot off when I goddam feel like it," the woman said, and for emphasis leaned more weight down until Rob heard the thin case start to crack. "Who the hell you people think you are, coming into town and bothering folks, anyway? Bet you even dyed your damn hair black, thinking we're too stupid to tell."

"You tell him," agreed the old woman without looking up from her quilting.

Rob realized this creature outweighed him, and her huge hands looked as if they could twist off his head like a bottle cap. She wore a crew cut, a loose T-shirt with no bra, and jeans with splits in the knees. She was fat, but clearly there was hard muscle beneath it. A musty, sweaty smell surrounded her.

He pushed the rocking chair back and stood. He looked up into her dark, opaque eyes. Quietly, careful not to sound belligerent, he said, "If the gentleman doesn't want to talk to me, I'll be on my way. I'm not trying to start any trouble here."

Hicks laughed and shook his head. "Lordy, you done said the wrong thing."

This distracted Rob just enough so that he didn't see the punch coming. A ham-sized fist slammed into his left eye and knocked him back between two rocking chairs into the brick wall. His head struck with a solid, melon-sounding *thunk*. Stunned, he would've slid to the concrete porch, but the immense woman grabbed him by the shirt and yanked him forward. She slapped him, both flat- and back-handed. The blows seemed to come from far away. He never lost consciousness, but he was too dazed to defend himself.

The woman dropped him back in his chair. His entire head felt numb, and his vision wavered. For an instant it was like two different TV signals battling for the same channel. Then he heard an off-key twang, and his sight cleared just as the woman grabbed his guitar from its case and raised it like a club.

My guitar, he thought calmly. Then the pain and rage hit simultaneously, and he was suddenly back in the moment. With no time to think, he reflexively kicked her in the groin as hard as he could.

It felt like trying to punt a sack of wet cat litter. The big woman let out a squeak and dropped the guitar; Rob caught it in midair. She took a step backwards off the porch and sank to her knees in the grass beside the flagpole.

Rob checked his guitar for damage, and when he looked back, the woman was on her feet. She snapped open a large pocket-knife with a practiced toss of her wrist. She whispered furiously, "I'm going to cut your heart out, peckerwood."

He held up the guitar to block the blow, closed his eyes, and gritted his teeth against the anticipated slashing.

A vehicle skidded to a halt in the street. *"Tiffany!"* a sharp female voice said.

Rob peeked out from behind the guitar. Bliss Overbay stood outside a pickup truck stopped crossways in the street. Dust from her sudden stop hung in the air. She wore dark pants and some kind of official-looking jacket over a white shirt. Two long braids hung from beneath a weathered baseball cap.

The big woman said, "You stay out of this, Bliss."

"No. You want to bust heads, Tiffany, you'll have to start with mine, and it's too early in the morning for that."

Rob just stared. It was hard to say what surprised him more: Bliss's appearance out of the blue, or the fact that this female Gargantua was named Tiffany.

"You been getting away with this shit for twenty years," Bliss continued, "and it's time for you to grow the hell up. We ain't in school, and you can't just beat up anybody you feel like."

"Grandpa Rockhouse said he was pestering him," Tiffany said, like a guilty child confronted by a strict parent.

"Bullshit, Tiffany. He's littler than you, and he's a stranger, and you don't need any more reason than that to start a fight. You're my cousin, and I've known you all my life, and I know you're a *bully*. But not today."

"You ain't the boss of me, Bliss," Tiffany pouted. "You ain't Mandalay. I could snap your skinny ass in half."

Bliss's expression darkened with her own anger. "You think?"

Tiffany took a step toward her, but Bliss simply raised her left hand and made a motion with her fingers. Tiffany stopped dead, her eyes wide.

"That's your ass talking, Tiffany, because your mouth knows better," Bliss said as she lowered her hand. "Go home. Don't make me do what you know I will if I have to, just because you woke up on the bitch side of the bed today."

Rob glanced back at Hicks. The old man sat very still, his eyes locked on Bliss. The amusement had gone from his face, although Rob couldn't read his new expression.

Finally Tiffany sighed, and her huge shoulders slumped with defeat. She put away the knife. Bliss also visibly relaxed. Rob heard the creak as Hicks again slowly rocked.

"Lots of fuss over nothin', if you ask me," the quilting woman muttered.

The same truck Rob had seen twice before stopped behind

WISP OF A THING

Bliss's vehicle. An old man so small, he could barely see over the dashboard leaned out the driver's side window. "Get in, Tiffany," he said.

"Yes, Daddy," Tiffany said. She climbed over the tailgate, and the whole vehicle creaked in protest. The two bone-thin boys scurried to get out of her way, while the other enormous girl shifted to one side to redistribute the weight.

Tiffany settled in with her back to the cab, then fixed her eyes on Rob. In his experience, most fat people had little pig eyes, but Tiffany had huge, menacing black orbs that looked like they might roll over white like a shark's. A jolt of pain shot through his head, and again two images fought for supremacy: one the street scene before him, the other a freakish variation in which the people in the truck seemed to have eyes like insects and big, folded bat wings.

He sat back down in the closest rocking chair and closed his eyes. An hour seemed to pass as he thought about random, idle things like what color he wanted his next pair of pants to be. He jumped when feather-light fingertips brushed the hair from his face, and realized only an instant had passed.

Bliss stood over him. "You probably shouldn't sleep for a while until we know if you've got a concussion," she said clinically. "Look at me."

He raised his eyes to hers. This close, she looked older than she had in the Pair-A-Dice, with little strands of gray at her temples. Her eyes were also a lighter shade of blue, filled with intelligence and compassion, along with something indefinably distant and sad. She said, "Well, your pupils aren't dilated, so I reckon you'll just have a lump. But you might want to get some aspirin and some ice."

Annoyed, he waved her hands away from his face. "Never mind that, where do you find the cops in this town?"

Bliss said patiently, "Talking to the police about Tiffany won't do you any good."

"So people can just attack you with a knife in broad daylight, right on Main Street, and nobody *does* anything?" He struggled to rise.

"Calm down. I just meant—"

All his life, people had told Rob to calm down when he got upset. It had led to conflicts with parents, teachers, friends, and the occasional law enforcement officer. He'd even punched the TV executive who told him to calm down after informing him that his contract required him to perform two days after Anna's death. There was no surer way to send him over the edge into genuine, ranting fury than to tell him not to do it.

So now he jumped to his feet and roared, *"Don't you fucking tell me to calm down!"*

Bliss jumped, startled by his vehemence, and for an instant her expression filled with such rage that it seemed possible she'd hit him, too. Then it was gone, and she said quietly, "Please."

Rob had to remind himself to breathe. The anger he'd glimpsed in her eyes had short-circuited his own, and that single, muted syllable slipped through his rage and ran a light, cooling touch over him. Bliss had also somehow changed in that same instant, and now he saw the woman who'd been onstage the night before, as gentle and soulful as a medieval painting of the Virgin Mary. He felt suddenly enveloped in an almost absurdly metaphysical calm that drained all his fury as surely as any therapist's technique.

He closed his eyes, disoriented by the rush of peace, and out of habit ran his hand through his hair. When he withdrew it, he saw blood on his fingers. "Uh-oh."

"Let me see." Bliss turned him and stood on tiptoes to examine the spot where he bled. He found himself facing Rockhouse Hicks. He winced as Bliss touched his scalp. "Enjoying the show?" he said to the old man.

"Ain't nothing to me, one way or the other," Hicks said.

"You didn't have to call for help."

"Son, I didn't call nobody. We just watch out for our own."

Bliss finished her exam. "You need a couple of stitches."

"I'll be all right," Rob said. "Now, are you going to tell me where the police are in this town, or do I just dial 911?"

"The police won't do anything about Tiffany. She's been that way her whole life, and nothing helps it. The Gwinns only come into town every three months or so, so it's best to just stay out of her way." He started to protest, but she cut him off. "And if the police went looking for her, they'd never find her. The Gwinns live way back in the hills, and the people up there take care of their own."

"Really," he said, with a pointed glare at Rockhouse.

"Really," she said patiently. "You stood up to her, and most people around here don't do that, so maybe she'll skip the next couple of trips into town until she knows for sure that you're gone. That means nobody will see her until next spring." She waited for him to say something else, but he simply scowled.

"Okay," she said when it was clear he was done. "Come with me and we'll get you stitched up."

"Oh, are you a doctor, too?" The back of his head began to throb.

"I'm an EMT," she said, and turned her shoulder to display the patch on her sleeve. "Nearest doctor is an hour and a half away. The local fire station is fifteen minutes up the mountain. Everything the doctor would have, I've got there." Then she walked to her truck.

Rockhouse's eyes followed Bliss, and Rob thought he saw real, genuine animosity in them. That was odd, considering they'd played together so well onstage, although he knew from experience that musicians didn't have to be friends in order to sound great. There were more undercurrents here than among the contestants of *SYTYCS?*, and that was saying something.

Bliss sat down in the driver's seat, put the truck in gear, and looked back at him. "Well? You coming with me, or you just going to stand there and bleed?"

Rob put his guitar back in its case. "Thanks for the Southern hospitality," he muttered to Rockhouse as he went to the truck.

"Bless your heart," the old woman called after him.

9

Bliss drove past the closed gas station at the far end of town and turned left at the light. Almost at once, the road became a shattered ribbon of potholes and rippled pavement. The way the truck bounced on the uneven blacktop made Rob's head hurt more. He tried to look at Bliss, but couldn't keep his vision focused. Just like the Gwinns in their truck, there were two overlapping images, and he couldn't make his eyes decide on just one.

Bliss tapped her thumbs on the steering wheel in time with her racing mind. Just when she'd thought herself free of whatever effect this stranger had had on her at the Pair-A-Dice, there he was on the street, *her* street, about to be pounded senseless. She *had* to act; her own people's laws and rules would not allow her to simply ignore it and drive away. Now he was in her truck, under her protection, and shortly she'd be alone with him, *touching* him. Would that same desire return?

They arrived at a small volunteer fire station, a cinder block square with one big garage for a single fire truck. A basketball goal hung over the door, which sported many ball-sized dents. Rob hoped they were better at fighting fires than they were at pickup games.

He stepped out of the truck, and his head swirled the moment he stood upright. "Hang on," Bliss said calmly as she slipped one hand around his waist and draped his arm across her shoulders. It was a professional reflex, and by the time she belatedly realized she was touching him, it was clear he had no more effect on her than any injured person. She wanted to laugh at her own worries.

"I don't need any help, I can walk," Rob protested weakly as they crossed the driveway.

"I could tell," she said. "Must be some newfangled kind of walking I haven't seen before."

"I didn't mean right *now*," he said as she guided him to the building. She propped him against the wall while she unlocked the door, then helped him inside.

He winced as the fluorescent lights flickered on, revealing the white utilitarian room used as both kitchen and staging area. "Going down," she said, and dropped him into a folding chair at the table. He sat with his eyes closed.

Bliss put down a white cloth, then carefully arranged bandages, needle, and suture thread on it. "I should shave around the cut before I sew it up, but I'm guessing you won't want that."

"No, thanks."

She dipped her fingers in a small container and smoothed the hair down away from the cut. "No problem. This curdled possum fat works just as well."

Rob jumped and looked around, then scowled when he saw the Vaseline label. "Very funny."

"It's *kind* of funny. Now, be quiet or I'll stitch your mouth shut, too. I'll be right back."

She went outside and returned with something he couldn't see. She pressed it to his scalp around the cut.

"Ow. What is that?"

"Spiderwebs."

"Ha ha."

She held up her hand, with a bundle of the fine threads between her thumb and forefinger. "Seriously. It does wonders to stop bleeding."

"Spiderwebs," he repeated.

"The night wind didn't give us any sickness or injury that it also didn't give us the cure for." Immediately she wanted to kick herself. *Why am I mentioning the night wind?* Trying to change the subject, she said, "Folks can live a long time using stuff like spiderwebs and pine needles."

"Like that old bastard at the post office?"

"Yeah, he's lived a long time, all right."

"Peggy at the motel said he was a couple hundred years old."

Good God, she thought, *even Peggy is forgetting herself when it comes to this boy.* "Oh, she was just exaggerating. I'm sure his family feels like he's been around that long, though. Still, he's a heck of a banjo player."

"And that quilting lady? The one who looked like a dried-apple doll?"

She snorted. "That's just Momma Rita."

"Margarita?"

"No, Momma . . . Rita. She's seventy-five years old, and lives all alone with her old blind husband. Believe it or not, they got about a hundred and twenty direct descendants." She snorted. "And not a blessed one of 'em is of any account."

One of her long braids fell in front of him, and he found himself focusing on the individual strands looped and twisted together. As her movements caused the braid to sway, his slightly fuzzed mind went through a list of connections: a black racer snake, a bullwhip, a horse's mane, and finally a hangman's rope. A lyric struck him:

> *Her dark hair*
> *will weave a snare*
> *for your broken heart*
> *but she's not the one*
> *for you*

He hoped he'd remember to write it down later. And he wondered if, instead of a lyric, it was a premonition.

The split in Rob's scalp was deep but not wide, and less than an inch long. Bliss could've stitched it in her sleep, and as she worked, she tried to puzzle out both why this boy had affected her so deeply the night before, and why he left her cold now that she was alone with him. He looked like a Tufa, but there was none in him; she'd been almost sure of that anyway, and now she was positive.

"So how'd you get the name Bliss?" he asked.

"The granny-woman who delivered me named me."

" 'Granny-woman'? Your grandmother?"

"No, sort of a . . . community grandmother. Like a midwife. She delivered almost all the children around here, and it was a sign of respect to ask her to sing a song that names the babies." She dabbed at the cut, then asked, "You were down at the Pair-A-Dice last night with Doyle and Berklee Collins, weren't you?"

"Yeah. I noticed you, too. You were—*ow!*—incredible, and I wanted to talk to you, but you ran off before I could."

"Once Rockhouse and the boys get you started, you're lucky to get out before dawn. They're all retired, they don't have to get up

WISP OF A THING

early and go to work. I told 'em I'd come by, but not how long I'd stay."

"And you wrote that song you sang?"

"Yeah." If he noticed the slight hesitation before she answered, he didn't mention it.

"What was it called?"

"Er . . . 'Lament for the Storm.' Silly, I know."

"So why are you doing *this* instead of playing music full-time?"

"Under the circumstances, you should be grateful that I am. Besides, all anybody really wants to hear is what's on the radio, and I don't have any interest in playing that."

"So you know a lot of the songs from around here?" he asked before he'd even consciously formed the question.

"Some," she said. "Why?"

"Well . . . I'm looking for one."

"Which one?"

"Don't know. Someone told me about it. Said, 'If you sing it, it'll heal your broken heart, and the heart of anyone who hears it,' and 'It would be on a hill, carved in stone.'"

"That's all you've got?"

"Pretty much." He found himself holding his breath, awaiting her reply.

"Never heard of anything like that," she said. The thread pulled tight, and he heard it snap. "There. Good as new in a few days. Go see your regular doctor to get these out."

He tenderly felt around the cut. As she'd said, pine needles protruded from his scalp like an acupuncture treatment. "It still hurts."

"It'd hurt worse without 'em." She wrapped the towel around the bloody tools. "You'll probably have a black eye, too. Now, let's walk around a little, make sure you didn't do anything more serious."

She helped him to his feet and led him through an adjoining door into the garage, past the fire truck. They went into the backyard, which bordered an overgrown field slanting down toward the valley. Beyond that, the ever-present Smoky Mountains formed cool blue and gray curves. The view, like all those in Needsville, would've been breathtaking if the sun hadn't added to his headache. The light seemed extra bright, the way it did after a summer thunderstorm.

Bliss stood in front of him to again check his pupils. "Don't squint."

"Can't help it."

He managed to open his eyes enough for her, and she nodded approvingly. "I think you'll live."

"Will I be able to play the piano?"

"Of course."

"Good, I always wanted to do that." As his eyes adjusted, Rob noticed something in the field. "What're those?" he said, pointing at a spot where some white stonelike objects rose above the tall grass.

"What?"

"*Those.* Those things sticking up there."

"Some old family cemetery. They're all over the place around here. This is the second-oldest town in Tennessee, you know." Her blasé demeanor masked her frustration and confusion. *What the hell* are *you?* she wanted to scream. *How can* you *see that graveyard when there's not an ounce of the true anywhere in you?*

Impulsively, Rob walked into the field toward the cemetery. "Hey, where are you going?" Bliss asked, following him. "Maybe you should go back and sit down for a while."

"A minute ago, you said I needed to walk around."

Before she could think of a reply, they'd reached the spot. A waist-high, rusted iron fence surrounded the tiny graveyard. Inside it, the ground was mostly bare, as though grass did not grow there very well. Four headstones and a smattering of foot markers delineated the burial plots, all adorned with the surname SWETT.

"So how come the Swetts bury their kin all the way out here behind the fire station?" Rob asked.

"They used to have a house here, but the family's gone now. The last one sold it to the city for a dollar to use as the first fire station, in fact. Until it burned down."

"The fire station burned down? That's ironic."

She nodded. "I was in high school when it happened. One of the firemen fell asleep on the toilet with a lit cigarette. He got out, but the old building went up like rice paper."

Rob opened the gate with difficulty; the hinges were rusty and stiff, and the tilted ground had caused them to seize up at an angle. The grass stopped growing in a straight line exactly beneath the edge of the gate; he wondered if the ground had been treated with something.

"That's not very polite," Bliss said. "You don't know these people."

"'I beg the pardon of the dead, should I tread upon their head,'" Rob said with mock solemnity. It was part of a poem he and his friends used to chant when they'd play hide-and-seek in the church graveyard. In his peripheral vision, he saw Bliss make another hand gesture, similar to the one he saw back in town. "Hey, you just did it again."

"Did what?"

"That hand thing. Like you did to Queen Kong that made her stop dead."

"I was shooing a bee." Another insect, small and fluttery, popped up around her face, and she made roughly the same move again to chase it away. "See?"

He knelt before the tallest tombstone. It read THOMAS SWETT, 1824–1901. The letters were cut so deeply, the normal weathering had not yet obscured them. Beneath the name was an inscription:

THROUGH HIS WINGS THE BREEZE SHARP RINGING,
WILD HIS DYING DIRGE WAS SINGING,
WHILE HIS SOUL TO EARTH WAS SPRINGING,
BODY LIFELESS FOR THE FLIES.

Rob ran his fingertips over the chiseled letters. *On a hill,* the man had said. . . . "That's not from the Bible, is it?"

"I'm not sure." *Oh, hell,* she thought. *He had to notice that.*

He moved to the next marker, whose name was illegible, although the words BELOVED DAUGHTER and the dates 1832–1837 indicated it was a child. Beneath that was another inscription.

"Am I reading this right?" he asked. " 'Buried in a keg'?"

"Yeah. It means she died at sea, and her body was kept preserved in alcohol until they could bring her home. She was literally buried in a keg of rum."

"You're making that up."

"No, it was more common than you'd think."

"Why didn't they just bury them at sea?"

"Because for some people, the sea's not home. Don't you want to be buried somewhere near home?"

He recalled Anna's funeral, in the graveyard of the church they'd both grown up attending, and where they planned to be married. "Never thought about it," he lied.

The name and date on the next stone, FERLIN EDWARD SWETT, 1802–1855, were legible, but lichen covered part of the inscription beneath it. He was about to move on, when he noticed the word "feeble." That seemed such an odd word for an epitaph that he knelt and picked enough of the green cover away to make out the phrase:

> HE FADED INTO DARKNESS, SIGHING
> THOUGH HE CALLED, NO ONE REPLYING;
> ONE LAST FEEBLE EFFORT TRYING,
> FAINT HE SUNK NO MORE TO RISE.

"What does that mean?" Rob asked.

"Who knows? Probably some old Victorian poem or something. I'm not a tombstone-ologist." She knew she sounded tense, but Rob was too engrossed to notice. He looked back and forth between the two headstones.

Long forgotten, the man had said. *Carved in stone.*

"You know . . . these inscriptions could almost be two verses of the same song. Except the more recent one would be the *first* verse, since it talks about what happens at the point of dying, and the older one is what happens afterwards. What do you think?"

Nervous perspiration trickled between her shoulder blades, and it took real effort to sound casual. "Hm. Well, as fascinating as this is, you seem to be recovering nicely, and I need to take you back to town so I can get on to work."

"Yeah." He stood and wiped his hands on his jeans. "Thanks, by the way. For helping out back in town, and for the stitch job."

She nodded. "Glad to do it."

He took out his phone and began taking pictures of the inscriptions.

"What are you doing?" she almost shouted.

"Just taking pictures. That way I can play around with the words later."

"You'd steal someone's epitaph and turn it into a song?" She couldn't keep the fear from her voice, but luckily it came out as outrage.

He looked at her oddly. She seemed offended all out of proportion. "Wow. I'm sorry, are these some of your people?"

"No," Bliss said. "It just seems . . . rude."

"What I really hope to do is find the poem these came from."

"Oh." She fought to appear calm. "That's sensible, then. Come on, let's get you back to the Catamount Corner."

He started to protest, but suddenly his head swirled and he truly just wanted to lie down back in his room. He followed her back to the station, where she finally gave him some aspirin.

They were about to drive away when she abruptly stopped the truck at the end of the driveway. She searched his eyes for any gleam of the true, no matter how small, but found none. "You're really *not* from around here, are you? I mean, no family from here, no history, nothing."

"No. Sorry."

She shook her head. "You sure look like you've got a good bit of Tufa in you. Hell, you and I could be brother and sister."

"That's a weird thing to say."

"No, I'm serious. You don't have *any* family ties to this area?"

"Not a one. It's just a coincidence."

They rode in silence back into town, and she dropped him off in front of the Catamount Corner. He carried his guitar through the empty lobby to his room, where he fell facedown on the bed. But he couldn't sleep; the words from the two grave markers kept running through his mind, finding their own meter and melody.

He knew from experience that there was no fighting the muse when she struck. He pulled up the pictures on his phone, quickly transcribed the words to a piece of motel stationery, and began quietly noodling on his guitar, trying out the stanza in different ways, breaking it at different points. It worked best as a simple 4/4 rhythm, a basic chord progression, simplest thing in the world. . . .

"Soul to earth" was a weird metaphor, he realized. Souls normally sprang to heaven, not earth. And yet it couldn't be a euphemism for decay, because the next line explicitly covered that. He knew of no branch of Christianity that allowed the soul to return to the earth; so what religion had these people practiced?

And "through his wings"; what could that mean? Wings were reserved for angels, yet the subject of the verse was clearly not yet dead.

His cell phone rang and he jumped. He set the guitar aside and answered it. "Hello?"

"Hey, tough guy," Doyle said, amused. "I hear you had a donnybrook on Main Street this morning."

"Yeah, with some Neanderthal hill woman named Tiffany."

"She's a monster, all right. So did she beat you up too much to come over for that dinner tonight?"

"Not at all. I don't know how much fun I'll be, but I could sure use some home cooking."

After Doyle gave him directions and hung up, Rob got online and tried a search for the poem or song that had inspired the epitaph. He got no results that fit. This thrilled him even more, for it meant he might be on the track of the secret, magical song that had brought him here. And they were right where the man had said they'd be: on a hill, long forgotten, carved in stone.

10

The Collins's trailer home looked isolated and vulnerable in the twilight. The trees around it were thick, old, and more densely packed than the rest of the forest. A creek ran along one edge of the lot, crossed by a small decorative bridge.

Rob parked next to Doyle's truck beneath a solitary old oak that shaded most of the front yard. One branch had grown so long and heavy that halfway along its length, a makeshift metal brace supported its weight. The yard was neat and boasted no half-assembled cars or sleepy dogs, something Rob realized he'd expected to find.

Berklee greeted him at the door. She wore khaki shorts despite the chill and a criminally tight white T-shirt, and looked absolutely stunning. She held a beer, and the slight red flush to her cheeks said it wasn't her first of the day. She stepped aside to let him enter and said, "Hi, glad you could make it. See you found us okay."

Rob tapped the brim of his Royals cap. "Sorry for wearing a hat indoors. I know better, but I've got fresh stitches and Vaseline in my hair, and I just didn't think I could stand shampoo on it just yet."

"You're not the first person Tiffany Gwinn's made get stitches," Berklee said sympathetically. "Seems like every town's got someone like her, doesn't it?"

Berklee took his jacket and hung it on the rack by the door. The trailer's living room was furnished in matching couch and recliner, while the little dining area had new-looking table and chairs. Everything was neat and organized, in contrast to the cliché image of trailer people. Rob took a seat on one of the barstools in front of the counter that divided the kitchen and living room.

Doyle came down the hall in jeans and a dark sweater. "Well, look who took on the Queen Bitch of the Mountains and lived to tell about it. Quite a shiner you've got going there."

Rob touched the skin around his left eye. It felt tender and hot. "Apparently, I don't *have* to tell about it, everyone already knows."

"Someone usually gets their head busted when the Gwinns come to town. You ever hear of Great Kate Gwinn?"

"No."

"Back about seventy years ago, she was the biggest moonshiner around Needsville, in every sense. They say she weighed seven hundred pounds, but I figure there's a thirty percent exaggeration factor in that. She lived up at the Gwinn house, but she was too big to get out the door, so nobody ever arrested her. The local cops told the feds, 'She's catchable, but not fetchable.'"

"Wow. If she was around now, she'd have her own reality show. What happened to her?"

"When she died, they just put sides and a top on her bed and knocked down a wall to get her out. Took a dozen men and two mules to drag her the ten yards down the hill to the family plot. People all switched to white lightning for a month in her honor."

"Switched from what?" Rob asked.

"Moonshine."

"What's the difference?"

"White lightning's brewed during the day, moonshine's brewed at night."

Berklee dropped her empty beer into the garbage with a loud clank. "I hear Bliss—" She said the name with disdain. "—bailed you out."

Rob nodded. "Ran off the monster, then stitched me up. Probably saved my life. Definitely saved my ass."

Berklee folded her arms. "That's Bliss, all right. The answer to every man's prayers."

Doyle kissed her on the cheek. "I keep telling you, honey, green ain't your color."

"Hmph." Berklee shrugged off the kiss and opened the fridge for another beer.

To Rob, Doyle said, "Bliss knows a lot of different things."

"No kidding. All she had to do to run off that psycho bitch was this." He made an approximation of her hand gesture.

Berklee, just closing the refrigerator, gasped and made a motion with her left hand in response. She caught herself about halfway through, and tried to turn the movement into an innocuous tapping on the counter. But Rob caught it.

"What was *that*?"

"What?" Berklee asked innocently.

"What you just did." He imitated it as accurately as he could.

Berklee glanced at Doyle, who shrugged.

"Oh, it was nothing, you just startled me," she said dismissively. "It's stuff we used to do when we were kids."

"Like what?" Rob pressed.

"Just . . . stuff," she said desperately, unable to come up with anything else. "Excuse me, fellas, I have to pee." She practically shoved Doyle aside to run down the hall.

Rob looked at Doyle. "So are you going to tell me?"

"Son, I don't know and I don't *want* to know. Women around here are crazy on a good day. They all get these superstitions from their mommas when they're young, and they never quite shake 'em."

"And you're not superstitious?"

"Not a bit," he deadpanned, then knocked on the wooden table.

When Berklee returned from the bathroom, Rob did not bring up Bliss or the hand gestures again. They sat around the kitchen and drank beer until Berklee produced the casserole from the oven.

"So you both lived here all your lives?" Rob asked as they ate.

They nodded. Doyle said, "I reckon it's true, you can take the boy out of the mountains, but not the other way around."

"And now he's got his own business," Berklee said.

"Yeah, long as you quit running off my help."

Berklee blushed and smiled, and Doyle laughed. Rob said, "What am I missing here?"

"I came by to bring Doyle his lunch one day, and he was up under a car working on it," Berklee explained. "I was feeling kinda silly, so since his legs were sticking out, I bent down and unzipped his pants on my way into his office."

"Where she found me sitting at my desk," Doyle added.

"Seems he'd hired this Barnes boy without mentioning it to me," Berklee said, "and now the poor kid came staggering in, bleeding from where he'd smacked his head when he jumped 'cause somebody opened his fly."

They shared more stories as the empty beer cans piled up. Later, Doyle lit a fire in a pit in the backyard, and they sat under the stars, surrounded by the sounds of the mountain night.

At last, after a long period of silence except for the fire's crackling, Rob turned to Doyle. "You know who I am, don't you?"

"Yeah," Doyle said guiltily. "Knew you looked familiar, so I looked you up online."

Berklee looked from Rob to her husband. "Who is he? Is he famous?"

"I guess," Rob said. He gazed into the fire. "I was a contestant on that TV show, *So You Think You Can Sing?* I made it all the way to the finals. Me and two other idiots. The producers were going to fly my girlfriend Anna in for the show, to surprise me."

"Her plane crashed," Berklee finished in a small voice. "I remember. Oh, my God, I'm so sorry."

"Me, too," Rob agreed. "It was all such a stupid situation. I only auditioned on a dare, I can't stand shows like that. They celebrate all the wrong things about music, you know? Technique over talent, skill over soul. I mean, I write my own songs and that's what I want to play, not the stuff a bunch of market researchers pick out. But I kept getting selected for the next round, and before I knew it, there I was, in fucking Hollywood."

The flames blurred in his vision. He realized as he spoke that he had yet to just *talk* about what happened, to anyone.

"You sang George Jones," Berklee said.

"Yeah. I don't know why, really. The damn producers kept wanting it to be 'Wind Beneath My Wings.' But I told them I'd either sing what I wanted, or just sit there without making a sound. They weren't about to take that chance."

"So why are you here?" Doyle asked gently.

"Because God wants me to suffer, I guess."

"No, I mean, why are you here in Needsville?"

"The truth? You'll laugh."

"No, we won't," Berklee assured him. Sympathetic tears streaked her face.

"I had to do the final show, right? I'd signed a contract, and only your own death gets you out of that. So I was backstage at the Fox Theater in Atlanta, where they were staging it, and I was a wreck. Really. They hadn't given me any time to myself to deal with things, I guess because they knew if they did, I'd just collapse into jelly. I was waiting in this stairwell all alone, and it . . . just . . . hit me. She was really dead.

"And then this guy appeared. He was dressed like one of those old country music guys, with the sequins and the fancy boots, but he couldn't have been more than forty. He sat with me while I was crying, and then he told me he could help. He said . . ."

He trailed off. *I'll sound like a lunatic,* he thought.

"What did he say?" Doyle prompted.

Rob took a deep breath. "He said, 'There's a song that heals broken hearts. I'm not kidding, and I'm not exaggerating. Go find this song, learn to play it, and all that pain you have inside will be gone.'"

Doyle and Berklee exchanged a look.

"I didn't believe him, needless to say," he continued. "But he told me to come here, to Needsville, and get to know the Tufa. He said it was one of their songs, and since I looked like them, they'd share it with me. He said they'd been around since before the wind rounded off the Smokies, and that I'd find the song I wanted 'on a hill, long forgotten, carved in stone.'"

"So you came here," Berklee said.

"Had nothing better to do," Rob said. "I didn't really want to be around people I knew. I knew the sequin cowboy was nuts, of course. But I couldn't stop thinking about his story. And after I read about the Tufa online, I decided it might be the kind of vacation I needed. Away from everything that reminded me of her."

"The Tufa don't have their own songs," Doyle said. "They know the same ones everyone else does. There's no mystery to them. They're just . . . folks."

"Well, except for Bliss Overbay," Berklee said bitterly. She finished her beer and crushed the can between her hands. "Right, Doyle? She's a mystery, ain't she?"

Doyle looked at her over the top of his beer. "You're doing that thing we talked about again." He tapped his can with one finger to indicate her drinking.

"How do I know you're not?" she shot back. "Doing that *thang,* I mean?" She drew the word out into a long, accusatory snarl.

"Because I have never, ever in my entire life slept with Bliss Overbay," he said calmly. "And I never will. I love *you.*"

"And I love you so much, I can't imagine life without you," she said sarcastically.

"Is that you or the beer talking?"

"I was talking *to* the beer," she shot back.

"Whoa, guys, I didn't mean to start anything," Rob said.

"Oh, this was started long before you showed up," Doyle said. "Berklee and Bliss have what y'all city folks call 'issues.' Never mind that they're both damn near thirty years old and all this stuff happened in high school. Some people just can't let things go."

"Well, *some* of us didn't run off to college," Berklee snapped. "Some of us had to stay here and work and watch all the boys ignore us and chase after that smug heifer. You ever think about that?" Berklee seemed about to cry.

With no malice, Doyle said simply, "You're right, I ran off to college. And then I ran *back* to you."

Rob stood. "Look, maybe *I* should run back to the motel. My head really hurts, and if I drink any more, I can't outsmart these mountain roads. Thanks for dinner, guys."

A coyote howled in the distance. Rob froze, every sense alert, to see if the eerie voice from the previous night would reply.

"What is it?" Doyle asked.

"Shh!" Rob hissed. "Listen."

"It's just a coyote," Berklee said, her voice slurred. She pronounced it "ci-yo-*tay*," and giggled.

"Just wait," Rob said.

The response came, just as it had the night before, a long lilting wail that almost, but not quite, hid its human origins in mimicry.

"There!" Rob said triumphantly. "I heard that in town last night. What is that?"

Doyle shrugged. "Sounded like a dog to me. They holler back at the coyotes sometimes."

"No, that's a person," Rob insisted. "Someone howling back."

"Girls howl at the moon sometimes, y'know," Berklee said woozily.

"Hush, sweetie," Doyle said gently.

Then the cry came again, considerably louder and closer.

"Well," Doyle said quickly, with stiff nonchalance, "I, uh, guess we'll turn in as well." He nudged Berklee with his elbow.

"Yeah. Nice to see you again, Rob," Berklee said, and unsteadily got to her feet.

"I'll call you tomorrow, maybe we can have lunch or something, grab a beer after work," Doyle said as he practically shoved his wife toward the trailer. By the time Rob reached his car,

Doyle and Berklee were inside with the door locked and all the lights off. He lowered the car's window, but heard nothing over the chorus of insects that filled the darkness. There was no additional howl, either human or animal.

Bliss sat in her bathtub, feet propped on opposite corners, a wet rag over her eyes. Only a single candle in a jar provided light. She had both windows open, and the breeze grew cold almost as soon as night fell. She ran some more hot water into the tub and resumed her attempt to relax.

She felt the weight of the house almost the way normal people felt the clothes against their skin. This spot had housed Overbays for longer than most could imagine, and now she was the last one. Well . . . not entirely, of course. The last true one, if not the last with the true. And she was alone, and childless, and probably barren, and definitely not going anywhere.

A coyote's cry broke the silence, followed by the inevitable response. She sighed and sank farther into the water. That second sound felt as heavy as the very mountains around her. Once it could make her cry; now it got only a weary exhalation, bubbled into the bathwater just below her nose. She closed her eyes and slid all the way under, enjoying the moments of silence and peace it granted. Soon enough, she would emerge from the warm water into the cool night, a pointless symbolic rebirth that gave no sense of change or future. For the moment, she'd forgotten the upheavals promised by her dreams.

The same Kate Campbell song ran through her head:

> *I have seen hope and glory fade away*
> *I've heard old folks talk of better days*

When she broke the surface, her cell phone was ringing. She got out of the bath, dripped water across the tile floor, and fished the phone from her jeans. "Hello?"

"It's Mandalay," the voice said. "Are you feeling the wind?"

Her wet skin was pebbled from the chill. "I sure am."

"It has a message for you. And a job. Watch for the sign. Bye." The line went dead.

Bliss shoved the phone back in her jeans pocket, in the process dislodging two guitar picks. Both fell into the bath and floated on the surface. As she reached for them, a gust of wind rippled the water and blew the two picks together.

She picked them up. Here was her sign, just as Mandalay had said, and it sure wasn't hard to interpret. Only now, her chills had nothing to do with the wind.

11

When Rob returned to the Catamount Corner, he parked next to a dust-covered SUV with Michigan plates. Otherwise, the street was deserted. He double-checked the post office porch, but it, too, was empty.

He heard angry voices as he got out of the car, and it took him a moment to realize they came from above him, through a partially open window. The dim blue light from a laptop computer glowed on the room's ceiling, which was all he could see from his angle. Shadows moved through this light, as one of the arguing people paced the floor. A female hand reached through the opening and flicked cigarette ash into the night.

Rob smiled wryly. There were at least ten NO SMOKING signs in each room. This must be the couple that had checked in while he was out at the Pair-A-Dice the previous night. They sure didn't sound like honeymooners, though.

"That's not what you said before!" a male voice said.

"I know, but that was before we were married!" a woman responded.

"So everything's magically different now just because we wear these stupid rings?"

"Yes, it's different because it *counts* now! Now your stupid little fuckups affect *me,* too!"

"You said you had all these issues worked out!"

"Well, I was wrong!" The woman paused, then added in a calmer voice, "There, I said it. That should make you happy."

Rob quietly shut his car door. He carried his guitar onto the porch and settled into the swing. Except for the voices above him, the night was quiet. Only a dozen streetlights were needed to go all the way down Main Street, and three of them had failed, so the darkness seemed like a heavy tent held up by these isolated poles. He felt like a small child hiding under a blanket, safe and deliciously frightened at the same time.

He plucked lightly at the strings of his guitar as occasional phrases drifted down from the argument.

". . . flirting like that with every guy who . . ."

". . . not change who I am for you . . ."

". . . don't respect me at . . ."

". . . trust me as far as you can . . ."

As he played, the voices above him provided the harsh, chopping rhythm. He echoed their words in his head and tried to fit them to his tune.

". . . goddammit, I have every right to . . ."

I have every right to feel this way. . . .

". . . not my fault that people just like being around me . . ."

It's not your fault, you always say. . . .

". . . work all damn day and come home to . . ."

At night I feel like you just don't care. . . .
". . . don't like to do any of the things I like to . . ."
There's nothing that we like to share. . . .
Finally he heard a door slam, and then silence.

It was the first time since Anna's death he'd been moved to write about anything other *than* her death. He worked on the tune a bit more, barely touching the strings, until the combination of alcohol and headache finally won out. He quietly went to his room, wrote down the lyrics, and slept.

This time, a *smell* woke him.

A fetid odor filled his room. It reminded him of the old junior high bathrooms that were never really cleaned and thus constantly smelled of urine, feces, and sweat. This odor was similar, although he also caught whiffs of dirt, like a freshly turned garden.

He sat up and winced at the fresh pain around his stitches. Except for the moonlight outside the open window, the room was dark. The blowing curtains made shadows across the floor. He remained very still as his eyes adjusted, and listened for the slightest sound.

Then, despite the silence, he had the very definite sense that someone else was in the room.

Had Tiffany come back to knife him in his sleep? He imagined her on tiptoes, like a cartoon elephant sneaking up on him. But there was no place for anyone her size to hide.

"Hello?" he said, his voice raspy from sleep. There was no response.

He considered turning on the lamp, but decided against it, since it would blind him as well as any intruder. He carefully slid out of bed. He wore only his boxers, and when his bare feet hit the cold wooden floor, it creaked under his weight. As he crept to the door, the night chill raised bumps on his skin.

He stopped. *Wait a minute,* he thought. *Chill? I didn't open the window.* In fact, he was certain he'd closed it before he went to bed, so he wouldn't be awakened again by the strange cry.

The first real moment of panic struck, and he stood with his back against the locked door for a long time, waiting for anything in the room to move. But nothing did, and by then, the smell had almost vanished.

At last he felt along the wall for the light switch. In the sudden illumination, he saw every detail of the lace-encrusted room, nothing odd or out of place. No furtive figures dashed for cover. He was just about to chide himself for his excessive imagination when he noticed something shiny and wet on the floor.

He knelt beside it. The spot of mud was in the shape of a small, bare human foot. He spotted another one closer to the bed, then saw a whole trail of them, half-dry and rapidly disappearing, that led from his bedside to the floor beneath the open window.

"What the hell?" he said softly to himself.

He leaned out and looked down at the wall below his window. An agile person could climb the gutter drain and then get access to his room. But who would *want* to?

His fingers slid into something wet. On the windowsill was the muddy outline of a hand. He put his own down next to it; the print was smaller, but the fingers were long and slender, reaching past his own, almost like some kind of monkey. He envisioned a half-simian gargoyle creature perched on the sill, watching him with big, night-vision eyes, like a giant lemur.

And the print seemed to have six fingers.

The smell was almost gone now, as were the prints. Soon they'd be only amorphous patches of dried mud. He couldn't tell anybody, because there'd be no proof. And what if this was all just some weird hallucination brought on by the whack to his head?

"You're losing it, Rob," he told himself. He closed and locked the window, turned off the light, and went back to bed. He was asleep again almost instantly.

The next morning Rob managed a shower, enduring the agony as he washed the blood, Vaseline, spiderwebs, and pine needles from his hair. Luckily, the scab around the stitches held. He opened the window and let the cool air and bright sunshine flood into the room, dispelling the night's heebie-jeebies. As he expected, the muddy prints on the sill were now indistinct patches of dried dirt that blew away in the morning breeze.

He got dressed and went downstairs to the Catamount Corner's dining room. A heavyset man with a goatee and glasses, his eyes red from sleeplessness, sat alone at one of the three tables. Rob assumed he was the male voice he'd heard from the porch. He had the general cast of the Tufas—dark hair, dusky skin, and big white teeth—but the qualities weren't so obvious as they were in the locals. A road map lay open on the table in front of him, and he was comparing it to notes on an iPad. They nodded at each other as Rob got coffee and sat at the table closest to the door.

Rob opened his notebook to the lyrics he'd scrawled the previous night. They seemed awfully trite in the clear light of morning, but they might work as a start. With a little tweaking . . .

A tall redhead entered the room, glanced at Rob, and smiled. She sat down opposite the goatee guy.

"Sleep well?" the man asked sarcastically.

"Like a baby," the woman said, deliberately blithe.

"I bet," he snorted. "Look, if we're just going to fight all—"

"We're only going to fight if you start it."

"Can I finish my sentence?"

"Sure." She waved her hand dismissively.

"I was saying, if we're just going to fight all day, maybe I should go do the cemeteries alone. You can do whatever you want."

"Oh, yeah, lots to do here."

He rubbed his eyes. "If I don't go check these last couple of graveyards, then I'll always wonder about them. It would be stupid to leave without doing it. I'll do it as fast as I can, and you can, I don't know, read a book or something."

"Fine. Next year I pick the vacation. And no more of this idiotic grave-robbing."

"It's grave-*rubbing*. And it's for our kids, too, if we ever have any."

"Our kids won't care who's buried in what little town. They probably won't even care where *we're* buried. I think it's a little morbid, anyway." She stood. "I'm going up to the room. You do what you want." She gave Rob another smile as she passed his table; she was long and athletic and clearly aware of her effect on men.

When she'd gone, Rob realized her husband was glaring at him. "That's my wife you're drooling over."

Rob shrugged apologetically; he *had* been staring. "Sorry. Didn't mean anything by it. She's just pretty to look at."

The other man nodded sadly. "Yeah. I'm sorry, we've just been fighting nonstop for a week now. It seems like everything I do or say just pisses her off, and—" He stopped. "Well, you're not interested in our problems, I'm sure. How'd you get the shiner?"

"One of the local Southern belles rang *my* bell yesterday." Rob turned to show his stitches.

"Ow. A *girl* did that?"

"She was bigger than me."

"I hope so." The man reached across the empty table between them and offered his hand. "Terry Kizer."

"Rob Quillen." Kizer's grip was soft, his hands a bit pudgy. "Nice to meet you."

"Likewise." He looked more closely. "Have we met before?"

"Don't think so."

"You sure look familiar."

"Hey, let me ask you something," Rob said, glad to change the subject. "Did you see anyone strange around this place last night?"

"Strange how?"

"Somebody sneaking around, being nosy."

"No. Although my wife said she thought somebody was watching her undress last night, through the window." His eyes narrowed. "It wasn't you, was it?"

Rob shook his head, which made him wince. "Never saw her before this morning." He wondered anew if he'd imagined or dreamed the whole thing. But no, damn it, the dried mud had been there on the floor and windowsill this morning.

"So what brings you to Needsville?" Kizer asked.

"Oh, this and that. You guys honeymooning?"

Kizer looked around, then said softly, "No, we just said that so we'd get the biggest room. We're actually here to research my genealogy. It was supposed to be a fun trip, tracing my ancestors and all."

"And it hasn't been?"

Kizer chuckled ironically. "No, not a bit. But at least nobody's hit me in the head yet."

"So how do you go about doing genealogical research?"

"Mostly you prowl libraries and cemeteries. A lot's on the Internet now, too. But I've hit a dead end, and I know I've got some family buried around here, so if I can find them and see who else is buried with them, I'll know where to keep looking."

"Your wife doesn't share your enthusiasm?"

He aimed his eyes at the ceiling, toward his room. "You could say that. Plus most of the cemeteries are old and grown over, and you can't even read the tombstones half the time."

"I saw one like that yesterday. Out behind the fire station. Seemed to be mostly the Swett family."

"Hey, that's one of mine," Kizer said, a glimmer of excitement in his eyes. "Where'd you say it was?"

"Behind the fire station, just outside of town. If you want, I can show you where." He had nothing else to do, and Kizer seemed like a nice guy.

"That'd be really cool," Kizer said appreciatively. "I need to go upstairs and grab my stuff. Meet me out front in about ten minutes?"

"Sure."

Kizer used the key ring remote to unlock the doors on his SUV. The inside was littered with evidence of a long trip: wrappers, audiobooks, CDs, and odd socks. As they settled into the seats, he asked Rob, "So which way, captain?"

"Huh?" Rob said, looking up at the second-floor windows and pondering the intruder.

"Which direction?"

"Oh. That way. Down Main Street."

"Are you okay?"

"Oh, yeah, sorry. Just thinking. Did you say that your wife thought someone was watching her last night?"

"Yeah. But she generally thinks that most of the time."

"I imagine she's usually right."

"Yeah."

Rob nodded at the street. "Head that way, and I'll show you where to turn."

As they drove past the post office, Rockhouse was back in his usual place on the porch. The old man waved, and Rob noted the six fingers, just like the much smaller print on his windowsill.

Ten minutes later, a bored Stella Kizer walked down Main Street, hands in the pockets of her jacket, lost in bitter thought. Her marriage, the goal she'd pursued her whole life, was disintegrating around her, and she seemed powerless to stop it. None of the fairy tales she'd loved as a child, none of the sermons preached by her minister, had prepared her for the reality of a partnership defined, it seemed, by all the things each did to annoy the other. Often she'd lie awake, watching Terry sleep and considering how he'd feel if she died . . . or, alternatively, how *she'd* feel if *he* did.

Now she was stuck in the world's most isolated and backward town—"second oldest in the state," the frighteningly countrified woman who ran the hotel said with pride—while her husband continued his necrophilic pilgrimage. Ever since he'd discovered his family's link with the mysterious Tufa, he'd been obsessed with tracing his lineage, as if it might somehow tell him something about himself he didn't already know.

That made her smile: the idea that Terry, so supremely self-absorbed, might not know something about himself. She almost laughed.

"Life sure is funny, ain't it?"

She looked up. Rockhouse Hicks smiled at her from the post office porch. The sun was in her eyes, so she couldn't see him clearly, just a vague impression of an old man in a rocking chair. "Excuse me?"

"Especially when you get married," he continued as if she hadn't spoken. "You get up there and say 'I do,' but they don't tell you 'how to,' do they?"

Stella shielded her eyes with her hand. "I'm sorry, do I know you?"

"Naw."

"Then . . . why are you talking to me?"

"Just being neighborly. Pretty thing like you should be used to that. I bet men been neighborly to you your whole life."

She walked up onto the porch in order to see him more clearly. He wasn't the first dirty old man she'd encountered; since puberty, she'd dealt with the unwanted attention of older males. When she rejected or ignored them, they often turned hostile, and she knew how to handle that as well. And today she was particularly in the mood to deal harshly with anything masculine that crossed her path.

"Look, I'd appreciate it if you'd mind your own business. What if I were your granddaughter and some old man started coming on to her? How would you feel?"

"Well, if she was as pretty as you, I'd at least understand it. Men have to be men."

She scowled. That sounded enough like a threat that it made her a bit nervous. "I'm married, too, you know."

"Yeah, but you ain't happy about it."

She folded her arms. "Now, why would you say that?"

"I seen your husband drive off with somebody else in his truck earlier."

She blinked a little. They knew no one in this town; Terry had found it on a map and made reservations on the Internet. He hadn't mentioned anyone accompanying him when he'd rushed through the room, grabbing papers. "Who?" she asked coolly.

"Had dark hair, that's all I could see. Lots of people around here do."

Stella was taken aback. Could Terry really be having an *affair*? Could he have met some local woman on the Internet, come here to tryst with her under the pretense of this genealogy research, and then picked these fights in order to have time alone with this new paramour? Was he that devious, that resourceful?

"I don't believe you," she said at last.

"Suit yourself," Rockhouse said with a shrug. "But a pretty girl like you shouldn't be alone."

"I think I can manage." She turned to walk away, then froze. Standing ten feet behind her was the most handsome—no, the most *beautiful*—man she'd ever seen. Her stomach dropped, her mouth went dry, and her whole body seemed to surge with sensation. When he smiled, she thought she'd pass out.

"Hey, there, little lady," he said, and his voice made her whole body shudder. "My name's Stoney. What's yours?"

12

"So where is it?" Kizer asked.

Rob scanned the field behind the deserted fire station. Everything was just as he remembered it, but he saw no sign of the tombstones poking above the waving grass. "It was right there," he said in disbelief. "I swear."

"Maybe we're not in the right spot to see it," Kizer said helpfully.

"I was standing right here yesterday and saw it," Rob grumbled. "Right *here*," he repeated with certainty.

"Hm. Well, It didn't show it on any of my maps, so maybe you made a mistake."

"Look, I walked up to them and touched them. I read the inscriptions off them. I took pictures with my phone. I'm telling you, they're here somewhere."

He marched out into the grass, toward the spot he *knew* the graveyard had occupied the day before. Kizer followed, a little wary now. "It really isn't that big a deal," he called, but Rob ignored him.

"Goddammit," Rob muttered as he stomped through the weeds, "it was here, I swear to God." Yet now he saw no sign of the fence, the tall tombstones, or even a cleared space where they might have been.

His foot slipped into a small hole. *"Shit!"* he cried as he fell; his head hit the ground right on the place Bliss had stitched. Pain shot through him like he'd been stabbed in the skull. *"Ow!* Oh, *goddammit!"* He curled on his side and cradled his head.

"You okay?" Kizer asked as he rushed to him.

Almost immediately, the pain faded to a dull ache. "Yeah, just hit the same goddam spot again." When he gingerly touched it, he felt fresh blood. "Oh, great. Can you see if I ripped the stitches?"

Kizer scrutinized his scalp. "No, they're still there. Just busted the scab. It's not bleeding much."

Rob blinked into the sun, which seemed brighter now, harder on his eyes. With Kizer's help, he got to his feet and brushed the dirt off his jeans. He turned to say something, then froze.

Behind Kizer, no more than thirty feet away, he saw the tops of the headstones above the grass. "I'll be damned. It's right there."

"Where?" Kizer said, and turned around. He couldn't speak for a moment. "But . . . I mean, we just . . ."

"I know, but there it is."

Kizer took several pictures of the cemetery's perimeter. Then he tried the gate, which didn't budge. "Is it locked?"

"Just a little rusty," Rob said. "Try it like you mean it."

Kizer leaned against it, and the gate protested as it swung open and allowed him to squeeze inside.

Rob remained outside the fence, looking out at the waving grass. Under the crisp blue sky, it was postcard-beautiful, and although he had to squint into the sunlight, he felt a weird tingle inside. It was almost like he was looking at something alive, as if the rolling peaks with their wispy clouds were the curves of great, soft women reclined beside each other as far as he could see.

A gust of wind, cold like the one that came through his window at night, blew over him. *Curnen shares your song,* a voice seemed to say in his head. *Curnen hears your heart.*

He blinked. Where had *that* come from? "Did you hear something?"

"No," Kizer said absently.

"Huh." He looked around, but saw no one else.

"I can't read any of these," Kizer complained, breaking the reverie.

"What?"

"The inscriptions. They're too worn down to read. Which ones did you see 'Swett' on?"

Rob went inside the fence and looked at the monuments. The surfaces were weathered and flat, including the ones on which he'd read the poems the previous day. "What the—?" he muttered, and knelt before one. He pressed his fingers to the now-smooth surface. "Okay, maybe I got hit in the head harder than I thought, but I swear to God, there was a readable inscription here."

"It's not there now," Kizer said.

Rob couldn't believe it. Plainly, the stone had not been recently altered. The barest hints of the words could be seen, but not nearly well enough to be legible. So how had he read them yesterday?

"I can feel something here," Rob said. "I just can't make it out."

"All right, let me at it," Kizer said. He pulled some paper and a charcoal stick from his backpack and pressed it against the stone. Working quickly, he covered the paper with broad, wide swaths of gray, against which the monument's engraving plainly stood out. "Well, what do you know?" He moved the paper and looked behind it. "That sure did come out plain for something that's so messed up, didn't it?"

"Yeah. Is that who you're looking for?"

"One of them, yeah. Thomas Swett. They called him 'Bullman Tom' because he once beat a bull in a tug-of-war. He's on my mother's side at some point, I'll have to check when I get back to the hotel. Now I just need the rubbings off the others to get names and dates for more research." He looked up at Rob. "Thanks, man. I know it seems kind of loony, but this means a lot. I might never have found this place without your help."

"Glad to do it."

As Kizer went to work, Rob stared at the other Swett tombstone that only yesterday had borne a plain, legible inscription. Now it, too, was unreadable.

"That's some weird shit, these epitaphs," Kizer said.

"Yeah," Rob agreed. "Have you run up on anything like this before?"

"No. Seems odd that somebody would take the time to chisel so many words into a rock, doesn't it? Most people just had the name and dates, maybe a short Bible verse."

"Maybe the Swetts were big shots around here."

"Hardly." He carefully rolled the rubbings and placed them in a tube that hung from his bag. "We'd call them white trash if they were around today, I'm afraid."

Rob nodded absently, his attention drawn back to the wave pattern of wind across the grass. When the breeze reached him, he felt the odd tingle again, but did not hear the strange voice.

Kizer dropped Rob off at the Catamount Corner. Without going inside, Rob got his car and drove out to Doyle's gas station. Doyle's father sat on a pillow atop two milk crates, his back against the building, reading a magazine. He looked up as Rob got out of his car.

"Howdy," he said. "Car still starting okay?"

"Yeah, so far," Rob said. "Is Doyle around?"

"In the garage," he said, pronouncing it "ghee-raj."

Rob found Doyle under the hood of a spotless black Gran Torino. The owner clearly treasured it. "Hey."

"Hey," Doyle said with a smile. "How's it going?"

"A little weird," he said honestly. "After I left your place last night, somebody snuck into my room while I was asleep, and . . ." He trailed off, suddenly aware of how ludicrous he sounded. "Ah, forget it, the more I think about it, the more I figure I must've just been dreaming. Mainly I just wanted to see if you knew how to reach Bliss Overbay."

"Somebody snuck in your room?" Doyle said. "Like a burglar?"

"I don't think so. I think it was somebody's kid: I found little muddy footprints all over the place. The creepy part is, I was in there asleep when it happened. And they would've had to have come in through a second-story window." He didn't mention that the handprints seemed to show six fingers; the story was already strange enough.

"That *is* creepy," Doyle agreed.

"So do you know how to get in touch with Bliss?"

He wiped his hands on a rag. "I might have her number around here somewhere. Mind if I ask why?"

"I don't know. Mind if I ask why you want to ask why?"

"The folks around here—the hard-core pure-blood Tufas—have their own way of doing things. And they're like a tribe, with important people at the top. Bliss is one of those important people."

"Important how?"

"It's complicated, and there's a lot I don't know. But I've heard people say that among the Tufa women, she's the second-highest authority. There's not much business in Needsville, so I can't afford to alienate anybody by being indiscreet. Especially someone with any sort of influence."

"I want her to take a look at the stitches she put in. I fell down this morning, and I might've torn 'em loose." Since that wasn't technically a lie, Rob had no problem meeting Doyle's eyes when he said it. But he mainly wanted to talk to her about what had happened at the graveyard.

The mechanic thought hard. "Well . . . okay." Rob followed him into the office, where Doyle wrote the number on a Post-it note. "Better tell her you got it from me, though."

"Why? If I don't, will she wave her hands at me?" He wiggled his fingers, intending to be funny.

Doyle turned red, although his voice stayed even. Rob couldn't tell if he was angry or embarrassed. "No, but she might not talk to you if she thinks you got her number some underhanded way, like off the Internet or something."

"Sorry, it was a bad joke. But seriously, what is all that hand-waving stuff? Is it religious or something?"

"When you were a kid, did you believe in Santa Claus and the Easter Bunny?"

"Yeah."

"It's kind of like that. We were all raised being told that some silly stuff was true. And even though we're all grown up and know better, it's settled in our heads so well that we still act like it's true sometimes."

"That doesn't make any sense."

He shrugged. "Best I can do." He went back into the garage,

picked up a socket handle, and stuck his head back under the Torino's hood.

"Well, thanks for the number," Rob called after him, worried that he'd alienated his only real friend here.

As Rob drove away, he swore he saw Doyle on the phone in the office, talking earnestly with someone. It was a momentary glimpse, really no more than an impression, and he knew that thinking Doyle was calling to warn Bliss had to be a reflection of his own paranoia. Didn't it?

13

When Rob returned to the Catamount Corner, a Tennessee State Trooper's car was parked next to Terry Kizer's SUV. As he got out, the young officer appeared from inside and came down the steps toward him. He had the Tufa hair and skin. "Are you Mr. Robert Quillen?" he asked in that flat, emotionless policeman's way.

Rob's first thought was that he was being arrested and would be forced back on the TV show. "Yes, sir. What can I do for you?"

"I'm Trooper Alvin Darwin. I need to talk to you in an official capacity, Mr. Quillen. Might have a missing-persons case on our hands, and you might be a witness."

"Who's missing?" Rob asked.

Before Darwin could answer, Terry Kizer came out the front door. "Hey, Rob. You didn't see Stella while you were out, did you?"

"No." Rob looked at Darwin. "Is that who's missing?"

Again, as Darwin started to speak, Kizer jumped in.

"She wasn't in our room when we got back, and she didn't leave a note or anything. But we found her purse down the street." He indicated the area around the post office, where Rockhouse sat alone on the porch. The shadow was too deep for Rob to tell if the old man watched them.

"You ask that old guy?" Rob said.

"Mr. Hicks said he hadn't seen her," Darwin said. "Said he'd been there all morning."

"Yeah, his word and a dollar'll get you a cup of coffee," Rob said.

"And you haven't seen her since breakfast?" Darwin asked.

"Nope."

"And Mr. Kizer was with you immediately after breakfast?"

"For a while. We went gravestone-rubbing. Was she carrying any money?"

Kizer nodded. "Yeah, and it was all there when we found it: traveler's checks, credit cards, everything. I'm starting to get really worried."

To Darwin, Rob said, "I'm impressed. I thought you had to wait twenty-four hours to declare someone missing."

"I need to ask you some more questions," Darwin said, ignoring Rob's comment. He gave Kizer a serious *be quiet* look, then turned back to Rob. "You never know which details turn out to be important. Can we step inside?"

"Sure."

"So tell me what happened this morning," Darwin said as he poured himself a cup of coffee in the little dining room. Kizer sat tapping nervously on the tabletop near the window.

"I showed Terry this old graveyard behind the fire station, and he did some rubbings on some of the tombstones. Then we came back here, and I drove out to Doyle Collins's gas station."

Darwin looked up sharply. "Behind the fire station? The old Swett family plot?"

"Yeah."

For an instant, Darwin looked puzzled and angry; then he smiled, once again the friendly good ol' boy. "How long have you been in town, Mr. Quillen?"

"Two days."

"And which side are you from?"

"Side of what?"

The trooper's eyes narrowed. He seemed to see something he hadn't noticed before. "Oh, I'm sorry. I thought you were Tufa. You look familiar."

"You're not the first to think so."

Darwin turned his attention back to his notebook. "You know about what time you and Mr. Kizer got back?"

"Around eleven thirty."

Darwin put away the notebook and stirred creamer into his cup. "Mr. Kizer, you have those rubbings handy? Just so I can verify it in my report."

Kizer looked annoyed. "Shouldn't we be looking for Stella instead of worrying about that?"

"Every deputy and forest ranger within a hundred miles is doing just that, and if she doesn't turn up soon, we'll start calling up volunteers. My job is to figure out when she left and why she went wherever she is." He looked back at Rob. "So you ever see the two of 'em fight?"

"Hey, I'm right here in the room, you know," Kizer said.

"No, I never saw them fight," Rob said. It wasn't a total lie, since he had only *heard* them the night before, and the little scene at breakfast couldn't really be called a "fight."

"Look, we have ups and downs like anybody," Kizer said defensively. "If you're married, you know what I mean."

"I surely do," Darwin admitted. "Would you mind getting those rubbings for me? Just so I can be honest when I say I saw 'em."

Exasperated, Kizer left. When they were alone, Darwin asked Rob, "He seem nervous when you two were out this morning?"

"No," Rob said truthfully.

"Think he's violent?"

"No. Do you?"

Darwin shrugged.

"Wasn't it Terry who called you?" Rob asked.

"True enough. The lady who runs this place saw Mrs. Kizer leave while you guys were gone, but nobody in town saw her after that. It's like she just walked off into the woods, which seems kind of unlikely. From what he says, she didn't care much for the rustic life."

Kizer came back in, looking even more frustrated. "Well, I can't find them. I thought I put them down in the room, but they're not there, and they're not in the truck."

"No big deal, I'm sure they'll turn up," Darwin said. To Rob, he added, "Besides, you can verify his whereabouts, right?"

"Yeah."

Darwin put a lid on his coffee cup. "Then we won't keep you, Mr. Quillen. Mr. Kizer, y'all better come with me. We'll drive around and see if we can spot your wife."

Kizer followed Darwin out. Peggy Goins appeared, shaking her head as she gathered up the empty creamer package and swizzle stick. "That poor man. I can't believe his wife would just run off on him like that. Sure, he's a little overweight, but he's so nice."

"Sometimes nice doesn't count for much," Rob said. He watched through the window as Kizer and Darwin drove away.

"That's true," Peggy agreed. "Will you be wanting some lunch?"

"Hm? No, I think I'm going to go up to my room and lie down for a while. I bumped my head again this morning, and I've got a headache."

She patted his arm. "You rest, then. I'll make sure no one bothers you."

"I can't imagine who in this town would want to bother me, but thank you."

Peggy went onto the porch. Deputy Darwin and Terry Kizer were gone, and the rest of the street was deserted except for Rockhouse on the post office porch. She lit a cigarette and leaned on the rail, letting the sun fall on her face.

Across the street, young Lassa Gwinn stepped out of the Fast Grab convenience store where she worked. She was as round as her big sister, Tiffany, but on a much smaller scale, and radiated kindness. "What's going on with the poe-leece?" she called. "Somebody in trouble?"

"Fella done lost his wife," Peggy answered. "Turned his back on her, and off she went."

"Tall redheaded thing?"

"That's her."

"I seen her come out this morning. She was down talking to Rockhouse before."

"That ain't what he told the deputy."

Lassa snorted. "That a surprise? Saw Stoney down there, too."

Peggy felt claws of ice dig into her heart. "No you did not."

Lassa nodded. "I sure did."

"Was Stoney talking to the girl?"

"Didn't see that. But if a pretty girl disappears within a hundred yards of Stoney Hicks, what do you think? Ain't the first one, won't be the last." Then she went back into her store.

Peggy looked down the street at Rockhouse, and the urge to smack a shovel against his smug skull had never been stronger. Peggy took the final drag from her cigarette and tossed the butt into the street as she went back inside.

The school bus stopped at the end of the dirt driveway leading to the trailer. It was a single-wide, and there was a swing set beside it where Bliss Overbay sat waiting.

A lone ten-year-old girl got off the bus and waved at her friends. As the bus drove away, she trudged along the grass strip running down the driveway's center. She had her head down, and she hummed to herself.

Without looking up, she said, "Hey, Bliss."

"Hey, Mandalay. Got a minute?"

"Lots of math homework."

"It won't take long."

The girl shrugged. "Okay." She dropped her backpack on the cinder block steps and took a seat in the swing next to Bliss.

Although she was only a child, Mandalay Harris was the head of the Tufa First Daughters, and Rockhouse Hicks's equal and opposite. Time and memory worked very differently for the Tufa, especially the full-blooded ones, and Mandalay understood that more than any of them. Bliss often wished she could gaze into those dark, enigmatic eyes for hours, searching for the secrets the girl possessed, secrets older than the mountains around them. But for now, Mandalay walked the world as a ten-year-old girl, and Bliss operated as her eyes, voice, hands, and occasionally, fists.

"There's somebody in town who shouldn't be," Bliss said. "He looks like one of us, but he's not. There's not a drop of the true in him. I know it, Peggy knows it. You'd know it if you spent five minutes with him."

Mandalay kicked at the dirt with her Sleeping Beauty tennis shoes. "I already know it."

"But here's the thing. He found the Swett graveyard. He saw the inscriptions."

Mandalay frowned as she swung. "That ain't right, is it?"

"I don't know," Bliss said honestly. "But remember how you told me to watch for a sign last night? I accidentally dropped two guitar picks in the water, and the wind blew them together."

"He knows the music?" Mandalay asked.

"He's a musician, yes. And he knows the verses on the Swett stones are from a song."

"Then you have to go play with him."

"But—"

"The sign's pretty clear. The night winds want you two together. You fight them, they can make it a lot worse than a suggestion."

She remembered the surge of unwanted desire when she first saw Rob at the Pair-A-Dice. Had that been the winds, making sure she noticed him? "*Why*, Mandalay? Why him? Why me?"

Mandalay looked up at the sky, squinting her eyes against the sun. "Why him, I don't know yet. But why you . . . because you're the closest thing to what they want that the night winds can reach."

"Closest to *what*?" Bliss said, thoroughly confused. "You?"

"No, not me." Mandalay looked at her with that patient, vaguely superior air she got when something was obvious to her but to no one else. The soul behind her eyes did not belong to a ten-year-old girl.

Then Bliss got it. "Oh, shit."

Mandalay nodded. "Her time's running out. This season will be her last. When the final leaf falls from the Widow's Tree this year, she'll be lost for good. Lost to memory, lost to time. Lost to the winds."

Bliss could barely breathe.

"I don't know what the night winds want yet. And if I don't, Rockhouse don't. But he's got a bigger stake in this than I do because he started it. It's in his best interest to finish it once and for all."

"So is Rob here to help him, or—?"

Mandalay shrugged her little shoulders.

"That's not fair," Bliss said.

"I ain't arguing that. But it's what's coming."

"Does *she* know?"

"I don't know if she even knows her name after all this time. She's just a wisp of a thing now." The girl began to swing higher.

"No," Bliss insisted. "No, she's not. Not yet."

Mandalay jumped out of the swing and landed at the edge of the grass. "That's all I can tell you. It's all I know. I'm going inside now, I want to finish up my homework before *iCarly*."

Bliss made a hand gesture that conveyed respect, obedience, and affection. Mandalay returned it, started to walk away, then stopped.

"I don't know this for sure," the girl said carefully, "but we've always been able to have babies with human people. So we can't be that different from them, right?"

"Oh, we're different," Bliss insisted.

"No, that ain't what I mean. Cut us, we bleed red. Tickle us, we laugh hard. Whack us in the head, we get dizzy."

"I don't follow."

She smiled. The knowledge and maturity behind the smile, coming as they did from the face of a child, were terrifying. "You will. It's right in front of you." Then she went inside.

Bliss sat on the swing for a long time, watching her feet drag through the dirt as she slowly moved back and forth.

Exhausted, his head pounding, Rob fell asleep almost immediately. His mind dived straight into dreams.

He was alone, on a high spot that overlooked the valley. Here the great hills seemed different, sharper and edgier, as if they hadn't yet achieved their lyrical, rolling quality. Birds swooped through the skies, but they weren't buzzards or crows. They were immense and black, like ravens on steroids, and looked capable of snatching small children. In the distance, a single tree rose higher than the others.

Behind him, he saw a picnic table in a clearing, and beyond it a tree with a huge ball deformity in the trunk. An emu walked across the clearing, oblivious of him, and disappeared back into the forest. Then Rob saw an old man perched on one of the deformed tree's large root knobs. He had a pipe in his teeth, jet-black hair, and wore overalls and old-style workboots.

And he was, at most, three feet tall.

Rob approached this perfectly scaled miniature old man. In dream-logic, this didn't seem strange. "Hi," he said.

"Howdy," the old man replied.

"My name's Rob. Who're you?"

He tapped the root with the stem of his pipe. "You can call me Jessup. I'm the tree."

"You're the tree."

"Sure. Just like them."

He waved his pipe to indicate the woods around three sides of the clearing. When Rob looked again, he saw that each tree had a small person seated on it, near it, or in it. They were as varied as any group of normal people, men and women wearing jackets and jeans and T-shirts. They weren't moving around or speaking, and they didn't seem concerned with him, either.

Rob looked back at the little man. "You're all trees?"

"Sure." Wincing, the old man pulled off one of his boots and propped his painfully swollen foot on another nearby root. " 'Scuse me while I git comf'table."

Rob turned, and now Bliss sat at the picnic table, her chin in her hands. She was dressed as she'd been at the Pair-A-Dice.

"Are you the picnic table?" he asked.

She smiled. Her teeth were even, and white, and now shaped into little triangles, like shark's teeth. "No, I'm just me. The real me." Something rustled behind her, and he thought he caught a glimpse of shimmering, diaphanous, tightly folded *wings*.

Something leaped onto the table, and Rob jumped back, startled. The movement and color were identical to the mysterious shape that caused him to run off the road.

It was a teenage girl, with a halo of short, dark, and ragged hair around her face. She had enormous eyes, and she huddled behind Bliss, peering over the woman's shoulder. She wore a tattered orange dress, and her skin was dark from both sun and dirt.

Bliss turned very serious. "This is Curnen. She's my baby sister."

"Nice to meet you," Rob said. In dream-memory, he vaguely recalled that he'd heard the name before.

"Be nice, Curnen, and say hi," Bliss lightly scolded.

The girl rose so that Rob saw her whole face. It was small, and gentle, with full lips on a tiny mouth. Little bits of spittle formed at the corners.

"She doesn't have long before she's lost for good," Bliss said. "She wanted to meet you. That makes you special."

Suddenly Curnen leaped over Bliss, nimble as a monkey, and hit Rob hard. She wrapped her arms and legs around his upper body and they fell together to the ground.

Curnen crushed her lips against his, like someone who'd only seen other people kiss, and he was too startled to react. He hit the back of his head painfully, right on his injury—

And snapped awake in his bed, the girl hunched over him, her lips pressed to his.

14

Rob struggled to free himself, but the girl's wiry arms encircled his neck, and her legs locked around his waist. Her skin was slick with sweat and dirt. She smelled like a stream.

He got his hands between their bodies and felt the grimy texture of the ragged dress. It took all his strength to push her off him, and she landed silently on the balls of her feet and her fingertips, like a monkey. She stared at him, eyes wide, and he got his first clear sight of her: an unwashed teenage girl with the glazed look of mental retardation.

Her eyes cut toward the open window. Rob, still a little disoriented, realized a moment too late that she was going to leap for it. He reached for her just as she did, and his hand brushed her leg as she sailed past him.

She landed on the sill, again reminding him of a particularly graceful simian. The sky beyond was dark blue, nearing the cusp of sunset. The girl looked back at him, tensed to jump again, and he blurted, "Curnen, wait!"

She hunched down even lower against the sill and stared at him.

He blinked the rest of the way awake. Was that really her name? How did he know it? Wasn't that the word he'd heard in his mind at the graveyard? No, wait, in his dream Bliss had told him her name, and even introduced them . . . hadn't she?

"I won't hurt you, you just startled me," he said, keeping his voice even. He knew she could vanish out the window in an instant. "Please . . . come back inside."

She looked down, then out at the night, then back at him. Her eyes were too big for her head, and slightly glassy, and he wasn't sure she understood any words other than her name. But he knew now she'd been his mysterious mud-footed intruder.

"Come on . . . ," he prompted, hoping he didn't sound too much like he was calling a dog. "That's a girl, come on. . . ."

She lowered one leg. Her foot seemed elongated, the toes like a child's fingers. She flowed to the floor with feral grace and crouched low beneath the window.

He talked softly as he moved around the end of the bed. "Hey, it's okay, everything's okay, I just want to see you, that's all, just see you. . . ."

He knelt in front of her, and she trembled like a nervous colt. Grass and leaves were matted in her hair, which had been raggedly hacked or torn off short. Trickles of sweat wove tracks through the grime coating her skin. She should have been the rankest thing in the world, but this close, she smelled deliciously like freshly turned earth. He felt a weird, instant affection for her.

"Shh, that's okay, don't worry," he said, barely above a whisper. He reached out his hand to her, palm down, like he would to a strange dog. And that's how she responded, leaning close and sniffing it.

He slowly turned his hand until the palm was open to her. She leaned her cheek into it and closed her eyes. Her lips parted, and a sensual little moan escaped her. He risked stroking her with his thumb.

"Can you talk?" Rob asked softly. "Can you say anything?"

She responded with a sound that reminded him of a cross between a sigh and a purr.

"You're going to be out that window like a shot if I do anything else, aren't you?" he murmured. He moved his hand a little and scratched behind her ear. She leaned into it, and he saw more of her lithe, oddly shaped body. Her legs and arms really did seem too long for her, and she looked as comfortable crouched on all fours as most people did standing.

"So how do I know I'm not imagining this?" Rob asked in a whisper. "Or that I'm not still asleep and dreaming?"

The room phone rang.

Rob jumped. The girl shot through the window. When he looked out, he saw no sign of her. He slapped the sill in frustration, then answered the phone.

"Mr. Quillen," Peggy said brightly, "you have a visitor."

"I do?"

"You do. She's waiting on the porch. I'll tell her you're on your way."

"But who—?" Rob started to ask, but Peggy had already hung up.

He sighed, stared at the window, then went into the bathroom to freshen up. Whoever it was could damn well wait a minute.

Bliss Overbay reclined in one of the rocking chairs. She wore jeans and a black tank top under a denim jacket, and her hair hung loose and shiny. She was breathtaking, and he actually spent a moment just staring at her. "Wow," he said at last. "What a surprise."

"Pleasant one, I hope," she said.

"So far." She stood as he approached. Her smile, all dazzling Tufa teeth, was luminous. "So what brings you around?" he asked.

"Thought I'd see if I could take you to supper."

"Why?"

"Why?"

"Yeah."

"Does the word 'supper' mean something different where you're from? Because here it's just a meal at the end of the day when you've finished working."

He wanted to blurt out what had happened in his room, but fought down the urge. "Look, my head hurts. I don't think I'm up to a verbal skirmish right now."

"Here, let me see." She stood on tiptoe to check his injury. "Appears that you yanked on the stitches, but they didn't pull loose. What did you do?"

"Tripped and fell," he said, and left it at that.

"Did you get dizzy?"

"No, just clumsy."

"Well, you were lucky. So how about that supper?"

He was still fuzzy from sleep and the abrupt awakening, but she looked so adorable, so sweet, that he couldn't resist. He looked up at the sky. The sun was low, almost touching the mountains to the west. "Well . . . all right."

"Great. Come on, and bring your guitar."

Rob placed the instrument in the back of her truck, carefully nudging it down between the side panel and the old spare tire.

The dream had almost entirely faded, and as a result, he was ready to accept that the girl Curnen had been part of it, too. He shook the guitar slightly to make sure it was snug.

"You're particular," Bliss said.

"Found out the hard way that traveling with guitars is like traveling with kids. You can't leave 'em alone for too long, and you always have to make sure they're buckled in."

Rob closed the door, fastened his seat belt, and turned to Bliss. "So. Where are we going?"

"You'll see. It's a beautiful spot, especially to watch the sunset."

As they rode down the street, Rob noticed a new, odd detail about the town. He waited until they had passed all the buildings before remarking, "There aren't any churches. I thought church was a big deal to Southern people."

"There's churches, just not in Needsville or Cloud County," Bliss said. "Most of them are just across the county line. Have been as long as I can remember."

"And nobody built any in town?"

"Have you looked around? Except for the post office and convenience store, nobody's built anything new in years. It's not a place where much changes. Besides, not many people actually live in town. And a lot of folks don't like coming into town any more than they have to."

"Like the Gwinns?"

"Exactly. Here's what *I* always heard. Way back in the last century, before the Spanish-American War, a bunch of ministers came through here, setting up churches and schools and trying to bring the word of the Lord to us unchurched heathens. Around here they still talk about one in particular, Brother Bull Damron, this old 'holiness roller' who went around preaching against 'love songs' while he seduced every girl between fifteen and forty."

"What did he have against love songs?"

"It's not what you think. Around here, a song can be about murder, suicide, sex, torture, or war, but if it's also got a man and a woman in it, it's a love song. No sweet ladies in May for us, just plenty of jealousy and shame and false true lovers. Anyway, after they got a few converts, they went around renaming places, like changing Devil's Fork to Sweetwater. But they overplayed their hand when they said our songs were the devil's music. Even called fiddle-playing 'the devil's dream.' Music's too big a deal for us to put up with that nonsense, so we sent them packing. They tried to call down fire and brimstone on us, but we just laughed at them. Nothing's more fun than watching a hypocrite sputter and smoke."

"You sound like you were there."

"I've heard about it so often, sometimes it feels like I was." As if to end the conversation, she pushed a cassette tape into the old-fashioned player. Immediately, a woman's voice came from the speakers, perfectly clear despite the road noise.

"Who's that?" Rob asked.

"Kate Campbell. The song's called, 'When Panthers Roamed in Arkansas.'"

"Is she a Tufa?"

"No, she's from Mississippi. But she *is* a preacher's daughter."

They passed the turn-off to the fire station and continued up the forested slope. The truck swung with easy familiarity around the curves, and all signs of the modern world vanished. Rob could not even see a cell phone tower on any of the wooded summits. He had a momentary thought that no one would ever find his body if Bliss decided to dump him out here.

He ejected the tape so he could ask, "Where are we going?"

"On a picnic," she said brightly.

"A supper picnic?"

"Sure. Why not?" She put the tape back in the player.

Rob couldn't take his eyes off the hills around them. Most were still green, but there were patches where fall had taken hold and the scabby-red leaves seemed to mark open wounds along the slopes. The woods here, he realized, had the same overwhelming presence as those behind Doyle's trailer, only they were more majestic. They had a sense of ominous importance that he'd never before experienced. One tree in particular, its mostly bare branches towering above the others, looked to him like the groping fingers of a mighty giant drowning in the sea of gold, red, and green leaves.

Bliss pulled off the road and stopped the truck beside an enormous oak tree with a swollen lump in its trunk. This growth, easily the size of a small car, had split the bark sometime in the past, leaving two painful-looking scars grown black with time and decay. The tree shaded a concrete picnic table with a tin garbage can chained to it. "Here we are."

Rob sat very still. The area, the view, everything was identical to his dream. Even the tree with the huge lump in its trunk. He looked around for Old Man Jessup and the other diminutive tree people.

Trying to sound casual, he asked, "So what made it grow like that? With that big lump?"

"The park rangers say it's a fungus called oak gall," she said. "They have a scientific explanation for everything. But you want to really see something?"

She led him to the edge of the slope. It wasn't exactly a vertical cliff, but it fell away quickly, and a tumble down it could very easily be lethal.

The sun hadn't lowered at all in the time they were driving. If anything, it was higher, as if time had slightly rewound for them. He squinted and shielded his eyes against the glare.

Mountains rose to the right and left like great waves in a storm, and bracketed a panoramic view of the whole valley. Directly ahead, at eye level, big crows drifted back and forth against the sun, perusing the ground far below.

It was the same as his dream. No, it was *almost* the same. In his dream, the mountains had been taller, sharper, younger. And the birds were gigantic, practically prehistoric.

Needsville appeared ridiculously small, a few spot-sized buildings clustered along the gray black line of highway. In fact, Rob realized, the town looked out of place; the valley should be pristine and empty, with maybe the occasional farm, but only if it was worked by people who respected and loved the place. It wasn't meant to be settled by just *anyone*.

"See that?" Bliss said. She pointed to a gnarled tree thirty feet down the slope. "That hickory tree is nearly three hundred years old. It was here before George Washington was president."

"Shouldn't there be a marker or something?"

"So some Yankee tourist could cut it down for a souvenir?"

"Good point."

"Besides, he's a friend."

"The tree's a 'friend'?"

She nodded. "He's an old, tired man who wishes more people would listen to him before he dies because he knows things they'll need to know later on."

Rob's mouth went dry as he recalled the tree-folk in his dream. "Poetic."

"Is it?" Without waiting for an answer, she walked back to the truck, grabbed her guitar case and the picnic basket.

Rob retrieved his own guitar and followed. Should he tell her about the dream? Would she think he was a lunatic, or that the repeated bonks to his head had driven him slightly mad? And what would she say about the feral girl whom, in his dream at least, she claimed as a sister?

"So, why are we here?" Rob asked as they sat on opposite sides of the table.

"That's very existential for a picnic."

"You know what I mean. I thought maybe . . . you recognized me."

"Are you famous?"

Why the hell did I bring this up? he wanted to yell at himself. "Well . . . yeah, actually."

She skeptically pursed her lips. "Really?"

There was no backing off now, he decided. He said grimly, "Really."

"In what capacity?"

"I'm Rob from *So You Think You Can Sing?*"

Her face remained vaguely amused for a moment; then her eyes opened wide and she pressed her fingertips to her lips. "Oh, my God," she gasped. "You are."

"I am."

"Your girlfriend died. Flying out to surprise you."

"She did."

Bliss reached across the picnic table and touched his arm. "I'm so sorry."

"Me, too."

"I don't . . . I mean—"

"You don't have to say anything else," he said wearily. "It's all been said by now. But I appreciate your sympathy. Seriously, I do."

"Why didn't you tell me yesterday?"

"It's kind of hard to drop into casual conversation, especially when someone's sewing your head closed. Besides," he added wryly, "I asked Mrs. Goins at the motel to keep it secret, so I figured she might've already told you."

"She's not as gossipy as she seems."

"Well . . . now you know."

Tentatively, she took his hand. He hadn't held hands with anyone since Anna died, and the sensation of feminine fingers threading through his own made him jump. They sat in silence, the wind rustling the leaves around them. Rob looked down at the ground, where a train of ants detoured around one foot. It was always weird when his tragedy came up; only this time, he also felt unaccustomed relief.

In a voice as gentle as the breeze around them, she said, "Now I have to ask you: Why are *you* here? You don't know anyone, and you're not descended from the Tufa. Shouldn't you be at home or something? With your family?"

"Home's the last place I want to be. Everything there reminds me of her. And way too many people want to tell me how I should feel."

"But that doesn't explain why you chose *here*."

He thought before answering. "I'll tell you why, but then you have to answer a question for me. Agreed?"

"What sort of question?"

"Ah, that's cheating. You have to agree without knowing, otherwise I won't be able to trust your answer."

"Agreed, then."

He told her about the backstage cowboy and the supposedly magical song. He watched her face, but she betrayed no reaction. When he finished, he said, "So what do you think?"

"Is that your question?"

"No. But I'd like to know."

"It sounds like somebody was just yanking your chain. They knew what had happened to you and were playing a really cruel joke."

"So you don't know anything about it?"

"Why would I?"

"I heard you were high up in the Tufa chain of command."

She laughed. "Who told you that? Doyle Collins? Doyle's not a Tufa."

"So he's wrong?" Before she could answer, he continued, "Look, I'm sorry. Rationally, I don't really believe a word of it myself. But if there's even a chance . . . if a song exists that could get rid of this feeling, this *weight* . . ." He looked away and blinked his tears back under control.

"Sorry," he said. "Slips up on me sometimes. Now, my question. Are the verses from those tombstones behind the fire station part of a song? Maybe part of *that* song?"

She'd promised to answer, but she had older promises to keep as well. She said carefully, "I'm serious when I say that I've never heard of a song like the one you described. As for the graves . . . you weren't supposed to see them."

"Why not?"

"No, that's not what I mean. You weren't supposed to be *able* to see them. Would you accept, for the sake of argument, that there are ways of hiding things in plain sight? Ways of keeping people from seeing them even when they're looking right at them?"

He recalled the way neither he nor Kizer had been able to see the words earlier. "Like some kind of psychic cloaking field?"

"Yeah, that's not a bad analogy. Something that keeps non-Tufas from seeing things if they aren't deliberately shown them."

"A magic spell?"

She half shrugged, half nodded.

"But I saw them. And so did Terry."

A pit opened in her belly. "You showed them to someone else?" she whispered.

"Yeah, some guy in town doing genealogy. He said the Swetts were his ancestors, so I took him out there. And he saw them, too."

She waited for her stomach to hit bottom. How could this get worse?

"But I'm not a Tufa," Rob finished. "Not a bit. So how did I see them?"

She forced herself to stay calm. She said, "I've been pondering that myself. I can't explain it. But you *did* see them. They're verses from something that's sacred, and secret, and powerful to us. That's why we hide them."

"So what's the rest of the song?"

She shook her head. "I don't know. Honestly. I have no idea how the song ends."

"What's it about?"

"It's a dirge. A song written for someone's death. That's why it's used as an epitaph."

"A dirge," he said, thinking aloud, "could also be a song that takes away grief. And heartache is grief. But how can a song do that?"

She gritted her teeth against the urge to speak. He was so right, so close, and yet he had no business being. How could this non-Tufa comprehend, understand, *see* so much? What was she missing?

"Look around you, Rob. It looks beautiful and serene, doesn't it? But there's more blood soaked into these hills than you can imagine. And not all that blood sits quietly. On the right night, at the right time, if the right song is sung, you can see the shades in the moonlight. And that's no joke."

"I don't get it."

"Here, songs . . . do things. Cause things to happen. The right song at the right time can change everything."

"Like a spell," he said again.

"Like, yes. But more so."

"So the song from those epitaphs has the power to change things," he said.

Bliss nodded, but inside she was struggling to decide what she should do. Should she kill him now, and end any chance of the secrets coming out? It would be simple, and so easy to make it look like he'd slipped and fallen to his death.

But the night winds had blown them together. The sign was unmistakable. Two guitar picks floating on the water, like two musicians in the rivers of time, drawn together and lightly touching.

And then she knew what she needed to do.

She put her guitar across her lap.

It was a customized black Breedlove C22, with her name set in inlaid faux pearl letters along the neck. "We've talked enough," she said. "Let's play. This is another song by Kate Campell. See if you can follow me."

The spotless black truck was parked incongruously outside an old shotgun shack high on the mountain. In a few weeks, enough leaves would have fallen that Needsville would be visible below, through the bare branches. As it was, though, the vehicle and building were hidden from view.

Rockhouse Hicks sat on the tailgate, his banjo in his arms. He softly plucked the strings, just loud enough to cover the sounds of sexual activity coming from the shack. Inside, his nephew

Stoney Hicks was having his way with the woman from town. She was willing—they were all always willing—but she had no idea that she'd pay a horrendous price. Non-Tufa girls around here knew to avoid Tufa boys, especially full-blooded ones like Stoney Hicks. *Especially* Stoney.

The cries and grunts faded, and Stoney emerged, barefoot and clad only in his jeans. He was a staggeringly good-looking young man, with a face like a Native American warrior and matching jet-black hair to his shoulders. He stood six-four, and every muscle was chiseled perfection. He wouldn't have been out of place on a romance novel cover, were it not for the cold, selfish mockery in his eyes.

"Hey, Uncle Rockhouse," he said as he opened a cooler in the bed of the truck. "Want a beer?"

"No, thanks," he said. "How'd it go?"

The younger man grinned. "How'd it sound like it went? Had her on her knees begging before the door even shut. What are we going to do about her husband?"

"Us? We don't do anything. She'll take care of that, once you tell her to, just like she got us those tombstone rubbings."

"What's so important about 'em?"

"You don't be worrying about that. You didn't look at 'em, did you?"

"Nossir, you told me not to."

"That's good. Make sure you don't. You hear me, boy?"

"Yessir," Stoney said contritely. "So, uhm . . . her husband?"

Rockhouse shrugged and spit tobacco into the dirt. "Fella comes up in here, being all nosy and asking questions, something happens. Nobody'll be surprised. Nobody'll ask too many questions."

The door to the shack opened. Stella emerged, fully dressed but with unmistakably ruffled hair. She looked around until she saw Stoney, then gasped as if she'd been wandering in the desert and he was an oasis. "H-honey?" she said meekly.

"Fix your damn hair, will you?" he snapped at her, and she quickly went back inside. He took a long drink of his beer. "She's a good one, though. Knows a lot of city-girl tricks."

"Enjoy her while you can."

"Oh, I will." He finished his beer, tossed the can into the woods, and went back inside.

Rockhouse began playing "Carolina in the Morning."

15

"You're not bad," Rob said when she finished the song "See Rock City."

"Did you expect me to be?" Bliss replied.

"Not at all. I heard you at the roadhouse, remember? So who taught you to play?"

"Mostly my grandfather. He started showing me things when I was about six or seven. Oh, do I remember them snappy black eyes glaring at me when I'd done something wrong or fell back a little bit. But eventually he slowed down and I sped up, and he taught me a lot. What about you?"

"Self-taught. Bought a DVD and sat in my bedroom learning chords and writing songs all through high school. Better than leaving the house and getting beat up."

"And then you ended up on TV. How did that happen? Unless," she added quickly, "you'd rather not talk about it."

"Nah, it's okay. I had a band. Three other guys, but

they were . . . you know how some people are serious about what they do, but some people just do it because it's easy and then quit when it turns into work? That was them. Not their fault, but I wanted more. Anyway, whenever I'd complain about how that show just made musicians look stupid and shallow, they'd say I should audition. They were kidding, but one day I was at the mall, the auditions were going on, and I just went in."

"And you won."

"Better for everybody if I hadn't." He paused. "So what was your first time like?"

"Excuse me?"

"The first time you ever played in public."

"Oh. Well, let me see. I guess I was about ten years old. I was having a real hard time with the guitar Granddaddy wanted me to play, so Daddy bought me this thing, it was bigger than a uku-lele, but smaller than a regular guitar. They called it a tiple; you ever heard of it?"

Rob nodded. Her accent grew stronger when she talked of her family.

"There was a big barn dance coming up," Bliss continued, "and one of the men who organized it happened to come by the house one day and heard me singing and playing that tiple. He asked me to come down and told me, 'You don't have to play but one song.' And I think I played fifteen songs before they let me off the stage." She put her hands back on the guitar. "Now let's play something else."

As he settled onto the bench across the table from her, she began to play and waited for him to join in. He concentrated on following her melody, and at last he recognized it as an obscure country song called "Calico Plains." When they finished, he said, "That was great."

"Yeah," she agreed. "You're the first person I've met who knows that song."

"That's not the Pam Tillis version, is it?"

"No, it's Matraca Berg's original, off *Lying to the Moon*. Bought the cassette at a flea market."

"She's great, isn't she?"

"She's the real deal. Except she says the name wrong on 'Appalachian Rain.' The tradition is that it's 'latch,' like throw an 'apple *atcha*,' not 'apple *laycha*.'"

"I've heard it that way more than the other."

"That's true. Maybe eventually that's how we'll say it, too. 'Tradition' doesn't mean just passing down the old things, anyway. You also pass down a tradition of creativity, of being alive. Otherwise, it dies on its feet. So I guess if she needs to say it wrong to make the song work, it's okay."

"The one song of yours I've heard sure isn't traditional. Sounds like you're developing your own thing."

"Oh, I just piddle around with stuff. No one wants anything genuine, anyway. They want the same thing they've always heard. Like that TV show of yours. No one cares what the songs are about, as long as the singer can hit the high notes. That sort of thing bores me."

"The singer, not the song."

"Who said that?"

"Exactly."

She looked confused. "What?"

"Sorry, making a joke. Pete Townsend of the Who said that." He chuckled. "I'm thirsty now."

"There's bottled water in the basket. And our food."

He helped spread the cloth over the table, and they quickly set out her meal. When he bit into the first sandwich, the ham had a deep sugary taste different from any he'd had before. They talked about songs and musicians, and he told her stories of some of the odd people he'd met during his TV tenure.

When they finished eating, she picked up her guitar again. "Okay. This is my favorite Kate Campbell song. And it's pretty easy to follow, too, so feel free to jump in."

She began by playing the first verse without singing, so he could pick it up. He got most of it the first time through; as she said, the changes weren't that complicated. Then she sang:

> *Tangled vines cover the lattice*
> *They creep and crawl around the house*
> *Nobody lives there*
> *Only ghosts hang around*

"This is the chorus," she said.

> *I have seen hope and glory fade away*
> *I've heard old folks talk of better days*
> *And all that's left to guard the remains*
> *Are wrought iron fences*

"Wow, that's great," Rob said as they played the verse again without singing. "Great details."

"She's a master of that," Bliss said. "Now here's the second verse."

> *Sarah Mae bore two children*
> *One died at birth and one at Shiloh*
> *Now they're on a hill long forgotten*
> *Carved in stone*

Rob reached over the table and grabbed the neck of her guitar so hard, his knuckles turned white, silencing the music with a jarring *ching!* "Why the fuck did you pick this song?" he said, his voice choked.

The rage in his eyes caught her off guard, and she swallowed hard. "I just . . . we were listening to her in the truck."

"Yeah, and that was just a fucking coincidence, too, I suppose?"

He got up and came around the table. She scooted away. "Rob, stop it. It's just a song!"

"That was what he said to me!" he yelled.

"What who said?"

"The man backstage at the Fox! He told me the song I wanted was 'on a hill, long forgotten, carved in stone'!"

"Rob, I swear, I don't know anything about that! I just like the song, and—" *And it's been stuck in my head for days,* she finished to herself. Now she knew why.

He put his guitar down hard on the table and stalked away, trying to get control of his temper. What the hell was going on?

"Rob?" Bliss asked. She had to be very careful now, to sense the right things to say. She was certain the winds had brought her here for this conversation, this moment.

"If you want to help me," he snapped, "convince me this is a coincidence. Convince me there's no connection between what the guy who told me about the Tufa said in Atlanta, and the fact that you drive me out into the middle of nowhere and then tell me the same thing."

"I didn't tell you anything, I just played a song," she said.

" 'On a hill, long forgotten, carved in stone.' Which is exactly where I found those verses." He stared out across the valley. Either she was telling the truth, which seemed impossible, or she wasn't, and he was the focus of an elaborate multi-state conspiracy designed to do . . . what? Make him read the epitaphs? Who the hell went to that kind of trouble?

He sighed and kicked at the ground. "All right, look, I'm sorry. This is all just a little much."

She still kept a distance between them. "That's some temper you've got."

"Yeah. It gets away from me on occasion." He felt the same hollow, shaky shivers that drove him into the stairwell that night in Atlanta. "I'm okay now. At least, I'm not going to punch anything. Or anyone."

She moved closer. Suddenly she knew what to say. "I want to ask you something, and I really want you to think about the answer. Okay?"

He nodded.

She looked steadily into his eyes. "*Why* are you so angry?"

He snorted sarcastically. "Well, let's see, my girlfriend died, and—"

"No. You were angry before that, and before we played 'Wrought Iron Fences.' That 'whim' story might fool some people, but a man like you doesn't go up for that TV show unless he's angry." With certainty she said, "You auditioned to make someone eat their words. Who? The guys in your band?"

He shook his head and closed his eyes. "Anna. She was . . . disappointed with my career progress."

"She wanted you to quit music?"

"No, she wanted me to reprioritize it. Make it a hobby." He laughed at the inane cliché of it. "Get a real job."

"So you thought if you made it on the show, it would prove you had talent."

He nodded. His chest felt tight, and the back of his throat swelled.

She took his hand. They stood in silence, the wind rustling the trees around them. At last she said, "There's nothing wrong with feeling regret over this."

"Oh, it gets better. That surprise visit at the finals? It wasn't a surprise. She wasn't going to do it, but the producers were adamant she had to be there. I had to . . ." He wiped hot liquid from his cheeks. "I begged her to come. Pleaded. Promised her everything. And she came."

For a long moment there was only the wind around them. At last Bliss said, "That's a lot of pain to carry around."

"I know," he said. "That's why I came all this way, why I need to find . . . that song."

He couldn't hold it back then. He began to cry, big gulping sobs bereft of dignity or solace.

Bliss put her arms around him and pulled him close. This pain was real. The night winds could be capricious, even enigmatic, but she'd never known them to be deliberately, truly cruel. Whatever the truth about that night in Atlanta, they'd blown this sad man to her because he needed her help.

She rested one strong, small hand up between his shoulder blades. "Some things a song can't fix, Rob," she said softly. And she moved her fingers, making a sign.

He pulled away enough to look into her eyes. She met his gaze expectantly, eyes clear and strong. He was torn between the desire to kiss her right there on the spot, and tenderly protect her from anyone who'd come near her with rough intent. He sensed, though, that neither reaction was quite the appropriate one. Still, he leaned closer.

Their lips almost met. Then he turned away and walked to the edge of the slope. After a few moments she came and stood beside him.

"You didn't want to kiss me," she said, not asking but simply stating.

He looked out at the valley, eyes squinted tight from tears and the sun's glare. "Yes, I did. It just would've been the wrong thing, for the wrong reasons. But I do need your help."

"So what can I do?"

"Help me find the rest of the song. Whether it's magical or not, I need to do it. For myself, for Anna, and for—" He took a deep breath. "—for all the broken hearts in the world."

"Okay," she answered with certainty. The wind rustled the trees, and she knew what to do next. "But if I'm going to help you, there's someplace else I have to take you."

"Okay. When?"

"Now. Tonight."

And before he could say another word, the sun dropped behind the mountains as if the cord holding it up had been cut. They were plunged into twilight.

16

"Is something wrong?" Bliss asked as she drove.

Besides the fact that it got dark so fast, I worried that I was passing out? he almost said, but didn't. Instead, he decided to play his last card. The Tufa weirdness grew deeper with each revelation; he couldn't wait to hear her explain this one. "This afternoon, while I taking a nap . . . I met your sister Curnen."

Bliss didn't take her eyes off the road. She said, "Hm." *How could Curnen be so stupid?* she thought. Then she realized what time of year it was, and what *this* cycle in particular meant. When the last leaf fell, the curse on Curnen would become permanent and irrevocable; the girl would become a wild animal, lost to herself, her family, and the Tufa.

And what did this mean for her, for Bliss? The night winds had blown her into Rob's path, and she was doing her best to sense and follow their desires. Was Curnen, all feral instinct and instant gratification, working with or against the winds? If she was defying them out of selfishness and fear, then it would resolve itself soon enough. But what if the winds really *were* blowing both sisters into the path of the same man? What could be the reason? Or the ultimate outcome?

The immediate problem, though, was explaining Curnen, and many other things, to Rob. He'd already proved an enigma with his ability to see things that should be hidden to non-Tufas. She'd promised to help him, but how far did she dare trust him? What was the right thing to do?

Finally she said, "I guess you've got some questions about Curnen, then."

"Yeah. She's been coming into my room for the last two nights, hasn't she?"

"Did you get rid of something that looked like a piece of blue glass on the windowsill?"

"Yeah."

"That would've kept her out. So yes, she's probably been visiting you."

"Why?"

"She's not entirely . . ."

"Normal?"

"I was going to say . . . Well, normal's as good a word as any. No, she's definitely not normal."

"What is she, then?"

Bliss didn't answer. They drove in silence for several minutes, and eventually turned onto a gravel road. Finally Rob asked, "Hey, where are we going?"

"There's a place up here where some of the local musicians gather. I thought you might like to see it."

"What's that got to do with the magic song?" When she didn't answer, he asked, "Is Rockhouse Hicks going to be there?"

"No, Rockhouse isn't welcome. Most people have the same opinion of him as you do. The only place you're likely to hear him play is the Pair-A-Dice. That's neutral territory."

"You still haven't answered my question about Curnen."

"Yes." She paused. "You know the stories they tell about mountain people being all weird and cousin-marrying and inbred? They always leave out the reasons. Before there were roads, you could live on one side of a mountain and never see folks from the other side. They might be five miles away as the crow flies, but it'd be thirty miles up and down, and over dangerous trails at that. People didn't mix much, and there's still a few people around here who live like that. They keep to their own . . . for everything."

For a long moment, the only sound was gravel under the tires.

She continued, "And you really can't understand unless you're from here, which I thought you were at first, especially when you found that graveyard. That's still the damndest thing."

"But I'm not a Tufa."

In the light from the dashboard, he thought he saw her smile. "The Cherokee called us *Nunnehi*."

"You know," he said, annoyed, "I'm getting real tired of you half-assed telling me things. Either trust me or don't, but quit dangling carrots in front of me, okay?"

Bliss stopped the truck so suddenly, the tires slid on the rocks. When she turned to look at him, Rob noticed her eyes reflected light like an animal's.

"Rob, this isn't easy for me. I'm used to *keeping* secrets, not revealing them."

"Okay, then, let's take it one thing at a time. What's the deal with Curnen?"

She took a deep breath and closed her eyes. "Her parents were brother and sister."

Rob blinked. "And she's your sister?"

"Yes."

"So your parents—"

"No, no, we only have the same mother. My daddy was fine. Curnen's father was . . . well . . . an important person in these parts, at one time. And very, very good at getting what he wanted, even to the point of using threats and force. Which was why . . ." She looked out the windshield at the trees illuminated by the headlights. Dust from the abrupt stop drifted lazily through the beams. "It's hard to talk about something so personal."

"I know what you mean," he said with no irony. "So she's retarded? Or 'challenged,' I think they call it now?"

"'Challenged' is better because it's more accurate. Something was done to her, and she can't escape it. But she's resisting it the best she can."

"Why don't you help her, then?"

Bliss's voice choked. "Because I can't."

He wanted to ask more, but there was something in her voice, a pain so similar to his own that this time, he reached over and took her hand. At first she allowed it, then squeezed his fingers and pulled her hand free.

"I'm sorry," she said. "It slips up on me, too."

"Will she hurt me?"

"No. She wouldn't. If she's visiting you, she senses something about you."

"Like what?"

"A . . . kinship, for lack of a better word."

"Because of my hair?"

"No. Something deeper. Something painful."

He started to reply, but the memory of the way she'd snuggled her cheek into his hand overwhelmed him. The girl, like her sister, like Rob, carried around more pain than a being should have to. They were all three bound by it.

Bliss put the truck back in gear and drove on. Light showed through the trees ahead.

"Looks like a good crowd," she murmured. They rounded the last curve, and Rob saw two dozen other vehicles parked neatly parallel along the road. Past them stood a huge old barn. In the moonlight, the roof sported immense painted letters urging people to SEE ROCK CITY, although Rob couldn't imagine a lot of tourists passed it. Bliss parked at the end of the line.

Rob had heard many types of singing in his life, but never anything that filled the air like this music. He sat transfixed, as caught in the melodies as a deer in headlights. He distinguished fiddles, guitars, accordions, and each rang with a purity he'd never encountered, as if somehow the song reached directly into his heart and connected with his emotions.

"You all right?" Bliss asked with a knowing smile.

"I hope so," Rob said. "Unless I've died, and this is heaven."

"What if it's hell?"

"Like Mark Twain said, heaven for the climate, hell for the company."

This made her smile. "Come on, I want you to meet someone."

They grabbed their guitars, and Bliss took the cooler from the picnic basket. Then they walked up the road toward the barn. Rob saw a vast shimmering starfield above the trees, brighter than he'd ever seen before. He blinked as several dark objects quickly flew over just above the treetops, momentarily blocking the stars as they passed. They were too big for birds or bats, but he couldn't imagine what else they might be. Kites at night?

Bliss stopped and turned to him. "I almost forgot, I have to warn you about something. They'll offer you drinks. Mostly homemade, but somebody always brings beer. It's very important that you don't drink anything except the stuff I brought in this cooler."

"Why?"

She ignored the question. "I need your word on it. I know you're honorable, and if you say you won't do it, you won't do it."

"Why?" he asked again.

"I promise I'll tell you later, and you'll believe me then. But I need your word now."

He sighed. "Okay, I promise. I won't drink anything except what's in your cooler."

He followed her up the driveway, and almost immediately the music drowned out the sound of their feet crunching gravel. He didn't recognize the song, but it carried that eternal, timeless quality only the best tunes embody.

He glanced back the way they'd come. The road disappeared so thoroughly into the darkness that he worried it had vanished. "What if I decide to leave on my own?"

"You'd never find your way out," Bliss said. "Just like no one who isn't invited will ever find their way in."

When they reached the barn door, the dozen or so people gathered there all warmly greeted Bliss. They were big men and small wiry women, dressed exactly as Rob imagined working-class mountain folk would dress. To one side, a prepubescent girl danced on a flat board thrown on the ground while a young man marked time with spoons that echoed the tempo of the music inside. The girl watched her feet with grim concentration, the lace hem of her dress fluttering like a line of white butterflies.

A large man in overalls and an Atlanta Braves cap sat on an old crate at the side door, a cigar box on his lap. Moths and other insects circled the light above him. "Hey, Bliss," he said as he hugged her.

"Hey, Uncle Node. How are you doing tonight?"

"If things get any better, I might have to hire someone to help me enjoy it."

"Sounds like quite a crowd."

"Yes indeedy. Something in the air seems to've called everybody out tonight."

Bliss nodded toward the dancing girl. "Clementine's getting pretty good at that flatfooting."

He smiled proudly. "She sure is. I reckon by winter, she'll be ready to move inside."

"Reckon so, too. Noah Vanover, this is my friend Rob. He's a musician, too."

"Never woulda guessed with that guitar case," Vanover said with a grin. He offered his hand. "How y'all doing? Call me Uncle Node, everybody else does."

"Good to meet you, Uncle Node," Rob said. The man had an immensely strong handshake.

"Quite a shiner you got there," he said, nodding at Rob's black eye.

"Tiffany Gwinn," Bliss said. "Rob stood up to her and lived to tell about it."

"Now, that I would've purely loved to have seen."

Bliss dug in her pockets and produced what looked to Rob like two small rocks. "This should cover me and him," she said, and handed them to Vanover. They clattered against other stones when he put them in the cigar box.

"Always a pleasure, never a chore," he said with a smile. "Y'all have a good time."

They entered to the right of the bandstand. A pile of guitar, fiddle, dulcimer, and other instrument cases rested against the wall, and Bliss propped hers among them. She leaned close and yelled in Rob's ear, "It's okay to leave your guitar here!"

Rob nodded, a bit overwhelmed. The building's interior seemed bigger inside than it had appeared outside, like a hillbilly TAR-DIS. Bright overhead lights hung from wires spaced among the wooden crossbeams. Stacked in a stairstep fashion and covered with blankets, hay bales provided rough bleacher-style seating. The band riser was made of old shipping pallets covered with particle board.

At least three hundred people were crammed inside. They lined the walls and covered the hay bale bleachers, while perhaps a third of the crowd filled the hard-packed dirt dance floor in the center. Couples danced in old-style formality, but some individuals also flatfooted on pieces of wood just like the girl outside. And everyone sported the "Tufa look"—dark hair, dark skin, and seemingly perfect teeth.

"How often do you do this?" Rob hollered into Bliss's ear.

"There's something going on here most nights," Bliss called back. "Lots of people still don't have cable or the Internet. This is what they do instead."

He followed her around the dance floor. They all seemed to know Bliss; she waved, smiled, hugged, and shook hands with almost everyone they passed. Rob was sure she introduced him to a dozen people, but he couldn't hear a thing over the music and crowd noise. When they reached the hay bleachers, they sat with the cooler between them. He'd never seen anyone look so at home, so *happy*, as Bliss did at that moment.

The song finished, and the crowd applauded both the musicians and the dancers. The flatfooters held hands and bowed in a group: hefty men, skinny boys, and hard-looking women in long dresses. They gathered their boards and left the dance floor. Some of the musicians left the stage, and new ones took their place.

The squat little bandleader, who held a guitar that his stubby arms could barely reach, said, "Thank y'all. Hey, if you see a banjo player on one side of the road and an accordion player on the other, which do you run over first?" He paused for effect. "The accordion player. Business before pleasure."

The crowd laughed good-naturedly, while both the banjo and accordion players pretended to beat the man with their instruments.

"Play 'The Seven Nights' Drunk'!" someone called.

"Naw, not that ol' nonsense," the man said, and a chorus of boos responded. He just smiled and shook his head. "See, that's why I'd rather milk cows for a livin' and play just for fun. Then I can play what I want to!"

The round little man waved and left the stage to a smattering of applause. The other musicians milled around, waiting as the next performer came forward.

"See that girl?" Bliss said. She indicated a teenager who now stood at center stage, tucking a fiddle under her chin and talking to the old man who played lap dulcimer. "Page Paine. She's only four-teen. She may not be the best fiddler in Tennessee, but the ones that can beat her don't run in bunches. A guy from Nashville heard about her, wanted to sign her up and turn her into the next Taylor Swift."

"Didn't happen?"

Bliss shook her head. "Nope. That's not the reason she plays music."

Page stepped up to the microphone and said, "Hi, y'all." The crowd applauded again, and a few people whooped. Page smiled shyly. Her long-limbed, gawky body seemed to consist mainly of elbows and knees. "Heck, I ain't even played nothin' yet." There was some laughter at this. "This first number we call 'Knee Hig 'Em.' It's sorta made up."

"What does 'Knee Hig 'Em' mean?" Rob asked Bliss.

"'I don't understand.'"

Carefully, he repeated, "What . . . does . . ."

"No, that *is* what it means. It means, 'I don't understand.'"

"Oh, sorry. In what language?"

Before she could answer, the drummer, a long-bearded young man in a faded tie-dye shirt, counted four and the band began to play. The other musicians melded together and formed a mass of sound over which Page's fiddle *soared*. There was no other word for it: her skill was secondary to something ineffable, something spiritual that came directly from her soul and touched each person in the audience through the medium of her playing. Musicians dream of connecting this way, Rob knew, and to witness it—to *experience* it—gave him chills.

He recalled a book he'd read about the father of bluegrass, Bill Monroe. He'd talked of "the ancient tones," undernotes that sustained while the fiddler played the melody, allowing the music to fill more space than seemed possible. For the first time, Rob understood what the old master meant. Page certainly did.

When she finished, she bowed and tossed her hair dramatically. The applause was genuine and enthusiastic.

"Holy shit," Rob said as he clapped. "Do they realize how good they are?"

"Oh, yes," Bliss answered simply.

Page pointed her bow at the back of the room. "I do believe I see my cousin Bliss back there," Page said. "I bet we can get her up here if we try hard enough."

People turned to look and began shouting good-natured encouragement. Bliss looked at Rob, and he nodded. She hopped down off the hay and crossed the dance floor, once again running a gauntlet of well-wishers and friends. She didn't get her guitar, but instead climbed onstage and stood next to Page, who was half a head taller.

Page leaned down and whispered something to Bliss, who nodded. Then she said something to the band, and once again, the drummer counted off.

This song was completely different. It had a deep, primal rhythm that was more African than Appalachian, and Page played sharp percussive notes, not the soaring ones that filled every corner of the room. The crowd didn't dance, and most of the extraneous conversation dropped off, as if in respect.

Bliss stepped to the microphone and sang the first verse:

> *One time a man came up the mountain*
> *Looking for the promised land*
> *He brought all the evils his life had made*
> *With him in the palm of his hand*

Page leaned in to harmonize on the chorus. Unlike a lot of women's voices, they didn't aim for the higher registers, but kept their harmonies low, and bit off the end of each line:

> *The wind tried to blow him back down the hill*
> *The rain tried to wash him away*
> *But he knew at the top he'd find what he sought*
> *But not the price he'd have to pay*

Then Page, still playing, sang the next verse:

> *There he met a girl with the eyes of the sea*
> *And a soul as cold as the moon*
> *She laughed at his pain and then took his heart*
> *And mocked his eternal ruin*

Again they harmonized on the chorus, which they sang twice, and the band dropped away until the only sound was a single long, mournful note from Page's violin. Bliss stepped back to the microphone.

She taunted his love, and tainted his heart
With venom he'd never known
Her bitterness swallowed him and spit him forth
Half-eaten and without a home

Page joined her, but sang only a sad, mountain-style wail while still playing the same long, quavering note. Rob couldn't imagine how she kept both melodies straight, but the effect was chilling. There wasn't a sound in the place now other than the music.

Bliss sang:

When the sun arose it found only his bones
It kissed them and shed not a tear
The moon gleamed off them in the cold of the night
Until the mountain swallowed them dear

Then Page, along with the drummer and upright bass player, joined in on the final verse. The addition of these male voices added a last, sepulchral aura to the song.

So my love, don't climb with pain in your heart
Or bitterness filling your soul
The wind and the rain won't save you, my dear
From the arms that are waiting and cold

The other musicians built to a crescendo, then dropped off sharply, leaving only the long, wailing violin note quivering in the silence. Page snapped it off like a gunshot, and there was a moment of total, dead silence before the crowd began applauding and whooping its appreciation.

Rob was flabbergasted. The music being played here, by these people, was on a par with the best stuff he'd heard anywhere. It was the kind of music *he* wanted to play, the cosmic antithesis of the shallow, technique-oriented reality show crap that had inundated him. These were world-class players, and here they were in a barn in the middle of the Smoky Mountains playing for the sheer hell of it.

Below him, a big man packed into a too-small lawn chair looked up at Rob and smiled. "Want a beer?" he said, offering a can.

Remembering his promise, Rob shook his head. "No, thanks. Makes me act stupid."

"Drink is the curse of the workin' man," he said. "Course, work is the curse of the drinking man."

"And drink is the work of the cursing man?" Rob deadpanned. The big man howled in laughter, until Bliss's voice again came through the speakers.

"Thanks, y'all. I got kind of a surprise of my own for you, a friend of mine from the flatlands who's a heckuva picker. Rob, come on down. Rob Quillen, ladies and gentlemen!"

Rob hopped off the hay bleachers and followed Bliss's trail to the stage. If anyone recognized him, it didn't interfere with their enthusiasm; he saw no whispered asides or pointing fingers. Amazingly, he also felt no qualms, just an eagerness to join these players.

A teenage boy, shirtless beneath overalls and sporting a scraggly soul patch, stepped in front of him just before he reached his instrument. "I think you'll be wanting to use this instead." He held up an electric guitar.

Rob said, "No, I've got my own."

The boy smiled. "You can't rock the hills with a whisper, son."

Rob took the instrument to avoid any trouble, but as he put the strap over his head, he felt more complete than he had in months. The instrument felt amazing in his hands, perfectly balanced and as comfortable as if he'd been playing it for years. It was a first-generation Telecaster Esquire, with the finish worn in places by years of playing. He looked for a cord to plug into the jack, then realized there was a wireless unit taped to the strap. The boy who'd given him the ax turned on an amplifier, which buzzed and chirped when Rob touched the strings. He gave Rob a thumbs-up, then disappeared into the crowd.

Rob stepped onstage next to Bliss and Page, grinning. "What are we playing?"

The drummer pointed a stick at him. "One of yours."

"Mine? You don't know any of—"

"Tell us the changes, we'll be fine," one of the others assured him. It was a woman in her thirties, with tight jeans and short hair. Rob swore she hadn't been there a moment ago, but now she was, holding an electric bass.

At once he knew exactly what song to play, one that was musically simple enough the band could easily get it and run with it. "Changes are one-three-five, Bo Diddley style."

A wiry man with leathery skin and an eye patch carried a banjo onstage. "Care if I join in?"

"You ever played Chuck Berry on that thing?" Rob asked.

"Once. Down in Louisiana, close to New Orleans."

"Hop onboard, then. Everybody else clear?"

They all nodded as if playing a brand-new song off the tops of their heads happened every day.

Rob stepped to the microphone. "I'd like to thank everyone for making me feel so welcome. This is one of my own songs; hope you like it."

He began to play, and the others listened as he strummed the first stanza in full before he began to sing:

> On a hot summer night down in Bourbonville
> He left his wife in bed asleep and got behind the wheel
> Laid a long track across the county line
> To a hoppin' little roadhouse hid behind the pines
> A little girl was playin' so the place could hop
> He jumped into the crowd and found the center stage spot

The drummer caught the beat after the first few bars, and then the bassist and one-eyed banjo picker followed. After only the briefest disharmony, they sounded like they'd played the song a thousand times. Grinning like an idiot, Rob charged into the chorus.

> Play it hard, little bluesgirl
> Make that bottleneck scream
> Let me feel every word that you're sayin'
> So I know that you know what I mean
> A man's gotta die of something
> And I don't care if I bleed

When he paused after the chorus, Page contributed a long, heartrending fiddle riff that caught him so by surprise that he almost missed the cue to begin singing again.

> She saw him in the crowd and flashed him a smile
> Said I'll be done here in just a little while

If you come around back and bring some Johnnie Walker
  Red
I'll do things to put the fear of God in your head
He couldn't say no, couldn't walk away
He had to dance as long as she had to play

This time he nodded for Bliss to harmonize with him on the chorus, and she did, taking the high end and adding just enough Joplin-y growl to really accent the song's grit. She sang as if she could read his mind.

Make your move, little bluesgirl
Let that leather jacket fall to the floor
Kick those army boots under the bed now
I'll hang the do-not-disturb on the door
Your fingers get my skin all a-twangin'
And your mouth makes me holler for more

Rob jumped into the air, came down with his feet spread wide and tore into a solo. He wasn't a show-off, he believed in sacrificing everything for the sake of the overall song, but this time the music burned out of him. He felt sweat run down his cheeks and nose as he huddled over his guitar, and he finished with a flourish and a full 360 spin. The reaction was ecstatic.

The banjo player stepped forward and took the next solo. It brought a spontaneous cheer from the crowd; Rob couldn't blame them.

When he stepped to the microphone again, he decided to really see how good these guys were at following him.

"Wait a minute!" he cried, and waved his arm for the band to stop. They did, right on cue, except for the steady rumble of the bass and the tapping on the drummer's hi-hat, just as Rob imagined it.

The crowd, smiling and clapping, waited to see what he'd say. He felt as if they hung on his every word, that he could do no wrong, and that the musicians behind him would accurately anticipate his every move, on a song they'd never even *heard* before. He never wanted this moment to end.

"You folks would call this a love song, wouldn't you?" he asked the crowd, and was rewarded with cheers. "Well, I've learned a lot about love songs over the past couple of days. This song used to have a happy ending, where the guy runs off with the girl, but that doesn't seem right, does it?"

The crowd booed and shouted "No!" and "Uh-uh!"

"Yeah, I agree. I mean, the guy is cheating on his wife, and in your love songs, he wouldn't get away with that, would he? So I've kinda made up a new verse just now, to end it differently. Tell me what you think."

He turned to the band and shouted a four-count before launching into the final verse.

> He was wobbly on his feet when the lights came up
> She slipped out the back, he tried to catch up
> When he reached the alley, there was nobody there
> 'Scept a single guitar pick and a long black hair
> "See you in hell," he heard her ghost voice say
> "I died here twenty years ago this very day!"

The crowd roared its approval, and with a wild cry of abandon and joy, he launched into the final chorus. The band came in right on cue. Both Bliss and Page leaned in to harmonize, and they held out the final crescendo until he swung his guitar up and dramatically brought it down. The crowd applauded, cheered, and whistled, and Rob watched them with amazement. He felt Bliss thread her fingers through his, and glanced over at her. She was smiling, and he thought at that moment he'd never seen a more beautiful woman in his life. He took Page's hand, and when the others had lined up with them, they bowed in unison.

When he stood, his eye fell on a woman in the crowd who looked for all the world like Stella Kizer.

He froze and stared. She followed a tall, ridiculously handsome man as he worked his way to the back of the room. She momentarily turned toward him, and he saw that her face was drawn tight and tired, with dark circles under her eyes as if she hadn't slept in days. In fact, she looked so different, he wasn't entirely certain it *was* her, and she vanished into the approving throng almost immediately.

By the time Bliss handed him a bottle of water from her cooler, Rob was exhausted. He wiped sweat on his shirttail and drank half the bottle at once. Another group of musicians was onstage now, and he followed Bliss into the cool outside air. Everyone he passed told him how well he'd played.

At the edge of the clear space around the barn, a group of small children stood together tossing bread crumbs and corn to three enormous emus that had emerged from the forest. The birds, skittish and uncertain, caught some of the pieces in the air, which made the kids laugh. The noise caused the birds to back away, but they didn't run off into the darkness.

Bliss led him to a bonfire, deserted except for some teenagers banging rough tunes on bongos. A canvas camping chair stood empty, and he held it mock gallantly for Bliss. Then he dropped

to the ground beside her. The night's breeze was the perfect temperature to take the edge off the fire's warmth.

"That . . . was . . . *amazing,*" he said, still grinning. "I've never
played with anyone who could follow stuff like that without
rehearsing. *I* sure can't do it."

"Good thing you were leading, then," Bliss said. In the orange
glow, she appeared untouchably beautiful.

"Do I get my explanation now?"

Bliss smiled tiredly. "Yes, you do. I know what I need to know
about you."

"Which is what?"

She looked at the people milling outside the barn and clustered around the fire. "Ah-ha. There's Annie May Pritchard."

She pointed across the fire, where a teenage girl danced to the
sultry beat provided by the drummers. She had black hair in a
ponytail and her eyes were closed. She wore low-slung jeans and
a tank top that left her stomach exposed, and her bare feet stirred
a small cloud of dust.

"What do you see?" Bliss asked.

"A pretty girl dancing."

"That's all?"

"What else should I see?"

"Look harder."

He did, then shook his head. "Sorry. Maybe if I knew what I
was looking for—"

Bliss licked her lips. He'd played with the Tufa, with *her* Tufa.
Even if Mandalay was right about why, it didn't change what had
happened. And now she had a promise to keep. "This'll hurt for a
second," she said, and before he could respond, she thumped him
solidly right on the stitched lump.

"*Ow!*" he cried, and closed his eyes against the pain.

He felt her hands on either side of his head from behind, holding him in a rock-solid grip. "Don't close your eyes, Rob. *Look.*"

He blinked. Across the fire, he saw the same young girl dancing, except . . .

"Holy shit," he whispered.

It *was* the same girl, the same Annie May Pritchard, but now she wore a shimmering wrap that alternately covered and revealed a lean, supple body. Her skin shone in the firelight, alive with rainbow colors. Tall, pointed ears rose from her hair. And from her back sprang two enormous, gossamer wings that flexed to the same rhythm.

He blinked again. Once more, she was just a dancing teenage girl.

He sat very still until Bliss removed her hands. "So what did you see?" she asked quietly.

"I don't have a clue," he replied honestly, his voice barely louder than the crackling fire. "What was I supposed to see?"

"Tell me what you *did* see."

"It looked like that girl there turned into . . . Tinker Bell or something."

Bliss nodded. "Not far off."

"And exactly *why* did I see that?"

Cut us, we bleed red. Tickle us, we laugh hard. Whack us in the head, we get dizzy. Now Mandalay's words made sense. "Somehow, your blow to the skull the other day opened you to . . . well, things most non-Tufa people don't see. I realized it when you saw those tombstones behind the fire station, and then when you were able to find them again after you reinjured yourself. And when I heard you play, at our picnic and here tonight, I knew that it was the truth. Even though you're not Tufa, apparently the right whack to the right head will do it." *We can't be that different from them,* Mandalay had said. "I know it sounds squirrelly, but you *saw* it, didn't you?"

He swore that when he focused on Bliss's eyes, her ears were tall and pointed in his peripheral vision. Yet when he looked directly, they were as normal as his own. "You didn't slip anything in that water, did you? Acid or something?"

"No." She looked into his eyes as her heart pounded out a foxtrot in her chest. "So. Do you believe me?"

"I'm looking for a magical song, I'm in no position to judge." He should've been afraid, or at least nervous, but he felt inexplicably safe with her. "So what are you people?"

She looked down, summoning the courage to break the Tufa's greatest taboo. Carefully, she said, "We were here before the first tribesmen came over from Asia and became the Native Americans. We were here when the first Europeans laid claim to these mountains, as if they were something you could own, like a hat or a gun." She gestured at the trees. "The forest is our home. When you enter it uninvited and unaccompanied, you enter our world and have to abide by its rules. Many who do, are never seen again. But the ones who *are* invited, who are brought by us—"

Before she could continue, a vehicle missing its muffler came out of the night. An old station wagon parked awkwardly, right in front of the barn.

Bliss got to her feet. "You have *got* to be fucking kidding," she whispered.

The door opened, and Rockhouse Hicks lurched to his feet. He held unsteadily on to the door. "Y'all havin' a hell of a time, ain't you?" he said in a loud drunken voice.

17

Vanover got to his feet, and although the music inside the barn didn't stop, several big, grim-faced men emerged as if they'd somehow heard Rockhouse arrive. They lined up on either side of Vanover.

"Well, butter my ass and call me a biscuit," Rockhouse said. His hair was disheveled, and spittle hung in his beard. If he was intimidated, it didn't show. "Y'all got quite a shindig going here."

"Just turn around and go back the way you came, Mr. Hicks," Vanover said. "None of us want any trouble."

"Hell, me neither, boys." Rockhouse closed the station wagon's door. A couple of the men jumped at the sound. Rob couldn't figure out why this old man made these big, strong farmers so tense, but they all looked like they expected violence to erupt at any moment. "I'm just here to fetch my nephew home before he gets into any trouble. I told him not to come up here, but he's got a new city girlfriend and wants to show her off."

Without taking his eyes off Rockhouse, Vanover said, "Jim, go fetch Stoney Hicks. I saw him polecattin' around inside earlier." One of the big men nodded and went inside.

Bliss grabbed Rob's arm and pulled him into the shadows near the edge of the forest. "I thought you said Rockhouse never came here," he whispered.

"He never has before," Bliss said, her voice tight. *Of all the times to be saddled with a non-Tufa.* "Something's up. Just stay here and be quiet, okay? This doesn't concern you."

Bliss strode out of the darkness and stood in front of Vanover, facing Hicks. The beefy hill men looked visibly relieved when they saw her. Rockhouse belched a little, then squinted at her. "That you, Bliss?"

"You know it is, Rockhouse," she said, folding her arms.

Her presence took away a bit of his bluster, and he stood quietly until the side door opened and Jim led two people out. One was the tall, handsome young man Rob had noticed earlier. He held the hand of the girl behind him, and when the light struck her face, Rob saw that it was indeed Stella Kizer.

Before he even consciously realized it, he stalked out of the shadows. "Hey!" he yelled. "Stella Kizer!"

She turned toward his voice. Her face looked pale and splotchy, as if she'd been crying. She seemed to recognize Rob, and opened her mouth to speak.

Before she could, Stoney said simply, "C'mon, Stel." She lowered her eyes and turned away.

"Hey," Rob said as he reached the group, "I'm a friend of the lady's *husband,* and I'd like a word with her."

Bliss grabbed him by the arm. "Stay out of this!" she hissed.

He twisted out of her grasp. "Her husband's worried sick about her, and the cops are looking all over for her. I figure the least she could do is tell me what the hell she thinks she's doing so I can pass it on to them."

Stella looked stricken, torn between obeying her new paramour and talking to Rob. Stoney opened the back passenger door.

"So what's the deal, Stella?" Rob demanded. As he waited for her reply, he spotted several familiar rolled pieces of paper on the vehicle's floorboard. So *she* had the rubbings.

"Y'all best back off," Stoney said, his voice thick with alcohol and arrogance.

"I got no quarrel with you, friend, I just want to hear what the lady has to say for herself," Rob said.

Stoney stepped in front of Stella, his broad chest belligerently pushed out. Rob looked up into the handsome face's dull, almost lifeless eyes. "I ain't your friend, city boy. I'm about to sing your dyin' dirge."

"Stoney!" Rockhouse barked warningly.

A line from one of the tombstones behind the fire station jumped unbidden to the front of Rob's thoughts, and he fired back, "Yeah, well, I may just leave *your* body lifeless for the flies, pretty boy."

The onlookers gasped. The music inside the barn stopped dead. The only sounds were insects in the woods and a distant airplane far overhead.

"See what you done?" Rockhouse said to his nephew, his voice high with outrage. "Now, get in the goddam car, Stoney. *Now.*"

Stoney held Rob's gaze. "This ain't over, short stuff," Stoney said, then followed Stella into the car. Rob thought he caught a last, pleading look from her as the door closed, but before he could respond, the station wagon was already driving away in a cloud of dust turned hellfire red by its taillights.

The music picked up as if it had never stopped. Rob turned to Bliss. "They had her husband's tombstone rubbings in—"

She took his hand and yanked him away from Vanover and the other men, all of whom stared at him as if he'd grown a second nose. When she had him back in the shadows out of earshot, she grabbed him by the throat. He was astounded at her strength.

"If you ever do anything like that again, Rob, I swear to God, I'll kill you," she roared, although her voice was barely a whisper. "I'm not exaggerating for effect, I mean it. I'll physically *kill* you, and no one will ever find your body."

"You people take your epitaphs mighty seriously," he croaked, trying to get free of her grip. Maybe this was why she frightened Tiffany Gwinn.

"You just presumed to be something you most definitely are not. You represented yourself as something you can't possibly be." She yanked him close. "And your mouth wrote a check that I *guarantee* your ass can't cash. And that makes it *my* problem."

She released him and stepped away. He took a moment to catch his breath, and wondered if she'd done any permanent damage to his voice. "Okay, that was seriously messed up," he gasped. "Here's a hint—if something's supposed to be secret, you shouldn't carve it on your damn tombstones."

"What the hell do you know about it?" she snapped. *Calm down, Bliss,* she told herself, *you don't have the luxury of a temper.*

"You threatened to kill me," he said.

"No, I *promised* to kill you. I'm sorry about that. Just give me a minute, all right?" She turned her back and lowered her head. She'd completely blown everything, thanks to Rockhouse's unexpected appearance. Rob had seen the truth, but she'd had no time to explain it, to tell him what words and songs and stories really meant to her people, and why the wrong thing quoted at the wrong time could do irreparable harm.

He started to reply, but didn't. Despite the attack and her demonstration of an almost super-human strength, he was moved by the way she suddenly seemed small and fragile. He started to reach for her, when movement in the corner of his eye stopped him.

Curnen peered around a tree at the very edge of the forest. It was the first time he'd seen her standing fully upright. She wore a different tattered dress, this one a couple of sizes too big that fell off one shoulder, and her hair was haphazardly brushed back from her face. It was both comical and touching, as if she'd wanted to dress up and look nice but literally had no idea how.

She put her finger to her lips, then nodded that he should come closer. Bliss, still turned away, did not notice. Curnen repeated the gesture, and playfully smiled. She stretched one six-fingered hand toward him, tentative and shy, and he couldn't help himself. He reached toward her.

Her long, supple fingers closed around his hand, and she yanked him after her into the woods.

Bliss whirled. Rob had vanished, and only the vibration of the tree branches showed evidence of his passage. She caught a whiff of Curnen's distinctive odor. No doubt she'd appeared demure, and helpless, and like a lost little girl to him. And now he was gone.

The images from that first dream before she'd met Rob sprang unbidden to her mind: a white hand clawing out of a grave, and the two figures fighting, one in a blood-spattered dress. She felt a chill, and heard the wind rustle the trees far above. The bonfire flared, and the conversation outside the barn died down. Even the music paused. When the night wind spoke, the Tufa listened, but only a few could hear it clearly. She was one of them.

Bliss bit her lip, clenched her fists, and plunged into the forest after her sister and Rob. For a Tufa, the woods were as vast as the seas, and she was looking for a lone man adrift in them. But she had to try. At least she had a pretty good idea where they'd gone.

Curnen's grip was as powerful as her sister's, and Rob barely kept his feet under him as she pulled him through the dark forest. He deflected branches from his face with his free hand and yelled, "Hey, stop! *Hey!*" His mind flashed to the song Rockhouse had sung on the post office porch: *Young women they'll run / Like hares on the mountain.*

Then they burst into the open and her hand slipped away. He almost fell from the loss of momentum.

They'd reached a wide clearing. He looked back, but saw no sign of their passage through the forest.

The air around him felt warmer than at the barn. A stream trickled through the nearby woods, and he heard a glorious chorus of frogs. Above him, the full moon shone down so brightly, it was like silver-tinted daylight. Fireflies drifted through the air, hot gold against cool moonlight.

Curnen watched him silently from the far side of the open space. She swayed on her bare feet, with the same motion as her sister when she sang. Rob got a little nervous, wondering why she'd brought him here. He felt a pang of real panic.

"So, ah . . . what happens now?" he asked, trying to sound nonchalant.

As she'd done in his dream, Curnen leaped onto him. Her arms and legs wrapped around him, and he sat down heavily under her impact. She pressed her lips against his, and it took all his strength to push her away. He held her by the shoulders, and felt bones and wiry muscle beneath the dress. He wiped her excess spittle from his face and said, "Whoa, no, wait a minute, hold on."

Her big eyes looked hurt.

"Just—look, can we talk first? *Can* you talk?"

She looked down and shook her head.

"But you can understand me, right?"

Again she shook her head. Then she laughed, giddy and simian-like. Was she joking, or just insane?

She felt amazingly strong and solid in his arms, and as she wriggled on his lap, he tried to banish his unexpected physical response. "Okay, look, I think you're very, ah . . . *interesting,* but this really isn't the best way to get a guy to like you." He brushed some hair out of her face. Her big eyes seemed even larger as the moonlight glinted off them. "And anyway, you don't know anything about me."

She touched his chest over his heart, then mimed breaking a stick. Then she put her palm over her own heart.

Rob choked on unexpected emotion. "Well, I can't argue with that," he said, his voice ragged.

This girl was as beautiful as her sister, although in a wild way he'd never experienced. And she definitely aroused him. He hadn't been with anyone since Anna, and now all those denied feelings surged to the surface. His hand shook as he cupped her cheek. "Have you ever really kissed anyone before?"

She ignored the question, nuzzling into his hand. The moonlight shone off her full, moist lips.

The desire had grown too strong to resist. "Okay, just trust me," he said as he leaned up and kissed her again, with just his lips. She tasted of wild berries, and her breath smelled of fresh apples. When he pulled away, she whimpered very softly.

A tiny rational voice in his mind screamed variations of *What the* hell *are you doing?* but he was too entranced to acknowledge it. "Did you like that?" he said, moving his hands to her waist.

She nodded.

"Sometimes when people who really like each other kiss, they touch their tongues together." It was like explaining something to a child, which was totally at odds with the urgency he felt in his body. "Do you think you might like that?"

She nodded again.

"Okay. Now close your eyes, relax, and do what I do."

With her eyes closed, her body trembling, she looked impossibly young. But he'd passed the point of resisting his own impulses, and was motivated by both raging lust and overwhelming tenderness as he put his hand on the back of her head, drew her down, and touched his lips to hers. Their mouths opened and she tentatively met his tongue with her own.

Her hands brushed his face with light, fluttering fingertips, careful around his swollen cheek and eyelid. She shivered all over, making faint delicious sighs, and he let his hands move up her slender torso until his thumbs felt the swell of her breasts beneath the old, worn dress. When he stroked her lightly, she moaned into his mouth.

Her kisses turned into little nibbles that covered his chin and cheeks before returning to engulf his mouth. He let her dictate the pace, enjoying the way she delighted in each sensation. When she finally stopped and looked into his eyes, the simplicity of the tenderness he saw in them almost brought him to tears. He'd forgotten that look, and the feelings it inspired. "Hey," he said hoarsely, not wanting to cry, "maybe we should slow down a li—"

She jumped to her feet and pulled the dress off over her head. Beneath it, she was naked. She tossed it aside and then fell on him again. Straddling his body, she kissed him hard and urgently. His hands slid to her back, down to her hips, then up to her breasts. Her body felt more voluptuous than it had moments earlier; were her breasts now somehow larger? He took off his own shirt, holding her soft, warm, slippery skin against him, feeling her nipples slide deliciously over his chest.

Finally it was too intense for him, and he reached for the clasp of his jeans.

"I won't hurt you," he whispered. "Other people may have, but I won't."

A tear dropped silently from her eye to his cheek.

"That's not really her, you know," a voice said from behind them.

18

Curnen leaped off him, and he jumped to his feet. Bliss stood at the edge of the clearing.

Curnen crouched on the grass nearby, clutching the dress against her. Her limbs trembled as she tensed to either flee or attack. She *growled.*

"She's making you see what you want to see," Bliss continued. "We can all do that, to one extent or another. Look at her now."

He did. Now Curnen *was* the same girl he'd seen in his room, with long limbs, strange toes, and too-big eyes. In her gaze, he saw only animal wariness.

"The common term is 'glamour,'" Bliss said.

Rob got to his feet and moved away so he could keep an eye on both women. "Glamour," he repeated. "Like fairies use?"

"Rob, please, catch a clue here. Remember what I told you before? We were here long before the Europeans, even before the so-called Native Americans. How do you think that can be true?"

"So you're saying you two are *fairies*?"

With an impatient sigh, she nodded.

He remembered the dancing teenage girl. "That's what I saw back at the fire. A fairy."

"Yes."

"That's what all the Tufa are?"

She wanted to slap him. How many ways did he need to hear it? *"Yes."* And there it was: the secret known only to the night wind and her riders, spoken plainly in inadequate human words to a man she'd known three whole days. Mandalay and the other First Daughters would be so proud of her.

"But . . . you drive trucks, and work, and—"

"Yes, I drive a truck, and go to work, and watch TV and worry about the economy and terrorism. We don't live in a storybook, you know. We live in the world, just like you. We're just not . . . *of* it."

Curnen, back in her dress, slipped under his arm and pressed possessively against him. He was too startled by all this new information to resist. She reached for his face and tried to turn it down so she could kiss him.

"Curnen!" Bliss scolded. "Stop that. Not now!"

Curnen glared at Bliss and bared her teeth. She released Rob and moved toward her sister, but Bliss wasn't intimidated. "Don't mess with me, Curnen. Now, get out of here."

Curnen stopped, threw back her head, and howled. It was the same sound Rob had heard that first night outside his room, and again at Doyle's trailer. This close, it gave him goose bumps.

"Oh, stop it," Bliss said. She fingered the fabric of the dress. "Whose garbage did you raid to get this, huh?"

Curnen *slithered* away—no other word described the quick, sinuous motion—and vanished into the darkness.

In the silence, Rob realized he heard nothing except insects and animals—no music, or traffic, or even airplanes overhead. No songs from the barn dance. Could he and Curnen have really run that far? Finally he asked, "So she got that dress from someone's trash?"

"Yes. She's mostly like a wild animal. She digs things up, buries things, thinks only in immediate sensation."

"Because she's inbred?"

Bliss's eyes flashed with anger. "No. She's my baby sister, I helped raise her and she was as normal as anyone once, she just—"

Then suddenly Bliss began to sob. She turned away and leaned against the nearest tree. Just like Rob at the picnic, things she'd kept under tight control burst out with no warning, all the pain and misery and loneliness.

Rob went to her, and she fell into his arms. He felt her tears against his still-bare chest, and she let him hold her up as her legs collapsed. "I'm sorry," she said between cries, "I'm so sorry. I'm normally tougher than this, I just—"

"Shh, it's okay," Rob said. "Cry as long as you need to. You were there for me, I'm here for you." He looked around the clearing for a sign of Curnen, but the other girl was gone. Above him, several of the kitelike objects flitted across the face of the full moon. The brief glimpse told him nothing, although he swore they had human legs and arms as well as big blurry wings.

Bliss was a dead weight now, her arms around his neck. He lowered her slowly to the ground and knelt beside her, trying to gently disentangle her. "Shh, it's okay," he said, stroking her hair. It was soft and deliciously smooth beneath his hand.

"It's not okay!" she said fiercely, wrenching free to glare at him. "That was once a beautiful girl, with a voice like an angel! Now look at her!"

"Why do you let her live like this?" he asked. "What happened to her?"

"She lives like this because she has to," Bliss said, wiping furiously at her eyes. "She's the victim of someone's hatred, the worst kind of curse."

"Who?"

Bliss started to answer, but caught herself.

"Rockhouse?" he asked. "She's got six fingers like he does. Is that who did it?"

She said nothing.

He sprawled back on the grass, wet against his spine, and gazed up at the stars. "Christ on a stick, Bliss. I don't know what to believe here. You tell me you're fairies, and that your sister's cursed. You say I'm not a Tufa, but because someone smacked me in the head, I can see things only a Tufa can see. None of this makes any sense, you know."

He turned to look at her. She gazed up at the moon, her back to him. Fireflies lazily swarmed around her, as if their light might provide consolation. Her shoulders shook with sobs, but she made no sound.

He got to his feet, stood behind her, and put his hands on her shoulders. "I'm sorry. I know you're upset, and I'm not helping. Why don't you just take me back to the motel and we'll call it a night."

She turned and looked up at him. "No. I need to sing you a song."

"Why?"

"Because it's our story, and you deserve to know it."

"You don't have to—"

"Yes, I do." *Curnen has claimed you,* she wanted to say. *If the curse is broken, she'll be yours. If not, you'll go down with her now and you don't even know it.* But she only repeated, "Yes, I do."

She took his hands in hers, closed her eyes, and began:

When these hills were sharp as claws
Raked slow across the sky
We rode the wind that wore them smooth
And came to this place to die.

We thought our time had ended
As it does for all true things
But here we found a new green home
And room to spread our wings.

Oh, time makes men grow sad
And rivers change their ways
But the night wind and her riders
Will ever stay the same."

She hummed a stanza of the melody before she resumed singing. As if she'd somehow conjured it, the treetops above them began to sway in the breeze. He shivered.

We sailed the slopes and valleys
Played in the hollers and hills
Our songs filled nights with wonder
Our tears the storms fulfilled.

Till men came over the mountains
And brought their changing ways
We loved them back when they loved us
And loved the children that we made.

She looked into his face. Her dark hair fell away from her ivory shoulders. She held his gaze as she sang:

And now we are the same as you
Our blood no longer tells
'Scept on nights when we spread our wings
And ride moonbeams cross the hills.

Now you, dear stranger, know our tale
Even though you don't believe
So eat our bread and drink our wine
And you may never leave.

They stood quietly facing each other, holding hands. Another verse from that day at the post office went through his mind: *Young women they'll sing / Like birds in the bushes.* It was almost as if the song had been a warning about the Overbay sisters.

She looked into his eyes. "So what do you think?"

He searched for the right word. "I'm . . . enchanted."

She smiled, leaned closer, and softly, gently kissed him. It went on for a long time. It inspired no sexual passion, just a tenderness that drained away all anger and worry.

Curnen howled far in the distance. Coyotes joined in from all around, a chorus of loneliness counterpointing the lovers' connection.

"Don't worry, sister-girl," she said to the night. "He's still yours."

"What do you mean by that?" he said, but a yawn cut him off.

19

It was dark outside when someone knocked on Rob's door.

He blinked awake. The pressure in his bladder was horrendous. When he got to his feet, every muscle protested the movement, as if he hadn't moved once during his sleep. "Coming," he said, his voice raw in his dry throat.

Where the hell was he? The last thing he recalled, he was in the woods, in a clearing, with Bliss Overbay and her sister, Curnen, who had . . . Wait, what?

He rubbed his eyes and looked around. He was back in his room at the Catamount Corner. How the fuck had he gotten here? He squinted at the clock on the bedstand. The red numbers showed 4:14 A.M.

The knock came again. He opened it, squinting against the light from the hall outside.

Terry Kizer stood there, looking very tired and worried. "Can I come in and talk to you for a second?"

"Sure," Rob croaked. "'Scuse me for just a minute.

Make yourself comfortable." He went into the bathroom and epically relieved himself. Then he brushed his teeth and drank what seemed like a gallon of water.

"I've got to go home to Michigan today," Kizer said from the room. "I wasn't prepared for an indefinite stay here. But I'm coming back tomorrow to help with the search."

"She hasn't turned up?" Rob asked as he came out of the bathroom.

"No, not a trace," he said bitterly. "I mean, I can imagine her running off, even shacking up with some other guy for a while just to piss me off. But not without money, or her ID, or any of the stuff she swears she needs before she leaves the house. She's always thought she was smarter and tougher than everyone else, no matter where we were. So yeah, I think something's happened to her."

"What do the cops say?"

He snorted. "The cops think *I* did it, even if they don't know what 'it' is yet."

"No, I meant about your leaving. Do they know?"

"Yeah, they know. I'm going to get a lawyer before I come back, that's for sure." He handed Rob a folded piece of paper. "This is my phone number and e-mail address. You seem like a decent guy. If anything happens while I'm gone, could you let me know? Please? I somehow doubt the Mayberry Police will go out of their way to tell me anything except my Miranda rights, and then only after they beat the shit out of me."

"Sure," Rob replied. He almost blurted out that he'd seen Stella, but stopped himself at the last moment. He didn't want Kizer running afoul of Rockhouse. Or Bliss. He needed to think much more clearly than he was able to at the moment.

"Thanks," Terry said. He started to leave, then stopped. "*You* don't think I had anything to do with anything, do you?"

"Not a bit," Rob said honestly.

"Thanks," he said, sounding genuinely relieved. "Oh, Mrs. Goins asked me to give this to you, since I was coming up." He handed Rob a folded note.

When Kizer left, Rob sat numbly on the bed. His bones felt rusted and his head thick and cobwebby. He unfolded the note and had to blink several times to focus his eyes.

> *I'll call you in the morning. I imagine we have a lot to talk about. Bliss.*

She'd drawn a little design next to the message, a symbol he didn't recognize.

He pocketed the note, took out his guitar, and aimlessly picked the strings, skirting half a dozen melodies before deciding on one:

> *Oh, time makes men grow sad*
> *And rivers change their ways*
> *But the night wind and her riders*
> *Will ever stay the same*

He stopped, shook his head to clear it, and without thinking scratched the itching on the back of his head. He winced as the injury throbbed, and abruptly felt as if a hazy curtain had been drawn away from his eyes. He remembered everything clearly now. And he knew he needed help.

He drove way too fast out to Doyle's trailer, and pounded on the door with more urgency that he'd intended. The porch light blinded him when it came on, and Berklee peered through the safety chain gap. Her eyes were bloodshot. "Hey, there, Robby-bobby," she said. "What are you doing up this early? Or have you not been to bed yet?"

"Is Doyle here?"

"Naw, he went in early. Probably stopped to pick up his dad, too." She belched softly; the smell was rank and vivid.

Rob felt real sadness that such a beautiful and fiery woman seemed determined to dive so thoroughly into alcoholism. He wondered what she was like completely sober; he'd never actually seen her that way.

"Why don't y'all come on in and have a drink with me?" She undid the chain and opened the door all the way. She wore a robe cinched far too loosely. "I can be late to work. My boss couldn't care less."

"Thanks, but I think I'll try to track down Doyle." He didn't want to be alone with Berklee; a drunk woman with something to prove was more than he could manage, and Doyle was big enough to use him for a chamois cloth if he got the wrong idea.

He met Doyle's truck at the end of the driveway. They each rolled down their windows. "Hey," Doyle said with an edge of suspicion. "What are you doing here?"

"Looking for you. Berklee said you went to work."

"Forgot my lunch. So much for getting an early start."

"Can I talk to you?"

"Sure. Just back on up and—"

"No offense, but your wife's still half-lit, and this is serious. Can we go somewhere else?"

Doyle chewed on the ends of his mustache. "Yeah, I reckon," he said at last.

Berklee finished her morning beer as she watched Doyle's truck and Rob's car drive off into the gray predawn. She carefully placed the can in the recycle bin. Then she went into the bathroom, leaned on the sink, and studied her face in the mirror.

A harsh image gazed back from the glass. Even with the flattering effects of the vanity lights, she knew she looked awful. Without her "face," or the fake cheerfulness that got her through work, she appeared forty years old even though she wasn't yet thirty. The bags under her eyes could carry groceries, and the corners of her lips sagged in a perpetual frown. Even her forehead, once smooth and unblemished, was creased with lines from the perpetual nagging sense that she was incomplete, that something essential was missing. No, not missing: *taken.*

After nearly eight years, it still felt as if it had happened the day before. The way he'd rolled off her after bringing her to the greatest, most sublime climax she'd ever known, then sat on the edge of the bed and fished for his clothes on the floor. She could barely breathe or move for long moments afterwards, and then she felt only this *craving*, an irresistible desire to touch or be touched by him, something that took her over in those postcoital moments and had not lessened a bit in the time since. That stormy afternoon she'd reached for him, for his strong broad back and tousled ebony hair, only to have him shrug away and mutter, "Stop it, will ya? Dang." She felt the reproach like a knife to her belly, and withdrew her trembling hands. He stood, his magnificent form lit in the gray light from outside as he pulled on his shirt. "I gotta go. Your parents'll be home soon, and your ma don't like me."

Her mother . . .

The day her mother took her outside to the front porch and gave her "the talk" had been scorchingly hot. Her mother wore a thin cotton dress and no shoes, and the porch swing squeaked as they sat. Yellow jackets buzzed around the flowers. There had been a breeze, hot and steaming, appropriate for the subject matter. Berklee had been fifteen years old.

The talk included a lot of religion, a smattering of practical advice on birth control, and the solemn warning every non-Tufa mother gave her daughters in Needsville: "Now, them real Tufa boys will make you feel everything a woman's supposed to feel when she's with a man, but if you don't make the sign, they'll own you. You'll never be able to feel anything with any other man, and if they don't want you—and them true-blood Tufas never want you twice—it'll just build and build until you can't bear it no more. These hills are filled with the bones of girls like that; don't you be one of 'em." Then her mother had taught her the hand gesture that would allow her to dance with these devils and not pay the piper.

But that rainy afternoon with Stoney, a little high and a lot amazed that anyone so gorgeous would bother with *her,* she'd forgotten the warning. She wanted to get back at Doyle, who'd gone off to college and left her alone in Needsville. So she brought the big Tufa to her bedroom in her family's house, and in Stoney's arms, beneath his dominating weight, she felt utterly beautiful for those few moments, as if his attention had somehow erased every bit of self-doubt she'd ever known.

Fifteen minutes of ecstasy. And now a lifetime of aching, unfulfilled need.

As he'd left her that day, she begged him to stay with her, promised obscene acts and utter devotion. Her family's empty house felt tomblike the moment the screen door slammed, and as his pickup drove away, she'd screamed in torment because her mother had been horrifyingly, utterly right: She could imagine no other man touching her, ever. And even though she'd allowed Doyle to claim his husbandly prerogative when she could find no way to avoid it, each time was private, thorough agony. And he *knew* she hated it; they'd been celibate for the past two years.

Tears trickled down her face. Nothing could take it back; nothing could cure it. It was done. *She* was done. And yet she didn't take the step so many other girls had taken when left in this state. There were two reasons for that: One was the forlorn but still present hope that Stoney might one day want her again, that she might experience that amazing sensation of being transcendently beautiful. And two—the most frightening of all—was that she wasn't sure this addiction wouldn't also follow her to the other side. Perhaps Stoney was surrounded by the haints of girls like her, all still tied to him and aching for corporeal pleasures they could never again experience. She would sometimes lie awake at night, wide-eyed, contemplating that.

Rob and Doyle sat across from each other at the Waffle House near the interstate, outside a town called Unicorn. It had taken half an hour to reach it, but Rob didn't feel comfortable talking anywhere near Needsville. He wanted to be completely off the Tufa radar until he decided how much he could really trust Doyle.

When they parked, he'd noticed a bumper sticker on another truck: IF IT AIN'T KING JAMES, IT AIN'T BIBLE. The presence of this sign of normal Southern Fundamentalism filled him with relief.

The waitress, attractive except for a ton of blue eye shadow, left two empty cups and a carafe on the table. Doyle said, "Alsie, you mean you ain't even gonna bring us coffee that's been saucered and blowed? What if I burn myself?"

Alsie gave him a pretend scowl. "Doyle Collins, I am not your momma. I figure you're smart enough not to scald your pretty little tongue." As she walked to the next customer, Rob wondered if her hips were doing an authentic Southern sashay.

Alsie stopped at the only other occupied booth, where a tired-looking woman sat with a six-year-old boy. She had the long straight hair and denim skirt that marked a Pentecostal believer.

The boy loudly sneezed. "Cover your face when you do that," his mother admonished.

"You don't want to spread your germs everywhere," Alsie added.

"Germs and Jesus, that's all I ever hear about," the boy said in a voice too weary for his age. "Germs and Jesus. And you know something? You can't see neither one of 'em."

Doyle grinned, poured coffee in his cup, and asked Rob, "So what's the big secret?"

Rob nodded toward the waitress and asked softly, "Is she Tufa?"

"Alsie? Nah. Well, maybe a smidgen. No more than I am, at any rate. Why?"

Rob paused, then decided to plow ahead. "Did you hear about that woman who disappeared in town yesterday?"

"Yeah."

Rob drank his coffee and made a face. "This tastes like mud."

"Well, it *was* fresh ground this morning," Doyle deadpanned.

Rob ignored him. "I didn't see germs or Jesus, but I *did* see that girl last night at this barn dance Bliss took me to. And some weird shit happened there, man."

Doyle sipped his coffee. "Like what?"

"You'll think I'm nuts if I tell you."

Doyle sat expectantly.

"Well . . . Bliss told me some stuff about the Tufas. And while

207

it's loopy, I gotta tell you, I halfway believe it. Especially after meeting her baby sister."

"Who?"

"Her sister, Curnen."

Doyle looked puzzled. "Bliss doesn't have a sister."

Rob was silent for a moment before saying, "Really?"

"Yeah, I've known her all my life, she's an only child. Her mom got that thing, endometriosis, right after she was born. Couldn't have any more children."

"So . . . you don't know anyone named Curnen Overbay?"

" 'Fraid not."

Rob looked down at the greasy coffee in his cup. Now he wasn't sure how to proceed. "Well . . . do you know a guy named Stoney?"

"Stoney Hicks? Big guy, looks like a Chippendale? Oh, yeah, I know *him*."

Rob leaned closer. "I need your word that this doesn't go any farther. Okay?"

"Okay."

"Last night, this Stoney guy was dragging around that woman who disappeared yesterday. She looked like she'd been awake for a week. Do you know where he hangs out?"

Doyle's eyes narrowed. "Why?"

"I need to talk to that girl. Let her know her husband's all torn up about the way she's treating him. I tried last night, but there were too many people around."

Doyle shook his head. "I wouldn't go poking around, trying to find him. His uncle's that old guy you had the run-in with at the post office, Rockhouse Hicks. Between the two of them, they've got some mean family and friends." He looked out the window at the sunrise, and his tone changed. "Besides, I ain't never known

Stoney to have to *make* a girl come with him. They just kind of drop their panties if he nods at 'em. Don't matter what promises they've made to someone else."

It took Rob a moment. "Wait, you mean him and Berklee?"

Doyle nodded. Rob never imagined such a common gesture could encompass so much sadness and regret.

"Wow," Rob said.

"Yeah," Doyle agreed.

Rob pressed on. "I'm sorry to hear about that, really. But I need to find this girl and talk to her. Her husband's not a bad guy, and he doesn't deserve the hassle he's getting from the cops over this. If she's where she wants to be, that's fine. I'll pass along the word and everyone can get on with their lives."

"I wish I could help you, but honestly, I ain't seen Stoney myself in probably six months. And anyway . . ." He seemed to want to say more.

"What?" Rob prompted.

Doyle thought it over. "This is going to sound kind of strange. You see . . . Stoney likes to use the fact that he's real good-looking to get girls to do things for him. Nothing, like, mean or anything, he doesn't hit 'em, he just kind of . . . I don't know, uses 'em up. Wears 'em out. Lots of the girls he's dated died within a couple of years after he broke up with 'em. From just kind of giving up on things."

"Giving up," Rob repeated.

"Yeah. They don't eat, they don't go to school or work, they just . . . quit. Quit life. Some even kill themselves. Happened to two girls I personally knew back in high school. Damndest thing."

"And nobody thought this was weird?"

"Weird's relative around here. Our most famous local murder was over a spelling bee."

Rob just looked at him.

"I'm not making it up. Back in 18-something-or-other. A schoolmaster and his student who won the big county-wide spelling bee got ambushed by the head of another school who was jealous 'cause they won. True story." He drank some coffee, then followed it with water to wash down the taste. "Y'all may think this is silly, but there's stuff in this valley that . . . well, it goes back a long ways. Most folks outside of here consider it superstition and bullshit like that, but around here, it *works*. It's for *real*. Now, I ain't saying I believe in it or anything, but I *am* saying that I'd be stupid not to, given everything I've seen over the years. And on top of that, the girls all have their own special secrets that the boys don't never know."

"That's true everywhere."

"Not like it is here with the Tufa girls."

Rob could only nod in agreement to that. "So you're saying that I should just forget about finding Stella Kizer?"

"I'm saying that if Stoney's got his hooks in her, it won't change anything if she goes back to her husband." He leaned over the table and lowered his voice. "I saw one girl's suicide note, man. Jillie Rae Keene. She said it was like Stoney took part of her soul away, and without him, she could never be a whole person again. It was downright *spooky*."

"But Berklee got away from him."

He took on a depth of sadness Rob had never imagined. "Sure, she did. And now she drinks herself to sleep every night. She's right, if I hadn't gone off to college, everything would be different. But I did, and Stoney was still here, and . . . I think she's just taking the slow road instead of the interstate like some of the others did. But she's going to end up in the same place."

"I have to try, man. I can't really explain it, but I *have* to. Nobody, and I mean *nobody,* tried to help me when I needed it. They were all hyenas, snapping around for scraps, or just ignored it like it didn't matter to them. I can't let myself become one of those people."

Doyle looked at him seriously. "It ain't your problem. Live and let live. Respect boundaries, like they say on *Oprah.*"

"I can't," he said sadly. "Not this time."

20

Bliss climbed the trail, her back sweaty despite the cool breeze. The path wound through the woods, so well hidden that only someone with her background could follow it. Here the trees had never been cut, no fires ever thinned their ranks, and once anchored firmly into the soil, they were as immovable as the mountain they crowned. She heard deer scamper away in the shadows, the smaller movements of more phlegmatic raccoons and possums, and felt the presence of other things that lived only around the Tufa's sacred places. She wished she had time to bask in it, to reconnect with that huge tug in her belly that led ultimately into the heart of the night wind itself. But this was First Daughter business, and the hike alone had taken an hour and a half. She'd started just before sunrise, after dropping off her note for Rob, and it would be past noon before she reached her truck again. Worse, she was almost entirely sure this would be pointless. But unless she tried, whatever she did next would be misinterpreted and scorned.

Despite a lifetime in the mountains, she found this climb so arduous, her calves burned, and she wanted nothing more than to sit down, catch her breath, and then descend. But she recognized that urge as part of this spot's defenses, and while she couldn't ignore it, she used the annoyance it generated to urge her on. She didn't *have* to walk, of course; the Tufa had much faster and easier ways to get around. But the meeting she sought needed to be arranged in the proper way.

At last, through the final grove of trees, she saw the bare top of the mountain. Smoke curled into the sky from a stone chimney that emerged straight from the ground. In a few minutes, she stood before the rock wall built into the side of the hill, with its gray, ancient wooden door. Railroad ties provided steps for the last few yards, and planks made a crude porch. Music played softly from a cheap radio. She knocked.

"Whozat?" a man's voice demanded.

"You know goddam well who it is," Bliss said. "Let me in."

The door opened, and Rockhouse Hicks peered out. In the shadowy interior, he seemed bulkier and more threatening, but of course she knew the secret of that. "What do you want?" he muttered when he saw her.

"Shouldn't you be on your way to the P.O.?"

"So? You ain't my keeper."

"That's lucky for you. I figured you might have quite a head, drunk as you were last night."

"Don't remember much about it."

"Convenient. But we need to hash out what to do about Curnen and Stoney."

"You do what you want, they ain't nothing to me," he said, and started to shut the door.

She blocked it open. "I don't want to be in your damn hobbit hole any more than you want me here. So stop being a jackass and work with me."

"You ain't my equal, Bliss, so don't take that tone with me. Mandalay wants to talk, she can bring herself up here, just like you did."

"I carry Mandalay's song, you know that. Stop stalling."

He looked at her. The smug superiority he showed in town was completely gone, and he now appeared as a weak, tired old man. His overalls were stained with mud, and his beard held crumbs and bits of food. When he turned just so, the light revealed two long, untended hairs protruding from one ear. He said, "I ain't got nothing to do with that retarded sister of yours no more."

"She's not *retarded,* you self-righteous bastard," Bliss hissed. In her head, she added, *She's cursed. By you.* She followed him inside.

The dwelling consisted of one room with a fireplace, a table with two straight-backed chairs, a rocking chair, and a bed. The walls were stone, sealed with mortar that had crumbled in places and allowed gray lichen and mold to grow along the seepage stains. It made the place smell like an untended armpit. All the furniture was handmade, squared off and crude. The blankets on the bed were tattered and faded. Only the five banjos in their stands gave evidence of any recent attention. The heat and light from the hearth fire were overwhelming when the door closed behind her.

"And she's not just my sister," Bliss continued as she unzipped her jacket. "She's your daughter."

"Ain't nothing to me," he said as he turned off the old radio and settled into the wooden rocker before the fire. He picked up an old quilt and arranged it over his legs. "She turned her back on me when I needed her most. When the last leaf falls off the Widow's Tree, she'll be gone. No more of that damned *howling* all night."

Bliss knelt and shoved the chair around so that he had to face her. "You made a big tactical error with her, Rockhouse. You backed her into a place where she doesn't feel like she has anything to lose. What happens if she decides the hell with you and your rules?"

"Hmph," he said. He spit into the fire, and it sizzled. "That girl ain't got long. Then it won't be nobody's problem no more."

She stood and walked away, fighting the urge to make him follow his saliva into the fire. It was hard to remember that this tired, pathetic creature was also the mean, vindictive monster who sowed malice and spite from the post office porch. What did it feel like to live alone, in one room beneath the top of a mountain so isolated, no one ever visited unless they were pissed off enough to make the climb? To know that you inspired only hatred, fear, or disgust? But then she remembered all he'd done, and her pity burned away like his spit.

A small object on the table caught her eye. She picked up a tiny ax, no more than five inches long. Its metal head gleamed, and the edge shone like a scalpel. Beside it rested a walnut. "Reliving past glories?" she said, with no attempt to minimize the sarcasm.

"Kiss my ass, Bliss," Rockhouse mumbled without looking.

"And we got Yankees, too," she said. "There's one that Curnen's been sniffing around."

"Ain't Curnen that brought him to y'all's barn dance, now, is it?"

She ignored him. "And Stoney's picked up a Yankee girl with a husband. That was stupid, Rockhouse, even for him. Now there'll be all sorts of attention."

"Ain't nobody gonna find nothing they ain't supposed to find. Always been the way. Still true."

"What if it's not? What if things are slipping? What if the night winds want it that way?" When he didn't reply, she slammed her hands on the table, and he jumped. The tiny ax fell to the floor. "*Dammit,* Rockhouse! This affects us all, not just your people! All the Tufa stand to lose now. If there's any chance, we have to work together to stop it, or at least turn it aside so it glances off."

"Yeah?" he said contemptuously. "What'll you do about it, Bliss? Sing a song?"

"Maybe," she said. "I know the right song to sing."

"You know part of it," he said. "And you can't find the rest, not without Mandalay's permission. And that little girl ain't even bleeding age yet. And as for them Yankees . . ." He trailed off with a cold little smile.

"What?" she asked darkly.

Now the Rockhouse everyone in Needsville feared turned and smiled up at her, his feebleness replaced by smug arrogance. "I know what that boy with you found out behind the fire station. I know he done told that other Yankee boy, the fat one with the wife, all about it. You think them rubbings are dangerous, but I done took care of them. And as for that gee-tar-playin' boy . . . well, even though he's probably caught up in your sister's curse now, I didn't want to wait. I done took care of him, too."

"What did you do?" Bliss demanded. Rockhouse's grin faded, his eyes closed, and his chin dropped to his chest. "What did you *do*?" she repeated, and shook him. But although he still breathed, she knew he was no longer in the room.

She drew back and slapped him so hard, it knocked him from the rocker, then left him sprawled on the uneven plank floor. The wind whined through the chimney when she threw open the door, momentarily causing the fire to flare up. That same wind rustled the trees above her all the way down to her truck.

———

Rob considered his strategy as he drove the deserted highway back to Needsville. He turned up the music, which always helped him think. Sirius was tuned to an all-bluegrass station, and he sang along with a sprightly version of "Shenandoah."

There was one solid hint about how to proceed. Something about that line from the epitaph had stopped Stoney dead the previous night, and even gotten Old Man Rockhouse's attention. Why?

As he topped a hill, an emu stood in the center of his lane. He didn't want to pass it on the left, because he might collide with another car coming over the next rise. He stopped ten feet from the bird and honked, but the animal stayed put.

He put the car in park and got out. He waved his hands at the bird. "Hey! Move, will ya!"

The bird blinked. Then its head turned slightly, toward something behind Rob.

He caught just the hint of a movement in the corner of his eye, but it was enough to make him duck, and the ax handle swished through the space an instant earlier occupied by his head.

He spun around. He was being *ambushed*.

Well, fuck me, he thought. He looked Hispanic and had attended a Kansas City public high school, so he knew how to fight when he had to. And if they were swinging ax handles at him, he definitely had to.

Rob dived right at the man who'd tried to blindside him and tackled him to the pavement. The ax handle skidded away across the blacktop. He straddled his attacker's chest and punched him in the face, sending a jolt of pain through his own hand. The guy clutched his nose and cried, "Shit!" He had black hair and dark Tufa skin, and looked barely old enough to drive.

Then someone else hit Rob hard across the back with what felt like a baseball bat. He cried out in agony and surprise, then reflexively jumped to his feet. The blow made him gasp for air. He kicked the fallen man hard in the groin to put him out of commission, then turned to face the second attacker, his fury rising until it blanked out any sensation of pain. "Come on, you son of a bitch!" Rob croaked.

The second man, also a young Tufa, brandished a shiny aluminum bat and took a wild, clumsy swing that Rob easily avoided. Despite the pain, he body-blocked the second man into the car's fender. The bat clanged off the hood and landed in the road. Rob head-butted the man and drove his knee hard into his crotch. With a thin moan of pain, the second man joined his friend on the ground.

Rob blinked, momentarily dazed by the skull-to-skull contact, then retrieved the baseball bat and stood over the two men. Both curled fetally and clutched their groins.

His back felt numb and hot, but he knew the pain would return soon enough. The urge to pound them into hamburger was incredibly strong, but he managed to hold back. "What the *hell!*" he yelled at the two. "Who the hell *are* you guys?"

"Get . . . the fuck out of Needsville," the first man wheezed.

Rob slammed the end of the bat against the pavement next to the man's ear so hard, the tarmac cracked. "Says who? Stoney Hicks? Rockhouse?"

"You just need to go, man," the second man added, his voice whiny from pain. "Ain't no songs for you here."

Rob felt under the driver's seat for the can of spray paint he'd gotten from Doyle. He put one knee on the first man's chest and sprayed bright red paint all over his hair and face. "I'll know exactly who you are if I see you again, asshole," he snarled. "Tell Hicks Junior and Senior that they need to send full-grown hillbillies next time." He turned to mark the second man, but he'd already staggered off into the weeds, and Rob didn't feel like chasing him.

Beyond him, for just an instant, Rob thought he saw a third figure, wide and distinctive. But the shadow he imagined to be Rockhouse Hicks vanished the moment he looked straight at it.

Breathing heavily, Rob got back into his car and, hands shaking, drove into town. He repeatedly counted to ten until his temper got back under his control.

Back in his room, he went into the bathroom and gently removed his shirt. A purple bruise ran across his shoulder blades, and it was already tender to the touch. A few inches up, and the guy would've knocked his head clean off. He dug out the piece of paper Doyle had given him with Bliss's phone number on it. He got no answer, and no machine picked up.

Whom could he go to? The police would do nothing. Doyle had his own problems, and Bliss was unavailable. Even the only other stranger, Terry Kizer, had left town. He was on his own.

He paced for a long time, trying to walk off the rush from the fight. Finally an idea struck him. He turned on his laptop and searched for the address of the closest public library. He wanted archives of the local newspapers, to verify Doyle's story of Stoney Hicks's former flames. If he could show Stella that the big lunk was such bad news that his girlfriends actually died, perhaps she'd find the strength to break free of him.

Needsville had no library or newspaper, which didn't really surprise him, but a quick search revealed a library located in the nearby town of Cricket. The link to the library went through the town's main Web site, where he found the odd description under the title, "Welcome Ye to Historic Cricket."

> The world watched in 1875 as famous British author, statesman, and social reformer Roy Howard dedicated the new town of Cricket. It was to be a cooperative, class-free society, a Utopia where artisans, tradesmen, and farming families could build a new community through agriculture, temperance, and high moral principles. Today, in a gentle mountain setting little changed by twenty-first-century technology, this would-be Shangri-la survives. More than two dozen of its decorative, gabled buildings remain, and Cricket's dual Victorian and Appalachian heritage is everywhere visible.

A Victorian village in the middle of the Smoky Mountains? Why had he not run across this before? He clicked on the link to the library.

> Visitors to the Roy Howard Library will find it just as it was more than a century ago, when Cricket's early colonists enjoyed its reading pleasures. The collection of Victorian period literature and all furnishings are original to the building. The library was the pride of the colonists and many first editions were donated by admirers and publishers, along with unique and notable works of art.

He Googled directions, checked the library's hours, then logged off and tried Bliss's phone number again. He still got no answer. If she had caller ID, she'd think he was stalking her.

21

It took Rob an hour to drive to Cricket on the winding mountain roads. He had to sit ramrod straight the whole way, because reclining against the seat was too painful. The bruise across his back was now livid black, with purple and yellow edges, and it hurt to take deep breaths. This was turning into the most violent vacation of his life.

As he approached the strange little town, he noticed that the area felt completely different from the country-side around Needsville. It was nothing he could identify, yet the sun seemed brighter, the breezes cleaner, and the trees less gnarled and voluptuous. It felt, he realized, *normal*.

Finally he rounded a curve and arrived in Cricket. He felt as if he'd driven into a storybook. A dozen small, elaborate buildings lined the highway, all built in an unmistakably English style. They were painted in colorful pastels, and connected by wooden sidewalks. He parked next to the visitors' center and went inside to ask directions to the library. The docent indicated the next building.

A churchlike spire rose from the metal-plated roof of the Roy Howard Library. Despite the docent's assurances, Rob thought at first the library was closed, since no light showed from within. When he tried the door, though, it opened with a gentle chime.

The library's interior consisted of one big room, with shelves along every available bit of the walls. There was, in fact, no real lighting, only the tall windows that managed to provide enough illumination, at least on a sunny day. There appeared to be no other patrons.

The librarian, a tall woman with freckles and glasses, blinked in surprise at his black eye, but quickly masked it behind a professional smile. The nameplate on the circulation desk said THELMA BREWER. "Welcome to the Howard Library. I have to tell you not to touch anything without putting on these." She tapped a box of disposable cotton gloves. "Were you looking for anything in particular?"

Just before he asked about the newspaper, he had an idea, and dug out his phone. "Tell me, does this—" He showed her a photo of the tombstone with the inscription clearly visible. "—look familiar to you?"

"The stone, or the words?"

"The words."

She took his phone and looked it over. "I can't quite make it out."

The inscription was perfectly clear to Rob, and he smiled wryly. "Hang on. Here's what it says." He quickly retrieved the cloud file with the transcribed words.

"Oh!" she exclaimed. "Yes, this is very familiar. Now where's that book—?" She went to the card catalog. "Part of our charm is our complete lack of anything useful like a computer, on top of which the books here use an obsolete cataloging system. There's not a volume here more recent than 1880."

"You must get a lot of requests from researchers."

"Not really. Most of what we have here is available in later editions in regular libraries. The physical volumes themselves are unique, but their contents aren't. Except for, ironically, the one you want." She found the card and went to one of the freestanding shelves.

Rob patiently waited as she searched for the book, until a painting on the end of the shelf unit caught his eye. It was a small canvas, displayed in an outsized, carved wooden frame. A group of fairies—*here we go again,* he thought—stood among flowers and weeds, watching the fairy in the center. This subject's face was hidden, but he wore an odd cap, and he raised a double-bladed ax above his head. Hickory nuts, scattered at his feet, seemed to be the blow's target.

Rob moved closer. It was really hard to see clearly, but he swore that the figure immediately to the right of the woodsman, watching with adoring eyes, looked *familiar,* down to her seeming awkwardness in her clothes.

When he realized why, he got goose bumps along his arms. Even with the painting's stylization, it was clearly the image of Curnen Overbay.

That wasn't the only familiar face, he realized. Directly across from the man with the ax, with an expression of mixed petulance and apprehension, was the old man from his dream, who'd sat on the stump of the gall-afflicted oak tree and complained about his foot. Here he hunched with his hands on his knees, a look of uncertainty and fear on his pointed little face.

Rob was still staring when Ms. Brewer discreetly cleared her throat behind him. "Sir?"

He turned around. "Did someone local paint this?"

"My heavens, no. That's a famous painting by Richard Dadd. *The Fairy Fellers' Master-Stroke.* It's one of our most prized pieces. And that's not his watercolor copy, either. You'll find that in London's famous Tate Gallery. This little treasure is the original."

Rob looked around at its isolated location. It couldn't be seen from the door, or even from most places in the room. "You don't believe in showing it off."

"You're not the first person to say that," she chuckled. "We've left it exactly where it was when it was first placed here. The original residents of Cricket didn't show it off, either. Now, watch this." She took out a small pen-sized flashlight and moved the circle of illumination across the painting.

The image was almost done in three dimensions, with layer upon layer of heavy oil paint creating a sense of depth. "Holy shit," Rob whispered, then added quickly, "I mean—"

"In this case, that reaction is entirely appropriate," Ms. Brewer said. "Dadd painted on this one canvas for eight years while he was confined in an asylum after he killed his father." She seemed happy to share information with someone who appreciated it. "Now, would you like to see your poem?"

He followed her back to a reading table, where she opened a large and ornately illustrated book. Words in elaborate calligraphy covered the two displayed pages.

"This book is *The Secret Commonwealth.* It's a collection of Scottish fairy folklore written in 1690 by an Episcopalian minister. It's pretty well known, and the text itself is available on the Internet. But this particular edition has one very special addendum."

Gently she placed the book facedown and opened the back

cover. A folded piece of paper lay nestled into the spine. Yellowed with age, it was thicker than normal paper and covered with handwritten words. The top edge had been glued to the inside of the cover.

She very carefully unfolded it. "This poem is called 'The Fate of the Tyrant Fae,'" Ms. Brewer said.

"Who's Fay?" Rob asked.

"'Fae' is another term for fairy. Not in the Tinker Bell sense, but in the sense that the Fae were the original ancestors of the Celtic tribes. They occupied places like Ireland long before the Irish settled there."

He fought to sound nonchalant. "Fairies, eh? No kidding."

"Well, it's folklore, of course, not anthropology. Although a lot of those New Agers claim that fairies are real, and that they can see them. I think they just spend too much time at their Renaissance Fairs and not enough time in the real world." She tapped the poem with her cotton-gloved finger. "This is a verse epic about a man named Caisteal Guineach, who left Scotland to find the islands to the west, where people lived forever. There are many versions of this type of story in Gaelic literature."

Rob recognized two of the middle stanzas as the epitaphs, and smiled when he realized he'd been right about their order. Then he read the whole poem.

A tyrant fae crossed the valley
His list of pains he could not tally
To his cause no one would rally
And so he left to lead no more.

His old and feeble feet did fail him
His eyes grew dim and ears betrayed him

225

The error of his ways assailed him
As he came to a stranger's door.

With weakness spreading, he called aloud
"I have no place to spread my shroud
My folk are all beyond me now
May I stay with you until I die?"

The lord inside would not be fooled.
"You are that fae, once vain and cruel
There is no comfort here for you
Thoughts of rest you must deny."

The night's cold wind blew round him there
As truth and fortune both despaired
He went away with all his cares
To die beneath the moon's cold breast.

He walked through hills, he walked through dells
To himself he told old tales
Until at last his body failed
And he found the spot to wait for Death.

He faded into darkness, sighing
Though he called, no one replying;
One last feeble effort trying,
Faint he sank no more to rise.

Through his wings the breeze sharp ringing,
Wild his dying dirge was singing,

While his soul to earth was springing,
Body lifeless for the flies.

With wings too weak for soul's last flight
The dying tyrant perceived a sight
Death would take him not this night
Instead a wonder did appear.

But the final stanza was missing, carefully excised like a coupon clipped from the newspaper. "What happened here?" Rob asked.

"No one knows. According to notes left by the original librarian, it was like this when the library received it, back when the town was founded. Considering that he used to personally go collect late fees and overdue books from people's houses, I'm inclined to believe him. If one of the locals had mutilated a book, he'd have skinned them."

"Any idea *why* somebody would cut out the last verse?"

"Well, the academic gossip says this is one of those ancient symbolic books that held mysterious secrets coded into its passages. And whoever glued the poem in here originally might have thought the last verse contained some magical secret, or perhaps the code key to decipher everything else." She rolled her eyes to show how little she thought of this concept. "By removing it, the meaning of the symbols can't be decoded."

"And you don't think it's anything like that?"

"*I* suspect someone wanted to include the final verse in a card to his lady love, and lacked the patience to simply copy it. Sort of like those people who tear whole pages out of phone books to get one number. But be that as it may, I *do* know that this poem's complete text has never been found, because back in 1992, we had an intern who got a grant to try and find it."

He stared at the space in the book. "Sorta leaves you hanging, doesn't it? Don't know what 'wonder' appeared to him."

"You said you found two verses on tombstones?"

"Yeah, these two. Over in Needsville."

The mention of Needsville made her look up at him. "Ah. I thought you had the Cloud County look to you."

"It's just a coincidence. My grandmother was from the Philippines."

"Oh, I didn't mean anything by it. A lot of people come through here tracing their families, especially since Needsville doesn't have its own library. And, of course, all the town's records prior to 1925 burned up in the famous courthouse fire. So unless they want to drive to Nashville and try searching the state archives, they usually come here."

"Do you have a lot of Needsville material?"

"No, not really. We're more of a museum than a real library. We have nothing from the last century."

"So you wouldn't have back copies of the local paper?"

"No, you'd have to go to their office for that. The *Weekly Horn* covers Needsville. They're a small operation out of Unicorn, so you might want to call ahead and make sure someone's there before you drive all that way."

He took photos with his phone of the nearly complete poem—the library naturally did not have a copier—and made one last visit to the strange painting for a photo. There was no way, of course, that it could be Curnen, since the painting had been finished in 1864. Then again, Doyle swore that Curnen didn't even exist, and the artist had painted this while insane; should Rob take that as a warning?

22

On his way to downtown Unicorn, Rob passed the Waffle House were he'd plotted with Doyle. He wished he had time to stop for lunch, but as it was, he'd just barely make his appointment. When he'd called from outside the library, the editor said he'd only be in the office until three.

The *Weekly Horn* was between a State Farm Insurance agency and an antique store. As soon as he entered, a man with a gray crew cut, clad in a button-down shirt that barely contained the bulky muscles of his shoulders and arms, stepped from an office to greet him. He spoke with the nasal accent of the Upper Midwest. "You must be Mr. Rob Quillen."

"Yes, sir," Rob said, and shook the man's hand.

"I've seen you on TV. I'm very sorry for your recent loss."

"Thank you. Are you Mr. Howell?"

"Call me Sam, please. Mr. Howell's my dad. What happened to your eye?"

"Pulled out in front of a fist."

"Well, I went ahead and found the articles you asked about when you called. It's a shame when a young person takes their own life. So was the girl who died a friend of yours?"

"A friend of a friend," Rob said evasively. He'd told Howell only that he was passing through the area and would like to see the news articles associated with Jillie Rae Keene's death. "I just wanted to see what the official version of the story was, since we only heard the broad strokes."

"Not much but broad strokes to it," Howell said as he led him to the back. The place smelled of ink, sweat, and cigarettes. A stack of back-issue volumes bound in heavy faux-leather card stock rested on a table. "You know, we don't get many celebrities through here. We're pretty far from any beaten path."

"What about Bronwyn Hyatt?"

"She had her fifteen minutes, true enough, but she went back up in the hills with her family and, as far as I know, hasn't come out."

"I can understand that. I'm ready for my fifteen minutes to be over, too."

"That reminds me: Before you leave, would it be too much trouble if we took a picture together? Just for a 'look who stopped by' thing, I won't mention why you're here."

"Promise to Photoshop out my shiner?"

"It's a deal."

Rob looked around. The newspaper's equipment, except for the laptop computers, looked like it came from another era. "You run this place by yourself?"

"Mostly me. Got one full-time writer on staff, and some folks in the little towns around here who write up the high school sports and community news." He patted the stack of bound volumes. "One of these days, I'll get these all scanned and posted on the Internet, but until then, folks have to go through 'em by hand. And as you can tell from the dust, that doesn't happen very often."

"So where should I start?" Rob asked.

Yellow Post-it notes marked specific pages. As Howell opened the first book, he said, "I found the main ones for you. Here's the original news story."

Dated 2009, the indicated headline on the yellowed paper read, NEEDSVILLE TEEN SUICIDE BLAMED ON ROMANCE.

> The county sheriff reported that Jillian Rae Keene, 17, of Needsville, died Sunday from an overdose of prescription painkillers.
>
> Keene, daughter of Lloyd and Francis Keene of Pine Road, was found by her mother. A note found at the scene indicated the girl was despondent over a failed romance.
>
> Services will be held Wednesday at the First Methodist Church of Unicorn.

"That's it?" Rob asked. "That doesn't really tell me much."

"That's because there wasn't much to tell. But your question kind of jogged my memory. Look at this one."

He opened another book, to a page dated 2010. This headline read, LARK VALLEY TEEN FOUND DEAD IN APPARENT SUICIDE.

> County Sheriff Clip Rooker reported that Leigh Anne George, 16, of Lark Valley, hanged herself Monday in the family garage.
>
> George, daughter of Fred and Helen George of Lark

Valley Community, was found by her father. A note found at the scene indicated the girl was despondent over a failed romance.

Services will be held Friday at the First Methodist Church of Unicorn.

"Other than going to the same church, what's the connection?" Rob asked.

"They were both dating the same boy."

"How do you know?"

"Because who's dating who is all the women around here talk about, and I've got a wife. See this?" He held up an old photograph, covered with blue cropping lines indicating it had once run in the newspaper. A middle-aged couple, dressed for a funeral, descended the steps of a church. Next to them stood a tall, distinguished man in a white suit with a bolo tie. "That fancy fellow in the white suit is State Representative Sandy Stang, which is why this funeral was news. He was campaigning, and made sure we knew he'd be visiting the bereaved of his district so we could get a picture. But look in back of him."

Behind the grieving parents stood Stoney Hicks, looking uncomfortable in a suit and tie. Next to him, as faintly amused as ever, was his uncle Rockhouse. Except that Rockhouse sported an enormous walrus mustache instead of a full beard, both looked exactly the same as they did now.

"There's your Romeo," Howell said.

Rob got a chill. "So both these girls dated Stoney Hicks?"

"Yep."

"Was he ever implicated in their deaths?"

"Oh, hell no. They were suicides, no doubt. After the fourth or fifth one, though, people started to whisper."

"*Five* different girls killed themselves over this guy?"

"Yep."

"Did anybody ever date him and *live*?"

Sam chuckled. "That wouldn't make the news."

"People had to have noticed the pattern. Especially in a little town like Needsville."

Howell looked him over as if just noticing him. "You do look like you've got some Tufa in you. That why you're in the area? You got family there?"

"No Tufa in me at all, I promise you. I'm part Filipino, and the rest is all Kansas."

He narrowed his eyes, as if he didn't quite believe it, then shrugged it off. "Needsville's a funny place. You notice there aren't any churches there?"

"Yeah, actually, I did. Do you know why?"

"What I heard was . . . Ah, never mind. I was always told it's best not to talk too much about the Tufa. They've got a way, especially the true bloods, of finding out if you've spoken out of turn. Then bad things can start to happen to you."

"Like fairies?"

Howell's frown deepened. "Why would you say that?"

"It's what they say about fairies over in England. They call them 'the Good People' so they won't get mad."

"You sure know a lot. You positive you're not part Tufa?"

"Swear on a Bible if you got one."

He chewed his lip. "Son, let me speak to you like a father here. I'm an outsider, too, even though I've lived here over thirty years. I've seen a lot of weird things happen around Needsville. You take any one of 'em, there's always a rational reason for it. Add them all up, though, and it makes a different picture." Then he pointed to the newspaper. "And speaking of pictures, look here.

Recognize the guy next to your young Bluebeard? That is the legendary Rockhouse Hicks."

" 'Legendary'?"

"You bet. I've got all three of his albums. Actual vinyl albums. Far as I know, it's the only way you can get 'em."

Rob smiled skeptically. "I'm a musician, Mr. Howell, and I've done a ton of research on the music of this area. I never heard of him before I met him."

"To be fair, he wasn't ever really famous. But he *almost* was, and he probably should be." He went to the shelf filled with the other bound volumes and pulled out another of the big books, much older than the rest. He opened it unerringly to the spot he wanted, as he'd no doubt done many times. "I wasn't living here then, but the paper covered it."

The headline proclaimed, CLOUD COUNTY NATIVE'S STAR RISES, FALLS.

> Though his family did not have a radio, young Rockhouse Hicks would go into Needsville on Saturday night and ask someone sitting in their car if they could turn on their radio so he could hear Bill Monroe and Roy Acuff on the Grand Ole Opry. At age 5, he made his first banjo out of a Christmas peppermint can, and dreamed that someday he would join these legends on the Opry stage. But thanks to a cruel twist of fate, it never happened, and he hasn't released a recording in over twenty years.
>
> Hicks is no stranger to hardship. He lost his father, Grannett Hicks, to pneumonia when he was only 4 years old. He was 20 when he got fired from a quarry in Morristown for singing on the job. He then boarded a

bus for Nashville and talked his way backstage to meet his idol, Bill Monroe. Impressed by the young man's courage, Monroe auditioned Hicks on the spot. A week later, Hicks was in Fort Smith, Arkansas, singing on stage with the father of bluegrass.

"You do know who Bill Monroe was, don't you?" Howell asked.

"Might've heard the name," Rob said dryly. He skimmed the details of Hicks's brief career, looking for the point things went wrong.

After three albums, and three years with Monroe, Rockhouse finally had a solo hit with "Love Flew Away" and began his only tour as a headliner. But at his third show, he was caught backstage in a compromising position with an underage black girl. The racial attitudes of the times resulted in him being blacklisted, and the girl's age led to the end of his friendship with Monroe. Although he attempted a comeback on the coattails of the '60s folk revival, his difficult personality ended whatever chances he had of joining the likes of the Carter Family, Pete Seeger, and Woody Guthrie as icons for the new generation.

"That sounds like the guy I met, all right," Rob admitted.

Howell said, "I've found out some more stuff since then, though. Turns out that story isn't exactly accurate."

"What do you mean?"

"He wasn't caught with a black girl. I mean, that would've been bad at the time, but the truth was actually kind of worse. Probably the only thing that *could've* been worse. I've got it on good authority, from more than one local source, that he was actually caught with his pants down . . . with his own daughter."

Rob stared at him. His first thought, naturally enough, was Curnen, but that was absurd. This happened fifty years ago, after all. No telling how many kids the old shithead had scattered through the area. "Wow. Did he go to jail?"

"No, nobody pressed any charges—you just didn't do that to family back then. But it pretty much finished him up as a working musician. He got blacklisted everywhere. And the girl's boyfriend threatened to kill him, right before he disappeared. That is, the boyfriend disappeared, not Rockhouse. He never came back from Nashville, and no one's found a trace of him to this day. Everyone figured Rockhouse and the Tufas had something to do with it, but nobody ever got arrested. No body, no crime." He shook his head. "The Tufa are still like that. They take care of their own problems."

"Wow."

"Now, here's something you'll get a real kick out of," Howell said, and handed Rob a yellowed, fragile sheet of paper and three flat pieces of cardboard.

The paper atop the pile was a handbill that read:

ROCKHOUSE HICKS AND THE NEEDSVILLE BOYS
WE PLAY BANJO, FIDDLE, GUITAR

Singers of old time songs such as "Wayfaring Stranger," as well as love songs. We also have yodeling with part of the songs if that's the kind you like. We'll supply you all we know if you want that much. It takes 5 to 6 hours to play all we know.

COME BRING ALL YOUR SWEETHEARTS
AND FRIENDS!

Carefully Rob placed the ancient advertisement on the table and examined what lay beneath it. They were album sleeves: all showed Rockhouse Hicks dressed in the exaggerated cowboy gear of the time, grinning and clutching a banjo.

But it wasn't the clothes that caused Rob's chest to tighten so much that he struggled for breath. "Holy fuck," he choked out.

"Something, isn't it?" Howell agreed. Then he added with concern, "You all right? You're white as a ghost."

"I think I've seen one," Rob said. He turned the album cover over and looked at the copyright date: 1959. It certainly didn't appear to be fake.

"Would you like to sit down?" Howell asked.

"No, I'm . . . sorry, it just reminded me of something. About my girlfriend," he added, figuring the lie was infinitely more believable than the truth.

Howell nodded. "Stuff slips up on you. I was in the service in Vietnam. Still happens to me sometimes, too."

Rob forced himself to smile and sound casual. He held up his phone. "Do you mind if I take some pictures? I'd love to have copies of these album covers."

"Sure," Howell said.

As Rob photographed the covers, he tried to calm his thundering heart and put aside the truth of what he'd just learned. It was, by any stretch of the imagination, totally impossible; therefore, it could damn well wait a few minutes for him to think about it in detail. It took all his concentration to keep the phone steady in his hands.

"Too bad my main reporter Don's not here," Howell said. "He's part Tufa. He told me his dad was actually over in Needsville the day the old notions store got Rockhouse's first record in stock. Said old Rockhouse himself came in, to see everyone buy his new record. The lady working in the store was new in town and didn't know him, so he asked her, 'You got that new record by that fella Rockhouse Hicks?' 'Sure do,' she said. And she went and got one, and put it on this old turntable they had up front.

They all stood there listening, and when it was over, the lady said, 'That boy sure can play the banjo.' Rockhouse kinda snorts and says, 'Heck, he ain't so hot. If I had my old banjo here, I could play as good as that.' She looks him over and says, 'You can't play the banjo.' 'Yes, I can, I just ain't got mine here with me.' So she goes in the back and comes out with this banjo somebody'd ordered from Nashville. She hands it to him, he makes a big production of tuning it, then jumps into 'Love Flew Away,' which was his first 45 single. You remember those?"

Rob managed a wry grin. "I've seen them in my parents' attic. What'd the woman say then?"

"She said, 'How'd you learn that record, it just came out?'"

They both laughed, although Rob's was mere politeness. He turned the top album over and read the brief liner notes. "A new down-home sound for the uptown crowd," they proclaimed. "Rockhouse Hicks turns his banjo inside out, with a freewheeling style not seen since Bill Monroe." A quote from Roy Acuff, in large italic print, claimed Rockhouse was "the best hillbilly picker runnin' around loose."

The black-and-white photo in the bottom left corner showed elaborately stitched cowboy boots propped next to an open door. The song titles blended standards such as "Your Cheatin' Heart" with odd-titled originals like "Rain of Toads," "My Roots Are Here," and "Chained to This Spot."

Suddenly Rob felt a fresh new chill. How weird could this get?

The very last song on his last album was titled "The Fate of the Tyrant." The poem from the Cricket library was "The Fate of the Tyrant Fae." Could it be—?

Howell tapped the song title. "That last song isn't on the album. As I heard the story, he was supposed to record it, and some folks say he did, but somehow between the time the cover was printed and the actual album was pressed, it got taken off."

"You ever heard him play?"

"No. Needsville is Don's beat. Tell you the truth, those real pure-blood Tufas like Rockhouse Hicks give me the willies. They have this air about them, like they're . . . different, sort of. You'd have to experience it to know what I mean." He chuckled at his own words. "But I guess you've probably run across that."

"Yeah," Rob agreed. "They can be very different."

As he walked to his car, Rob was numb with the shock of the information he'd found. Missing songs, mysterious albums, incestuous scandals: those were interesting—compelling, even—but at least they made sense in the material universe he used to believe existed. A track could be left off an album, an album could fade from popular memory, and of course, a father could molest his daughter. But none of those explained the realization that had turned him pale and breathless in Howell's office.

The face on the album cover . . .

. . . the face of young Rockhouse Hicks . . .

. . . was the face of the man who'd told him about the heartache-curing Tufa song, backstage in Atlanta.

23

On his way back to Needsville, Rob topped a hill and slammed on his brakes. Traffic was blocked in both directions. In the rearview mirror, he saw the car behind do the same thing, stopping an inch short of Rob's bumper.

He sat shaking, his heart pounding. On the satellite radio, Ricky Skaggs sang about Bill Monroe's Uncle Pen.

A pickup had gone off the road and smashed into a tree, and now a state police car, ambulance, and tow truck clustered near it. The trooper efficiently directed traffic, and Rob waited as a vehicle traveling the opposite direction made its way slowly around the wreck. The driver rubbernecked to see details.

EMTs carried the injured driver on a stretcher to the ambulance. The victim was huge, and the two big men carrying him visibly strained with effort. Rob recognized Bliss as the third rescuer, holding up the IV bag of clear fluid attached to the victim's arm; she didn't notice him in the line of cars. The ambulance passed Rob as it headed toward the interstate, lights and sirens blazing.

The trooper motioned Rob around the wreck. As he passed, a shudder ran through him as if he'd crossed some unseen barrier. The odd atmosphere of Needsville started at this exact point, and as he drove the rest of the way into town, it only got stronger.

At the Catamount Corner, Rob checked his e-mail and did a quick, fruitless search on the Internet. Evidently Rockhouse Hicks's musical career had faded so thoroughly that not even cyber-hicks who knew every concert played by Uncle Dave Macon could remember him. This both delighted and saddened Rob; the shit-heel deserved it, but at the same time, what a fate to befall a musi-cian who'd once shared the stage with the immortals.

The room phone rang. "Hello?"

"Hi," Bliss said. Her voice sounded a little odd. "I just finished my shift. Can I see you?"

"Sure."

"Okay. I'm at the hospital in Unicorn. I'll pick you up in an hour."

Forty-five minutes later, Peggy Goins pushed open the door be-hind the Catamount Corner, lit her cigarette, and nearly screamed. Her first thought was that the dark shape huddled beside the wall was a bear cub, which meant the momma bear wouldn't be far away. Then she sighed with relief.

Bliss Overbay sat on the ground, her back against the building, legs drawn up, and head down on her knees. She still wore her dark brown EMT uniform and cap. Peggy fluttered her hand over her chest. "Lord a'mercy, Bliss, you almost scared me out of my skin. I should be standing here just a skeleton, you know that?"

Bliss's eyes were red, and tears glistened on her cheeks. "I'm sorry, Peggy," she said in a trembling voice. "I just didn't know where else to go. I wanted to talk to you, but I didn't want to do it inside, and I just had to rest a little. . . ." She began crying again, the kind of big sobs kids make when they've lost the battle to be brave.

With her cigarette held safely aside, Peggy knelt and put her free arm around Bliss's shoulders. "There, there, darlin'," she said gently. "I know something's happened—now, you just tell Peggy all about it."

Bliss nodded. "Uncle Node. He went off the highway in his truck." She looked up and met Peggy's eyes. "Right at the county line."

Peggy's jaw muscles swelled as she gritted her teeth. "That six-fingered sonuvabitch."

"It was because of me, Peggy," Bliss blurted, still crying. "I stood up to him in public, and he couldn't do anything about it, but Uncle Node was right there with me, and I didn't think to protect him."

"Oh, sweetheart," Peggy said, and sat on the ground beside her. The gravel dug into her legs through her starched and ironed jeans as she let the other woman snuggle into her embrace. "You're not responsible. You're the regent, not the queen."

"The queen's in elementary school," Bliss said bitterly. "It *was* my responsibility."

"Bullshit, if you'll pardon my French. Uncle Node's been around almost as long as I have, and knew the risk of standing up to Rockhouse."

"I can't let him get away with it, Peggy," Bliss said, resolve finally breaking through the tears. "He hurts too many people.

That nephew of his alone has killed how many poor girls who did nothing to him but love him."

"Honey, ain't a girl in these mountains don't know what she's getting into when she lies down with a Tufa boy. It's just a shame the Tufa girls can't do it so easy. But then again, there's things we do that the boys can't even imagine." She remembered the looks on young men above her, long-haired and scraggly-bearded hippie lads, their eyes wide with wonder as they experienced just what a Tufa girl could do in an intimate moment. It had been a time of free love, and Peggy embraced it with a fervor that these now-nearing-retirement men no doubt still wistfully remembered. But that was too long ago in the world's years to dwell on now.

She nodded at the treetops looming over them. "What do you think is moving them boughs around?"

"The wind," Bliss said, like a child to a patient parent.

"That's right. That wind brought us here, that wind still guides us. And she whispers to you far more than she ever has to me. I'm sorry you never got to be just a girl and play and have fun with the boys, but you just weren't picked out for that. Until Mandalay is ready to step up, you're on one end of the stick, Rockhouse is on the other. If you jump off, he goes all the way up. And don't nobody want that, including him, I imagine. Am I right?"

Bliss thought about the rank, primitive place Rockhouse called home, and the solitude he endured because no one from her side trusted him, and no one from his own loved him. They only feared him, which kept them in line but also kept him isolated. She nodded. "Yes, ma'am."

"You here to see that boy Rob again?"

Bliss nodded.

"That sister of yours has been poking around him, too."

"Yes. She knows he's different. She thinks he can help her."

"Nothing can help that girl. And if he ain't careful, she'll latch on to him and pull him down with her."

"It's not all her fault, Peggy."

"No, but it takes two to tango, if you know what I mean."

"My God, Peggy, she was a *child*. She was *his* child."

"Only in the way outside people reckon things. She's a truer Tufa than you in some ways. She's a *sprite*, if you ask me, and I don't mean that ol' fizzy soda pop."

"She's just a girl who's trying not to blow away," Bliss said firmly. She was no longer crying.

Peggy hid her smile. Of course, she'd known just what buttons to push to get Bliss outraged, which in turn got her focused on something other than herself. "Well, you're family, you'd know better than anyone."

Bliss got to her feet and helped Peggy stand. "I have to meet Rob," she said. "I have to take care of some things before anyone else gets hurt."

With her cigarette still held safely aside, Peggy again hugged the younger woman. "You do what you have to do, Bliss. Listen to the winds, they'll tell you." Like a mother, she patted the younger girl on the back.

When Rob came downstairs, Bliss stood alone in the lobby. She walked quickly across to him, then stopped as she was about to throw her arms around him. Her beseeching look was so different from her normal demeanor that he didn't realize at first that she was asking his permission. He held out his arms and she leaped into them. When she squeezed, he hissed through his teeth at the pain across his back.

She drew back, concerned. "What's wrong? Are you hurt?"

"Just not so hard, okay? Here." He tucked her arms in close, so that her hands were flat against his chest. She snuggled against him. "There. Now—what's wrong?"

Bliss wiped her eyes. "Worked a bad accident out on the highway between here and the interstate. Uncle Node ran off a curve and hit a tree."

So *that* was the wreck. "Is he all right?"

"No, he's not. And we don't know if he will be."

She took Rob's hand and led him outside. It was now dark, and the night air was colder than it had yet been, heralding the approach of the mountain winter.

"I'm sorry," she said, and wiped at her eyes. "You do remember Uncle Node from the barn dance, don't you? He sat outside taking the money? Stood up to Rockhouse?"

"Yeah."

"I think his neck's broken. He may be paralyzed. He may even die." She took a deep breath. "I had to look into his eyes. . . ."

He put his hand lightly on her shoulder, a gesture that felt wholly inadequate. "I'm really sorry."

"Rockhouse did it, you know. Because of what happened at the barn dance. We embarrassed him in front of a crowd. He couldn't do anything to *me,* and if anything happened to *you,* it would attract too much attention after that girl disappearing, so he took it all out on Uncle Node."

He wondered if she knew about the boys who'd tried to beat him up. "Like every other crime around here, I guess calling the police would be a bit pointless."

She nodded. "It's not a 'crime' in any legal sense. That's why I'm scared, and angry, and don't know what to do." She shivered a little. "And it's cold." She turned to face him. "I suppose you've been going over the stuff that happened the other night. I bet you've about talked yourself out of believing most of it, haven't you? Well, it was all true. Every bit of it. And it's really important now that you believe it."

"Why is that?"

"Because you have to leave. Seriously. Rockhouse holds a grudge like a mountain holds gravel. Curnen has come to you, and you let her. That means *her* curse might very well take *you.*"

"I can't leave," he said seriously and carefully, "until I talk to Stella Kizer."

"You won't find her, Rob. Nobody will, not the police, not her husband, no one."

"Is she dead?"

"No, but she doesn't want to be found. She wouldn't leave if she could."

"If that's the case, then there shouldn't be any problem with her telling me that herself, should there?"

"No, but like I said, she won't talk to you. You won't be able to find her."

His eyes narrowed. "Maybe you're right. But guess what I *did* find today?"

"What?"

He sang the first verse of "The Fate of the Tyrant Fae" with a haunting, minor-key melody that insinuated itself into his head even as he sang.

If he'd drawn a knife and held it to her throat, he doubted she could've looked more frightened. "Where the *hell* did you hear that?" she gasped, and looked around the deserted street to see if anyone overheard. "Have you sung that for anyone else?"

"Why? Would it bring down the wrath of Rockhouse on me?" He made no effort to hide his irritation.

"You went to Cricket, didn't you?" she said, but her tone made it clear she wasn't really asking. "You saw the poem in the back of *The Secret Commonwealth*. And you saw the painting."

He said nothing. He wanted to tell her about Rockhouse's spectral appearance in Atlanta, and how it spawned this whole chain of events, but suddenly he didn't trust her.

Finally she said, "I'm guessing there's no chance you'll promise me to never sing that song again, anywhere, ever, is there?"

"Not without a better reason that the ones you've been giving out."

Finally she said, "Okay," and took a deep breath. "I need to tell you more, then. So you'll understand and believe me and never sing that song again because you know what will happen."

"So tell me, then."

"Not here. We need to go to my place."

"And why is that?"

"Because I have something there that will convince you."

"Will this 'thing' help me find Stella Kizer?" he said, knowing he didn't sound nearly as harsh as he wanted.

"Yes."

He thought it over. It could be another trap, one more deadly than a couple of hillbillies with baseball bats. But he'd learn nothing sitting in his motel room. Bliss was really his only link to the Tufa society, so he had no choice.

He gestured at his car. "My chariot awaits."

24

He didn't know what to expect. The idea of Bliss's "home" conjured up so many different images. Would she live in a dilapidated mountain shack next to an outhouse? Or a haunted, gabled mansion with only a single light burning in one high bedroom window? Maybe it would be a trailer, like Doyle and Berklee, or just a cave with a witch's cauldron hung over the fire at the entrance.

A narrow wooden bridge that did not inspire confidence appeared on the gravel road ahead of them. He slowed and crept onto it. Beneath it, he saw a shimmering creek whose depth he couldn't judge in the darkness.

"You don't have to go so slow," Bliss said, "it'll hold."

The car lurched slightly as one of the bridge planks shifted, accompanied by a loud clattering sound. "Ever seen *Sorcerer?*" Rob said, his hands tight on the wheel.

"I wrote a song about this bridge once," she said. " 'The Cider Branch Special.' That creek is called Cider

Branch, and when a car comes over at normal speed, you can hear the bridge rattle all the way down to the house. Lets you know you'll be having company in about five minutes."

Evidently, the bridge was accurate, for five minutes later, the headlights illuminated a mailbox with OVERBAY spelled in reflective stickers. Lack of space forced the final Y beneath the rest of the word.

The moonlit view that greeted him was breathtaking. The driveway led into a small valley, with a lake in the center. At the water's edge, with a back patio perfect for fishing, rose a narrow two-story house with big arched windows. He couldn't make out its color in the dark.

The gravel driveway widened into a parking area beside the house. From this spot, wooden steps led down to the water. Bliss got out and walked to the side door, where a security light snapped on as it sensed her movement. She searched her ring for the right key. By the time she found it, every bug in the valley swarmed around the light.

"Nice little piece of land," Rob said, impressed. "I bet it's gorgeous during the day."

"It's been in the family for a long time. We used to farm down there—" She gestured toward the opposite side of the lake. "—but I decided to let it grow back up. I'm not much of a farmer, and I enjoy woods more than fields."

In the moonlight reflecting off the lake, he saw the ripples of something big moving just below the surface. "You got an alligator in your pond?"

"Maybe," Bliss said as she opened the door. She swatted at the bugs as they tried to enter her house. "I sure wouldn't go swimming in it."

He couldn't tell if she was kidding, so he followed her inside. A tiny harp identical to the one on his motel room door chimed its little tune.

The kitchen looked like any country kitchen: dishes in the drain rack, little iron trivets hanging on the wall, hand-stitched hotpads piled next to the stove. Homemade magnets covered the front of the refrigerator, tiny country people painted on wooden silhouettes. All held crude little musical instruments.

"You live here alone?" he asked.

She nodded. "I put the last stitch in a quilt when I was sixteen. If a single girl does that, it's supposed to curse her to never marry. So far it's been true, and when I see some of the marriages around me, it doesn't feel like a curse."

"And you don't have any other family? Well, besides Curnen?"

"No. A train hit Mom and Dad one night on their way home."

"Wow. I'm sorry." He almost mentioned that Doyle claimed no knowledge of Curnen, but decided to keep it to himself.

A big covered pot sat on the stove. The burner wasn't lit beneath it, but there was a smell he couldn't quite identify. He asked, "What are you cooking?"

"Groundhog," she answered as she looped her key ring on a hook by the door. "But it's not cooking yet, it's just marinating."

"Groundhog?"

"Sure. Ran over it yesterday."

"It's *road kill*?"

She laughed. "It was fresh, I promise. I threw it in the truck and brought it straight home. Skinned it, cleaned it, and now I've let it soak overnight in warm salt water. Tomorrow I'll start it boiling."

"You boil it?"

WISP OF A THING

"Yeah. You open all the windows, boil it for twenty minutes, then throw the water out. You do that twice more, then you bake it."

"Why do you open the windows?"

"You ever smelled boiling groundhog?"

Before he could answer, she lifted the lid and peered inside. An eye-watering odor filled the room. Rob gagged and stepped around the divider wall into the dark living room. He groped along the wall until he found the light switch. If it smelled that bad just soaking, he sure didn't want to be around for the boiling. He fought down his gorge, then said, "I'll just wait in here until you finish with that."

"Okay," she answered, and he heard the scrape of a spoon inside the big pot.

He browsed slowly around the room. Photographs, old musical instruments, and odd symbolic knickknacks covered the living room's walls. There was no television or computer. One shelf of an old, heavy bookcase held a slender upright line of vinyl records pinned between heavy bookends. Rob glanced at the records, then looked again. They were thinner than normal albums, and their blank paper sleeves had faded yellow with time.

He pulled one out and slid it into his hand, careful to touch it only on the edges. The plastic surface was wrinkled in places, making the grooves look like terrain readouts on radar. The disks themselves were bare black plastic, and only dates were written on the sleeves: *5/23/68, 8/4/70,* and so forth.

He heard the lid clang down on the noxious groundhog, and called out, "Hey, Bliss, what are these? Home demos?"

"Do you always just pick things up without asking?" she said as she joined him.

251

"Just wondered what kind of albums you'd have. My curiosity took over. I'm sorry."

She took the record from him. "When my dad was in Vietnam, Grandpa and some of his brothers recorded some music, then took it over to Asheville to a place that could make them into records. It was fairly inexpensive, which I guess is why they're so thin and wobbly. They'd mail them to him, and he told me the only record player they had was a cheap plastic one with a burned-up motor that he had to spin by hand." She tilted the disk so the light struck its surface. "See how some of the grooves are almost gone? He played them so much, he plumb wore 'em out."

"You should get them transferred to digital."

She smiled patronizingly. "That would defeat the point, wouldn't it?" Reverently she returned the record to its place, then turned out the lights.

He followed her back into the kitchen and noticed a piece of blue glass on the windowsill behind the sink. "You trying to keep Curnen away?"

"It keeps away more than just her."

"Like what?"

"Other things that live in the woods that you wouldn't want in your house. Would you like a drink?" she asked as she opened the refrigerator.

"Sure." She handed him a beer, and took one for herself.

He popped the tab and was about to drink when he caught himself. "Wait a minute. If I drink this, will I end up 'under your spell'?"

She did not smile. "You think I'd do that to you?"

"I'm asking."

She took the beer from his hand and put them both down in the sink. "Never mind. This isn't really a social visit, is it?" She

WISP OF A THING

looked up at him, her expression grim. "Do you remember how I told you the Tufas were descended from fairies? That the real Tufas still have fairy blood, and all the things that go with it?"

He nodded. Hearing it spoken so simply, in a normal kitchen, made it sound even weirder.

"Well, I have a bunch of it," Bliss continued. "A bunch of Tufa blood, a bunch of Tufa magic. And I'm a First Daughter, just like my mom and my grandmother. The first girl child in the family. That's why I'm considered . . . well . . . a leader."

"Really." He tried for a neutral tone, but the skepticism seeped out.

Her eyes flashed. "I'm not *joking* with you, Rob."

"I didn't say you were. But it *is* hard to accept."

"Try *living* it," she snapped. "I have to exist in the mundane world, you know, not in some storybook. Knowing who and what I am, and having to keep it secret all my life, ain't very damn easy. I brought you here to convince you that you could get hurt if you stay and keep asking questions. And the only way to do that is to also persuade you I'm telling the truth."

He backed up a step. "If you try to poke that spot on the back of my head again, I won't take it real well."

"I promise I won't do that. But I want to show you something else I hope will help you believe."

She led him through the small dining room to a corner doorway almost hidden by an enormous china cabinet. She unlocked the door with a big, old-fashioned key. It opened with only a slight creak. An overhead bulb illuminated a steep flight of wooden stairs.

At the ninth stair, the steps changed from wood to stone. Nine more steps, and they reached the hard-packed dirt floor.

They stood at one end of a minelike tunnel that stretched

ahead of them into the darkness. Shelves lining the walls held old books, strange musical instruments, and odd *objects d'art* that Rob couldn't identify. Bliss threw another switch, and a hanging fixture at the far end of the tunnel revealed another door.

Rob followed her toward the second light. After a few steps, he risked a look behind him and saw the bottom of the steps much farther away than it should have been. He felt vaguely nauseated at this disorientation; he turned to her and whispered, "I think we've gone far enough, nobody'll find my body here."

"Yeah, it's a little weird the first time," she said without looking. "But it'll pass."

Again he looked back. Now there was nothing but darkness behind them, and the light ahead did not seem to be getting any closer. He felt the presence of the earth above him, millions of tons of house and valley floor that could collapse and crush them at any moment. "Have I mentioned my family history of claustrophobic insanity?"

She said nothing. He glanced back a third time, and when he faced forward again, the door was suddenly right in front of them. He looked back again, and this time he saw cellar steps just as they should be, thirty feet away down a low-ceilinged corridor. Had he not been with Bliss, he would've fled screaming from the sheer freakiness. "This part of that Tufa magic you were talking about?" he asked.

"Beats anything ADT has to offer for security," she said. She unlocked the door, braced one foot against the wall, and slowly pulled it open. It scraped loudly across the floor.

She led Rob into a small, musty room. The air here was cooler and drier than in the tunnel. The shaft of light through the open door fell on an oil lamp atop a small table. She took a match from the box beside it, lit the wick, and adjusted it for maximum light.

The room reminded Rob of an elevator shaft. The floor was a twelve-foot square paved with smooth flat stones, while the rock walls receded into darkness far above. A tapestry, six feet wide and at least fifteen feet long, hung from the unseen ceiling.

The cloth radiated both antiquity and, oddly, *sanctity*. Rob felt sure it would crumble in his fingers if he dared touch it, but the atmosphere of reverence was too great to seriously contemplate such an idea.

As the light played across its surface, the colors and images woven into the fabric seemed to move and flow. "Look familiar?" Bliss asked.

He nodded. "It's the same as that painting at the library. *The Fairy Fellers' Master-Stroke*."

"Not exactly. Look closer."

He did, and finally saw what she meant.

The tapestry depicted the same scene, but from the *opposite perspective*. Here the axman's face was plain, as were those of a whole new crowd of people behind him—including a young man in Victorian garb hunched over a sketchpad. The old couple with their odd wheelbarrow device, prominent in the background of the painting, dominated the tapestry's foreground. It was as if two snapshots had been taken of the same moment from two different angles. "Okay, that's weird," he said. "Explain it to me."

"I can't."

"That's not the best way to convince me of something."

"There simply is no real-world explanation. This tapestry is older than anyone can remember. I don't even know how it's stayed in one piece this long. What I *do* know is that it's been kept in my family for generations, and part of my role in the Tufa community is to protect it. Just like my mother did, and my grandmother, and so on."

He pointed to the artist diligently working at his sketchpad. "Is that supposed to be the guy who did the painting I saw at Cricket? The one who went insane?"

"Can you think of another explanation?"

He indicated the girl with the rapturous expression. "And that's your sister, Curnen?"

"Yes," she said with certainty.

"Somebody stitched her into a tapestry before she was born?"

She took a deep breath before saying, "Time doesn't work the same for everybody."

"I need more than a fancy beach towel to convince me of that, Bliss."

"Keep looking at it."

Rob was about to reply, when he noticed something so obvious, he couldn't believe he'd missed it before. The axman in the tapestry also had a familiar face, and when he looked more closely, he saw that each hand wrapped six fingers around the ax handle. "Is that . . . *Rockhouse Hicks?*"

"Yes."

"Really?"

"Yes."

He tried to cover his shock. Cavalierly, he said, "I suppose there's a story behind it?"

"There's *always* a story." She reached out and gently touched the fabric, tracing the edge of the axman's blade with her fingertip. "This man was the queen's forester, which was a title as well as a job. He organized the forest so that only the right trees were cut, and had absolute control over the people and animals that lived in it. But he wasn't the brightest thing in the woods, so he made a stupid bet that he could split a hickory nut in half with one stroke of his mighty ax. The queen, who adored gambling, got wind of it and came to watch, and this threw him off. He failed, and as a result, he was banished from the kingdom, and the forest."

"And this happened when?" Rob asked.

"Before we came here. Before the people of the forest followed the forester to this new land. Ironically, although he couldn't split one damn hickory nut, he managed to split the Tufa in two."

"And nobody's noticed that he's been around for hundreds of years?"

"Oh, that kind of magic's not hard at all. It's the same thing that makes people not see the cemetery behind the fire station. People notice what they want to. The people who stay in Needsville know to leave Rockhouse alone. The people who leave town forget about him. Visitors just think he's colorful. So he just goes on, piddle-assing with his music and being a bastard to everyone."

Rob pointed at the figure of Curnen. "So why is your sister there?"

With no emotion, she said, "Haven't you figured that out? I thought the six fingers would make it obvious. My sister is also his daughter."

The full meaning of this worked its way through his brain. He looked into her grim, unsmiling face. "Your mom was Rockhouse's sister?"

"Yes."

"And . . . so his musical career was ruined because he got caught with *Curnen*? His daughter, who is also his niece? . . ."

"Yes, it's just . . . Chinatown," she said wryly. Then she stared at him in surprise. "Wait, you know about his career?"

"Is it a secret?"

"It's very old news."

"That's the nice thing about the Internet. All news is current." He didn't want to bring Howell into it if he didn't have to.

257

She took a moment to collect herself. "Well, as for Curnen destroying his chance to be a star, yes, but no. He did get caught with her. But his career was ruined because he broke Tufa rules and tried to permanently leave Cloud County. That's hard for a Tufa to do. You've heard of Bronwyn Hyatt, haven't you? She joined the army to get away, but she ended up right back here, and quite a bit the worse for wear. The powers we worship and follow used the events of the war to bring her back, and they did the same thing to Rockhouse."

He studied the faces of Rockhouse and Curnen; there could be no mistake, it was *them*, but that story explained nothing, not least of which how the girl had stayed young while Rockhouse aged normally. "Rockhouse's fall happened almost sixty years ago."

"Yeah."

"And all this is possible because 'time doesn't work the same for everybody'?"

"Yes, yet again." She reached up and brushed the tapestry so lightly, it didn't visibly move; only the slight puff of dust that rose from it said she'd even made contact. "Rockhouse led our people across the ocean to the west, and they settled here. But eventually other people began to arrive, the first human settlers, and as our folk and theirs began to mix, he got restless. He saw that the Tufa were losing their identity and becoming more like these newcomers. So he decided we should all only breed with each other, to keep the Tufa bloodlines pure, and with a lot of persuasion and manipulation, he managed to get my mother pregnant with Curnen."

"How did your father take that?"

"It wasn't pretty. But as you can imagine, Rockhouse's whole save-the-tribe-through-incest program never really caught on. Most of the Tufa just ignored him and went on their way, blending in and falling in love with whoever they wanted."

WISP OF A THING

"What did Rockhouse do then?"

"At heart he's a petulant child. He just said 'screw it,' and struck out on his own. Picked up a banjo, a pair of cowboy boots, and some songs. Took Curnen and her boyfriend, Brushy Dale, with him. Brushy was his guitar player, and Curnen sang backup. They did all right for a while. The night winds will let us leave, as long as our intentions are pure. But once the winds realized he never intended to return, they made sure he had no choice. They used his own proclivities to disgrace him." She paused. "When Brushy Dale learned what Rockhouse had done to Curnen, he pulled a knife and threatened to kill him, in front of a bunch of other people backstage at the Opry. That's how everyone found out."

"Where is Brushy now?"

"No one knows. Well, maybe Curnen, but she can't say. He never came back to Needsville, and Rockhouse swears he left him in Nashville."

"You don't believe it?"

"Not for a fucking moment. I think Rockhouse cursed Brushy just like he did Curnen. I don't know exactly what he did to Brushy, but he cursed her to become a wisp of a thing, a ghost that's never actually died. She's fought it, but he's strong, especially when he wants to hurt someone. Fewer and fewer people remember her, and when the last leaf falls from the Widow's Tree this year, she'll be lost entirely."

Rob nodded, but said nothing. What was there to say? This was so much to absorb, it left him speechless. The lump on his head tingled and itched, distracting him as well. But he finally said, "I have a story for you now. I wasn't going to tell you, because I thought it sounded ridiculous, but after what you've told me . . ."

Like her, he reached up and gently touched the fabric. He heard a sharp intake of her breath, but she didn't try to stop him. He lightly tapped the face on the fabric, making the tapestry ripple. "This was the guy who told me about the magic song that night in Atlanta. Rockhouse Hicks. As he looked on his old album covers. I didn't recognize him the way he is now, old and with a beard. But it was him." He turned to Bliss and smiled without any amusement at all. "I'll believe your fairy tale if you'll believe mine."

Bliss stared at him. "That's not possible."

"That's a little pot–kettle, don't you think?"

"No, that's not what I mean. He *couldn't* have been there. He can't leave."

"He's chained to this spot?" Rob asked, wondering if she'd recognize the song title.

"Yes. So you didn't see *him*. You saw a haint. An apparition."

"A ghost?"

"No, not a ghost. He's not dead, it wasn't his spirit."

"Then what was it?"

She waved her hands in front of her face. "Stop badgering me, let me think."

He returned his attention to the tapestry. Now that he understood its secrets, he saw lots of other familiar faces: Peggy Goins and her husband, Marshall, were there; the portly MC from the barn dance; even Stoney Hicks. Or was he just projecting onto these stylized visages?

"We need to go," Bliss said abruptly. She took his elbow and pulled him out of the chamber, pausing to lock the door behind them. She was silent until they reached her kitchen.

"What happens now?" Rob asked.

"I don't know. Nothing else tonight. Just go back to the motel and wait. I'll catch a ride in the morning and pick up my truck."

"I don't want to—"

"Just *do it*!" she exclaimed, and glared at him. "Jesus fucking Christ, can't you let something go for one night? I'll get in touch with you tomorrow and we'll figure out what to do, okay?"

He stared at her, his own anger rising. "Okay. Thanks for the interesting evening."

"You're welcome," she snapped back.

A wave of utter weariness hit Rob as he opened his car door. His shoulders ached, his eye throbbed, and his stitches itched maddeningly. He wanted nothing more than to be asleep in his own apartment back in Kansas City, with the old box fan providing white noise.

His eye was drawn to movement on the lake. Something like an upside-down canoe momentarily broke the surface, and ripples outlined by moonlight spread from it. That made sense, he thought; a place where fairies played fiddles probably would have a monster in every pond.

He shook his head and was about to climb into the car when he looked up. Curnen perched on the top of the car, hunched down on all fours, her face level with his.

"*Yah!*" he cried, startled. He had neither heard her nor felt the car shift under her weight. She immediately put her finger to her lips. Rob glanced back at the house, but the lights stayed off and Bliss did not emerge.

Curnen wore the same tattered dress, and her hair was matted with leaves. In the moonlight, her eyes appeared all pupil, with no visible white. Her fingers tapped softly and impatiently on the car's roof.

He swallowed hard and whispered, "Hi. Don't take this

personally, I like you and everything, but under the circumstances, I really don't want to get in the middle of things between you and your sister." *Or you and your father,* he thought but didn't say.

Curnen scooted forward until he thought she'd fall onto him, but she maintained her balance. Then she began to hum. Rob recognized it at once: "Wrought Iron Fences."

She made a scribbling motion with her hand, as if she were writing something on a piece of paper. She stopped, and gestured to indicate the bottom of the imaginary page. Then she mimed cutting off that section. She cocked her head and waited for him to respond.

His eyes opened wide. He looked back at the house to make sure Bliss wasn't watching, then whispered urgently, "You know where I can find the final verse?"

She nodded.

"Where?"

She jumped off the car onto the gravel. Her feet crunched no louder than a squirrel's might. Then she took his hand and gently tugged, indicating that he should follow her into the woods.

He recalled the last time she'd dragged him through the forest. "I've heard some weird stuff about you, Curnen. You promise this isn't a trick?"

Curnen stepped close and looked into his eyes. He saw the resemblance to Bliss now, in the line of her jaw and the way her eyes suddenly locked on his. Curnen's gaze was different, though, and not in the way he expected. Bliss had mystery in her eyes; Curnen's were wide open and innocent.

Or, damn it, was that a trick as well? Part of the Tufa's so-called enchantment?

Curnen nodded once, seriously. So now it was up to him; did he trust her, or not? "Please don't lie to me, Curnen," he said softly, with all the honesty he could summon.

She made an *X* sign over her heart with one long finger.

"Then what the hell," he muttered, and let her pull him across the yard toward the dark trees.

25

The forest felt more like a jungle, deep and overpowering. Once they were far enough away that Rob could no longer see Bliss's house behind them, Curnen tightened her grip and yanked him along as she'd done before. He ran blind, unable to guess what direction they traveled, worried only about keeping up with her. She was silent as a viper; he made more noise than Metallica.

After several minutes, they abruptly stopped. Winded, he leaned against the nearest tree and waited until he caught his breath. The cool air made him shiver, even though the exertion drenched him in sweat. He tried to recall what he'd learned of hypothermia. Curnen stood very still, her eyes on something up in the trees.

He followed her gaze, but saw nothing in the shadowy branches. He recalled the strange shape in the lake, and wondered what other bizarre nocturnal creatures might roam these woods. "What is it?" he asked softly.

Suddenly an owl's high, trilling *wooooooo* came from the branches above them. He recognized the sound, yet a shiver still ran up his damp, bruised spine. Curnen ripped a foot-long strip of cloth from the hem of her ragged dress and frantically tied it into a row of knots. The owl hooted once more, and Curnen threw the knotted cloth in its direction. She made a series of quick rapid hand gestures, and in the silence Rob heard the heavy wing-beats as the owl flew away.

He couldn't see her face, but her body visibly relaxed. He thought owls were considered good luck and signs of wisdom; evidently to her, though, they carried a darker meaning.

She took his hand and again pulled him after her. They emerged from the woods onto an untilled field, nestled in a narrow stretch of flat ground. Old plowed furrows were now overgrown with weeds and saplings. To their right, the moon illuminated a small cabin; smoke rose from the chimney, and lights blazed in every room. A small satellite dish was clamped to one corner of the roof, and a weed-choked, skeletal tractor filled the side yard. Several cars and trucks were parked in the dirt driveway.

Their path took them toward the house, and Curnen slowed as they neared it. Rob heard voices inside, and thought this might be their destination. Then Curnen yanked him to the ground and slapped a hand over his mouth. She pointed.

The door opened with the protest of wood against wood. Rob heard the sounds of wailing and weeping from inside. A man's voice called out, "For God's sake, Viney, shut up. The dead can't sleep when their kinfolk holler too loud."

"You won't burn that feather crown we found in his pillow, will you, now?" a woman sobbed. "The devil'll get him for sure."

Another woman stood silhouetted in the door, a plate of food in her hands. "Feather crown ain't from the devil, Viney, it's from the Christian Lord. You got it backwards, you ain't never had it right." She placed the plate on the ground and stepped back inside. The door closed and audibly locked.

Rob looked questioningly at Curnen. She pointed.

A shambling figure emerged from the trees. At this distance, it looked approximately human, but moved in a slow, foot-sliding manner. It reminded Rob of all those zombie films he'd watched as a teen. The figure went straight to the shack, picked up the plate of food, and disappeared back into the forest.

Curnen, obviously relieved that they weren't noticed, pulled him along much more slowly this time. They reached a small clearing that sheltered another tiny graveyard. Unlike the Swett family plot, this one was completely neglected; the iron fence had fallen in places, and weeds hid all but the tops of any tombstones that hadn't fallen or crumbled to pieces. Incongruously, a fresh pile of dirt indicated a new, open grave. Curnen guided him around the edge of the clearing, toward the narrow trail opening he saw on the opposite side.

His pants snagged on a briar bush growing beside one of the old grave markers. He stopped to free it, and muttered "Dammit!" when he felt the thorns tear his fingers.

"You must be a Yankee," a voice said from the darkness.

They both froze. Except for the slight wind, everything was silent, until the voice spoke again, right behind them. "That's a green briar that's snagged you. They grow over Yankee graves. Wild roses grow from the Johnny Rebs."

Rob's heart thundered as he freed his pants leg and turned. The hunched, shambling figure they'd seen earlier watched them, holding the plate left outside the cabin. The smell of dry, rotted fabric filled the air. Rob could not make out his face, but his eyes twinkled in the darkness.

"That you, Curnen?" the figure said. Curnen nodded. "And who're you?" he asked Rob. "You a Yankee or a *damn* Yankee?"

"What's the difference?" His voice sounded higher and shakier than he'd hoped.

"Yankees come to visit. *Damn* Yankees come to stay."

"I'm her friend," he said, and nodded at Curnen.

"Dangerous hobby," the figure replied.

Curnen made an inarticulate warning noise.

The figure did not seem intimidated. "Be careful, little missy. If I don't eat your sins, nobody will."

"Eat her *what*?" Rob asked. This guy gave him a serious case of the creeps.

"People die, I eat their sin." He held up the plate. "Last meal. Left beside the body to soak up everything wrong they done. I eat it so they don't take it with 'em." He waved what looked like a biscuit at Curnen. "She's likely to die in the woods, no one to tend her, sit up with her, bury her. I'm the only one who might find her." Then he pointed at Rob. "You run around with her too much, you're likely to end up the same way."

"I'll be all right," he said with a conviction he didn't entirely feel.

He shrugged. "Your life. She's carrying a curse, you know."

"I don't believe in curses."

Rob's eyes could just make out the man's big, full-toothed Tufa grin. "Curse don't care if you believe in it or not. Do you know what she is?"

Curnen stepped between the two men and growled again.

"She's a *wisp*, friend." The figure illustrated the word with a blowing noise. "Most of her ain't even there no more. She'll be all gone soon."

He turned, walked to the open grave, and sat on the mound of dirt. He sighed and shook his head. "Look at this. Time was, no one would've left a grave open overnight. They would've been afraid of the bad luck. Now, nobody remembers all them old ways. Nobody cares. Pretty soon, they'll forget *I'm* out here just like they have your girlfriend there." He continued to eat. "Then I'll be in a mess, huh?"

Curnen snarled in the man's direction. Then she pulled Rob after her, back into the woods. Rob looked back over his shoulder, and caught one last glimpse of the sin eater. He sat on the pile of grave dirt, shaking his head and laughing to himself.

Low branches forced them to scurry along in a crouch. The bruise across Rob's shoulders tingled and throbbed. Curnen had less trouble, but in a few places had to stop and wait for Rob to get through a particularly narrow passage. She showed no impatience with him, though, and helped as much as she could.

They slid down a hillside to the bank of a small creek. The water sparkled in the moonlight, and Curnen knelt to drink. She picked up two small, smooth river stones and pressed one of them into his free hand. Then she led him along the edge of the creek until they reached a line of rocks that formed a footbridge across the water. She crossed nimbly, and waited for his considerably slower passage.

The high bank arched over their heads, and they walked under it until they found a gully they could climb. At the top, a vaguely man-shaped boulder jutted from the ground like a sentry standing watch over the creek. The moonlight didn't reach it, but Rob thought he saw many lines of runelike scratches along its surface.

The moonlight *did* touch Curnen's face. She gazed at the rock, and tears silently poured down her cheeks, cutting through the dirt. Her lips trembled with emotion.

"Are you all right?" Rob asked, touching her shoulder the same way he'd touched Bliss's.

Curnen nodded at the rock, then clasped her hands together and put them over her heart. Then she held up her left hand, made a circle with the thumb and forefinger of her right hand and slid it over her ring finger. Or what he assumed was her ring finger, since she had the extra digit.

Rob remembered the story of Rockhouse's fall. "That's Brushy Dale's grave?"

She shook her head, hard. She touched her heart, then pointed at the rock.

Rob realized what she meant. "That's . . . Brushy?"

She nodded. Her face contorted with sorrow.

He put his arms around her without even deciding to do it. She shuddered against him just as Bliss had done in the Catamount Corner lobby. He stared at the rock, seeing its humanlike shape even more clearly now. *Surely not,* he thought. Rockhouse couldn't turn someone to stone. He wasn't some fucking Medusa . . . was he?

At last Curnen pulled away and wiped her face. She took a couple of deep breaths, then held up her stone and took it to the boulder. At the base were many small piles of similar rocks. She kissed the one in her hand, knelt, and placed it reverently on the ground. She motioned for him to do the same. He was about to do so when movement caught his eye. He looked up and almost yelled.

Up the slope from the boulder, silhouetted against the night sky on a ridge, stood a deer. No, he corrected himself— a *stag,* and a gigantic one at that. Two large, wiry dogs accompanied it. Suddenly Curnen *howled* beside him, and he almost dropped his rock. A moment later, the dogs cried in response, and he realized they were *coyotes.*

She nudged him and indicated the rock in his hand. Quickly he put it next to hers. When he looked back, the stag king and his coyote courtiers had vanished into the night. He hoped that meant it was okay to travel through their forest.

They moved laterally along the ridge until it opened into a wide and well-marked trail. Curnen scurried ahead up the slope, and although it was easier, Rob still couldn't keep up. At last he saw her waiting beside a lone tree in the middle of a small clearing.

It took him a moment to realize where they were. This was the base of the Widow's Tree, the enormous tree that could be seen from just about anywhere in the valley. As he waited to catch his breath again, he saw that the bark was scarred up to a height of about ten feet with names and dates.

"Wow," he said when he could manage the words, "how long has this been going on?"

By way of answer, Curnen took his hand and pressed it against one carved name. He traced the *B,* then the *R,* and realized who it must be. And he also understood that if the name was here, it meant more than he'd initially thought.

"Brushy wasn't just your boyfriend, he was your *husband,* wasn't he?"

She nodded.

He had to swallow past the lump of emotion in his own throat before he could speak. "I'm really sorry."

She stepped close, stood on tiptoe, and kissed him on the cheek. She turned away, then impulsively kissed him a second time, on the mouth. It left tingles when she withdrew.

Curnen pulled him around the tree and up the hill. The ground rose sharply until Rob had to release Curnen's hand and pull himself from tree trunk to tree trunk up the slope. His arms, legs, and spine screamed in protest, especially the hot bruise across his back.

Curnen stayed just ahead of him, nimbly crawling on all fours. She glanced back often to check his progress, evidently unaware of or uninterested in the agony she put him through.

He stopped for a momentary rest, and when he looked up, he saw her just ahead, stretched out on her belly behind a log. He fell next to her, and again she put her hand over his mouth to quiet him.

He angrily slapped it away as he tried to catch his breath. Between the pain and exhaustion, his lungs could barely expand. "Goddammit, Curnen," he wheezed, "if you don't—"

She kissed him, then quickly touched his lips with a single finger while he was still startled. Her urgency was plain. He nodded, gasping, and waited until his breathing returned to normal. This kiss also left a tingle.

Little patches of foxfire glowed on the decaying log sheltering them. Curnen put a finger to her own lips and pointed ahead of them. He carefully rose to look.

A saggy, decrepit *dwelling* squatted on the side of the hill, its back wall buried in the earth. "House" was far too dignified a term for it, since he could see even in silhouette that boards had sprung loose from the sides and most of the windows lacked glass. Smoke curled from the chimney, blotting out the stars as it rose straight into the sky, and dim illumination came from oil lamps placed on the windowsills. Between the boards he saw the flickering light of the fireplace within.

He heard low, thick voices and the occasional loud, metal *plink*. Several figures sat on the porch, watching a pair of men in the yard. They all seemed able to see by nothing but moonlight. Some of them were enormous, round people, and others seemed thin and almost skeletal. The bigger ones were women, he realized; this must be the brood that had produced Tiffany Gwinn.

"Five points," a man's voice said after one loud *plink*. "That's fifteen."

Another *plink*. "That's ten, you mean."

"Dang it," the first voice muttered.

Something beeped musically. "Will you put that dang thing away?" one of the men in the yard complained. "I can't concentrate on tossin' these washers."

"I'm gonna beat this level," a boy's voice said, distracted.

"All you do all day is play them video games," said a voice Rob recognized as Tiffany Gwinn.

"It helps my ADD." He pronounced it "Aye-Dee-Dee."

"I'll pay attention to your deficit," Tiffany snapped as the boy fled into the house.

Rob dug his fingers into the soil. For the first time since he'd arrived in Needsville, he felt real, bone-deep *terror*. Less than a hundred feet away was an entire clan of people who would no doubt be quite happy to make sure he never left this mountain alive, and his only ally was a girl who was either inbred, cursed, or both. Had this been Curnen's plan all along?

But Curnen made no move to give them away, and pointed to a spot farther along the slope beside the cabin. In the moonlight, he couldn't resolve the scene into anything that made sense. Half a dozen structures resembling low doghouses, complete with peaked and shingled roofs, were scattered irregularly among taller objects poking at odd angles from the ground. Was it debris from the house? Discarded auto parts or farming equipment? A kennel?

Then the tall objects resolved into tombstones, and the small, low sheds appeared to be shelters covering certain graves.

If the final verse had also been chiseled as an epitaph on one of those markers, there wasn't nearly enough light to see it, especially if the letters had been weathered away. Also, there was no way to reach the graveyard without being seen by the people on the porch. And the flash from his phone would surely be noticed.

He slid back down next to Curnen. "So the last verse is in that graveyard?" he whispered.

She nodded.

He wished the girl's eyes were more normal; their opaque blackness unnerved him. "They'll see us if we try to go to the graveyard right now. We'll have to wait until they go inside."

She reached to his face and touched her fingertips to his cheek. In the moonlight her expression was so tender, it made something ache deep inside him. She leaned toward him, but he gently pulled her hand away. "Not now, Curnen, okay? We'll talk about this later."

Her expression turned eloquently sad, and he felt like a jerk. Whatever the reality, she clearly believed in the curse, and behaved accordingly. All she wanted from him was basic human kindness. And like everyone else, he was denying her.

"I'm sorry," Rob said gently. "Look, you know I'm your friend, right? Do you have any other friends?"

She shook her head.

"See? Then I'll be your friend, and that makes me special, okay?"

She tilted her head a little. If she tried, would she be able to make him feel as aroused as she had in the clearing? Or was her ability to manipulate him shattered now that he knew its source?

He shivered. The night was cool, and sweat soaked his clothes. Curnen silently piled leaves around them, forming a crude nest. Then she lay down beside him and scooted as close as she dared.

A guitar rang out from the Gwinn cabin. Someone yelled,

"Awright, now," and began to clap along. Feet stomped on the porch, the thud accompanied by an occasional cracking sound.

Rob smiled as he recognized the song, although he never imagined it played so harshly. He pulled Curnen close, and she nestled against him. He wondered if anyone had ever treated her like this before, or if everyone, including her own family, was either scared or desirous of her?

As loud as he dared, he sang to her:

> Down in some lone valley,
> In a lonesome place
> Where the wild birds do whistle,
> And their notes do increase
> Farewell pretty Saro,
> I bid you adieu,
> But I'll dream of pretty Saro
> Wherever I go. . . .

By the time he reached the second verse, he could tell by her breathing that she was asleep.

26

Bliss stood on her patio looking out at the lake in the moonlight. She felt the soft breeze as something flew behind her, then heard the faint, delicate tap as feet lightly touched the wood.

When she turned, Mandalay Harris stood there, dressed in a *Fresh Beat Band* pajama top and a pair of cut-off shorts.

The girl made a gesture of welcome, and Bliss replied with the appropriate hand signal. "It must be important if you're calling me over here in the middle of the night," Mandalay said. "What's up?"

"Something happened that I can't explain," Bliss said. "And it *is* important."

Mandalay hopped up on the patio rail. "Tell me about it, then."

Bliss related Rob's story of being accosted by the younger Rockhouse Hicks. Mandalay listened without interrupting. When she finished, Bliss said, "And I don't know what to do now."

"Wow," Mandalay said.

"I could use something a little more concrete."

"It wasn't a real haint, obviously. Rockhouse ain't dead. So . . ." She looked up at the sky, where a lone cloud scudded across the moon. "The night winds must have sent it."

Bliss's heart almost stopped. "You can't be serious, Mandalay."

The girl shrugged, as if what she'd suggested meant nothing. "You know another explanation, you throw it on out here and we'll see if it runs around."

"But they don't . . . They've never . . . They don't get involved that way."

"They never have before," she agreed.

"But why would they do it now?" Bliss almost shouted.

As if it were the simplest thing in the world, she said, "They want your friend Rob to come here and do something none of the Tufa can or will do."

"So the night winds brought him here by telling him some bullshit story about a magic song, and once he got here, they made Tiffany Gwinn smack him so hard that even though he has no Tufa in him, he can see things that should be visible only to us?"

"Well, duh," Mandalay said. "Look, it's pretty plain. None of us would have anything to do with 'The Fate of the Tyrant Fae.' We know what it is, and what it does, which is why Rockhouse keeps hiding it. But the night winds clearly want it found, and sung. They made sure it got put on tombstones, stuck in the back of that book in Cricket, even put it on the cover of one of Rockhouse's albums. They've basically rubbed our noses in it forever. But we haven't done anything with it, and they're tired of waiting."

"Why?"

"Why are they tired of waiting, or why do they want something done?"

"Both."

She hopped down off the rail. "Rockhouse's time is over, I'd guess."

"And Curnen?"

"Curnen's a lost cause, Bliss. I'm sorry to say it, but you know it's true. Every time I see her, there's a little more gone. My stepmom doesn't even remember her anymore. It's sad and it's awful, but it's beyond our control."

Bliss clenched her fists. She forced herself to stay focused on the bigger picture. "Rockhouse is what holds us together. He may not lead both tribes, but he's the reason we're here. If he loses his power—"

Mandalay smiled. "You remember what Bronwyn Hyatt said when she got back from Iraq, don't you? We have to change and evolve, we can't keep hiding from the world."

"If Rockhouse loses his power, Mandalay, we don't know who will step in."

She sighed. "Tell me about it. I'd be lying if I said that didn't scare the pee out of me. But if it's what the winds want, I'll just have to suck it up. Put on my big-girl panties, like my stepmom says."

"So if all that's true . . . why did I play that Kate Campbell song for him? That song had the lyrics that the haint of Rockhouse told him in Atlanta. Why am *I* in the middle of this?"

She moved close to Bliss and took the older woman's hands. "Nothing lasts forever. Not Rockhouse, not us. Bronwyn had it right: Everything living has to change, or die. You're part of the change."

Bliss felt the absurdity of being lectured by a ten-year-old. "And what about Rob?"

"When he got the ability to see our reality, he also got tied to it."

"Did the winds kill his girlfriend?"

"I don't know. I'd like to think not. But whatever got him here, he's doing what the winds want now. That means we have to help him."

"*We.* You mean *me.*"

"Okay, you. That's why they gave you the Kate Campbell song."

Now things fell into place, but it did not reassure her. Not at all. "I'm supposed to help him take down Rockhouse?"

Mandalay nodded.

"How?"

The girl smiled and shrugged. "Wait and see which way the winds blow."

Rob lay awake, listening. The player wasn't very good, skipping whole chords and apparently unconcerned with meter, and the singing was atrocious. Unlike what he'd experienced at the barn dance, this music was *ugly*. When it finally stopped, he disentangled himself from Curnen and peeked over the log.

Dawn began to lighten the sky. Mourning doves called from the woods. The oil lamps in the windows had either gone out or been extinguished. Only two people remained on the porch, and just when he thought they were asleep, one of them leaned over and spit into the grass. Two big, lethargic dogs under the porch raised their heads.

"Curnen," he whispered. She awoke with a start. He placed a hand gently over her mouth. "We have to go check this now, if we're going to. It'll be daylight soon. But there's still people on the porch."

She nodded and carefully looked over the log. He heard her make a low growling sound, barely audible even to him.

The nearest dog's ears perked up, and it crawled out to stand beside the porch. It was some mongrel beast with a head like a hyena, all teeth and jaw muscles. It looked around the yard, past their hiding spot, then turned to rejoin its compatriot.

Curnen growled again. The dog froze, looked up at the sky, and howled. Curnen continued to growl, and the beast cried out three more times. Then she fell silent, and the dog went back under the porch.

"You hear that?" one of the men from the porch said. "That sum'bitch howled four times and quit."

"So?" the other man said with a yawn.

"Daddy always said if a dog howls four times and stops, means somebody in the house is going to die soon."

"That's horseshit," the second man said.

"Yeah, well, it happened to the Potters down by Jonesborough. Their dog did that, lightning hit the house the next day, and it plumb blowed up."

"That's because they had a meth lab in the basement, dumbass."

"So what you want us to do?" a third man demanded, annoyed. "Go kiss the dog's ass or something?"

"I don't know, I'll have to go ask Momma." He went inside, and after a moment the other two followed.

At the instant the door closed, Curnen slithered over the log and dashed to the graveyard. The tattered dress flapped behind her as she ran. Rob expected the two dogs to bark and bring the Gwinns running, but the animals did not stir.

Curnen threw herself to the ground behind one of the grave shelters. Next to it rose a seven-foot tombstone carved in the shape of a cloth-draped pylon. It tilted awkwardly on the slope, and Rob was afraid it might tumble down on top of her. But it remained solid, and she motioned for him to join her.

Rob crouched low as he ran and slid to the ground beside her. An awesomely repulsive smell swamped the whole area, originating at the three outhouses just up the hill. He gagged, blinked back tears of nausea; then he looked up at the tombstone, eager to find the missing verse in the dim morning light.

The surface read only, KATE OVERBAY GWINN, BELOVED WIFE AND MOTHER, 1882–1922. So this was the grave of Great Kate, the bootlegger too fat to arrest. And her maiden name was Overbay. Bliss had called Tiffany her cousin, so he shouldn't be surprised.

He checked the two other sides he could see from his position, but those were completely blank. Could it be on the side facing the house? That would be just his luck. He turned to Curnen and whispered, "Where is it?"

But the wild girl had vanished.

Oh, shit, he thought. Even crouched behind the grave shelter, it was light enough that he'd be spotted by the first Gwinn who looked out the window. They'd torture him, then kill him, and his body would never be found. Tiffany would use his testicles for castanets.

He heard movement near the house, and watched one of the dogs walk out into the open, stretch, and hike its leg at a corner of the foundation. Someone moved inside, big feet thudding on old, creaking wood.

He glanced at the woods behind him. He'd have to make a break for it and hope he could lose himself in the trees. He had no idea which way led to Needsville, or even the nearest road; but with the sunrise to mark east, he could at least ensure he was running in a straight line away from the Gwinns.

Then, something wriggled under him, beneath the ground.

Startled, he moved aside. Was it a mole? Then he realized it wasn't moving horizontally under the surface, it was burrowing its way up through the soil, *from inside the grave of Great Kate Gwinn.*

He stared and almost screamed when a corpse-pale, dirt-encrusted hand clawed up into the air.

27

The hand *waved* at him. This hillbilly zombie knew he was there.

Then it curled and dug its fingertips into the dirt. Rob's heart threatened to rip its way out through his ribs and flee on its own.

Another hand burrowed out beside the first, only this hand clutched a letter-sized envelope. Then the two hands spread the ground between them, widening it into a opening big enough for a dark-haired head to emerge.

Curnen peeked out, only her eyes above ground level.

Rob sagged against the tombstone, shaking as the adrenaline burned itself out. "God *dammit,* Curnen," he breathed.

She saw Rob and waved the envelope at him. He grabbed it, and she ducked back down the hole.

He turned the envelope over in his trembling fingers. It was age-tarnished and sealed with wax. He felt a single small piece of thick paper inside. He folded the envelope and stuffed it into his pants pocket, figuring this wasn't the best place to examine it. It was almost full daylight now.

Ten yards down the slope, almost to the forest, Curnen emerged from a hole hidden behind a clump of weeds. He wondered if she had burrows in graveyards all over the area. Before he could dwell on that creepy thought, she waved for him to follow as she dashed down the slope into the trees.

He needed no extra encouragement. He ran as hard as he could down the hill. Just as he reached the tree line and safety, a voice behind him yelled *"Hey!"* followed by a dog's furious barking.

"Wait for me!" he cried to Curnen, barely able to see her ahead of him. She flitted gracefully through underbrush that threatened to snag and trip him. Within moments, she was gone, and he could only continue straight down the hill away from the Gwinns, hoping he'd catch up with her somewhere ahead.

He just barely cleared a log directly in his path. When he landed on the other side, the wet leaves slid out from under his feet and he tumbled out of control. He grabbed at every tree and branch he rolled past, until suddenly the ground was gone and he fell through the air.

Something slapped at his palm and he clutched it with both hands. It was a thick, old grapevine and it held his weight, but now he dangled off the edge of a gully, twenty feet above the creek they'd earlier crossed.

He shifted his grip and wrapped one leg around the vine as well. He was five feet below the edge, which curved out over the creek. He'd be seen if he pulled himself back up, and the drop would land him painfully atop a jumble of smooth, slick river stones.

Dogs barked in the woods above, and men shouted instructions and curses. The overhang hid him from view, and the vine seemed solidly anchored to a tree above him.

He stayed as still as he could and listened. The dogs were much closer, and now he could make out words.

". . . some gubment sum'bitch . . ."

". . . cut his balls off and feed 'em to him . . ."

". . . let the dogs rip him up . . ."

Rob spotted several thick, knobby tree roots protruding from the bank. He could use them to descend, but not with his pursuers nearby. Now the dogs were so close, he heard their paws crunch on the leaves overhead, along with the much heavier steps of their masters. They barked right above him, but could not see him beneath the overhang.

"God-dang it," someone said, "he must've jumped down there and run off."

"Ain't nobody going to make that jump, ya dumb-ass," another voice responded. "These stupid dogs lost him." One of the dogs yelped as it received a solid smack of disapproval. "He must be hid up around here somewhere, maybe up in a tree or something."

Rob's shoulder muscles seemed about to rip loose from the bones, and the bruise across his back felt like a hot metal strip against his skin. He gritted his teeth so hard, he could barely breathe.

"Hey!" the first voice said. "Look!"

"Aw, *shit*."

Rob carefully turned his head. Curnen crouched on the other side of the creek, drinking water from her cupped hands. She ignored both Rob and the men above him.

"God-dang it, it's that wisp of a thing again," one of the men said. The braggadocio left his voice. "Poppa Rockhouse said we shouldn't have no truck with her."

"Gimme that rifle."

Curnen stood and raised her arms over her head, her palms upward. Her face was pink in the dawn. She kept her eyes on the Gwinns, opened her mouth, and emitted a soft throaty *hiss* that grew louder until it was almost a roar. As she did, a breeze rustled the trees above her.

"Put that gun down, she's going to call up a storm on us."

She whistled sharply three times, and the wind grew stronger. One of the dogs resumed barking. Rob heard another smack, and the dog yelped and softly whimpered.

"*Stop* that, man!" one of the Gwinns said, his voice trembling.

"What's wrong with you? You're shivering like a dog shitting peach pits."

"I'm still thinking about the way that one howled this morning. And now we run up on this bitch, it's just too much."

"Hey!" a new voice called from farther away. Rob again recognized Tiffany Gwinn. "Momma says for y'all to quit fooling around and get your asses back home. *Now!*"

The wind continued to rise, and now the tops of the trees creaked and groaned under it. Some squealed as they rubbed together. Brown and red leaves ripped free of their branches.

"Some gubment man was poking around the house," one of the men responded. "We chased him down here."

"Momma don't care! She says if she has to get off the porch, she's going to tan all of your hides, she don't care how old you are!"

"Hell, come on," the first man said, resigned. "We ain't going to find him with that girl running around. It must've been her, anyway."

Their voices faded as they tramped back up the hill. The wind died down as well. Curnen motioned that it was all clear.

Rob awkwardly climbed down the tree roots until he reached the ground. He fell against the muddy rise, gasping, his arms burning. Curnen splashed across the stream and knelt beside him.

He could not remember ever being in so much physical pain. His back and shoulders hurt so much, it brought tears to his eyes. She stroked his hand, making little sympathetic whimpers. It was so touching, it made him smile, and gradually the pain faded.

"That was . . . fun," he gasped.

She smiled, then impulsively kissed him. He didn't resist. Then she helped him sit up, and he pulled the envelope from his pocket.

He'd broken the wax seal during his wild escape. He withdrew a small rectangle of paper, clearly the one excised from the book in the strange little library. The missing stanza read:

> *Around him stood the myriad fae*
> *Whose love had grown to hate's decay*
> *They bound him to the spot he lay*
> *"You can do no harm while you be here."*

He stared at these words, trying to make them coherent, but it didn't help. What was so almighty special about this last verse? He looked up at Curnen. "Hon, maybe I've just been smacked around too much lately, but this doesn't make any sense at all."

She looked down in hard thought, then held out her left hand, fingers spread so that all six were obvious. She gestured with her right hand as if stroking a long beard.

He nodded. "Rockhouse."

She stood and pretended to stomp things on the ground and silently laugh; then she looked up at the sky in mock terror, mimicking those being trampled.

"Rockhouse treats people like that," he said, and she nodded. Then she stood very straight, chin high and eyes almost closed. She made a tall motion above her head, as if she wore a crown.

"Because he's a king?"

She nodded, then tapped her forehead.

"Because he's a king . . . he thinks?"

She shook her head. She made a wide, expansive gesture, then tapped her forehead again.

"Because . . . *everyone else* thinks he's a king? That's why everyone's scared of him?"

She nodded emphatically.

He looked at the verse again. *You can do no harm while you be here.* A light went on in his mind. "Wait . . . they took his crown away, didn't they? When he couldn't split that hickory nut. He's not the fairy feller anymore."

Curnen bounced up and down, nodding. She no longer looked mentally handicapped or physically distorted; she was an angry, melancholy girl glad to be shed of a terrible secret. She watched him closely.

He continued to think through the implications. "So Rockhouse still has influence because no one knows he lost his job as king. And if the last verse of this song gets out, they will. *That's* why it was hidden."

She wiggled her hand to say *close enough* and nodded.

"It doesn't heal broken hearts, then, does it?"

She shook her head sadly.

He closed his eyes and waited until the disappointment passed. Then he got to his feet, his tennis shoes slipping on the rocks. He put the verse back in his pocket. "I'm going to try to help someone, a girl who's been . . . bewitched, I guess, by Stoney Hicks. I may have to make this song public in order to do that."

She nodded.

"Will you get in trouble?"

She shrugged, then nodded. *Probably.*

"Then why did you help me?"

She touched her own heart, then his, and again mimed breaking sticks. Then she pretended to take half of his broken stick, and half of her own. She put them together to make one whole. There was no guile or deceit in her eyes.

He let his hand brush her cheek. "Honey, I'm sorry, but I barely know you. Can you take me back to my car?"

She looked down, and nodded. Tears ran freely down her face; he could almost feel her heart breaking. How could she care so much about him when she hardly knew him? Could she really hear what was inside him, under the self-pity and sadness and rage? Not even Anna had been able to do that, and she knew him better than anyone.

Impulsively, he pulled her into a hug. He felt her small, hard body against his, and from deep inside him surged a wave of unexpected tenderness. "I can't stay here with you, Curnen, I'm sorry," he said, amazed at the lump choking his voice. "But before I leave, I'll do my best to help you, too. Then . . ." He let his words trail off, because he realized that with Curnen, he didn't have to say anything.

Above them, a crow flew over, and its cry sounded mocking to Rob's ears.

28

Bliss awoke with a start. Dawn illuminated the room in shades of gray, not yet bright enough for colors.

She lay curled up on the couch in the living room, her father's old fiddle on the floor beside her. The fire had died overnight, and her breath made little puffs as she yawned. She stretched, and the comforter slid to the floor. She'd slept in her shirt, underwear, and socks, and she felt goose bumps on her bare legs.

She looked down at the fiddle. She had no clear memory of removing it from the shelf after Mandalay left, but did recall scratching on it with her usual abysmal technique. Although she could make a guitar recite Shakespeare, she was almost completely inept at the fiddle. Her father, though, had been able to coax light and shadow from that same instrument.

She recalled drifting off with her hands touching the strings, imagining that through them she was able to connect somehow with the man who'd once played them with such finesse. Earlier she'd poured herself a big glass of Gwinn moonshine and tried strumming idly on her guitar, but it did nothing to soothe her pain. The alcohol, though, made her drowsy, and eventually she'd fallen asleep. All she recalled from her dreams was that same image of a deathly hand clawing out of the ground.

She went to the bathroom, then into the kitchen to start the coffee. She couldn't take another day off, yet the thought of driving to work and then dealing with either the endless hours of waiting or another life-threatening accident filled her with weariness. Avoiding the decision, she went back into the bathroom, brushed her teeth, gargled, and went out to the back porch.

The sun had not yet topped the mountains, so the air was filled with murky illumination that hid the edges of almost everything. The wind was cold on her bare legs and quickly insinuated itself under her baggy shirt. A bird flew over the pond and snatched an insect from its surface. A dove called out from the forest.

Something in the corner of her eye caught her attention. She turned and looked past the side of the house toward the driveway and the road beyond. She stared for nearly five minutes before the incredibly obvious discrepancy penetrated her brain.

Rob's car was still there.

Doyle awoke on the couch, swung his feet to the floor, and jumped when they touched something soft. Berklee lay curled up on the floor beside him, arms wrapped tight around herself against the night's chill. She wore sweatpants, a T-shirt, and no socks.

He lifted her under her arms and guided her onto the couch. Then he tucked the blanket around her. As he started for the bathroom, she said woozily, "Doyle?"

He stopped. "Yeah."

"Had a bad dream," she murmured, like a sleepy child.

"What about?"

She frowned a little, trying to remember it. "Seems like . . ." Then her eyes snapped open wide and she sat up, almost screaming. Doyle rushed over and took her in his arms, feeling her whole body tremble. She stammered, "Something . . . coming out . . . reaching up—"

"Shh, it's okay, I'm here," he said, stroking her hair.

She felt like a frightened rabbit in his embrace. "Something was . . . a hand came out of a grave . . . reaching for me . . . trying to kill me."

Doyle frowned. Had he dreamed the same thing? The image sure sounded familiar, but then it could've come from some horror movie he'd once seen. "Well, it was just a nightmare," he said gently. "It's daylight now, it can't hurt you."

"I'm scared, Doyle," she said into his chest. "I don't want to die. I feel dead already sometimes, but I don't want to die for real."

"You're not going to die," he said, and kissed the top of her head. She cried softly in his embrace.

Peggy Goins looked at her husband asleep beside her. He'd left the usual circle of saliva on his pillow, and now snored like a trolling motor at full throttle. His gray hair stuck out at odd angles from his square block of a head. She climbed out of bed, nudged her feet into her slippers, and pulled on her robe.

A quick look at the parking lot told her Rob had not returned to the Catamount Corner. She sighed; he must be with Bliss. The girl, bless her, was out of her depth with real leadership decisions.

Still, as with all the true Tufa, Peggy understood that Bliss's status could be neither revoked nor questioned. Mandalay led them and Bliss was her regent, just as Rockhouse led his people, and that was that. As the wind blows, so the trees bend.

She started the coffee and went out back for her first cigarette. She saw no sign of Curnen around the Dumpster, which was usually a good omen. But something bothered her nonetheless. She'd had that same dream again, of the hand clawing out of a grave. This time it was crystal clear, almost a vision of a real occurrence, and if she'd believed the dead could truly walk again in this world, she'd be frightened.

More than the image itself bothered her, though. She knew that if the dream came to *her* so clearly, it must've at some level touched all the First Daughters, and maybe everyone with any Tufa blood at all. Most would write it off as a nightmare, something inspired by a scary late-late show or a bad plate of food. But ripples traveling that far always came from something that made a huge splash, and Peggy wished she knew the source so she could be ready for it.

Rob emerged from the forest into Bliss's backyard. The sun peeked over the mountains just enough to flood the valley with light that twinkled off the dewy grass. His legs ached, his shoulders felt as if they'd been pulled off his body and then reattached, and he was both sweat-soaked and chilled. He kept checking his pocket to make sure the piece of paper hadn't magically vanished, although the words were safe in his head.

He looked behind him. Curnen stood at the edge of the forest, half-hidden behind a tree. Her expression was unreadable. She watched him sadly, steam rising from her sweaty skin. Then she flitted away.

Rob collapsed into his car, wincing as he settled back into the driver's seat. He started the engine and let it idle as he endured the sudden wave of exhaustion. He couldn't wait for the Catamount Corner's soft mattress and heavy blankets.

He glanced at the house. Bliss sat on the side steps, watching him. She wore a robe, sweatpants, and a white T-shirt, and her long hair hung loose around her shoulders.

"Hi," she said. She didn't smile or show any other emotion. "Wondered why your car was still here."

He forced himself to his feet, but leaned on the door for support. He hoped it looked nonchalant. "I found it," he said.

"Your car?"

"The last verse of 'The Fate of the Tyrant Fae.'"

She didn't visibly react.

"And I know why that asshole Hicks wanted to keep it quiet, too. So quiet, he buried it with Great Kate Gwinn."

"Curnan showed you." It was not a question.

"Yeah, well, I've got it now, and I'm about to go shove it down that old bastard's throat. Then we'll see if I don't talk to Stella Kizer."

"Wait!" she cried, and ran to the vehicle. She knelt by his door. "If I take you to where you can find your friend's wife, will that be enough? Will you keep the song a secret until . . ." She trailed off. What *was* the right moment to destroy the Tufa?

"You know what it says, don't you?"

"Not the words. But the purpose."

"And what do you think about it?"

"I think that you need help. And not just to find that Kizer woman."

"You *want* me to take down Rockhouse, then?"

"I think you're being guided by the powers that guide us, and they want it. And I'm willing to help."

He thought about it. "The Gwinns didn't see me, but they saw Curnen. They may figure out what we took. I was going to wait until tonight, but now that I think about it, I should go see Rockhouse now. Make him tell me where to find Stella Kizer."

"You're exhausted, Rob. Look at you."

"I'm fine. A cup of coffee and I'm good to go."

"Then give me five minutes. You have your guitar, right?"

"Yeah. Why?" But she was already inside. He yawned and felt his TM joint pop. He'd kill for a nap right now. Still, if he had a real chance to find Stella Kizer, and to wipe that smug grin off Rockhouse's face, he wasn't going to miss it.

Bliss stripped as she ran through the house to her bedroom, where she threw on jeans, a flannel shirt, and her tennis shoes. Then she quickly called the station and told them she'd be out again today. Her boss started to berate her, but she used her voice and Tufa skills to mollify him. She would put in extra hours to make up the time, she assured him. After all, she'd hardly missed any time before this, and never at short notice, so he could afford to cut her some slack. He grudgingly agreed, and she put that worry aside.

That done, she grabbed her denim jacket and rushed back downstairs to rejoin Rob before he had time to really think about things.

"You sure this is the right way?" Rob demanded as, still following Bliss's directions, they turned off the overgrown gravel road onto a path that would've bounced a tank driver out of his vehicle. Bliss had her hand braced against the roof so her head wouldn't slam into it. He could imagine nothing other than a tractor ever using the two ruts down which they now proceeded, and any moment, he expected the sound of protesting metal as the car's oil pan or tailpipe was ripped away.

"This is where to find Rockhouse's people," Bliss answered. "Remember how I told you they had their own place, just like we have the barn where you played? We're going there."

"Will they be there this early in the morning?"

"They'll be there."

The road dead-ended at what looked like a huge patch of briars and saplings. Rob stopped the car. Bliss said, "Just push through. It's not as thick as it looks."

"What's on the other side?"

"Like I said, Rockhouse's place."

"Another barn?"

"Look, will you just drive? It'll take me twice as long to describe it as it will for you to see it for yourself."

Choking down the spike of anger, Rob muttered, "All right, whatever," and pressed the gas pedal down slowly until the bumper parted the briars. He gritted his teeth against the sound of sharp thorns scraping against metal, and struggled to hold the steering wheel straight. She was right, though; the passage took maybe fifteen seconds, and they emerged into an open space that made him slam on his brakes despite their sluglike pace.

They looked out over a gently sloping mountainside, cleared of all but a few trees. An old mill, its big wheel immobile and partially buried in a dry creek bed, dominated the scene. The walls had been removed, so only the frame and semi-intact roof still stood, like the ruined gate in *Rashomon*. The mill mechanism inside had been taken apart, leaving only pieces too big to carry, including one of the grinding stones.

And behind this, black and dark in the morning sun, was the wide mouth of a cave.

It stretched thirty feet across the hillside, ten feet high at the center. It descended almost at once, but there was light visible far down and back. Music also drifted out, distorted by the stone walls so that it sounded harsh and arrhythmic, like the songs played by the Gwinns.

"They have their barn dance in a *cave*?" Rob said as he took out his guitar.

"It used to be a bootlegger's hideout. They'd meet up here to play and run off some moonshine. For a long time, it was the biggest cash business in Cloud County. But then they made beer sales legal, and somebody opened a liquor store in Unicorn, so the demand dried up."

Skeletons hung from the arched opening like ghastly, primitive wind chimes. Three were deer, one must have been a bear, but a third looked unmistakably human, even though it was missing its skull, hands, and feet.

Rob pointed at that skeleton with his guitar case. "Must be the last person who crashed this party. So we just walk in?"

"You do. Remember the scene when Rockhouse showed up at the barn? It'd be the same thing if they saw me here."

"Rockhouse knows me."

"Rockhouse is sitting on the front porch of the post office, trust me. I'll keep him busy. Besides, you're not looking for him, are you?"

"Stoney knows me, too."

"Stoney saw you once, when he was drunk. He won't remember you."

"I have a black eye. That's pretty obvious."

"Only if you're looking for it. Unless you mention it, no one in there will see it. They'll just see a Tufa they don't know coming to jam with them."

"I'm not a Tufa."

"*Stop* it, Rob. People who think they have Tufa blood in them are always coming to Cloud County, looking for their roots. Some stumble onto our barn dance, some find this cave. It's not that unusual, and more than likely, they'll just let you play and hope you go away soon."

"More than likely," he repeated doubtfully.

"You won't get better odds."

"How do I get past the guards?"

"There are no guards. They don't need them. It's like our dance—you can't find it unless you're meant to, or unless a real Tufa brings you. And I mean, look at it. Would you go in there if you didn't have to?"

He looked at the cave, back at Bliss, then at the cave again. "It's a little too Orpheus for me."

"Yes, but she's not Euridice," Bliss said. "The best you can hope for is Persephone."

"Yeah," Rob said. Rationally, he knew he should walk away, that he was liable to learn that *Deliverance* was in fact a documentary if he entered the cave. But rationality had nothing to do with his presence here. "Are you taking my car back, then?"

"I don't need a car," she said. "Just be careful, don't eat or drink anything, and get out as soon as she says she's not leaving."

"You're so sure that's what she'll say."

"As sure as I am of the sunrise. It's not her fault; it's just the way things work."

"Even if I sing the song?"

"Won't matter. Rockhouse isn't here."

He laughed coldly. "Right. Okay, then."

He started toward the entrance, then looked back. Bliss was already gone. Reflexively he looked up, but the sky was clear and empty.

29

Steps carved into the stone led down toward the light and music. Beer cans, broken glass pipes, and crushed Styrofoam cups littered the way, growing thicker as Rob descended. He gingerly stepped over a discarded condom.

The path narrowed to a tunnel that turned just ahead. A thick electrical cable was attached to the stone wall near the passage's roof, and a series of copper pipes ran along the ceiling. He stopped and listened. It sounded like at least two dozen people talking, laughing, and singing. Guitars, mandolins, and banjos rang out, completely lacking the sense of fun and skill he'd heard at the barn dance. These people had no interest in harmonizing, in weaving any sort of musical spell. They just played for themselves, even if they all played the same tune.

Heat surged up, making him sweat like he was in a sauna. Worse, the smell was awful: body odor, burning chemicals, and human waste. He wasn't sure he could stand it without gagging.

He looked back and up at the entrance. The blue sky outlined the skeletons, especially the one he suspected was human. The bones swayed in the faint wind and clacked softly together.

His belly knotted with tension, but the sleep deprivation also gave him a sort of bravado. He stood up straight, flexed his fingers around the guitar case handle, and entered the cavern.

It was a great upside-down bowl, the center thirty feet high. A pinpoint of daylight was visible at the top of the dome, which was good since it let the smoke from the fires escape. He counted three: one at the center of a group of men, the other two small ones that heated water for a row of tubes and pipes set up on a series of tables. He realized with a start they were brewing methamphetamine down here, as well as making moonshine. The very air was probably filled with poisonous fumes. So much for rustic backwoods charm.

Then he noticed the people. They had the same black hair as all the Tufa, as he himself did, but that was where the similarity ended. Clad in ratty overalls and well-worn clothes from the last century, they milled about muttering and laughing. He saw wide-flared jeans, tube tops decorated with peace signs, and even grunge-style tattered flannel. Everyone looked sullen, and as Bliss had predicted, no one glanced his way.

More than their clothes were distorted, he realized. There was something indefinable but definitely wrong in their physical appearance, a contradictory spindliness and softness that gave the impression of insects rather than people. They didn't move; they scuttled, or crept, or just sat still like spiders waiting for prey to cross their path.

Around the central fire clustered the musicians, their instruments battered from misuse and lack of care. It was the photo negative of what he'd seen and experienced at the barn dance, and it both disgusted and frightened him.

He walked slowly, stepping around rocks and bodies he hoped were only passed out. He kept his face neutral, but looked around for Stoney Hicks and Stella Kizer. Stoney, at least, was a good head taller than anyone else in the cave, so he'd be easy to spot.

He reached the circle of musicians. He waited until they finished an atrocious version of "Companions Draw Nigh," then said, "Hi. Mind if I sit in?"

Only one of them looked up at him. He had a beard down to the middle of his chest, and only two visible teeth, one in each jaw. "If your ass'll fit on the box," he said. His eyes were all iris, and the skin around them was a creased, dried-parchment map of his hard life.

Rob sat on the indicated apple crate, opened his case, and took out his guitar. By the time he got it situated, the banjo player had begun a too-fast version of "Little Omie Wise," and the others jumped right in. It took Rob several bars to catch up.

The banjo player began to sing in a voice so pure and high, it made Rob think of a castrato:

I'll tell you a story of little Omie Wise,
How she became deluded by John Lewis' lies.

He told her to meet him down by Adams's Springs;
Some money he would bring, and some other fine things.

Rob knew the song, but now he felt the words with an intensity he never expected. He found it hard to breathe and his eyes began to water, not from the mishmash of fumes but from tears that happened so fast, he didn't notice them until they dripped onto his hands. He wiped them furiously and choked down the guilt, despair, and hopelessness that swelled inside him.

He looked around the cave again. People milled about in groups now, still unconcerned about or unaware of his presence. Bliss was certain Stella Kizer was here, but where? In one of the side caves, some blocked with curtains? Were these like the little rent-by-the-hour bungalows behind the Beehive Truck Stop on Highway 69 in Kansas?

As if on cue, one of these curtains was pulled back and Stoney Hicks emerged. He was naked to the waist, and his jeans were unclasped. He looked like a black-haired, black-eyed barbarian god, every muscle chiseled and defined. His skin gleamed with sweat, and his hair was tangled, but that did little to dim his glory.

He turned his back to the room and urinated on the cave wall, then hitched up his pants and joined one of the groups. He sipped from the mason jar they passed around.

A moment later, Stella Kizer stepped from behind the same curtain. She wore only a ragged blanket tied under her arms. If she felt self-conscious, it didn't show: she had eyes only for Stoney. She stood demurely behind him, waiting for him to acknowledge her presence. Her face was drawn tight, and her hair also a tangled mess. The sophisticated spitfire he'd met at the Catamount Corner was totally gone.

He took a deep breath to shake off the despair and started to stand up. But then the music hit him again:

> *He hugged her, he kissed her, he turned her around*
> *He threw her in deep water, where he knew she would drown*
> *He jumped on his pony, and away he did ride*
> *The screams of little Omie went down by his side.*

Rob shuddered as the emotions in him seized up, choking the physical breath from his body. Everything he thought he'd gotten past resurfaced, filling him with more despair than he'd ever experienced. What the fuck was happening?

Through hot tears he saw Stoney turn to Stella and painfully pinch her ass through the blanket. She did not cry out, but she clutched the fabric to keep it from falling away.

The singer crooned,

Two boys went a-fishin' one fine summer day,
They saw little Omie go floating away.

Rob stopped playing, hunched over his guitar, and began to sob. No one noticed or tried to console him. The music continued:

They sent for John Lewis, John Lewis came by,
When confronted with her body, he broke down and cried.

Rob stood up. The others ignored him, except for Stella. She stared, astonished to see him and confused by his tears.

He no longer cared about her. He kicked his guitar case aside and stumbled away from the fire toward the cave entrance. But he was disoriented, and somehow found himself in one of the side tunnels. He kept moving into the dark, crying aloud and feeling like each sob might snap him in half. He *was* the worst person in the world, he'd sold out everything he believed was important for a few minutes in the spotlight, and even Anna had been sacrificed on the altar of his narcissism. Just like Omie Wise, she'd died because she trusted him and came to him when he asked her to. Now he deserved to die slowly and painfully, each bit of agony an atonement for the hurt he'd inflicted on others. How had he ever thought he could do good? Real men did good. He was a petulant, whiny boy.

Although he'd gone around several turns in the tunnel, the singer's voice seemed just as pure, just as loud.

> *My name is Rob Quillen, my name I'll never deny*
> *I murdered little Anna, she fell from the sky."*

He got tangled up in another curtain, this one much heavier than the others. He swiped at it with his hands as it fell over him, then finally grabbed two thick handfuls and pushed forward.

The curtain dropped away. Light blinded him.

He saw blue sky directly ahead and the tops of trees far below.

Then his momentum carried him out of the tunnel and into the air.

He screamed in free fall as he tumbled three hundred feet to the base of the cliff below.

30

It was midmorning by the time Bliss got into Needsville and stepped onto the post office porch. As she'd
told Rob, Rockhouse was there, all alone and slowly
rocking. She stood with her arms folded and waited to
be acknowledged.

When it was clear she wouldn't be, she said, "Most
men grow their beards for winter and shave them in the
spring. But you just have to be contrary, don't you?"

The old man stopped rocking and turned to look at
her. He was clean-shaven again, and his cheeks were
pink with the freshness of it. "You taking another day
off? You'll be out of a job if you keep that up. Those are
tough to come by these days, especially if you get a name
as a slacker."

"Don't worry about my job," she said.

"Whoo-ee, you sound pissy. About to get your month-
lies?"

Bliss sat in one of the other chairs. "Why'd you grow
that beard, anyway?"

"Sometimes a man just needs to get hairy. Has to let nature have its way for a while. If you're one of them modern girls who shaves her privates, you know what I mean."

"My privates are none of your business."

"Your momma never shaved hers."

Bliss narrowed her eyes. "That's beneath even you, Rockhouse. And you won't piss me off, so you might as well stop trying."

"Don't sound like I need to," he said with a self-satisfied wink.

"You're mad at me because I tried to broker a truce about this whole situation, aren't you? Didn't even matter that I came up to your place to do it, out of respect for your position. You took it as an insult, just like when we stood up to you at the barn dance. And you took it out on Uncle Node."

He looked away from her, at something in the far distance. "You know, before the power company cleared out trees for the phone lines, the top of that hill used to have a whole stand of sugar maples. Still get them damn saplings in the spring from seeds that just won't give up trying to sprout, even after all this time. They ain't never gonna grow to trees, but they come back every spring and have to be cut down. Kind of like the people who think they're smarter than me."

"Really?" Bliss said dryly.

He looked at her with a bully's smug amusement. "Girl, you ain't nothing to me. *Nothing.* You think you can protect that little snot Mandalay until she gets growed up and haired over, well, I got news for you: I could rip that little whore to pieces right in front of you and there wouldn't be a damn thing you could do. I *let* her stay, because I get tickled watching you folks sneak around and try to outfox me. And you, Miss Bliss? You're a joke. A baby-sitter who has to take orders from the baby."

Bliss was not intimidated. She leaned toward him and said,

"Keep rambling, old man. Keep acting like you never missed that stroke in front of the queen."

Pure hatred blazed from his eyes, and his features distorted as something behind them tried to escape. But it was only for an instant. Then he smiled and said, "This ain't the first time someone's tried to shellack me. Won't be the last. For me, that is. Might be the last time for them. Every spring there's fewer and fewer saplings to cut down."

Bliss started to fire back, *But this is the first time the night wind's done it.* She held back, though, as a new thought struck her.

Rockhouse *didn't know.* He thought it was another plot, this time by Mandalay. He had no idea the night winds themselves were not just facilitators this time, but *instigators.* They'd sent the apparition to Rob. They'd sent the Kate Campbell song to her. They'd probably even planted the suggestion that Rockhouse grow a beard so Rob wouldn't recognize him right away.

"What's wrong with you?" Rockhouse said, bringing her out of her reverie.

She stood, straightened her jacket, and said, "Maybe you're right, Rockhouse. Maybe this time you'll outfox us all again. But sooner or later, you'll slip up. And then what happens, huh?" She patted him on the arm. "You have a good day, old man. Stay warm. Fall's coming, and you never know when there might be a chill in the air."

"Why, thank you kindly," he said mockingly. "And speaking of falls, shame about that boy from the TV show. Must've been a suicide, or maybe just an accident. Reckon we'll never know."

Bliss went cold inside, but kept it off her face. "What does that mean?"

"You'll find out. Surprised I had to tell you about it."

"You're pathetic, Rockhouse."

"You know they say trouble comes in threes. First Uncle Node, then your boyfriend. I'd be watching my back if I was you."

He turned to look back into the distance, dismissing her from his presence. Bliss forced herself to walk casually back to the Catamount Corner, where her truck was still parked from last night. She drove with the same nonchalance until she knew she was out of his sight, then floored it.

Rob wasn't sure how much time had passed before he opened his eyes. He saw blue sky, which was also the last thing he remembered seeing. He'd read "An Occurrence at Owl Creek Bridge" in high school, and wondered if he was still in mid-fall, heading toward certain death below. He didn't seem to be moving, though, and no wind whistled past his head.

He shifted a little and felt solid ground under him. He reached down and touched rocky dirt. Okay, he was on the ground, but there was no way he was still in one piece. Was he split open like a grape, then? If he moved his hand another inch, would he encounter one of his own internal organs? What would the texture of a disembodied pancreas feel like?

Slowly he turned his head. He saw the tops of trees, now above him instead of below. A flock of starlings rose noisily from their branches. He wondered if they were going to circle back and begin to feed on his shattered remains. He'd seen crows and blackbirds picking over road kill, and was glad these little guys wouldn't have to worry about traffic.

Then he heard a woman singing.

He followed the sound with his eyes. He wondered if there was no pain because his spine was severed somewhere below his neck.

Then he saw her. She was younger than he was, with long black hair and a strong, lean body. She wore tight jeans and a black tank top that showed off her curves to excellent effect. At the moment, she was on her knees, weeding a patch of flowers that was clearly some sort of shrine.

And she was singing.

John Lewis, John Lewis, will you tell me your mind?
Do you intend to marry me or leave me behind?
Little Omie, little Omie, I'll tell you my mind.
My mind is to drown you and leave you behind.

He raised up on his elbows. It didn't hurt. In fact, nothing about him hurt, not even his eye, the bruise on his back, or the stitched lump on his head. When he looked down at himself, there were no injuries, no blood. Except for a little dirt, he was spotless. There could be only one explanation for that.

She looked up and stopped singing. "Back with us?"

"I always thought the idea of sexy angels was just a gimmick to sell lingerie," he said. "But I'm not going to argue."

She smiled. "Careful. My boyfriend has a direct line to God."

He sat all the way up. He wasn't even stiff. "I expected heaven to be more pastel. Kind of Maxfield Parrish. But I can live with this."

"You're not dead, wise guy."

"Really?" He looked behind him, and there it was. He sat at the base of the sheer cliff he was certain he'd fallen out of. There were several cave openings toward the top, far too high for him to have survived. "I'm pretty sure I fell out of one of those."

The girl laughed, low and sexy. "Sure you did."

He got to his feet. Everything was there, and everything

worked. There wasn't even a fresh scratch or new bruise. "I did. I remember it very clearly."

"And I suppose something just flew in and caught you at the last moment?"

Now that he was upright and the last cobwebs were gone from his brain, he looked at the girl more closely. "You look familiar."

"So do you."

"I was on TV for a while." He offered his hand. "Rob Quillen."

"So was I. Bronwyn Hyatt."

Her grip was as firm as any man's, and he recognized the name. "Yeah, I know you. Well, that is, I know *of* you. You were in the army, got rescued on live TV. Killed how many enemy soldiers?"

"More every time it's told. And you were on *So You Think You Can Sing?*"

"That's me. What's this?" he said with a gesture at the flowers.

"A memorial. My older brother used to bring me here when I was a little girl. He taught me the basic chords and how to sing harmony. He also showed me how a man was supposed to behave around a girl he respected and loved. Set the mark pretty high for my boyfriends later. Too bad I never held 'em to it, like I should have."

"I take it he's no longer with us?"

"No. He died back in the spring."

"I'm sorry. Was he sick?"

"He was stabbed."

There was nothing polite he could say back to that, so he resumed looking around. He spotted something half-hidden behind some rocks. He picked up the neck of his now-smashed guitar, still attached by the strings to the bridge pegs. "Look at this."

"Needs more than restringing, I think. It must've pissed off somebody."

"No, this is mine. It fell just like I did. From up there."

She put her hands on her hips in annoyance. "Well, maybe whoever or whatever caught you only had two hands and did the best he or she could."

He tossed it aside. "Ah, it's no great loss."

"That's a terrible thing to say about a musical instrument."

He chuckled. "*John* Hiatt wrote a whole song about that. He related to you?"

"He spells his name differently from mine."

They were quiet for a time. The sadness in her eyes touched him, and he asked gently, "I don't mean to pry, and it's totally none of my business, but . . . you said your brother was *stabbed*?"

"Yes. By my ex-boyfriend."

"Yikes. That's tough."

She nodded. "More than you know. They were arguing about me. Hard not to feel responsible somehow." She returned to the flower bed. "I laid awake thinking that for a lot of nights. If I'd done this, or said that, then it might not have happened. It was all my fault."

"I know what you mean," Rob said slowly. The numbness grew within him, threatening to choke him anew. "Had a lot of those nights myself."

"But I realized something," she continued as she weeded. "Something real important."

"Which was?"

"I didn't hold the knife."

He knelt opposite her and began helping. There weren't many weeds, but they had long roots that clung tenaciously to the soil. "Sometimes you don't have to."

"Yes, you do," she said firmly. "Someone kills for their *own* reasons, not yours. And they carry the responsibility for it, not you."

"Your boyfriend get that message from God?" he said with a half grin.

She laughed. "Maybe. He did help me understand it."

They worked together in silence after that. For some reason, Rob felt it was important to help Bronwyn spruce up her memorial. By the time they finished, it was almost noon, and he was starving, thirsty, and exhausted. He realized that except for his brief nap at the bottom of the cliff, he hadn't slept in nearly two days.

"Thanks," she said as they stood. "It went a lot faster with your help."

He tried not to appreciate her sweaty cleavage, but failed. "Always honored to help a war hero. I don't suppose you could give me a ride? My car's up there."

"Sorry, I didn't drive. But there's a trail over there behind that stand of cedar trees. Meanders a bit, but goes right to the top. Comes out by the old mill."

"Thanks." He paused, then said, "I know Bliss Overbay. And her sister, Curnen. They've told me some wild things about the Tufa, but you know what? I believe them. So . . . thanks for catching me."

She said nothing, but just enigmatically smiled. As he turned to walk away, she called, "There's one more thing I learned about sadness."

"What's that?"

"It'll follow you as long as it knows you're watching. So don't look back."

"I'll remember that," he said. He walked on, then turned, but as he'd now learned to expect, Bronwyn Hyatt was gone.

Bliss's truck burst through the briars and nearly rear-ended Rob's rental car. She jumped out and yelled, "Rob! Rob!"

She ran to the mouth of the cave. "Rob!" she called down, her voice echoing back at her. There was no reply. She took a deep breath, made a gesture of protection, and went quickly down the steps.

The cave was empty.

She gagged on the smell, and almost vomited. But there was no one present. All the fires were out, and even the meth equipment was cold. It looked like it had been abandoned for months.

"Rob!" she yelled. "Goddammit, Rob!"

Her cry bounced around the great rock dome. When it faded, only absolute silence remained.

She climbed the stairs. She felt as if she'd been pummeled, and the slight headache from last night's moonshine only added to it. There would be nothing to do but look for his body at the bottom of the cliff.

She was about to cry when a voice said, "I thought you couldn't go down there."

He stood beside his car, disheveled but clearly in one piece. She ran to him and threw her arms around him. "What happened?" she demanded. "The cave's empty."

"Beats me. It was hopping when I left."

"Left? Where did you go?"

He made a long, descending whistle.

"Are you all right?"

"I'm fine. Better than fine, actually. Nothing hurts anymore. At all."

She hugged him again. "I'm really glad to hear that. Really."

"But I still need to talk to Stella."

"Y'ain't gonna find her this way," a new voice said.

Rob and Bliss both turned. An old man now sat on the hood of Rob's car. He wore overalls and a sweat-stained Jack Daniel's baseball cap. The shade from the bill hid his face. Something about him struck Rob as familiar, but with all his recent odd experiences, he couldn't place it.

Bliss stepped toward him. *"Where are they?"* she said through her teeth.

The old man spit on the ground. "Rockhouse knows this boy's been diggin' around." He indicated Rob, then pointed at Bliss. "And you spooked him good this morning. So he's moved things."

"He can't just *move* things," Bliss insisted.

The old man grinned; he showed only three teeth. "Rockhouse can do a whole bunch of things he don't tell people about."

"I'm not trying to spook anybody," Rob protested. "I just want to talk to my friend's wife."

The old man snorted. "Nobody dragged her anywhere, you know. She went on her own two feet."

"Well, Pops, if that's true, why does everybody want to keep me from hearing her say it for herself?"

The old man shifted his foot, and suddenly Rob recognized him: Jessup, the strange tree gnome from his dream. Now he was normal sized and dressed in regular clothes, but the face and voice were the same, and he rested an identically swollen foot on the car's bumper. "All right, no need to get all cattywompus about it," Jessup said. "He's moved down to the Pair-A-Dice."

Bliss gasped. "No way."

"Yes indeedy way. Moved his whole bunch down there. Maybe for good, I don't know. Least until all this blows over."

"That's . . . he can't *do* that."

"He surely did."

Bliss turned to Rob. "The Pair-A-Dice is neutral ground, it's where we can all meet and play together without fighting. If he's moved his bunch into it, he's broken his own agreement with the community." She turned back to the old man. "You're sure about this?"

"Course I'm sure!" the old man said. "Go see for yourself if you don't believe me."

"Oh, I will." She stamped back to her truck.

Jessup slid from the fender and, favoring his swollen foot, moved aside. "Will Stoney be there?" Rob called to Bliss as he opened his car door.

"Where else?" She was already in the seat and buckled up.

An impossibly strong gust of air struck then. Rob knew the Kansas straight-line winds, and this was stronger. He covered his eyes and peeked between his fingers.

The wind sheared the leaves from the trees with the ferocity of a bladed weapon. Where moments earlier, the colors of autumn were everywhere, now he saw bare branches appear, still swaying from being suddenly denuded.

"Oh, no," Bliss said, so softly it was barely a breath. The Widow's Tree waved in the distance, more branches newly stripped. She had no time.

Before Rob even turned his key, Bliss gunned her truck's engine, made a wide 180 turn across the uneven ground, and roared away. Rob knew he couldn't find the Pair-A-Dice by himself, and wasn't even sure he could remember how to get back to town. He tried to catch up, but the rental car just couldn't handle the roads like the truck. By the time he reached blacktop again, she was long gone.

31

Doyle wiped his hands as Rob finished an extremely condensed version of the last twenty-four hours. He left out most of the really strange bits, including the poetry fragment and the fall from the cliff, but it was still a wildly improbable tale, and hearing it spoken aloud only reinforced that.

"So the upshot of this is you need directions to the Pair-A-Dice?" Doyle summarized as he closed the hood on the old Chevy pickup. "Or did I miss something?"

"I need *help*," Rob said. "Even if I find it, I can't just march in there by myself."

"No, if Rockhouse's people are crawlin' all over it, that wouldn't be too bright," Doyle agreed. "But really, this ain't any of your business. If your buddy's wife wants to be with Stoney—"

"I *just want to hear her say it*!" he almost yelled. "And I want someone else to hear it, so we can both go to the cops and tell them Terry's wife is not a crime victim."

WISP OF A THING

A car pulled up outside, and a moment later, Berklee appeared silhouetted in the garage door. She wore low-rider black pants and a top that revealed her navel. She carried a small cooler, evidently Doyle's lunch. "Am I interrupting anything?" she asked guardedly. "I can come back later."

"*You* know," Rob said to her, now unable to keep the desperation from his voice. "You know what Stoney Hicks can do. I just want to make sure my friend's wife is with him because she wants to be, and she's not being forced into anything."

Berklee froze as if Rob had just pointed a gun at her: eyes wide, mouth open in a gasp that never quite appeared, weight rocked back on her heels. She and Doyle exchanged a quick glance. Then she composed herself and said carefully, with tight faux casualness, "I'm not sure I know what you mean. I knew Stoney in high school, but—"

"Oh, come *on*," Rob snapped.

"Uhm," Doyle said quickly, "as a rule, we don't mess in Tufa stuff."

"I thought you were part Tufa, both of you."

"Yeah, and you're part Japanese or whatever—"

"Filipino."

"Yeah, but you wouldn't go to the Philippines and start telling 'em what to do, would you?"

He had a point, which took some of the steam from Rob's annoyance. He threw up his hands and said, "Look, you don't want to help, don't. No one else in town seems to care, either. It's just some stranger, she's there because she wants to be, nobody's business, yadda yadda. Just give me directions to the damn place, and I'll go do the best I can by myself."

In a tone neither angry nor annoyed, Berklee asked, "Why do *you* care?"

He looked at her seriously. "Because I know how Terry Kizer feels, and I can help."

Doyle and Berklee exchanged another look. "Would you excuse us for a moment?" Doyle asked.

Rob went outside the garage. The winds were still stripping the trees, making the branches sway and crack, and he squinted against the peppering dust. He'd given it his best, most persuasive shot, and if it didn't work, then he'd just have to go into the Tufa den alone. If he could even find it.

The tall tree he'd seen from the mountain outside the cave waved in the wind. Its limbs were now almost totally bare; only a few leaves remained, fiercely rattling like flags on a ship.

All his recent exertions caught up to him. His shoulders throbbed, his head alternately pounded and itched, and his black eye tingled maddeningly. Even his hands hurt. A musician should take better care of his hands.

At last Doyle and Berklee emerged from the garage. Neither looked happy. "All right," Doyle said. "Daddy'll watch the station while we're gone. What exactly do you want us to do?"

Rob felt an immense flood of relief. "Doyle, you don't know how much I appreciate this," he said with genuine feeling. Then he turned to Berklee. "Are you sure you want to go? It might get a little rough. And, you know, Stoney'll most likely be there."

"If he's not, then your friend's wife won't be, either," Berklee said. She had a distant, haunted look about her. "And yes, I want to go."

He nodded. In answer to Doyle, he said, "All I need you to do is stop anyone from messing with me once I get going."

"Get going doing what, exactly?"

Rob smiled coldly. "The very thing that brought me here."

Bliss reached the Pair-A-Dice. Vehicles already filled the parking lot. She clipped one old station wagon as she parked, but neither her truck nor the other vehicle would notice one more ding in the paint. She slammed her door closed and stalked between rusted old flatbeds and huge vintage Buicks, batting leaves from her face. She looked at the distant Widow's Tree towering above the forest and felt her stomach tighten. What should've taken weeks was now being done in hours, if not minutes. In a triumph of utter vindictiveness, Rockhouse wanted to ensure Curnen was gone for good.

Bliss stopped at the entrance and listened. Over the wind she heard the muffled noises of many people inside. When she pulled the handle, though, she found it locked.

She stepped back and kicked the door hard. "Open this goddam door now!" she yelled. Her voice had a timbre she rarely used, something her mother taught her and then warned her to employ only sparingly. "It's like when you beat a dog," she'd explained. "If you do it all the time, eventually the dog don't notice."

The dogs noticed this time. The door creaked open and a face peered out. It belonged to a man in his late teens, and seemed to be covered in red paint. "Miz Overbay?" he asked in disbelief.

She yanked the door from his grip and pushed past him. "What the hell happened to you, Cartille, you look like you got licked by a damn tomato. And where is that bastard uncle of yours?"

Cartille said nothing and quickly disappeared into the crowd. She pushed through the tightly packed mob until she reached the stage, where Rockhouse sat alone, tuning his banjo. The old man looked up, looked away, and then did a perfect double take. "What in the—?"

Bliss snatched the banjo out of his hands. "You and me,

fart-knocker," she growled so only he could hear. "In the kitchen, now."

He sputtered, "You ain't got no—"

Bliss slammed the instrument into its case, then made a hand gesture at him, another of the ones she'd been warned to save for special occasions. He drew back as if physically slapped. "You're crazy," he whispered.

"No, I'm pissed off. Now follow me." She grabbed him by the strap of his overalls and pulled him to his feet. He felt small and fragile to her, but she knew that was as deliberate a disguise as the way she made sure no one else in the room paid any attention to them. She slammed the kitchen door shut behind them, leaned back against it, and crossed her arms. The rowdy noise that came through the horizontal service window did not distract them.

"Honey, you must be on the rag something fierce to come stompin' in here like this," Rockhouse said.

"You insufferable old glob of possum spit," she hissed. "Tell me why you did this."

"Just felt like playin' me some music, that's—"

Before she even realized it, Bliss had slapped him so hard, her fingers were instantly numb. The blow knocked him onto the griddle surface, which luckily was not heated for cooking. He clutched the appliance to keep from falling, then turned and looked back over his shoulder at her. His eyes were black with rage. "You done made—"

She hit him again, this time a short punch to the kidney guided by her skill as an EMT. He groaned and fell to his knees, clipping his chin on the edge of the stove.

She was breathing rapidly now, and sweat coated her body under her clothes. She'd never physically attacked anyone before, and the thrill was almost sexual. "Now stop jerking me around," she whispered hoarsely, "and tell me what you're after."

He got slowly to his feet. Blood ran from his chin down onto his shirt. "Careful I don't git ahold of you like Stoney does his girls," he said as he eased himself back onto his chair.

She laughed. "Not a chance, old man. We're equals, remember?"

"Equals," he repeated dully.

"But since you brought it up, what's the deal with Stoney and this Yankee girl? I know he's done with her by now; why won't he just send her back to her husband?"

Rockhouse laughed. "Says she gives the best blow job in the valley."

"That's not it."

He wiped his chin and stared at the blood on his palm. "Ain't nobody broke my skin in a coon's age," he muttered.

She took a step toward him, and he flinched. She felt a rush of power. *"Tell me,"* she repeated.

"Her husband done found some of the poem on the Swett gravestones," he said with a sigh. "Too much of it for my tastes. Needed to get hold a'them rubbings he made, but none of us could sneak into Peggy Goins's place without her knowing. So we had her go git 'em. That woulda ended it, except Stoney decided he liked having a Yankee girlfriend."

Bliss gasped. The utter cruelty of what he'd revealed was more than she'd imagined even Rockhouse capable of. A debilitating enchantment that could never be broken doomed the hapless Stella to waste slowly away for no more reason than Rockhouse's convenience. "You mean you ruined that woman's whole life for nothing more than some *drawings*?"

"I didn't ruin nothing!" Rockhouse cried, suddenly furious. "It was *you*! You brung that Yankee boy around, showing him everything. You showed him the Swett plot, you took him up to y'all's singing."

Bliss slowly shook her head. For the first time in her short life, she truly felt her authority. "I always knew you were small, Rockhouse," she said softly. "I never knew how *pitiful* you were until now. I can't believe you ever scared me."

He smiled, his eyes atwinkle with malevolence. "You best be scared, Bliss. If that song gets out, if I go down . . . you all go with me. Including that little snot Mandalay."

She laughed. "Do you think I'd mind? You really ain't paying attention. The only reason I care is because I don't want to lose something so important to our people. You brought us here by pretending it was your idea, even though everyone knew you'd been kicked out on your fat ass. We've all played along because it's in our nature to do it, but you knew eventually we'd outgrow you. That's why you tried to keep us pure, and when that didn't work, you trotted out that idiotic music career. Did you really think the winds couldn't find you just down the road in Nashville?"

"So what's your big plan, emergency girl? How you gonna put a bandage on this?"

"All right, here's what's going to happen: I keep Rob from blowing your cover, and you drag your vermin back to their cave. This place stays neutral. Stoney sends his playmate back to her husband. And you take the curse off Curnen."

"It's too late for that." For emphasis, the wind rattled the sign on the roof.

"Not until the last leaf falls off the Widow's Tree. That's my deal. No negotiating." Then she made the hand sign that offered a binding agreement.

Rockhouse licked his lips. "And if I don't along with it?"

"If that song comes out, then you go down, and the Tufa have to acknowledge that they're free to leave. And they will. Whether I go with you or them is up to the night winds, but you lose the power to order people's lives around. You become what you really are." She stepped closer. "You got no choice, old man."

Without meeting her hard gaze, Rockhouse began to make the proper gesture in response that would seal the agreement. Just then they heard a commotion outside, and Rob's voice came over the speakers.

"A tyrant fae crossed the valley. . . ."

"Oh, no," Bliss breathed.

32

Ten minutes earlier, as Rob followed Berklee's car in his own, he made sure his iPhone noted the route. He could then retrace it to the service station, and from there to Needsville, if he needed to get back to town in a hurry. It felt good to be a bit less lost.

When the Pair-A-Dice finally came into view, Rob felt a sudden rush of panic. Even though it was the middle of the afternoon, the parking lot was full, just as it had been that first night. Apparently, Rockhouse could make his half of the Tufa drop everything at a moment's notice.

Doyle and Berklee parked at the edge of the lot, where they wouldn't get blocked in, and Rob followed suit. Doyle opened the trunk, pulled out a small eighteen-inch crowbar, and slipped it into one of the big leg pockets of the coveralls. Then he glanced back at Rob. "Got a couple of drop-forge socket wrenches here. They make quite a knot if you hit somebody hard enough." He produced a large Case knife from his pocket. "And I got this."

"No thanks," Rob said. "I'm really not trying to pick a fight."

"They might not see it that way," Doyle pointed out. But he closed the trunk without further comment.

They walked across the parking lot together, just as they'd done on his first night in town, only now a cloud of leaves formed a violent miniature tornado right in front of them. And once again, they heard music and laughter as they neared the building. Berklee nervously clutched Doyle's hand.

The Widow's Tree was visible in the distance, its great form swaying in the wind. Only a small clutch of leaves remained at the very top; the rest of its limbs were bare. Rob remembered the names carved in the trunk, and the sad realization that Curnen, too, had lost the person she loved most.

Just as they reached the entrance, a voice said, " 'Scuse me, y'all."

A big, potbellied man in overalls and a Confederate cap came around the building's corner. He carried a ten-pound mallet hammer easily in his right hand, like a trailer park Thor. "This is a private ay-fair. I'm betting you folks ain't on the guest list."

The man outweighed Rob probably by a hundred pounds, and had the mean, thick-browed look of so many rural bullies. Although the hair underneath the cap was Tufa black, his chin stubble was mostly white, except at the corners of his mouth, where it was stained dark yellow from tobacco juice. Matching streaks ran down the curve of his belly, marking times he hadn't spit far or hard enough.

"I just need to see the girl who's with Stoney Hicks," Rob said. "I know they're inside. It won't take five minutes if nobody gets too twitchy."

The big man smacked the mallet into his open hand. The sound was like meat hitting concrete. "You're not going in there, sonny-boy. You best just turn around the way you came before me and Mr. Whackie here get all over you."

Rob's temper began to sizzle. "I don't want any trouble, daddy-man, but I guarantee you I'm not walking away from it, either. All I want to do is talk to somebody, and I intend to do it. I suggest, if you don't want to get to know Mr. Whackie in a whole new way, you step aside."

"Whoa, now," Doyle said as he moved up beside Rob. His voice was low and even. "I don't see any need for everyone to get all huffy over this. Simple thing is, Mr. Gahan, if you pick a fight with Rob here, you're picking one with me, too. I know you used to beat up my daddy in school, you tell me every chance you get, but that was a long time ago. As you can see, my friend here ain't afraid of a scrap, and I don't think you're quite up to a double-header, especially with your bad hip."

Mr. Gahan's little pig eyes narrowed, and he stayed silent for a long moment. "Y'all ain't got no business here," he finally muttered.

"True enough," Doyle agreed. "But sometimes you got to go where you ain't got no business."

Gahan scowled, spit at the ground, then turned and lumbered back around the corner of the building. Doyle let out a deep breath, and took Berklee's hand. "Dang," he sighed. "That aged me."

"Me, too," Rob said. "Thanks."

"Wait," Berklee said, and turned to Doyle. Her expression was suddenly fearful and desperate. "I'm not sure what'll happen in there, but I want you to know, I really do love you."

"I know," Doyle said sadly. "I love you, too."

Rob grabbed the door handle. "Here we go," he said, and pulled it open.

Much like that first time days ago, the place was crowded and alive with conversation. The energy, though, felt completely different. It was simultaneously edgy, annoying, and compelling, the kind of buzz that helped fights break out at the slightest provocation and hinted that people might return home minus body parts. He heard screaming, farting, moaning, and even what sounded like animal sounds that could only have come from the men and women crammed into the room.

Doyle leaned close. "These ain't good people," he said warningly into Rob's ear.

"Oh, I know." Rob recalled the scene at the cave, the way the music had burrowed inside him and latched on to the guilt and pain he carried. Would the same thing happen again? His conversation with Bronwyn had gone a long way toward easing it, but was the effect permanent? He'd find out soon enough, he supposed.

Then Doyle pointed across the room, where Stoney's poster boy mane towered over the crowd. Rob couldn't see if Stella accompanied him.

"Do you see a girl with him?" Rob yelled to Doyle. "Red hair, about thirty, real tired-looking?"

Doyle couldn't tell, and turned to ask Berklee. "Hon, do you see—?"

She stood absolutely still, staring across the room at Stoney with a look so pained and needy that it would've been pitiful under different circumstances. Without looking at Doyle, she gasped, "I'm sorry," and began pushing her way through the crowd toward Stoney.

Doyle stood stunned, then turned to Rob. "I got to go get her," he said, the pain in his voice audible even over the noise. He didn't wait for Rob to respond.

Rob worked his way around the edge of the room. He spotted one young man with an odd, bright red face, and realized it was the ambusher he'd spray-painted. He was sure he'd be recognized, but nobody paid any attention to him.

Finally he reached the bandstand. The same Peavey amps flanked it, and a small drum set was shoved as far into the corner as it would go. A banjo lay in its open case. A single microphone stood at the center.

He looked around again, making sure no one had spotted him. He saw no sign of Rockhouse. He took a deep breath, then stepped up on the riser, experiencing a whole new form of stage fright.

With the added height, he easily saw Stoney across the room. Berklee stood pleading in front of him, while Doyle tried to pull her away. Stoney's big arm draped casually over Stella Kizer, who regarded Berklee with both sympathy and weary jealousy. Stoney's expression was blank, maybe slightly amused, and certainly not the least bit concerned with the pain he was causing.

Rob tapped the microphone. The speakers thudded in response. "Uh, excuse me," he said, putting a drawl in his voice, "would Stella Kizer please come on up to the bandstand?"

Stella turned toward him. A few others looked at him oddly, but most ignored him. "Stella Kizer, to the bandstand, please," he repeated.

She was fifteen feet away, watching him with hurt, watery eyes, but would not detach from Stoney Hicks. The big man ignored Rob, instead watching Doyle drag his wife away through the crowd. Berklee was crying, one hand stretched imploringly toward Stoney, who couldn't have cared less.

Rob met Stella's eyes. *Please,* he mouthed to her. But she looked away, helpless in the grip of whatever power had its hooks into her.

He had no choice; it was time to play his hole card.

He took a deep breath and began to sing. The melody that had haunted him now rang through the speakers.

A tyrant fae crossed the valley
His list of pains he could not tally
To his cause no one would rally
And so he left to lead no more.

His old and feeble feet did fail him
His eyes grew dim and ears betrayed him
The error of his ways assailed him
As he came to a stranger's door.

Silence spread, like oil atop water, from the people immediately in front of him until it reached everyone in the room. By the time he finished the second verse, he had everyone's attention, including Stoney Hicks's. He met the tall man's eyes, with an occasional glance down at Stella.

With weakness spreading, he called aloud
I have no place to spread my shroud
My people are all beyond me now
May I stay with you until I die?

The lord inside would not be fooled
You are that fae, once vain and cruel
There is no comfort here for you
Thoughts of succor you must deny.

A commotion stirred in the back of the crowd, and someone pushed people violently aside to reach the stage. Rockhouse Hicks suddenly appeared in front of him, red-faced and gasping for breath. Blood stained his chin and the front of his overalls. His eyes were wide with fury and, Rob noticed, fear. The crowd moved away from the stage to give them both room.

A moment later, Bliss appeared behind Rockhouse and put a restraining hand on the old man's shoulder.

Hicks was clean-shaven now, and Rob saw the outlines of the man who'd lured him here in the old man's face. Meeting Hicks's hate-filled glare with his own, Rob continued:

> With wings too weak for soul's last flight
> The dying tyrant perceived a sight
> Death would not take him this night
> Instead a wonder did appear.

Anticipation now hung in the air like cigar smoke. His voice trembled a little as he began the final stanza.

> Around him stood the myriad fae
> Whose love had grown to hate's decay—

"You little piss-ant *bastard*!" Hicks screamed. He grabbed the microphone off the riser and swung the heavy base at Rob like a club.

Rob blocked it, wrapped his arm around it, and yanked it easily from the old man's hands. A great squeal of feedback shrieked through the room as the microphone fell from its holder and landed near the speakers. Hicks stumbled back, off balance.

"You goddam Yankee shitwad!" Hicks yelled as he charged forward. "You fuckin' jackrabbit cornholing—"

Bliss stepped in front of Rockhouse, her back to Rob, and made a forceful gesture with her hand. The room instantly fell silent. "No more," Bliss said carefully to Rockhouse; then she turned to Rob. "Stop."

"It's up to him," he said, and pointed at Stoney with the microphone stand. "He knows why I'm here."

All eyes moved from Rob to Stoney.

"Let her talk to him," Bliss ordered Stoney. "Then we can all get back to our lives."

Rockhouse started to say something, but Bliss whirled on him. "If you so much as open your mouth, old man," she hissed, "I will get on that stage myself."

Rockhouse slammed his mouth shut like an angry red-faced bullfrog. Bliss went over to Stoney and took Stella's hand. The woman looked like she'd been told the worst news in the world, but put up no resistance as she was led to the bandstand.

Rob stepped down and looked in her eyes. "Terry's worried to death about you, Stella, and the police think he might've even killed you. I don't want to force you to do anything, but if you want to go back, I'll take you."

She looked as frightened as anyone he'd ever seen. "I . . . can't . . . leave," she whispered, although it sounded more like a plea than a statement.

"Do you *want* to leave?" he pressed. "Because if you do, not a Tufa in this place is going to stop us."

She looked back at Stoney as if she were a starving woman and he the only meal in town. She sobbed, and in the expectant silence it echoed around the room. Then she looked back at Rob, her eyes wet with tears. "Yes," she said in a soft voice, "I want to leave."

He grabbed her hand. "Then we're leaving."

He'd barely turned away when he felt a big, meaty hand on his shoulder, and Stoney Hicks spun him around, yanking Stella from his grasp. "She's *my* girlfriend now," Stoney said.

That did it. Months of choked-down rage, stronger even than what he'd unleashed at the ambush on the road, surged up from the pit of Rob's stomach, exploded in his solar plexus, and poured out in a scream as he threw himself at Stoney.

His momentum drove the bigger man back against the edge of the stage, and they fell together onto the wooden platform with a thud like a cannon shot. Rob was in full berserker mode, astride the bigger man's chest and still incoherently roaring. He smashed Stoney in his smug face once, twice, three times with fast little snap punches, enjoying the wet crunching sound he got with the third one. His knuckles were smeared with crimson.

Then *everything* went red, followed by gray, followed by a roaring pain from the battered lump on the back of his head. He fell off Stoney and sprawled limp on the riser. Something wet and warm spread under his hair. His vision blurred and sparkled around the edges, and he had a momentary sense of total disconnection from the world around him. Then his eyes gradually refocused and the pain roared back. He looked up.

Rockhouse stood over him, brandishing the mike stand like a spear; no, like a king's scepter. Blood—Rob's blood—dripped from the weighted base that had slammed into the back of his head. Rockhouse looked different, too. He had immense batlike wings, tattered at the edges, and huge pointed ears that rose almost higher than the top of his head. His eyes, previously sun-narrowed to slits, were big and black, like an insect's. Rob saw his own face, slack-jawed and dazed, reflected in their shiny surfaces.

Rob turned his head slightly. Bliss stood behind Rockhouse, one hand reaching in slow motion for the microphone stand. She had graceful, curving butterfly wings and an expression of infinite sadness.

Almost everyone in the crowd now sported wings, in fact, along with sparkly skin and smooth, youthful faces. He wanted to laugh, it was so beautiful, but the impulse got lost somewhere between his brain and his voice. What an amazing sight: a room full of hillbilly fairies, all watching him.

Then he realized they weren't watching him. They were watching Rockhouse. With great effort, Rob turned his head back to the old man.

The microphone stand rose above Rob like a dark moon in a white sky. Big and solid, it would smash his skull if it came down hard enough. And one look at Rockhouse's face told him it would come down that hard. He wanted to move, to react, but he had to lie there and watch this weird TV show playing out in slow motion all around him.

Then he blinked, everything snapped back to reality, and he realized he was about to *die*. Desperately he shouted the last line of the song:

They bound him to the spot he lay
YOU CAN DO NO HARM WHILE YOU BE HERE!

33

Rockhouse's raspy breathing was the room's only sound. He looked down at Rob, his eyes actually brimming with tears. Rob felt a throb of regret that he'd hurt this ancient, petty, pathetic tin god.

Then Rockhouse screamed in rage, drew back his arm, and drove the microphone stand's base down at Rob's head.

Something shrieked like a wild animal as it flew over Rob and slammed into Rockhouse. The mike stand hit the ground an inch from his cheek, dropped rather than thrown. Rob pulled his blood-sticky head free of the riser.

Curnen was wrapped around the old man, hissing and screeching as she clawed his face, his hands, his clothes. Where had *she* come from? The tattered dress tangled around his hands as he tried to grab hold of her. She ripped into his skin, and blood splattered those nearest the fight. Rockhouse staggered toward the crowd, hands reaching blindly for help, but people moved out of his way. No one, not even Bliss, offered any aid.

They thrashed in the middle of the dance floor in a display of Grand Guignol flatfooting. *"Help!"* Rockhouse yelled. *"Get her off me!"* But no one answered his cries.

Curnen bent the old man's head to one side. Her suddenly-pointed teeth gleamed when she opened her mouth, and her head darted snakelike to the soft flesh of his neck. He howled in renewed pain and fury. An arterial jet of unnaturally bright red blood shot straight up and splattered on the ceiling. It was only for an instant, but Rob swore he saw Curnen with a fist-sized chunk of flesh in her teeth, ripped whole from her father's neck. Then they fell backwards into the crowd, which moved to surround them.

Rob tried to organize his rattled thoughts. For the moment, everyone had forgotten him. He rolled off the riser onto the floor, then got first to his knees and finally to his feet. Dizziness spun the room around him, and blood trickled down the back of his neck. Teeth gritted against the pain, he shook his head to clear it, which almost sent him to the floor again. But he stayed upright, and the last of the dazed sensation vanished. He looked around for Stella.

She huddled against the wall behind Stoney, her arms wrapped around her body as if she'd been punched in the stomach. Stoney watched the fight with slack-jawed amusement and surprise, smiling even as he wiped his own bloody face.

A shriek that could shatter glass cut through all the other noise. Berklee charged across the room, Doyle's pocketknife in her hand. Before he could react, she stabbed Stoney in the groin, holding the knife there and twisting it. He screamed, too, but she held the knife in place, using her whole body to push it deeper. He fell to the floor with Berklee on top of him, screaming a lifetime's worth of torment into his contorted face. His spells were broken, too.

Rob stumbled across the room and grabbed Stella by the arm. He looked around for Curnen, but the crowd still blocked any view of the fight between father and daughter. Doyle pulled a still-screaming Berklee off Stoney, and together the four of them made for the door. Then they were outside in the still-roaring wind, running for their vehicles.

Suddenly Stella yanked free of Rob's grasp. "I *can't*—!" she tried to say, her face distorted with panic.

"Goddammit!" Rob said, and grabbed her by the shoulders. "Listen to me! Your husband is worrying himself sick about you! Doesn't that count for *anything*?"

"But . . . what I *did*!"

"It wasn't your fault! It's over now!"

Her mouth moved, but the words wouldn't come. Instead, she wrenched away from him and ran, not back into the Pair-A-Dice, but across the highway into the forest. He started after her, but a wave of nausea made him clutch at the nearest car, and by the time his head cleared, she'd vanished.

He looked at the huge wall of green and wood before him, as solid in its way as any fortress. Stella, rather than face either her husband or her lover again, had chosen to burst through that wall and disappear into whatever lay beyond. And Rob knew he could not follow; these woods belonged to the Tufa, and anyone who ventured into them gave themselves over to Tufa rules.

Doyle was suddenly next to him. "We're going," he said urgently. "You need a ride?"

Rob shook his head, but the movement made him dizzy again.

By the time it passed, he heard Doyle's car roaring off down the highway.

He stumbled to his own car, managed to get the keys into the ignition and start the engine. In the rearview mirror, he watched the Pair-A-Dice entrance, but no one emerged. He considered going back for Curnen, but a fresh wave of nausea hit him.

Finally he put the car into gear and gunned it out of the parking lot. He headed back toward Needsville alone.

Moments later, Bliss burst out the door, dragging Curnen by one wrist. The younger woman snapped and snarled like a mad dog at the people inside. Her ripped white dress was streaked with Rockhouse's blood. None of them attempted to stop or follow the women. Rockhouse's high, keening moans carried over all the other noise.

The door slammed shut, and Bliss threw Curnen to the ground between two trucks. Curnen skidded on the gravel, then glared up defiantly. The dust raised by the wind surrounded her like the smoke of her fury. Blood soaked her face and upper torso. She growled, low and menacing, like a coyote.

Bliss gathered her hair and held it back against the wind. The dream she'd had the day before she met Rob included an image just like this. It had seemed ludicrous then. Then again, so had the dream's other warnings.

Curnen growled again. "You don't have to do that anymore," Bliss said wearily.

Slowly, Curnen got to her feet. She wiped her mouth with the back of her arm. It left a bright red streak across one cheek. She stood upright and faced her sister.

"How does it feel?" Bliss asked.

Curnen, in a whisper made raw and thin by disuse, said, "I don't know yet. Is he dead?"

"In all the important ways. What will you do now?"

She licked her lips and looked off, searching for words. "I think . . . I'll leave."

"Needsville?"

She nodded.

"Good God, Curnen, haven't you learned anything? That's what started all this. You *can't* leave. None of us can."

Curnen struggled to form the words. "Not for good. Just . . . until people remember me. Until I become myself again."

"You think you can do that better somewhere else? You're a Tufa. A *full-blood* Tufa. What better place than here?"

She shook her head. "No. Here I almost became—" Again she paused to search for the words. "—a wisp of a thing. I want to be more."

"You're all the family I have left," Bliss said.

Curnen stepped closer. "I will be back. I will."

They hugged. Then Curnen turned and looked up. The Widow's Tree was totally bare now, its limbs like black veins against the sky. She began to laugh. After a moment, Bliss joined her. Curnen's laughter became a howl, the only cry she'd been allowed for so long.

Bliss stared at her, and laughed at the absurdity. Then, above the roaring wind, the Overbay sisters howled together, expressing their amusement and triumph at the world. The sound reached every part of Cloud County.

34

Rob went directly to his room, pulled off his shoes, and put a folded towel on his pillow. He gave no thought to seeking medical attention, or to the common warning that those with head injuries shouldn't sleep. He slept for thirteen straight hours, the wind roaring outside. If he dreamed, he recalled none of it.

When he awoke the next day, it was almost noon, and the wind had gone silent. Dried blood stuck the towel to his hair. Without getting out of bed, he called Deputy Darwin and told him he'd seen Stella Kizer alive and well at the Pair-A-Dice in the company of Stoney Hicks. He said Doyle Collins could confirm it, and gave him the service station's phone number. Then he sent Terry Kizer an e-mail stating the same thing. He didn't try to sugarcoat it.

He took a shower, letting the warm water rinse the dried blood from his hair. The lump seemed bigger and more tender, probably due to the blow from the mike stand, but miraculously, the stitches still held. He'd get a real doctor to look at it as soon as he reached Kansas City. He shampooed around it, and felt much better as the sense of cleanliness spread. More than just the previous day's blood and dirt had washed away; for the first time since Anna's death, he felt *content*.

He dressed and quickly packed, anxious to leave Needsville as soon as possible. As he made the last check for anything he might have forgotten, his phone rang.

"Hey," Doyle said. He sounded very tired. "Sorry we ran out on you. How's the head?"

"It hurts. But it'll be okay. Did the cops call you?"

"Yeah. I backed you up. Your friend's off the hook."

"Thanks. Did they say anything about Berklee stabbing Stoney?"

"No. And no cops have shown up here. If I know the Tufa, they wouldn't call the cops even if she'd killed him. Which I guess she may have, judging by how much of his blood she had all over her."

"You okay with that?"

"I guess. He deserved it."

"And Berklee?"

"She's different. Real different."

"In a good way?"

"I don't know yet. She's still pretty pissed off. I've had to physically stop her twice from trying to find Stoney with a gun. I pointed out that stabbing him in the dick like she did was probably worse than actually killing him."

"But she's not . . . under his spell anymore?"

"Spell?"

"Or whatever."

"No, she ain't. That's something, I guess. I owe you one for that."

"I think we're even. Take care, and give Berklee my best."

There was a rustle on the line, and then Berklee said, "Rob?"

"Yeah?"

"You saved my life." Her voice was firm, certain, and completely free of the pitiful whine that underlined everything she'd said before.

"Well, I don't know about *that*—"

"I do. And you did. How's your friend?"

"She ran off into the woods. I haven't seen her."

"Don't blame her. It's like having a knife inside you. When it comes out, it hurts more than you can imagine. And if she never really understood what had happened to her in the first place, it's no wonder she freaked out."

"Think anyone will ever find her?"

"I doubt it. And I'm sorry."

"Me, too. Take care, Berklee."

"I'll try."

At the very top of the Widow's Tree, where the trunk grew sapling-thin, clung Curnen Overbay. She swayed in the soft, cool wind, the sun warm on her skin.

She looked out over the valley and beyond. Too far away for human eyes, she saw the straight line of Interstate 81 where it cut through the hills around Morristown. The cars zooming along it resembled robotic insects obeying instinctual migratory urges. Even at this distance, the harsh chemical smell made her sensitive nose wrinkle.

It was nothing, though, compared to the emotions burning

inside her. Something huge had happened to her, and she wasn't yet done changing.

The truth about herself flew around in her head like a butterfly unable to select a flower. She was a child of incest, and the victim of sexual abuse. She was a widow. She'd only barely retained even her basic humanity. If the leaves atop this very tree had blown away even a few moments earlier, she'd be running around in the forest forever, lost to herself and everyone else.

But she'd been saved from that. And now she had a debt to pay.

Or was it? Was it something owed, or something desired? A reward, or a need?

The tree swayed. The wind tousled her hair.

She'd married young, in human terms. Her love had been true, and he had tried his best to defend her against the evil. It wasn't his fault that he hadn't been strong enough.

Rob had been, because Rob had the wind at his back. Rob had saved her. And he'd tried to save the other woman, the stranger.

She put her cheek against the bark. Somewhere far below, back in Needsville, Rob was leaving. Alone.

Downstairs at the Catamount Corner, Mrs. Goins rang up Rob's bill. "I hope you've enjoyed your stay," she said as she ran his credit card through the machine. "It's certainly been eventful, hasn't it?"

"I'll never forget a minute of it," he said with certainty. "Thanks for being so nice to a stranger."

She smiled and seemed genuinely touched. "Why, you're very welcome, Mr. Quillen. Will you be coming back to visit? I noticed you and Bliss Overbay seemed to be getting along real well."

"I doubt it," he said wryly. "Vacation romances never last."

"Now, that's not true. Look at Danny and Sandy in *Grease*."

He laughed. "I don't think that's an example of real life."

"Real life is more like a song than you might think. At least, it is here."

He carried his bag outside and put it into his car. He took one last look around the little town, marveling at the secrets he now knew lurked below its surface.

He shielded his eyes with his hand and squinted at the post office. The old woman sat in her chair quilting, but there was no sign of Rockhouse. Was he dead? Had Curnen killed him? And if so, what would happen to the Tufa? Would they all now follow Bliss? Or would a new leader, even worse than Rockhouse, appear to take over his half of Needsville's fairies?

He looked down the street toward the mountains. For a long moment, he didn't know what he was looking for; then he realized he expected Bliss's truck to suddenly appear in the distance and pull up beside him, followed by an awkward farewell in which he would at least learn what had finally happened at the Pair-A-Dice. He waited a few more minutes before he realized she wasn't coming. He started the car, backed out of the spot, and drove away from Needsville for good.

Just past the Cloud County sign, an emu blocked the road.

Rob slowed to a stop, but the bird still didn't move. He honked, leaned out the window, and yelled. Finally, he put the car in park and opened the door.

When he stepped out of the car, the emu trotted off and someone emerged from the bushes.

It was *Anna*.

At least, it was for an instant. When he gasped and looked directly, it was Curnen.

She wore frayed jeans with holes in the knees, an old sweat-shirt and a denim jacket. From the mismatched look of them, he guessed they'd been scavenged from people's clotheslines. Her hair was pushed back from her face, and she carried a child's small pink suitcase, probably also stolen.

Still, she looked . . . *normal.* She stood upright, and the glazed look had gone from her eyes. She was dirty and mismatched, but then, so were most of the interesting girls he'd known. The child's suitcase was no sillier than Anna's Hello Kitty purse.

She waited silently, eyes downcast.

"Uh . . . hi," he said at last. He nodded at the suitcase. "Going somewhere?"

She did not look up. Carefully enunciating each word, she said, "I want to go away with you."

"Did you just *talk*?"

She nodded. "I can talk." Eyes still down, she said, "He sent me away after his music failed. He said it was my fault. I was a wild animal, he said, and shouldn't be around people. Or talk to them. Or sing, even to myself." She raised her eyes. "He doesn't have that power anymore."

"Did you *kill* him?"

She shook her head. "Some of us—" She paused as she sought the words. "—don't die unless we want to. The selfish ones never do. I hurt him. But he won't die."

"And you want to leave."

"Yes. With you."

"Wow. This is . . . sudden."

"Not for a Tufa. I know your song. It hurm . . . horm . . ."

"Harmonizes?"

She nodded emphatically. "Har-mo-nize-es with mine. Sorry, the big words are hard right now."

He bit his lip. "Curnen, I don't want to say. I owe you a lot, but . . . you're not *human*." Even though he knew it was true, he felt weird verbalizing it. She certainly looked human, and small, and sad. If he touched her, she'd be warm and alive. But in a blink, she could transform into something ethereal, otherworldly, *alien*.

Curnen nodded. "I know. But I can be her, too."

And again, for an instant, Anna stood there before him.

"No!" he yelled, and turned away. "Don't *ever* do that!"

"I'm sorry," she said quickly. "I won't do it again, I promise. Some people, some men . . . like that."

"Not me." When he looked, she was herself again. "I'm sorry, I know you want to leave, and I don't blame you. But I don't think I could handle it."

She nodded as if she expected his answer. "That's how all the songs end. But we each lost half our hearts. If we put our halves together . . ."

He said nothing.

Sadly, she turned and walked away. Her bare, rough-soled feet skitched against the blacktop.

"Curnen, wait."

She stopped halfway up the shoulder of the road. Her posture had already regained some of its primal slouch.

"You really *can* leave? I mean, it didn't go so well for Rockhouse. Or Bronwyn Hyatt."

She nodded. With a little smile, she said, "I am not chained to this spot. And the winds know I'll be back."

"And are you sure you *want* to? I mean, I live in a city, in a real flat part of the country. We don't have hills. We don't even have many trees. We have a lot of cars, and corn, and people, and noise."

She chewed her lip thoughtfully. "Do you have songs?"

He half smiled. "Yeah. Songs we got."

She climbed back down to the road. "Then I'm sure." She touched his face with her rough fingers. "But hear me, Rob Quillen. The pain of your loss will return. Less, but still considerable. I know you've worked hard to release it, but it can still take hold of you. I will help you sing away the fury, Rob, but I will not bear it for you."

"Okay," he said, although he didn't know exactly what she meant.

She grabbed his wrist in a grip like a hydraulic press. "You have to understand me. There are no half measures here. I am your girl. I will be your woman. But I will never be your victim. If you ever try to turn me into that, I will sing your dying dirge."

Her eyes were, for a moment, as cold as any reptile's. Rob recalled the brief glimpse of Curnen, blood-spattered and wild, with a chunk of human flesh in her teeth. Then it vanished and she was small, and fragile, and *his*. He felt it as surely as he did gravity.

And it felt good. Whatever the source, whether it was his own emotion or something impinged on him by her, it felt good. He felt whole.

"I'll be careful," he said sincerely.

"And I'll be patient." Then she kissed him.

He gently took her arm and guided her to the car. As he did, he glanced at the Cloud County sign and stopped. Something had changed about it. It still read, *Welcome to Cloud County, Tennessee,* and the painted mockingbirds still flew in the corners. But there was a difference.

"Hey, didn't that sign used to say something else?" He was certain there'd been more, an epigram or motto of some sort. Of course there had; he'd nearly crashed trying to read it.

Curnen shrugged. "I don't know. Until now, I could only see the back of it."

"Huh," Rob said. Then he helped her into the passenger seat and buckled the belt around her.

Then Rob Quillen and his fairy lover drove away into the west.

35

Twenty years later . . .

Denton Sizemore had no time to react. One moment the road was empty; then suddenly she was *there*, right in front of him. He hit a deer last year, just after he'd gotten his license, and knew how sickening that felt. This was far worse; the sound his truck made when it struck the woman would stay with him forever.

He dialed 911 on his cell phone as he jumped out of the truck. No one used this old highway anymore, and there were no houses within five miles. The only building was the abandoned remains of an old roadhouse nightclub, its parking lot overgrown with kudzu, two faded wood cutouts of what looked like dice or dominoes still mounted on its roof. This was the last place he'd expect to find a pedestrian, especially one who dashed into the road right in front of him.

He knelt beside her. From the way her eyes stared at the overcast sky, he knew she was dead, and he almost threw up. The emergency dispatcher asked him calmly to describe the victim.

WISP OF A THING

"Sh-she looks about thirty," he told the dispatcher. "She's got red hair, and she's wearing clothes like they did twenty years ago. No, I don't see a purse anywhere."

Following the dispatcher's instructions, he tentatively touched her neck for a pulse. Her head lolled to one side the way it could only if her neck was broken. He nearly screamed.

"Y'all, please hurry!" Sizemore said, tears filling his eyes. "I don't want to be alone here with a *corpse!*"

The dispatcher stayed on the phone with him until the police and ambulance arrived. The paramedics quickly loaded the body onto a stretcher and carried it away, while the state trooper sympathetically took his statement.

One of the paramedics, a woman with long black hair, put a hand on Sizemore's shoulder. He recognized her as one of the Needsville Tufas, although he didn't know her name.

"Don't feel too bad about it," she said gently. "It was an accident, that's all." She leaned closer. "And really, this woman died twenty years ago."

Sizemore didn't understand the strange comment, but the EMT's smile and touch eased his panic. She hummed a tune he almost recognized as she climbed into the ambulance and closed the door. Red lights flashing, it drove away into the mist.

All song lyrics are original, with the exception of two stanzas from "Hares on the Mountain," a traditional English ballad first printed in *One Hundred English Folksongs: For Medium Voice*, a landmark 1916 songbook edited by Cecil J. Sharp (1859–1924); one stanza of "Pretty Saro," another traditional English ballad, first published in Alan Lomax's *North Carolina Booklet* in 1911; and "Little Omie Wise," which first appeared in *The Greensboro Patriot* (North Carolina) newspaper on April 29, 1874.

And of course, "Wrought Iron Fences" by Kate Campbell, from her 1997 album *Moonpie Dreams*, and used by her generous permission. She gets honorary Tufa status for that.

The painting *The Fairy Feller's Master-Stroke* by Richard Dadd is currently on display in the Tate Gallery in London. Its presence in the United States is entirely fictional.